ROB WILLIAMS

Give It a Day

Rob Williams

Give It a Day
Published by Rob Williams through Winged Publications 2024

ISBN: 978-1-965352-30-4

Preface

Disclaimer: This Christian crime novel is not meant to be read by or to children, as it contains violence and disturbing mental images. The actions taken by the primary fictional criminal are roughly based on an actual serial molester of women in my hometown years ago. In no way does this novel promote the horrible practice of brutal attacks on women. This fictional work is also based on ideologies promoted by a professor I had while attending a university when I was young.

Give It a Day touches on the struggles of an aging Atlanta detective, John Rawlings, who has lost the love of his life. Though his wife, Sharon, was a woman of faith and provided stability within the family, the detective is not a Christian. Loneliness, combined with facing the diminishing physical abilities which come with aging, introduces suicidal thoughts. For the first time in his life, John feels lost.

John owns an antique .38 caliber handgun, which he reserves for the purpose of ending things. Join him, as he tries to convince himself that life is still worth living.

John's daughter, Heather, is facing her own life struggles with an increasingly distant husband and a hampered career. Her life, which has purposely been lived far away from her father, leaves her lonely and desperate.

After his Christian next-door neighbor Emily Johnson confides with John, he finds that she has an unexpected past. God forgives, but does that forgiveness change the past?

As Atlanta becomes terrorized by a serial mutilator of women, will John maintain the mental discipline to help solve this case or will an overwhelming state of personal depression destroy him? Will Shawn, John's younger ex-partner on the police force, have a role in stopping this serial criminal – or will he fail? What about sweet Emily's safety?

How many victims must suffer?
Where is God in all of this?

In dedication to my soul mate and wife, Gwyn,
my four children, my grandchildren,
and
to all in law enforcement who have placed their
lives on the line in service.

Chapter 1

Zack

STILL IN BED, John Rawlings contemplated whether his lungs were worthy of pulling in needed oxygen. He felt as if every ounce of life had seeped from his aching frame. In the dimly lit room, John's gaze moved to a mostly empty bottle of bourbon left on a nightstand. His redirected focus allowed his body to trigger its natural responses. John sensed his chest move, and air gently flowed across unwashed sheets and into his nostrils.

Still breathing. My body seems to think that I deserve to live.

The quietness of his surroundings amplified the subtle throbbing of blood pulsing through his temporal artery. He drew a deeper breath. Every muscle complained loudly when the aging detective pushed himself into a seated position on the edge of the bed. As blood scabbed knuckles cleared his morning eyes, the previous night's activity weighed heavily upon his body and mind.

Having been badly beaten by a man twice his size, he remembered his assailant standing over him as he lay on the pavement of a downtown Atlanta alley. John's bruised eyes had captured the faint flash of a knife blade, and adrenaline raced through his body. He couldn't remember whipping the nine-millimeter from his shoulder holster and firing. The reflexive motion was as smooth and quick as the snap of a released mouse trap. However, the sound of the shot played in his mind repeatedly. If his body wasn't in so much pain, he might have convinced himself that it was just a dream. But it wasn't a dream. The detective clearly remembered surrendering his issued sidearm to those conducting the investigation into the shooting.

It shouldn't have come to that. I should be able to take a man down without having to kill him. That guy whipped me like he was working a punching bag. Except for using a gun, I've become as slow as a turd rolling down a hill.

His stomach called him to move to the kitchen for breakfast, but his mind wasn't willing to force himself to stand. A multi-front war was being waged between his mind, spirit, and body.

I wonder how long this will go on? Well, I don't have to wait to find out. I can take control of this one thing.

John opened the bottom drawer of the nightstand and lifted a box from it. Its weight reassured him of the contents. Wrapped in an old T-shirt was a police-positive .38 caliber revolver. He opened the chamber, and it easily spun by a flick of his finger. Both the bedroom and his life appeared to be trashed, but not this off-duty personally owned gun. It was well kept. He purposely reached into the drawer and removed a smaller box containing a mix of hollow point and copper jacket bullets. Today, his choice was the hollow point. He rolled each one between his finger and thumb, prior to slowly slipping them into the gun.

I only need one, but it just doesn't seem right to do something like this half-way. All six are needed to make it right.

He spun the chamber six times and snapped it into place. His thumb pulled back the hammer before he raised the barrel to the right side of his head. John stared ahead at the photo of him and a woman on the bedroom wall. Closing tear-blurred eyes, visions of his deceased wife filled his mind. The photo had been taken while on a camping trip shortly after they were married. He felt that there must be no better sensation of peace on earth than tasting a cup of coffee while sitting around a campfire on a cool morning with someone you love. Distant memories flooded his mind. An afternoon of making love in a tent was as fresh in his memory as when it happened. There was something pure and primal about nakedness in the outdoors. John remembered thinking that this was how life was meant to be lived. He imagined life before the stress-filled norm of this current time, before the rat race that flooded streets, offices, and restaurants.

This was life before electricity, cars, people jammed into massive cities, air conditioning and indoor plumbing. Well, indoor plumbing is a good thing. But the rest....

Thoughts of that nude younger woman lying in the tent were replaced with more recent images of someone crippled with Amyotrophic Lateral Sclerosis. His life with her ended with the last view of her lifeless face in the coffin just before the lid was shut for the last time.

That wasn't her. She had already left – gone somewhere, where pain doesn't exist. To a place of quiet peace. She believed in that place and in God. Her faith never wavered.

John tried to imagine her in that realm of eternal bliss, but he found it impossible. He missed her so profoundly. She was more than the love of his life; she was his refuge at the end of each dangerous day. She provided him relief from the intensely stressful situations demanded by his job. Moving away from raging storms of violent and twisted humanity, he would return daily to her safe harbor.

He remembered her firm and loving control of their son and daughter. The couple had guided their children through uncertain teen years, and they went without as they provided college funding for both. His children left Atlanta for employment on the West Coast, and their perspectives on politics and life morphed into those common for that area of the country. Embarrassed by his conservative views, the distance between them grew even wider. His wife continually strove to maintain communication among members of the family. She was the bridge.

His kids initially made efforts to check on him after their mother passed away. Over time, closure about the passing of their mother made way for again focusing on their own lives. John was rarely given the opportunity to spend time with his grandchildren because his children were fearful that his views would rub off on them. Phone calls from them became rare. Nothing was the same under the dark cloud of his wife's absence. The house they shared was a constant reminder of all that he had lost, so it was avoided. He was now rarely home. It became only a place for sleeping.

She's gone, and my kids wish I didn't share this planet with them. I'm basically monitored while with my grandkids, so as not to corrupt them. I've become so inept at my job that I'm now a killer instead of a lawman. What a totally worthless piece of crap!

John had considered ending things for some time, but each time fear halted the effort. Today, he was calm. He pressed the barrel tighter against his head. There was no unsteadiness in the raised hand which held the gun.

This should be no different from firing a gun at the range. Take a deep breath, let it out, and gently pull the trigger. Years of practice should make this last shot perfect.

He felt something touch him. Opening his eyes, he found the chin of his mutt resting on his thigh. There was unspoken communication in those round brown eyes.

"Hey, Zack. You need to go outside, don't you?"

John lowered the gun and placed it on the bed. Releasing it from his fingers, he reached for the dog's waiting warm fur. Zack raised his head to meet his master's hand.

"Lately, I've left you alone way too much. It's not right. None of this is your doing. You're the one constant that remains. Message received."

The detective lifted himself to his feet. With this signal, Zack trotted off in the direction of the back door. Cool morning air greeted John's bruised face when he opened the kitchen door leading to the backyard. The dog spotted a squirrel and shot out of the house in pursuit. When Zack was within ten feet of his prey, the bushy tailed critter sped up an oak tree to the safety of a large branch. The dog momentarily gazed up at it before he hiked his leg in the air and peed on the base of the tree.

"There you go, boy," John spoke. "You tell him whose yard this is, Zack. At least one of us still knows how to take care of business. I'm here for you, boy. As for that .38 lying on the bed, I'll give it a day."

Chapter 2

Emily

UNCHARACTERISTIC SHOUTS from a usually soft-spoken young woman living in the house next door abruptly captured John's attention. He stepped onto his front porch in time to witness a black car accelerate with a loud roar, tires screeching and leaving tracks in the street directly in front of her house. As the thundering sound began to diminish in the distance, his focus shifted entirely to his new neighbor, Emily Johnson, standing on her porch. John hurried down his steps and approached her home. Cupped hands over her mouth, Emily's pregnant body shook almost uncontrollably.

John ascended the steps of Emily's porch and moved toward her. As he neared, their eyes met.

"I'm sorry to have disturbed you," she whimpered.

"There's nothing to be sorry about," John replied. "Are you OK?"

"How did he find me?" she mumbled.

"Who was that guy?"

"You shouldn't be involved."

"It's clear that you don't want this fellow around. You should call your husband."

"No! I don't want Ron to be hurt."

"So, he's after your husband?" asked John.

"Ron doesn't even know Billy."

John's eyes searched hers for an explanation. Breaking from his gaze, she nervously lowered her face.

"He's my ex-boyfriend, from three years ago," she explained. "I was so stupid. I don't know why I ever got involved with him. My parents tried to warn me about men like him. I was raised in church. When I left home, it was like I lost my mind or something. I found life exciting when I was with Billy. I was captivated."

"I know the type," said John. "If he had come around my daughter, I might have beat the living crap out of him."

"My parents are good Christian people and are anything but violent," replied Emily. "I got swept up in the thrill of being with him. With Billy, life was anything but dull. I woke up to who he really is when he punched an old friend of mine when he found us talking on a street corner. His eyes were filled with rage, and he told me that conversations with other guys were off limits unless he approved. I had been told about his temper, but that was the first time I saw it for myself. He scared me; he really scared me. After I left him, I began attending church with my parents again. My faith was rekindled like never before. I think I finally grasped my need for forgiveness and guidance from God. I prayed that Billy would leave me alone."

"If this guy is giving you a hard time, you need to let Ron know," said John.

"Billy wants me to leave Ron and come back to him. But if Ron confronts him, I'm afraid Billy will kill him."

"So, this guy is really bad?"

"Please don't tell Ron!" begged Emily.

"Your call," said John. "Are you sure that you're OK?"

"I'll be fine. I don't know why I told you about my history with him. I'm so sorry to involve you."

"Please don't hesitate to call on me if you need help," John offered, while handing Emily his card. Her eyes spoke appreciation.

"What happened to your face?" Emily asked, placing her delicate right hand against his cheek.

"I got into it with a criminal," he replied. "Comes with the territory; I'm taking a few days off. Give it a day, and it will be better."

"Does it hurt?" asked Emily.

"I'm a quick healer."

The young couple, Ron and Emily Johnson, had moved into the house next door to John a month earlier. John liked Ron, but he quickly became especially fond of Emily. Her personal faith reminded him of his own beloved wife.

As soon as John returned to his house, he placed a call to a friend in the traffic division at the station and gave him the tag number of the black car.

"2021 Camaro SS… belongs to a William Ian Crews," said the friend. "He has a rap sheet: four assault and battery charges, one for car theft, and a few speeding tickets. None of them were considered felonies, but I think this guy has been lucky. The car he stole was worth less than $5,000."

"Anything outstanding?" asked John.

"Doesn't look like it."

"Would you do me a favor?"

"I just did. You're on paid leave until the investigation is done. Sorry, this is as far as it goes."

"OK. Thanks."

When the detective met the sweet young Emily next door, he never considered her past had been shared with a violent man.

It appears I can still be surprised. I didn't see that one coming.

JOHN DOUBTED THAT Emily had seen the last of Billy Crews, so he determined to await another visit by the ex-boyfriend. He positioned a small table and chair on his front porch and spent time seated there each day with a cup of coffee and his laptop. The Camaro showed up on the sixth day. When the ex-boyfriend exited his car and approached Emily's home, John closed the laptop and watched intently. Crews rang the doorbell.

"I know you're in there!" shouted Billy. "I just want to talk."

There was no response from Emily. Crews paced the porch for several minutes before his fists pounded on the door. "Open it!"

"Hey, I'm trying to enjoy my cup of coffee over here," the detective called out.

"Shut up, old man!" bellowed Crews, pointing a finger.

"Free country, I can exercise my freedom of speech," jeered John, giving the younger man a middle finger.

"You think you can flip me off?" yelled Crews.

"Freedom of expression," shouted John, giving him the middle finger again, this time holding his hand higher.

"I'm going to come over there and cram that finger down your throat!" Crews barked, moving away from the door just before it flew open.

"Leave him alone!" cried Emily, stepping out onto the porch.

"See how crazy you make me!" Crews shouted, as he grabbed both of her arms.

"Please go," she begged.

John raced down his steps and onto the sidewalk. Billy's eyes were fixed on Emily's.

"The young lady wants you to leave," John shouted.

Crews shoved Emily against her front door, turned his wrath toward John and rushed down Emily's steps. John met him on the sidewalk. The younger man grabbed the detective and shoved him against his car.

"You need to stop!" warned John.

"Shut up!" yelled the younger and larger man, as he punched the detective's cheek.

"*Not again*," thought John. "*I won't go to the ground*

this time."

John attempted to place a police force trained hold on his attacker, but he was unable to get a firm grip on him. Slipping away, Billy reached to take the detective by the throat. John blocked Crews' hand with his left arm, and immediately slammed his fist into the eye of his assailant. Billy clutched his face with his left hand, while reaching for the passenger side car door with his right.

"You're a dead man!" blurted Billy.

A scream from Emily brought a man and woman onto the porch of the home which bordered hers on the far side. John caught a glimpse of a pistol being pulled from inside the car. As Crews turned in his direction, John pounded his nose with a calculated punch. The blow caused the younger man to hesitate. Adrenaline raced through the seasoned man's body, and John violently beat Billy's face with both fists. With the gun still in his right hand, a dazed Crews turned and staggered from the vehicle. The detective caught him from behind, tripped him with his foot, and used the combined weight of both men to bring him down. Billy's face slammed hard against the sidewalk, and the altercation was over. John placed a knee on the unconscious younger man's back, while gingerly pulling the gun from his limp right hand. Glancing in the direction of Emily, he found her terrified and clutching a porch post.

"I'm calling the police!" shouted the man on the far porch, dialing his cell phone.

"Please do," replied John. "I am the police."

"Did you kill him?" questioned Emily, releasing the post.

"He's out," answered John. "His head hit the sidewalk hard, but his breathing appears to be fine."

"I knew he was going for a gun when he opened the car door," Emily explained. "He always kept one strapped under the dash."

John turned his attention from her and checked the pulse

of the unconscious Crews. "His pulse is steady," he stated.

From the corner of his eye, he caught a glimpse of Emily approaching.

"I advise you to stay back," he cautioned her. "He might start thrashing around when he comes to."

While the neighbor attempted to explain the situation to the 911 operator over the phone, his wife comforted Emily. John moved his knee from Billy's back to the younger man's right arm. Shallow breaths comprised the only movement coming from the unconscious man. Within minutes, three squad cars and an ambulance were on the scene. One paramedic examined Billy, while another questioned Emily regarding her condition. When both paramedics began to attend Crews, John noticed Emily begin a conversation on her cell phone.

"She may have a difficult time explaining this guy to her husband," thought John.

Two officers escorted John into his house for questioning.

"Trouble follows you like flies on crap," accused one officer, once the three were inside the house. "You can't seem to stop digging a hole for yourself."

"He attacked me, and then pulled a gun," replied John.

"I hear this started when you flipped this guy off," said one of the officers.

"It started when the guy was harassing my pregnant neighbor," explained John.

"You're on paid leave, and you're supposed to be keeping your nose clean during this investigation," explained the officer. "You're not a rookie. You know that you are to deescalate a situation, not provoke it further."

"I was trying to pull that guy away from her house," said John.

"Well, you certainly did that!" shouted an officer. "Was this guy trying to break in?"

"I thought he might try," said John.

"Pounding on a door isn't the same as breaking in," said an officer. "Her safety wasn't in danger until you caused a scene which brought this woman out of her house."

"I made a scene?" blurted John. "This guy was yelling and pounding on her door! You didn't see or hear this guy. Emily had already indicated to me that this man was violent. I did what I could to get him off her front porch."

"You shouldn't have stirred things up," said an officer.

"I made a judgment call," said John.

"Unless this guy was actually trying to break into this woman's house, I don't believe she was in any danger," said the officer.

"I think she WAS in danger!" shouted John. "Like I said, I made a judgement call."

"You need to know when to mind your own business!" blurted one officer.

"Are you freaking telling me that if a pregnant young lady next door is in trouble, that I have to stand on my porch and watch it?" blurted John. "You can't be serious!"

"Why didn't you tell him that she wasn't home?" asked the officer.

"Because he knew that would be a lie," said John. "Her car was in plain sight."

"You should have done something to calm the guy down," said the other officer. "That doesn't include escalating a situation by yelling at a guy and then flipping him off."

"I got him off her porch," said John. "I redirected the guy."

"Talking with you is like talking to a brick!" shouted one officer. "You're not listening. You're under an investigation for shooting a guy, and this isn't the first time you've been investigated. You're already under the spotlight. I'm telling you, for your own sake, that this doesn't look good for you. Your judgment is going to be called in question."

Chapter 3

Board

A WEEK LATER, John opened his front door and found his younger partner Shawn Stone standing on the front porch.

"We need to talk," stated the six-foot four-inch muscular partner in his deep voice.

"Come on in," welcomed John. "I just put a pot of coffee on. Follow me to the kitchen."

Hearing the conversation, John's dog stood attentively.

"Everything is OK," John assured Zack, while reaching down to give him a quick scratch behind the ears.

"Have you thought about retirement?" questioned Shawn. "Man, you're fifty-six years old. You could have retired last year."

"We had that talk last year, remember?"

"Things have changed since last year."

"Is that what you're hearing at the station?" questioned John.

"I'm just saying that you might want to reconsider."

"Did Evans send you?"

"Leave Evans out of this," said Shawn.

"He knows that I would never last in a desk job. He probably put a bug in your ear to talk retirement with me."

"This is just me and you talking, here," assured Shawn.

"If the word has filtered down to the level of my partner, then it's clear that they are fed up with me being in the field," said John. "What ticks me off is that Evans doesn't have the guts to look me in the eye and tell me. Maybe he can't. Maybe the union would be all over him if he did."

"I'm just saying that you've earned your retirement," said Shawn.

"And you're trying to tell me what the word is. I appreciate it. Listen, I was born to be a cop. That's who I am. You know the score. I don't really have a family anymore. Being a cop is all I have left."

"You've put in, what, thirty-seven years? Man, that's a long time in this business. That's two years longer than I've been alive. Some detectives retire from the force and make good money in private investigative work. You could set your own hours; take only the cases you want."

"You're selling this really hard," stated John. "So, that's where things are going? Do I have a choice?"

"It's still a free country. There's always a choice."

"Alright, I'll give it consideration. I'll give it a day."

"I HAVE LITTLE CHOICE", thought John, stepping onto his back porch after Shawn's visit. *"Oh, technically I could fight it, but then I would be placing myself in a position where the powers-that-be would be looking for reasons to fire me. Nothing would be overlooked, and over time they would build a case for getting rid of me. Being fired would mean that I forfeit my pension and retirement benefits. The decision is in my face. I'll have to pull the trigger and commit to retirement."*

The next morning, John informed his superior of his decision to retire. Captain Larry Evans shook his hand, mentioned a couple of heroic deeds John had performed over the years, and promised he would submit the required documentation by the end of day.

"Tomorrow you can formally meet with HR and sign the paperwork," Evans informed him. "Just call them and set up a time to drop by. I'm sure that you know the retirement benefits already, but they will go over them with you."

"I'm sure he already has the completed paperwork in his desk," thought John, as he walked from the office. *"I bet all he needed was the date. He doesn't personally know about any of those things he said about me. He just read about them in my file. Since Rich Sullivan retired last year, Evans has been my Captain – but doesn't know me like Rich did. I guess it comes with the territory, being in this stage of my life. I hardly know any of the top brass anymore. Almost everyone I worked with during my career has retired or died."*

Approaching his work area, he spotted his partner seated at his desk.

"I did it," John said.

"Did what?" questioned Shawn.

"I pulled the trigger. I'm retiring."

"Good for you!" exclaimed Shawn, standing.

"Keep it down," John whispered. "I don't want the entire room to start in on me."

"Lips are sealed, Buddy."

"And I don't want the big party thing," John told his partner. "I don't want to make a big deal out of it, and I certainly don't care to make speeches."

"I'll give it a try, but I can't control what goes on here. Hey, do you want to do something, later?"

"What?" retorted John.

"We could shoot pool or go bowling tonight," suggested Shawn.

"No, thanks. It feels like it's been a long day already. I think I should just go home and see about Zack. I have a lot to think about."

THE FOLLOWING WEEK, John sat before the Atlanta Civil Service Board which investigated his shooting of a well-known criminal. After ruling that the shooting was justified, the board congratulated him on his retirement. He was also told that retirees from the force are entitled to continued visits with the department therapist. Members of the board suggested that he take advantage of the benefit.

"Any plans?" asked Shawn, catching John as he left the meeting with the board.

"Not sure at this point," replied John. "I still need to meet with HR again to iron out the retirement details. It's all pretty weird. It hasn't really sunk in yet. I've been on the force most of my life."

"The way I look at it is that your opportunities are wide open."

"Wide open… it feels more like a pitcher of beer being emptied out over the top of a table. It just runs off and onto the floor. I see it as both a waste and a mess. I was born to be a cop."

"You've been an amazing detective," Shawn said, placing his large right hand on the older man's shoulder. "I don't know where I would be without you. I've learned so much from you over the past eight years. Plus, I owe you my life."

"I was just in the right place at the right time. You'll be fine. Now it's your turn to look after a young detective."

"Do you plan to continue seeing the therapists?" asked Shawn.

John planted his right fist into Shawn's shoulder.

"Ough!" complained Shawn.

"It's much more therapeutic to beat on you. Why don't you come over for a beating from time to time? It'll be great therapy."

"I'll pass on the beating," said Shawn, rubbing his shoulder. "For such an old fart, you still have a mean punch!"

"OK, forget the beating. I hope you'll drop by anyway."

"You can count on it. Call me anytime."

"NOW WHAT AM I supposed to do?" thought John. As he turned the handle of the front door of his house, he heard his dog Zack barking in the backyard. He entered his home and placed his keys on a hook stationed on the wall near the front door.

I was home for three weeks awaiting the investigation, but this is different. There's a big difference between being home temporarily and being sent home permanently. The .38 is still loaded. That's still an option.

The barking from the backyard became louder and more prevalent. John decided to check on Zack. He made his way onto the back porch and spotted a strange man peeking in a back window of the house belonging to Emily and Ron.

"Hey!" yelled John. Running down the back porch steps and to the chain link fence that separated the yards, he loudly shouted, "What do you think you're doing?"

The startled man glanced in his direction, then turned and leapt over the fence that separated Emily's front yard from the back. Instantly, John took out his cell phone and took a quick photo of the departing man. He was impressed by the quickness of the fellow as he watched the man run toward the street. John rushed through his home and out his front door just in time to see the stranger run down the street, enter a parked car and speed away. Concerned about Emily's safety, he made his way to her front door.

"Hi, John," Emily greeted, as she opened the door.

"There was a guy peeking in a rear window of your house!" warned John.

"What?"

"Didn't you hear Zack barking?" asked John.

"I did, but I thought he was barking at a squirrel or something. You saw this guy?"

"I called out to him, and he ran away. I tried to catch him, but he made it to a parked car down the street. The car was too far away to read the tag number."

"That is so creepy!" said Emily. "What should I do?"

"This time you should tell Ron about it. Keep your doors and windows locked and the blinds closed – and pay attention if you hear Zack carrying on."

"I will. Thanks for looking out for me. When will you start back to work?"

"This was my last day – I retired," stated John.

"That's great! I'm glad that you're able to retire, but please don't run off to some retirement place in Florida. I'm so blessed to have you as my neighbor."

"I don't have any plans like that, for now. Do you think this guy could be a friend of your old boyfriend Billy?"

"The thing with me and Billy was personal. I doubt very seriously that any of his friends would even think about me now. No, I have no idea who this could be. This is so creepy! You're a cop. Do you know if there have been reports of peeping Toms in the neighborhood?"

"I intend to find out," John assured. "I'll certainly let you know."

John returned to his back porch, where Zack was waiting. Dropping into an outdoor chair there, he took the dog's head in both hands.

"Good boy, Zack. You did good. Anytime you see some weirdo next door, you let us know. Good boy."

John's eyes scanned the current state of his backyard, and he realized the extent of neglect he had given it over the past year. He had regularly mowed the grass, but nothing else. The shrubs growing along the back fence were wildly untrimmed. Weeds grew in the flowerbed under the birdbath.

It's obvious that there are things which need my attention.

He placed a call to his former partner.

"There was a guy peeking into a rear window of the

house next door to me. I took a photo of him running away. I'll send it to you. Have there been reports of peeping Toms in my area of town?"

"I hope that creep wasn't the guy who has been entering houses and doing things to women," replied Shawn.

"What guy?"

"We were issued a report this morning about a pervert who breaks into houses, ties women up, and does things to them. The creep has a slim build, medium height, but we have no facial descriptions. He wears a ski mask when he attacks them. Did you get a good look at this guy?"

"No mask, but I couldn't get a good look at his face. He was wearing a sweatshirt with a hoodie, and his face was shaded. I think he was a white guy, but I wouldn't swear to it. This creep was slim, and athletic. He jumped the fence like a gazelle and ran like the wind. Why haven't we heard about him before?"

"The first attack was last month and across town, but yesterday it happened to a woman in a different part of town," explained Shawn. "They think it's the same guy. We're looking at serial attacks. We now realize that it wasn't a one-time thing on a victim he possibly knew, and it isn't limited to one area. This guy is a real pervert. He has some kind of wacko fetish."

"What kind of attack are we talking about?" asked John. "Is he raping women?"

"Not so far," answered Shawn. "He ties them up, gags them, and takes a knife to their breasts. The pervert doesn't cut them badly enough for his victims to bleed to death, but enough to cause pain and disfigure. He's a complete weirdo. So far, that's the extent of it."

"What a sick SOB!" exclaimed John.

"You can say that again," said Shawn. "Both victims were pregnant women."

Chapter 4

New Life

BEFORE SUNRISE, the following morning, John rose as he normally did. He let Zack out the back door, made a cup of coffee, and dropped a bagel in the toaster. It suddenly occurred to him that he had no schedule to keep and nowhere to go. John no longer felt a sense of purpose.

Maybe if I hadn't beat up that jerk Billy... Evans harped on and on about me stepping into a matter that was none of my business. Maybe he was right. If I hadn't called out to him, maybe he would have gotten the message being sent by Emily by not answering her door. Maybe he would have left her alone on his own accord. Who knows? It's too late now. I doubt it would have made a difference. Evans probably wanted me to retire anyway.

The bagel popped up, and John immediately bathed it in butter. He heard Zack at the back door, and he sipped the cup of coffee as he opened it. It was as if the dog sensed that there was something not quite right with his master. Instead of standing near his food dish, he stayed close to John.

"What's with you?" John asked his dog. "Oh, I'm sorry. I forgot to feed you breakfast."

John placed the dog food in the dish, but Zack didn't seem to be interested. The former detective dropped to one knee and wrapped an arm around the dog's neck.

"I'll get in a new routine, you'll see," John said, stroking

Zack's head. "Everything is fine."

As he stood to his feet, the dog dropped his head into the dish. John sipped his coffee.

A new routine, and it can't consist of lounging around all morning in my underwear. This is stupid! First, I need to take a shower and clean this bedroom. It looks more like one belonging to a teenager, and probably smells worse.

As John stood by the unmade bed, he glanced at the nightstand containing the gun and ammunition. He sat on the bed and opened the drawer. Reaching inside John took out the gun, still loaded from the last time he held it. It felt like it fit his hand perfectly. He heard a whine from the doorway. Turning in the direction of the soft noise, he spotted Zack's eyes fixed on him.

"Come here, boy," he said, reaching out to the dog with his left hand. "You're right. I'm not even sixty. Maybe I'll consider doing a little private work."

He removed the bullets from the revolver and placed them back in the smaller box. Wapping the gun in the old T-shirt, he placed it back in the larger box. John purposefully eased both the box containing the gun and the smaller one into the drawer. John stroked Zack's head several times before shutting the drawer of the nightstand.

"Back to work," he announced.

John collected the dirty clothes from the floor, dropped them in front of the washer in the laundry area, and returned to the bedroom. There, he threw back the comforter and gathered the sheets.

Enough of this! I'm going to first take a shower, then wash the clothes and sheets. While they're washing, I'm going to clean this room. It's nasty! I'm even going to buy air freshener and blast this place. I have the time now to treat this house like somebody lives here. This place is depressing. No more. Enough of this!

After showering, John started the first load of wash. He retrieved the vacuum from the closet, replaced the bag, and began cleaning the carpet. He heard a clinking sound when he ran the vacuum under the bed. He turned off the machine and dropped to his knees. Peering under the bed, he spotted four empty bourbon bottles.

I don't remember kicking those under there. I must have been pretty drunk. What a sickening slob! From now on, I have a new rule. No drinking in the bedroom. I will drink at the table with a friend or while sitting in my recliner watching a game. The bedroom is now off limits for booze.

He carried the bottles to the kitchen trash. Zack heard them drop into the container and trotted into the kitchen.

"How have you been putting up with this?" he asked the dog. "You're looking at the new me."

Zack's head tilted to one side.

THREE WEEKS LATER, clothes were on the bedroom floor and a couple of empty bourbon bottles rested under the bed where John was sleeping. As with many who are on the verge of becoming alcoholics, big turnarounds are often short lived. The one good aspect was the fact that the drawer in the nightstand had remained closed.

The morning sun attempted to slip through a small gap between the bedroom curtains. John opened his eyes at the sensation of his hand being licked.

"Zack, what time is it?" he mumbled.

He reached out and patted the dog's head. John was greeted by a massive headache when he rose to a seated position. He clutched his forehead and fell back into bed.

"Oh, God! I feel like crap, and I didn't even go out last night to make a hangover worthwhile. I've got to get a handle on things."

This time, he rose slowly before dropping his legs over the side of the bed. He felt Zack's head resting on his knee.

"I know. You want to go outside and then have breakfast. I'm coming. I just need a little patience from you this morning."

John collected a half-empty bottle of bourbon from the nightstand and shuffled into the kitchen. He raised the bottle to his lips while opening the back door for Zack. Without taking the sip, he lowered it.

What am I doing? I'm going to kill myself... slowly, not quickly with a gun... but slowly. I need to find something to do with myself. Maybe a hobby? Hobby? The kitchen stinks to high heaven. What would Sharon think if she saw this place? What would she think if she saw me? I know she would slap the hell out of me. Maybe that's the problem. I don't have anyone to slap sense into me anymore. I've got to figure out how to do this on my own.

Chapter 5

Contact

"THAT'S WHAT I said," stated John, in a phone call with his daughter, Heather Littleton. "I've retired."

"What brought this on?" questioned Heather. "I can't imagine you without a badge and gun."

"I guess everything has its season, and that career is over."

"Are you alright?"

"I'm fine," replied John.

"Listen, I want to visit you," Heather said. "The kids and I can catch a flight. I'm sure you'd like to see your grandkids."

"I would absolutely enjoy a visit," replied a surprised John. "Your husband is welcome, as well."

"David is super busy teaching philosophy and psychology classes at the university. He's been given more responsibility this year, and he uses weekends to communicate with his graduate students who assist him with grading papers and lesson plans."

"Sounds like he isn't around as much as when you first married."

"He reserves at least one Saturday each month to spend with us, and usually we have two Saturdays as a family.

Have you told Chris about the retirement?"

"I plan to call your brother later today. Do you hear from him often?"

"We sometimes call, but visits are somewhat rare. We live different lives. I have kids, and he still doesn't have plans for a family. However, we've always been close."

"I'm afraid he considers me to be a cave man, or something," said John. "His brain is in another world. I'm not sure what he's working on now."

"He develops artificial intelligence based on reinforcement learning chip design, primarily used in cell phones."

"I don't even know what that means," admitted John.

"That stuff is over my head, too. However, when we get together it doesn't take long during a visit for us to revert back to being brother and sister."

"I'm glad that's the case, but he and I just seem to drift farther apart. On a more positive note, I'm looking forward to your visit."

"I need to tell you about one concern of mine," said Heather. "I'm a little worried about my kids having access to a loaded gun during the visit. I remember growing up with you having a gun in your nightstand, and I remember on one occasion seeing a gun under your pillow."

"You don't have to worry about that. I'll make sure that's not a problem. Weapons will be secured. I promise."

"I'll call later to give you the details about the visit. Bye, Daddy."

The call ended. John poured a cup of coffee and accompanied Zack out onto his back porch. He stood next to the couch of an outdoor furniture set he purchased two years before.

Daddy. That's the first time in years she's called me Daddy. Interesting.

He dropped onto the couch, took a sip from the cup, then placed it on a small coffee table positioned in front of him.

Seated there, he surveyed the current condition of the backyard.

"What a crap hole," John mumbled to himself, as he watched his dog relieve its bowels next to the neglected concrete birdbath. "I told myself that I would clean this mess up. What's wrong with me? My grandkids aren't going to find me living like this! I've been putting this off, but I won't give it another day."

After using a shovel to relocate Zack's deposit, he began pulling the weeds from the flowerbed at the base of the birdbath. Once accomplished, he scrubbed the birdbath with a brush. Before it was time for supper, the entire backyard had been weeded. John dropped back onto the couch on the porch and took a sip of coffee. It had now assumed the ambient temperature of the air, and he tossed the remainder out onto the lawn.

Tomorrow, I'll cut the grass and trim the azaleas. But before that, I need to purchase a locking gun case. I made a promise.

WHEN JOHN FIRST saw Heather and her kids at a distance in Hartsfield-Jackson International Airport, he suddenly felt overwhelmed. He wept.

God, what is wrong with me? I've become a basket case.

He quickly pulled out a handkerchief and pretended to only blow his nose, but he also wiped the tears from his eyes and cheeks. He then waved it to gain the attention of his daughter. All three approached him pulling suitcases on wheels. Stuffing the hanky back into the pocket of his jacket, he made his way to Heather.

"Can I help you with the bags?" John asked her.

"We're perfectly capable of handling them," replied Heather. "This isn't the first time the kids have traveled."

"I have a couple of child seats in the back seat of my car," John said. "I hope I have the right kind."

"I'm impressed!" exclaimed Heather. "I'm sure they will be fine."

"They've grown so much," replied John.

"How old are you, Charlotte?" John asked, turning to the grandchildren.

"Nine," she stated.

"I'm five!" Josh proudly volunteered.

"Nine and five!" exclaimed John. "Wow! You two are really growing up."

"Are you really my grandfather?" asked Josh.

"I certainly am," answered John. "The last time I saw you, you were little. I think Charlotte was about your age, and you were really small." Turning to Heather, "Are you up for supper, once we drop off the bags? I know a great restaurant, not far from the house."

"What do they serve?" interrupted Charlotte. "I'm mostly a vegetarian, but I hate Indian food."

John glanced at Heather, and she gave him a wink.

"Well, not Indian food," replied John. "It has most everything else. Hamburgers, steaks, pizza, fish, chicken, vegetables, baked potatoes, meat loaf…"

"What is meat loaf?" asked Josh. "That sounds weird."

"I'll tell you what," answered John. "I'll order it, and let you have first bite. That way, if you hate it, you'll know without ordering it."

"Ok," Josh said.

"It's a deal," said John, holding out his hand. "Shake on it."

Placing his small hand in the aging hand of his grandfather, Josh smiled. Dropping to one knee, John took him in one arm and held out the other to his granddaughter. She cautiously stepped close to him.

"I can't tell you how happy I am to see you both," said John.

"Almost everything you listed about that restaurant was meat," said Charlotte. "Do they have pasta?"

"I know that it offers spaghetti with a vegetable only sauce," answered John.

"That sounds OK," Charlotte said.

He released them and stood. As he held out both arms to his daughter, Heather stepped into his embrace. For the first time since she was a little girl, she buried her head in his chest. She took a deep breath, and John felt her body relax.

"I love you, kid," he whispered.

ONCE THE CHILDREN were in bed that evening, John and Heather settled onto his couch with glasses of wine. John sensed a sadness in his daughter.

"What's going on?" he asked.

"We're busy with kids and careers," she replied, faking a smile. "I never understood the demands of parenthood until experiencing it for myself."

"That's not the entire situation, is it? I haven't seen you in four years, but I know you. You can talk to me."

"We're just busy," Heather said, taking a sip of wine.

"David spending a couple of Saturdays each month with you and the kids, isn't much," said John. "What's with him being too busy for you and the kids?"

"We're separated, Daddy." She placed a hand over her mouth. Her eyes filled with tears.

"When did this happen?" he asked.

"Three months ago. I complained about the fact that he was rarely home during waking hours. He said that he had to focus on his career, and then suggested that we separate until the semester ended. I didn't understand how distant we had become until then. He moved out the following week. That's when he promised that he would spend at least one Saturday per month with us. So far, it's been two Saturday's each month."

"Another woman?"

"I don't know. I'm sure there are young and pretty

graduate students who play for his favor, mostly for grades and jobs within the department. Who knows?"

"Does he call?" asked John.

"Rarely, now. At first, he called daily. He talked with the kids each night before bedtime. Now, it's once or twice a week."

"How about communicating with you?"

"He talks with me a few minutes before reaching out to the kids" answered Heather. "The kids and I are in the house, and he still pays most of the bills. I work part time from the house, doing paperwork for a counseling practice. Because of David, I have contacts with several professionals."

"You have a PhD in psychology," said John. "You should have no problem getting full time work."

"Josh is only five," explained Heather. "I want to be there at the house for him. Plus, I've let David focus on his career until lately. It's been years since I've counseled anyone."

"I don't see this working out," said John. "I would like to jerk a knot in David, or better still, kick his sorry butt."

"I doubt that would help," Heather said with a chuckle. "I've never cheated. If it ends in divorce, he would be at fault. Any butt kicking needs to be reserved for divorce court. Besides, I want the kids to have a relationship with their father."

Heather began to sob hysterically. John moved over to her side of the couch and held his daughter. His emotions ran the gamut, from deep compassion for his daughter to intense rage at anyone who dared to hurt her. He imagined finding David in a bedroom with a young female student, and then dragging him out of the room by the hair of his head, before pounding his lights out.

Heather's right. I don't need to do anything that would make David out to be the victim. Still, I would love to get my hands on him!

"On the bright side," Heather began, wiping tears from

her checks with both hands. "You successfully introduced Josh to meatloaf. He loves it."

"Glad I could be of service," John said, before kissing the top of his daughter's head.

"Things haven't been good with David for some time," she admitted. "That's why I've avoided you. I didn't want you to know. I hoped that we would move past it."

"I thought you were afraid that I would be a lousy influence on the kids," said John.

"That was David's concern, and I was doing whatever I could do to avoid being divisive. I don't agree with your political thoughts, but I didn't think you would be bad for them. For heaven's sake, you and Mom raised me."

"Thank you. It means a lot. I really want to get to know them better. I've missed you so much."

"I've missed you too, Daddy. You're welcome to visit us in California any time, and I'll try to come see you more."

"What about David?" asked John.

"David's not even around. Screw him. If we get back together, he'll have to deal with it."

"I'm retired. I'm free to go wherever I want and when I want. I will absolutely take you up on visiting you all on the left coast."

It was like the weight of the world lifted from John's soul. He held his daughter tight. Suddenly, he felt twenty years younger. His mind flashed back to his suicidal thoughts weeks before.

Dear God! If I had shot myself, I wouldn't have been here for Heather and these kids. I can be such a selfish SOB. What an idiot!

"Wait until Josh sees what I plan for breakfast in the morning," said John.

"I remember you and bacon," said Heather. "Josh might like it, but my mainly vegetarian daughter would have a cow!"

"Have a cow! That's funny. I'm thinking about

Charlotte, too. There's a place with a breakfast buffet, and it includes lots of fresh fruit, muffins, and scones. I'm sure she'll find something she likes. Nothing would give me more pleasure than to see smiles on both their faces."

"I'm sure they'll like it," said Heather.

"You'll smile again," said John. "You don't deserve this, and there will be happy days in your future. I promise that I will be there for you, whenever or however you need me."

"I love you, Daddy."

Chapter 6

OTP

SEEING A LIGHT on in John's house at 6:00 AM, Shawn Stone pulled his unmarked patrol car to the curb. Almost immediately after he knocked, John opened the front door while holding a finger to his lips.

"We need to be quiet," whispered John.

"What?" mouthed Shawn.

"I've got company, and they're still sleeping. Come on into the kitchen. What's up?"

"Company?" whispered Shawn. "Since when do you have company?"

"I'm not seeing a woman, in case that's what you're thinking. I have family visiting."

"Family? Since when do you have visits from family?"

"My daughter Heather and the grandkids are visiting," explained John. "So, what's going on? What brings you here?"

"I've been placed on the case of the weirdo who terrorizes pregnant women, and it's gotten worse."

"Worse than cutting women's breasts?" questioned John.

"He still does that, but now he is carving letters on the abdomen of his victims."

"Letters?"

"He carves the letters OTP," explained Shawn.

"What do the letters mean?"

"No one has a clue. Some think the guy is a member of some weird cult, but I wonder if it's his initials."

"Could be his initials, but I doubt it," said John. "Carving his initials could really speed up the investigation. I'm sure you have people searching the database for someone with those initials. I don't think the guy's ready to be caught. My guess is those letters are probably a personal message about something. Combined with the cutting of breasts, it's possible carving letters into the belly of pregnant women has to do with pregnancy. Maybe the 'P' stands for pregnant. How many cases involve the letters?"

"So far, he's done it to two women."

"Two don't make for a trend, but this progression in the attacks is a bad sign," said John. "If law enforcement fails to get his message, I expect him to inflect even worse on his victims."

"We need to catch this guy. I really want to get my hands on this little turd."

"If it's the man I saw, you're right about him being a lightweight," said John. "What can you tell me in addition to what I reported after I saw the guy peeping on Emily? What leads do you have?"

"Nothing – no leads. The victims confirm the account you gave, that he isn't a big man. He uses fear to accomplish what he wants. He catches them from behind, places a knife to their bellies, and tells them that he will gut them and kill the baby if they put up a fight. He then pushes them face down, uses zip ties to bind their hands, and gags them."

"He doesn't use chloroform?" asked John.

"No. It seems that he wants them alert to experience the fear and pain."

"Sick bastard!" exclaimed John. "Does he molest them in any other way?"

"Not yet, but he seems to be more of a mutilator than a molester. He seems to get off on cutting women. It's where he cuts them that places him in a category of molester."

"This is one screwed up individual," said John.

"I wish I could get my hands on him," said Shawn, holding a clinched fist.

"He'd better hope that you get your hands on him before the husbands of those women find him."

"That's for sure," agreed Shawn. "I've heard that a vigilante group has formed - made up of the husbands. Those guys would rip him to shreds."

"So, how's your new partner?" asked John.

"She's smart, but we don't seem to be on the same wavelength," answered Shawn. "This is a serious case, and I need someone I can communicate with."

"You're welcome to keep me informed about what happens with this case," said John. "You can always bounce things off me."

"I know that you're concerned about your neighbor, Emily, but I need to be careful with what I share," replied Shawn. "You aren't a cop anymore, and I could get in trouble if certain people found out that I was talking to you about this case."

"You do need to be careful about that," agreed John. "I want us to talk, but on the other hand, I hate the thoughts of coming between you and your new partner."

"I need to pick your brain on this one," said Shawn. "At least, for now."

"What else is going on with you?" asked John.

"That's pretty much the focus of my police work."

"What about your personal life?"

"What personal life?" replied Shawn. "I'm swamped with this case."

"That case can't be 24/7. What else is happening?"

"I feel like I'm basically working and sleeping," answered Shawn.

"Well, I'm glad that you're sleeping. A case like this one can keep you awake."

"Talking about sleeping, have you ever had a dream that you couldn't shake the next morning?" asked Shawn.

"It comes with the job," replied John. "Are you dreaming about these attacks?"

"Not really. Last night I dreamed about having a horrific case of diarrhea."

"Oh, come on man!" blurted John. "If I was a shrink, I'd say you're messed up."

"Yeah. So, I dreamed that I stopped at this place to use the bathroom. It was a large restroom, about 20 by 20 feet square, with four nasty toilets... out in the open room. There were no stalls. Two of them didn't have toilet seats, so I picked one near a wall with a seat. It also had a roll of TP hanging on the wall. I dropped down onto the toilet, and it was like my butt exploded. It was bad, man. Really rank... nasty."

"Gross," John chuckled. "OK, that's all I care to hear about your weird dream."

"You haven't heard the weirdest part of it," said Shawn. "Next, I heard a female voice outside and noticed the door opening. And here I am, sitting on this nasty crapper and stinking up the place. In the dream, I called out for her to not come in. Then I heard her yell at me through the door that I was in the women's restroom! She was screaming at me."

"Nope, that's enough!" exclaimed John. "Enough!"

"I've been having a lot of weird dreams," said Shawn. "I'm not sleeping good."

"Stress of the job," replied John. "You're probably frustrated with trying to find this guy who attacks pregnant women. I often had vivid dreams when I was working a nasty case. Sharon would wake me up. I guess I talked in my sleep sometimes. I didn't realize how much I leaned on her until she passed away."

"She was special," agreed Shawn.

"Your mind can do weird things because of our line of work. I remember a case where I found a guy with his throat cut ear to ear. I heard the gurgles of his last breath, so it must have just happened. Looking into the gash in his neck, I could see his esophagus and his windpipe…both cut into. The only thing holding his head on was his vertebra housing his spinal cord. He bled completely out. Within no time his lifeless eyes were staring straight up. I stayed with him until they took him away."

"Somebody must have really hated that guy," said Shawn.

"When they performed the autopsy, the doctor found eleven single-edged razor blades in his stomach," explained John. "It was ruled a suicide. The guy cut his own throat. His fingerprints were on a straight razor found nearby."

"The guy did this to himself?" questioned Shawn.

"Apparently," answered John. "I couldn't get that guy out of my mind. Over the next week or so, I would see the guy in the corner of my eye…standing in a dark alley, as I passed by it at night. I would then focus my eyes on the alley, but he wasn't really there. He really got to me. I knew my mind was playing tricks on me."

"Did you go to the department shrink?" asked Shawn.

"No. I think talking with Sharon helped more than going to him would have. I usually didn't unload on her, but I did about that one. After I lost her, I felt crippled. I'm not the same. I'm sure you were able to tell that something has been off since she died."

"Yeah, you haven't been the same," agreed Shawn. "Has it gotten any better since you retired?"

"A little better," answered John. "I don't know if it's retirement; you know the lack of stress. Maybe it's getting to know my neighbors, Ron and Emily. I don't know. It could be just spending more time with my dog, Zack. You know what they say. A dog is a man's best friend."

"I'm glad that you like your neighbors, but maybe it has

more to do with this visit from your daughter Heather and grandkids. What's she doing here?"

"She and the kids decided to pay me a visit," answered John. "This visit has been like icing on the cake!"

"It's been a while since they've last visited," said Shawn.

"Too long," added John. "I can't tell you how nice it is to have them around."

"I'm glad things are better."

"Hey, let me give you a suggestion regarding your weird dreams," offered John.

"Yeah?"

"Hold off the booze," advised John. "Since Sharon died, I started taking a drink at night before going to bed. Before long, I was drinking heavy before crashing. Eventually, I started drinking as soon as I came home from work. To be honest, it didn't really help with the dreams. I was just able to fall asleep easier. Don't go that route. Do something else. You're always welcome to drop by here and talk with me. Always."

"I may take you up on that," said Shawn.

"I mean it."

"We can still have a beer, right?" asked Shawn.

"Absolutely. I want to know more about that weirdo case. Does he carve the letters with the same instrument that he uses on the breasts?""Now, tell me which one of us is sick," replied Shawn.

"It's important," said John.

"What difference would that make?" asked the younger man.

"Just tell me," demanded John.

"No, those women said that he used something else."

"That means he premeditated the lettering," said John. "It wasn't something that he did based on a trigger he experienced with one of the women. The lettering was planned. He's proceeding along a planned course. It's deliberate, and I expect matters to become worse."

"What do you mean by worse?" asked Shawn.

"I expect him to escalate. I expect him to be more demonstrative in whatever message he is giving, and I'm afraid that means future victims will suffer more."

"I want to get my hands on this guy!" blurted Shawn.

Chapter 7

Decisions

"IT'S MURDER NOW," stated Shawn, as he stood on his ex-partner's front porch.

"I was afraid of that," John responded, fully opening the front door of his home. He motioned for his former partner to come inside.

"I thought maybe he was just a weird sicko," said Shawn. "I didn't expect this."

"Two visits from you in one week. I'm glad you dropped by."

"You asked me to keep you informed," said Shawn. "However, my new partner wouldn't like me talking to you about an ongoing case. I don't feel right about leaving her out. I need your experience, but I can't officially bring you in. You're off the force now."

"Sounds like I may have put you in a bad position. Sorry. I don't really want to get between you and your partner."

"Caitlin and I just don't seem to click like we do," said Shawn.

"Coffee?" offered John.

"Sure," replied Shawn. "You said that you were afraid this pervert would inflict more on his victims if the police didn't fully understand his MO. How did you know?"

"I've seen it happen before. What else has changed?"

"It's with this pregnant prostitute who was found with her throat cut," explained Shawn. "She had OTP carvings on her belly, but this time he carved the word ONLY beneath those letters. Any ideas?"

"My guess is that it could indicate what the letter the O stands for," observed John.

"Some think that, and others think that it means ONLY whatever OTP stands for. Previously, the victims have been women alone at home. Why would he change to a prostitute?"

"His actions have been well publicized on the news, so I would guess most pregnant women in the metro Atlanta area are taking precautions," explained John. "It appears that he is now going after easier targets, like prostitutes."

"Why murder?" questioned Shawn.

"Some prostitutes are real fighters. They're often in dangerous situations and some know how to take care of themselves. It's possible that she struggled with him and managed to pull that ski mask off. If she saw his face, it's doubtful that he would allow her talk to a sketch artist. She had to die."

"Some at the precinct are afraid that the next victim will also be killed," said Shawn "Once he crossed that line, most think he'll continue."

"Unfortunately, they're probably right," agreed John, with a sigh. "He may have unintentionally crossed that line. Not only does he have a vigilante group of angry husbands after him, but now he also has a pimp that probably wants him dead. Pimps can be ruthless, especially when someone messes with their business. Once this hits the news, pimps will be doing a better job of guarding their girls."

"I hadn't thought of that," said Shawn. "If he keeps this up, he may have an army of pimps after him."

"Army of pimps?" asked Heather, stepping into the kitchen. "Sounds like the title of a B movie."

"It does," chuckled John.

"Did we wake you up?" asked Shawn.

"Do I look like I just woke up?" asked Heather.

"No, you look good," Shawn replied.

"I see that you're no longer in uniform, big guy," observed Heather.

"I like detective work," replied Shawn.

"But I've always had a soft spot in my heart for a guy in uniform," she said, with a wink.

"You're a married woman," quipped Shawn. "So, behave yourself."

"That's right; behave yourself," added John.

"What's with the talk of an army of pimps?" she asked.

"A prostitute was murdered," answered John.

"Risky profession," stated Heather.

John silently nodded. His eyes spoke of the gravity of the situation, and Heather's jovial mood suddenly sobered. She'd witnessed those eyes before when her father was working a major case.

"There's more to it," she said. "There's more to it than just a random killing of a hooker, isn't it?"

"I probably should be going," said Shawn, avoiding to answer her question.

"I'll walk you out," volunteered Heather.

She took him by the arm and led him though the kitchen and to the front door. Opening it, she turned and placed a tender hand on his chest.

"Be careful out there," she whispered.

Their eyes met. Shawn's were filled with questions.

"I'm always careful," he replied, as he brushed by her and stepped onto the porch.

She watched his muscular and exceptionally broad shouldered frame make its way to the unmarked car and drive away. By this time, her father had moved behind her.

"That's one handsome man," she whispered to herself.

"What's going on?" John asked.

"Nothing," she said.

"I know you. I raised you. What's with your sudden interest in my ex-partner? What's going on in that head of yours?"

"Who said that I'm interested in him?" asked Heather.

"You're a married woman and you live on the other side of the country. Don't play with Shawn."

"I'm not playing with anyone," replied Heather. "I can tell that he's working a dangerous case. He wouldn't be coming back to talk with you about it if it wasn't. I just told him to be careful."

"You're concerned for him," observed John.

"Shawn's a good guy."

"I also heard your comment about his looks," said her father.

"So, you're going to monitor my personal thoughts now?"

"He has a partner, and they'll be careful," said John. "They'll look out for each other."

"You don't really believe that. If he was truly confident in his partner, he wouldn't be dropping by here to talk to you without her."

"How did you become so smart?" John asked.

"I have a PhD, don't you know," Heather answered with a smile.

"You didn't learn to read people through years of sticking your head in books."

"You two are not so hard to read," said Heather. "Remember, you said that you know me. You've known me since I was born. Well, I've known you too since I was born. I was raised by a cop, and I understand cops. Shawn's not just an ex-partner. Through the years, you've had several partners. I stood at the kitchen door and watched you two at the table. He's special to you. I can tell."

"Life is short," said John. "Your mother is gone. Your brother never calls or comes to visit. It's been years since you and the grandkids have visited. Shawn has been here. You're right. I've had partners, but Shawn and I are more like family."

"I'm sorry. I should have visited. I should have brought my kids around, even if David didn't want to come. I've tried to be a good wife, and I've tried so hard to support him in his career."

"I understand," said John.

"You have no clue what's it's been like," said Heather. "You and Mom were like two sides of a coin. It was like you were glued to each other. David and I haven't had that. I feel like I'm dying inside. He doesn't care. I feel so alone. For the past couple of years, I've wrapped myself around my children. They're all I have. I don't have what you and Mom had. I've never had it. I hoped after years of marriage that it would develop into that, but it's been the opposite. He's grown further apart from me."

"I'm sorry," John said, taking his daughter into his arms.

Heather's body trembled. Her tears soaked her father's shirt, as she buried her head in his broad chest and cried. After a few minutes, she relaxed. She took a deep breath and let it out. Heather released him and wiped her face with both hands. John stepped away and shortly returned with a box of tissues.

"I'm the one who's sorry," she said. "I won't stay away like this anymore. I promise. I need you. My kids need you, whether they or David know it or not. They need you."

"Do you think he'll move back in?" asked John.

"I'm exhausted with it all. I'm so tired of this. I'm almost to the point of not caring. I'm tempted to move back to the Atlanta area and put the kids in schools here. You're right. I'm educated. It's not like I'm unable find a job and take care of the kids myself."

"Is that what you want?" asked John. "I would love that."

"What I want is for my husband to love me and the kids more than his career. At least that's what I keep telling myself. But I'm so tired of this. David is still paying the bills for us, but that's it. Legally, I'm still married, but it certainly doesn't feel like a marriage. To be honest, I expect to see divorce papers in the mail any day. They could be waiting for me at home now. I'm tired of the stress. I feel used up, but I'm only thirty-one."

"You're not used up," said John. "You worked on your dissertation while you were taking care of two young kids. I can't imagine changing the diapers of one child and chasing another around, while earning a PhD. You're tough, but the relationship with David is a heavy burden. You'd be a different young woman if you were out from under that load. I realize that it's a tough thing to say, but he isn't doing right by you. I'd lay odds that he has another woman. I'd like to get my hands on the pointy headed prick! Why are you putting up with him?"

"I hate the idea of divorce," said Heather. "You and Mom didn't raise me to have a failed marriage. Part of my thinking tells me that I need to get out from under this sham of a marriage. But in my gut, it just feels wrong to leave him. I don't want my kids coming from a broken home."

"You're not the one who left," John reminded her. "Like they say, it takes two to tango. Both partners have to want it. You can't have a marriage by yourself."

"I have another week before we fly back to California," said Heather. "Maybe I'll see if any of the local universities here are hiring. Georgia State is downtown."

"If all else fails, you could set up a family counseling business. You have a PhD in the field."

"No, I'm not up to that," said Heather. "I would feel like a hypocrite. I couldn't counsel families after having a failed marriage of my own. Also, like you said, I need to get out from under the weight I'm carrying. I'm not sure that I could carry the burden of other suffering families just yet."

"That's my girl. I like the fact that you're not just waiting for David to call all the shots. I didn't raise you to be a doormat."

"I've missed you, Daddy."

"I've missed you too."

"I want my kids to get to know you better," said Heather.

"I would love that."

"Just don't fill their heads with your conservative Republican crap!" she said with a chuckle.

"Where's Zack?" questioned Josh, while stumbling into the kitchen.

"He's out back," replied John.

"Can I bring him inside?" asked Josh.

"Sure, but don't you want breakfast first?" replied John.

"After I see Zack," answered Josh, as he moved quickly to the rear door.

"He loves that dog," stated Heather.

"It's normal for a boy and dog to get along," said John. "You should get him a dog."

"Maybe one day, but there is just too much going on right now," Heather said while opening the refrigerator. "Looks like you're out of eggs."

"I can take us all out for breakfast," offered John.

"That can get expensive. There was a grocery store a few blocks over. Is it still open?"

"No, the larger chains put it out of business," answered John. "Get the kids dressed, and I'll take us out."

"I'll agree to it this morning," stated Heather. "But I plan to make breakfast tomorrow morning."

"It's a deal," said John.

Heather called Josh to come in from the backyard. She woke his sister. and told them both to quickly get dressed. Within minutes, John gathered his keys from the hook by the door and they were out of the house and heading for John's car.

"There's something under the windshield wiper of your car," said Heather. "Maybe Shawn left you a note."

John pulled a folded paper from under the wiper.

"This isn't from John," he whispered.

"Let me see," she said, returning a whisper.

"Later."

"I want to see it now."

John ushered the kids into the backseat. Once they were buckled in their seat belts, he held the note out for Heather to read while placing a finger to his lips. After reading it, her hands began to tremble.

"No other fingerprints should be on this," John stated, pulling the note away from her touch and placing it in the pocket of his jacket. "I've already messed up by touching it myself"

In bold type, it stated:

"YOU'LL NEVER FIND ME WITHOUT OPEN EYELIDS.

I'M WATCHING YOUR PRETTY DAUGHTER – AND HER KIDS."

Chapter 8

Note

"SHAWN NEEDS TO SEE this note," said John.

"Of course," agreed Heather, somewhat shaken.

"We promised the kids breakfast," John reminded his daughter. "I've already contaminated the note with my fingerprints. Let me first go inside and put the note in a zip lock bag to protect it from additional contamination. I'll give Shawn a call once the note is secured. After you and the kids are in my car, lock the car doors until you see me coming out."

Heather nodded her head and proceeded to do just as she was told. Soon, John returned to the car and slid behind the steering wheel.

"Who's hungry?" he asked, turning his attention to the innocent faces in the back seat.

"I am!" shouted Josh.

"I'm still asleep," mumbled his sister Charlotte.

"I went inside to get you two something," announced John. "I guess Charlotte is too sleepy to care."

"What is it?" Charlotte asked, sleepily.

"You can have these after breakfast!" he told his grandchildren while holding two candy bars so they could clearly be visible to the children. "I'll give them to your mother for safe keeping. If neither of you want them, I'm sure that your mother will be glad to eat them."

"I thought candy bars were off limits," said Charlotte.

"I can't seem to control your grandfather," Heather replied, attempting a smile.

"Chocolate?" asked Charlotte, now bright-eyed.

"You bet!" answered John. "And Shawn is going to join us for breakfast."

"Is Shawn my uncle?" asked Josh.

"No," answered Heather. "Why would you ask that?"

"He seems to be always around since we've been here," replied Josh. "I thought maybe he was part of the family, or something."

"You're so stupid," said Charlotte.

"Don't call your brother stupid!" warned Heather. "Both of my children are exceptionally smart. Now, apologize to your brother."

Normally, Heather would have been more concerned with name calling from one of her children, but she welcomed the diversion from the troubling note. She also felt a sense of comfort knowing that Shawn would join them for breakfast.

When the waitress arrived at their table, John announced that everyone would be enjoying the buffet. Each confirmed to the waitress their desire for drink, and then stood to begin their pursuit of buffet items. Heather's weary eyes met Shawn's as he entered the restaurant, but the large detective's attention was fixed on her father. Shawn was a striking figure. It was almost impossible for clothes to hide his tall muscular build, and his movements in his stride quietly spoke of both athleticism and confidence. John pulled the bagged note from his pocket and handed it to his former partner. Heather felt protected in the company of her father and Shawn, and her demeanor changed. Allowing the two men to have a private conversation about the note, she led her children to the buffet. Food wasn't the only thing on her mind, as she helped her children select items from the buffet. Almost captivated by the presence of the younger detective, she found herself repeatedly glancing back at him.

"We found this note on the windshield of my car this morning," John whispered. "Sorry. My prints are on it. I didn't expect this. I initially thought the note was from my neighbor Emily."

After glancing at it, Shawn placed it in a pocket inside his coat. As he did, Heather caught a glimpse of the weapon strapped FROM his shoulder as she watched him from the buffet.

"David hates guns, but I feel pretty good about this one today," she thought.

Heather attempted to guide her children in their selections at the buffet, but her attention was split between them and Shawn. She felt herself drawn to him. Soon, their plates were filled. As she led her children back to the table, she met John and Shawn as they approached the buffet. Heather felt a warm sensation move through her body, as Shawn placed his huge hand on her shoulder.

"I'm on this," Shawn whispered. "Just be vigilant in watching your kids. I'm on this guy."

"I would love to have you on ME," Heather thought as she mouthed, "Thank you,"

"Man, your boy loves bacon!" Shawn observed, pointing to the eight slices of bacon on Josh's plate.

"What am I going to do with him?" asked Heather, rolling her eyes.

"Well, he can't put it back, can he?" teased Shawn.

"Not another slice of bacon!" Heather called out to her son, spotting him cramming a piece into his mouth.

"He's in the South, now," said John, grinning.

Heather guided her children back to the table, as the two men examined offerings of the buffet.

"Shawn," John whispered to his ex-partner.

"What?" asked Shawn.

"After you turn that note in, come back to the house,"

John instructed Shawn. "Bring your partner, this time. This note places me squarely in the investigation. My involvement can be in the open, now. Plus, it's best for your relationship with your partner."

"Will do," replied Shawn.

"SO, THIS IS WHERE the notorious John Rawlings lives," detective Caitlin Reeves stated to her partner, as she and Shawn stepped onto John's front porch.

"The one and only," Shawn replied, while knocking on the front door.

When the door opened, Caitlin came face to face with Heather.

"She doesn't look much like a middle-aged retired guy," commented Caitlin. "Shawn, are you sure you this isn't your girlfriend's place?"

Before Shawn could answer the question, Heather spoke. "I'm Heather, John's daughter. Come on in. My father's inside."

John stood to greet Shawn's new partner. Caitlin quickly approached him and offered her hand.

"Shawn's said so much about you," Caitlin began, looking the older man dead in the eyes. "I hope you're enjoying retirement."

"Great to meet you, Caitlin," replied John. "The note I gave Shawn certainly puts a damper on retirement. What do you think about it?"

"My first question is why would this guy threaten you and your family?" Caitlin asked.

"I saw a man peeking in my neighbor's window a while back and I confronted him," John answered. "It's possible that he found out that I'm an ex-cop and he wants to send me a message. I have to say that it caught me off guard."

"The note was a printout containing Times New Roman font," said Caitlin. "It could have come from one of thousands of home ink jet printers in the area. There is nothing special about the paper stock. Is there anything that might indicate that it came from someone other than this serial molester? Any cop with the years you put in is bound to have made enemies."

"That's a good point," said John. "I sort of assumed it was from this pervert, but you know what they say about the word assume."

"Yep," Caitlin answered. "It makes an 'ass' out of 'u' and 'me.' My father taught me that one. Has anyone you arrested in the past come after you later?"

"I run into them from time to time, but most aren't in a hurry to go back to prison," John answered. "They also know that if they attack me, I carry all the time. It's in their best interest to back off."

"True, but Caitlin has a point," added Shawn. "Before now, Heather and her kids weren't in the picture. She's right about not assuming things. I think this sicko is the primary candidate for the note, but I wouldn't put it past somebody you put away."

"I don't find any of this the least bit comforting," interrupted Heather. "I thought the note came from this weirdo who is terrorizing the city. Catch him, and the matter is settled. Now, you're saying this note could have come from anyone my father has arrested over the past three decades?"

"It's probably the weirdo," John said. "But Caitlin is absolutely right. We shouldn't limit our thinking to just this one guy."

"Should I take the kids back to California?" asked Heather.

Caitlin and Shawn turned their attention toward John. Heather's father dropped his head and answered.

"It might not be a bad idea; just until we have a clearer picture of who is behind this."

"I hate this!" blurted Heather.

"Me too," mumbled John.

THREE DAYS LATER, Heather and her children landed back in California. She placed a call to her husband, who had been staying at the house during her absence.

"David, we're back in California and should be at the house within a couple of hours."

"I wish you had given me a heads-up earlier," David replied. "I thought you were coming back next week. The house is a bit of a mess. Last night, I had a group of friends over to the place and haven't had a chance to clean up."

"I don't know that I want to hear the details," said Heather. "Is it bad enough that I should call Maria to clean it?"

"Call her," answered David. "Sorry. I'm at work now, but I'll go over and unlock the house for her. I'll leave it in her hands because I will need to get back to the university."

"We've used her for years, so I trust her," replied Heather.

When Heather arrived, she found Maria busily vacuuming downstairs. Due to the noise of the machine, she didn't notice when Heather entered the house.

"Maria!" Heather called out.

"Mrs. Littleton – good to see you," Maria replied, turning off the vacuum. "Most of the downstairs has been cleaned, but not your bedroom upstairs. The kids' rooms upstairs are fine."

"Thanks so much, Maria, for coming at such short notice," Heather replied.

Heather instructed her children to take their luggage to their rooms upstairs. As she rolled her own bag into her bedroom, her heart sank. The wildly unkept bed still slightly smelled of sex.

"*I can't sleep in here,*" she thought. "*I'll take a pillow and blanket to the couch for at least tonight – maybe from now on. That's it. This isn't my bedroom anymore. This house isn't my house anymore, and my husband is not behaving at all as my husband. I'm done. I'm ready for a divorce."*

She called her husband a second time since arriving in California.

"David, I want a divorce, and I want the house on the market next week," she told him. "I'm calling a lawyer this afternoon, and I suggest you do the same."

"Are you sure?" asked David.

"We're done," answered Heather. "I'm thinking about taking the kids back to Atlanta in the future, so your visitation will need to be there – if you're interested."

"Of course, I'm interested," said David.

"Really? When was the last time you even talked to them? I will tell you this. I am taking sole custody of the kids, and you may have visitation rights in the summer – if you wish. Our lawyers will work out the equity of the house. I'm through with you. I am going back to my family in Atlanta. My kids need their grandfather, and I plan to be there should he need me. You and I are done. I suggest that you refrain from causing me or the kids any problems. If you agree to my terms, I promise not to do or say anything that would hurt your career in any way, and I will spare you from embarrassment."

"Are you trying to threaten me?" asked David.

"I'm not making threats, just stating the facts," answered Heather. "Think carefully."

"A couple of weeks with your cop Dad, and you seem to be acting like one." said David.

"Maybe after a couple of weeks I remembered who I am. I wish you well, but don't screw with me."

"Don't screw with me? Do you hear yourself?"

"Loud and clear," answered Heather. "I suggest you hear me loud and clear."

ALONE IN HIS house again, John missed the sounds of his grandchildren playing with Zack. He missed the company of his daughter. John stepped out onto his back porch to find his dog peacefully sleeping.

"Well, it's back to just me and you, boy," he said to Zack. "Shawn and Caitlin are busily trying to ascertain who is behind the note, and it's for the best that Shawn no longer confides in me without the new partner. Heather and the kids are in a much safer environment, for now. It's up to us to look out for each other."

John pulled the police positive pistol from a pocket of this jacket and opened the cylinder to check the recently loaded rounds of ammunition. He took a seat on the outdoor couch and snapped the cylinder shut. Studying the slight movements of Zack's chest as he breathed during sleep, he considered the loneliness he felt since Heather and his grandchildren left.

It's good that I didn't pull the trigger that day. Heather and the kids needed me during their stay. Nights with her and the kids around the kitchen table were the best...even better when Shawn was here too. They breathed life into this house again, and they did the same for me. It's too quiet now. Zack's not much good for conversation.

He placed the pistol back into the right outer pocket of his jacket and pulled an unopened pint of bourbon from an inside pocket of his coat. Holding it in his left hand, he contemplated the first sip.

It's been over a month, but I'm sure it tastes the same. I don't know...once I start...oh, what the hell.

Just as he placed his right hand on the cap, he was interrupted by a call on his cell phone. He set the bottle down on the porch and took the phone from the left outer pocket of the jacket.

"Heather?" John answered.

"Hi, Daddy," he heard Heather say.

"I was just thinking about you," he said.

"I just signed the divorce papers, and I made flight arrangements for me and the kids to fly out tomorrow," Heather announced.

"What?"

"We're coming back to Atlanta, if that's OK," said Heather.

"You're always welcome, but we still haven't determined who sent this note," replied John.

"I've given it some thought. You protected our family all my life while I was growing up. I trust you to protect me and the kids. No one is better. I want to move back to Atlanta. I plan to leave my car in California to be sold, instead of driving it across the country. Are you up for picking me and kids up at the airport tomorrow at 7:00 PM?"

"Absolutely, but are you sure you want to do this?" John asked.

"I'm done with David, and I'm done with California. We need you. The kids need a stable family life, and I need you right now."

"I'll be at the airport," promised John.

After the call ended, he picked up the bottle and headed inside. John opened a small cabinet over the refrigerator and placed the bottle inside it.

I'll give it a day. Family is coming tomorrow.

John stared at the bottle of bourbon. Mental pictures of Heather and his grandchildren flooded his mind. He took hold of the bottle and twisted the cap off. John poured the contents down the drain of the sink and flushed the smell away with water. He went outside to the garbage can provided by the city and tossed in the empty bottle.

"No, I won't give that a day," he pronounced before closing the lid of the garbage can. "I think it comes down to either the bottle or the family. I'll take Heather and the kids, hands down."

John went to his bedroom and reached for the small gun

case in the top of the closet. Dropping it onto his bed, he then opened it with a small key that he kept on his key ring. Inside was a box of .38 caliber ammunition and the old T-shirt. He quickly emptied the bullets from the revolver and placed each one back into the ammunition box. He wrapped the pistol in the old T-shirt and placed the box of bullets and the gun back inside the gun case.

I'll give it a day on this one, for sure…more like several.

"Good night, my old friend," he spoke to the .38 as he closed the case. "You have a special purpose, but I'll let you rest for a time."

He locked the case with the key and placed the case on a shelf in the top of his closet. John retrieved his shoulder holster that hung from a nail inside the closet and strapped it on his body. Moving to the nightstand beside the bed, he placed his index finger on the biometric fingerprint sensor to unlock an electronic small gun case that rested on it. Once opened, he took a loaded nine-millimeter pistol from inside and closed the case.

"You and I have been charged to protect members of the Rawlings family," John addressed the gun. "Lives depend on us."

John secured the safety and slid it into the shoulder holster. Fixing his eyes on the photo of him and his decreased wife, he stood at attention before it.

"Sharon, I promise you that it will be over my dead body that any bastard harms Heather or those kids. You have my word."

Chapter 9

Lily

"PLEASE HELP ME!" blurted Emily Johnson, in her call to John. "I'm having contractions, and my husband is an hour away at a jobsite."

"I'll be right over," replied John.

John pounded on the front door of Emily's house, and immediately heard her calling to him from inside. When he entered her home, he found her standing at the door of her bedroom. She gripped the doorframe with her left hand, her cell phone in her right hand. The sunlight coming from the bedroom window revealed a splattered coating of liquid on the hardwood floor between her feet.

"When did your water break?" he asked as he made his way to her.

"Just before I called. I took a childbirth class, so I knew this meant I was not in false labor."

"This is your first child?"

"Well… not exactly."

"Not exactly?" questioned a slightly confused John. "Alright, there's a hospital only ten minutes away. You'll be fine."

"But my doctor is at Georgia Baptist."

"He may have to make other arrangements. The important thing is that we have you under a physician's care.

You'll be fine."

"How do you know?" she questioned as he began to lead her out the front door.

"I was a cop for a long time, and we were trained regarding childbirth. Besides, I have two kids of my own. This is not my first rodeo."

"Please take my car," insisted Emily. "I have all the paperwork and a bag of clothes in the trunk. The class told us to be prepared during the last trimester."

"Sure," replied John.

"The keys are in my purse. It's on the couch."

After starting the car, John immediately turned on the emergency flashers. Years of experience in handling cars during pursuit of criminals showed as he smoothly made his way through traffic. Emily was impressed with his coordination. It was as if her vehicle was an extension of his body. As he drove, Emily placed calls to both her husband and her doctor redirecting them to the other hospital. A block away from the hospital, she turned to John.

"I had a miscarriage when I was with Billy," Emily explained. "Ron knows. I was honest with him about it before we married."

"It's important to have honesty in a marriage," John replied. "Is that information contained in the paperwork?"

"Yes."

"Good. Good. You did the right thing."

They pulled into the ER entrance to the hospital, and John tapped the horn of the car twice, before putting it in park and rushing to the passenger door of the car.

"You don't have to make a scene," she said.

"It's fine," he said, opening the front passenger door.

As he helped her from the car, an attendant approached with a wheelchair.

"Her water broke, and this isn't the first child," John explained.

"I've got her from here," the attendant calmly stated.

John popped the trunk and gathered the bag containing clothes and paperwork. He handed it to the attendant.

"All the paperwork is contained," he explained.

As Emily eased herself into the wheelchair, her eyes were fixed on John's. "I'd never met a real hero before meeting you," she said.

"Not a hero; I've just been around the block a few times," John replied. "I've just been fortunate to be at the right place at the right time on a few occasions."

"You're a hero!" she blurted as a contraction started.

"Never argue with a woman in labor," said the grinning attendant.

"You're right about that one," said John.

"You can park it right over there," informed the attendant, pointing to the ER parking area.

"Thanks," said John.

John watched him wheel her away and into the doors of the ER, before moving the car. He remembered the panic he felt in his heart when he had rushed his wife to the hospital to give birth to his daughter. John remembered the sinking feeling he had when he learned the station had called an ambulance for his wife when she went into labor with his son. He had been in a shootout with a criminal at the time. During his wife's pregnancy with Chris, in the days before cell phones, John carried a pager so that she would be able to contact him, but he never heard it go off. After he was informed about her being taken to the hospital, he checked the pager. John saw the code he and his wife agreed to use to notify him that she was in labor.

I guess my son Chris and I had trouble connecting from the beginning.

John considered the fact that a gun wouldn't be allowed in the hospital. He removed the gun and shoulder holster and placed them both in the glove compartment of Emily's car. After locking the car, he hurried through the ER doors and was instructed that she had been taken to a preparation area for the delivery. He took a chair in the waiting room. Within a few minutes, a nurse told him that it would be best for him to wait in a different waiting room designated specifically for those awaiting childbirth. He relocated himself to the other waiting room and informed the administrative person at the desk that he was there for Emily Johnson.

"So, are you about to be a proud grandfather?" she asked.

"I'm already a grandfather," he replied. "My grandkids are due to visit tomorrow evening. Emily is my next-door neighbor. Her husband is working at a remote jobsite, and she needed a ride to the hospital."

"She's fortunate to have you for a neighbor."

He dropped into a seat in the waiting room. A daytime soap opera was being shown on the TV."

I can't believe those things are still on TV.

He shuffled through a stack of magazines which dealt with pregnancies and care for children, until he found an outdated news magazine. He flipped through several pages, but he couldn't take his mind off his earlier conversation with Emily.

So, Emily and Billy Crews were having a child together. This explains a lot. It better explains why Crews was so attached to her. He wasn't just a passing fad for her during rebellious years. A natural connection is formed between people when a child is involved. The tragedy of a miscarriage can either strengthen that bond or stress it. This puts Billy in a somewhat different light.

He attempted to focus his attention on an article in the magazine, but after several minutes he laid the magazine aside. He felt tired. John took a deep breath and rubbed his eyes with both hands before spotting Ron heading in his direction.

"Man, I'm so glad you were there for her," greeted Ron, reaching his right hand out to John. "You are quite the hero."

"Glad I could help," replied John, shaking Ron's hand.

"I'm about to be a father!" blurted Ron.

"Congratulations."

"Any word on the delivery?" Ron asked.

"Not yet."

Ron walked over to the nurse at the desk, explained to her that he was Emily's husband, and asked about her status. He was told that she was currently in delivery.

"Is she OK?" asked John, upon Ron's return.

"In delivery right now," replied Ron. "Seems to be going OK."

"Good. Do you two know whether it's a boy or girl?"

"A girl."

"Have you two picked a name?"

"I believe we settled on Lily, after Emily's grandmother. My grandmother was named Phyllis, but we can't quite picture a baby girl with that name."

"Lily is a good name," said John. "I like it. Emily insisted that we take her car. It's in the ER parking lot."

"Whenever you are ready to leave, would you mind just parking it at the house?" Ron asked. "I can get the keys later."

"Sure."

After about twenty minutes, a doctor in scrubs stepped into the waiting area and called out, "Ron Johnson."

Ron leapt to his feet, waved his right hand in the air, and quickly made his way to the physician. After a few seconds into the conversation a large grin spread across the new father's face. John watched as he shook the hand of the doctor. Ron turned to John, gave him a "thumbs up" before following the doctor through double doors. John returned the gesture.

Ron and Emily, both called me a hero today. It's remarkable how little it takes for someone to perceive a person as a hero. I happened to be at the right place at the right time on a couple of occasions. It's as simple as that. Emily knows so little about me. She has no clue of my complete failure in establishing an enduring relationship with my son. I'm so lucky that my daughter has re-kindled her relationship with me. That certainly came out of the blue. Re-establishing relationships with my grandchildren certainly wasn't my doing. Heather did that. I can't take credit for any of it. Emily certainly doesn't know about my failures in my law enforcement career... one that resulted in me blowing a guy away instead of taking him in. Hero? Let Emily think what she wants; let her be happy. I'm sure that I'll let her down in a big way, at some point. I'm just glad I was there for her when she went into labor. It's the least a neighbor could do. Life is about to change forever for that young couple. Lily will experience the mistakes that a couple makes with the first born, but she will also experience the undivided attention that the first born enjoys. I've never seen Ron so happy. My part is done. Time to take Emily's car back to the house.

John rose from the chair and made his way toward his neighbor's car. Whenever John previously visited the couple, Ron had seemed to be a man of few words. Emily always dominated the conversation. On the way to the hospital, Emily had given John a glimpse into the soul of her husband.

I have a deeper respect for Ron, now that I understand that he was willing to marry a woman who had lost a pregnancy with her ex-boyfriend. Baby Lily is fortunate to have a father like Ron, instead of a hothead like Billy.

John dropped into the driver's seat of Emily's vehicle. Without the stress of getting Emily to the hospital, John immediately noticed its feminine characteristics for the first time.

I didn't even pick up on all this stuff enroute to the hospital. It seems that even my attention to detail has gone to pot.

A small pink heart dangled from the rearview mirror on a string. The steering wheel sported a pink cover, and there was a matching pink umbrella wedged between the driver's seat and the center console. He opened the glove compartment and retrieved the gun and shoulder holster. After starting the engine, a disturbing thought crossed his mind.

I hope Lily is truly Ron's child. Emily is an attractive young woman, but for Ron's sake, I hope Lily develops some of Ron's physical features. He deserves that peace of mind.

Chapter 10

Preacher

THE DAY FOLLOWING LILY'S birth, John paid his next-door neighbor a second visit at the hospital. Stepping inside Emily's room, he found a strange man seated in a chair beside her.

"Is this your father, Emily?" asked John.

"You just missed my mother and father," she answered.

"I'm Emily's pastor, Matt Wright," stated the man, as he stood to his feet and held out his right hand.

"John Rawlins," replied John, clasping the right hand of the minister in his. "I'm her next-door neighbor."

"So, you're the man who rushed Emily to the hospital!" exclaimed pastor Wright. "She was so fortunate to have you as a neighbor."

"I believe God had him there for me," Emily piped in.

"He absolutely may have been an instrument of God," agreed the pastor.

"Let's not get carried away, here," said John. "Let's just leave it as me being in the right place at the right time. I don't see myself as being God's instrument, or any such thing. My wife was a believer, but I'm pretty much outside the church. There isn't anything holy about me."

"God doesn't have to limit Himself to only Christians to do His work," said pastor Wright. "Jesus said that if His people stay quiet, that the rocks would cry out. I believe the Creator of the universe is much more capable than to be forced to rely on only believers to do His work. If Christians fail to be used by God, they miss out on partnering with God. Believers would miss out on that blessing, but God can act as He sees fit."

"You believe that God uses people who aren't in the faith?" asked John.

"I do," answered the pastor.

"Are you one of those preachers who is open to all religions?" asked John.

"I didn't say that I think all roads lead to heaven, but I certainly think there is insight to be gained from all who seek God," explained the minister.

"I don't mean any offense, but I'm not really one who seeks God," said John. "Like I said, my wife was a strong believer – but not me."

"It sounds like your wife passed away," observed pastor Wright.

"She did, of ALS," answered John.

"I am so sorry for your loss," said the minister. "I know that sounds like just a cliché, but I do understand loss. I had a son who was killed in an auto accident when he was a teen."

"I can't imagine…," said John. "Losing a child is probably the worst. I can't imagine losing my daughter."

"The loss of an immediate family member can be devastating," agreed the minister.

"Why don't we focus on the birth of Lily?" asked John.

"You are absolutely right," agreed the pastor. "This is a time for celebration."

"I'm going to ask you two men to step out of the room for a few minutes," announced a nurse, as she entered the room while pushing a cart that held the infant. "It's time for little Lily to nurse, and time for me to examine her mother."

"Say no more," said John, making his way out of the

room.

"There are seats in the waiting area around the corner," said the nurse. "I'll come for you when I'm finished here."

"Of course," said pastor Wright.

Once seated in the waiting area, the minister continued his conversation with John.

"I hear that you're a retired detective," said pastor Wright.

"That's right," replied John.

"I have a lot of respect for those who put their lives on the line for other people," said the minister. "My son was planning to join the Air Force after graduation, but he didn't live long enough to do so. As a father, I was concerned a bit about his safety while serving in the military, but he lost his life as a civilian."

"It seems senseless, when a young person dies," said John. "Life can be cruel. Your profession involves convincing people to worship God. Why does God allow things like that? What answer do you have for people? My wife was the rock of our family. Why did God allow her to suffer for so many years before she died?"

"I certainly don't have all the answers," said pastor Wright. "All I know is that this place isn't heaven. Terrible things happen here. God can give us strength when they do."

"So, you're not one of those TV preachers who tell people that God loves them so much that He is going to make them rich if they hand over their hard-earned money to some ministry?"

"No, I don't tell people that," answered pastor Wright. "God doesn't need your money."

"What? Reverend Wright, I have never heard any preacher say that."

"First of all, please don't call me reverend," said the minister. "You can just call me Matt, if you will. The members of the congregation call me Pastor Matt. Listen, do you really think that the Creator of the universe is poor and needs you to pull Him out of poverty with your charity?"

"Probably not, since you put it that way," answered John. "So, you don't take up a collection in your church?"

"We do take up a collection."

"I'm confused," said John. "You just said that God doesn't need my money. So why the collection?"

"I believe that God wants to partner with people in His work," said the minister. "We encourage people to give, but not because they are meeting God's needs. God isn't poor. The scripture says that a person is to be cheerful giver. Giving does something for the soul. There is something spiritual about sharing what you have. God wants us to partner with Him in meeting the needs of others by people sharing what they have. We do what we can toward meeting physical needs of people, but the act of cheerfully giving helps meet a spiritual need of the one who shares."

"I get that, but I'm sure that you get a cut of whatever people give to the church," said John.

"I do," said pastor Matt. "There is a board of directors at our church who determines my salary, and they handle that. The church meets at a renovated grocery store that went out of business. The board pays for the rent, utilities, cleaning, and items – like chairs for church members to be seated. The church helps support two missionaries abroad. We also have a large food pantry that helps us meet the needs of people who are having a hard time, and occasionally we help pay utility bills of those who are financially struggling. Each year, the board openly presents an accounting to the congregation of where every dime is spent – including my salary."

"I respect that kind of transparency," said John.

"You're welcome to come by and check us out," invited the pastor.

"Thanks, but I don't belong at your church," said John. "I'm not a believer. I tried reading the Bible when my wife was alive, but it didn't make sense."

The nurse interrupted their conversation by informing them that they could return to the room. She also told them that Emily was currently nursing the baby, but the act was covered by a baby blanket.

"What didn't make sense to you?" asked the minister, as the two began making their way back to Emily's room.

"I began reading the Bible from the beginning of it, but none of it made sense," answered John. "First of all, I can't believe God created the entire universe in six days. Secondly, when I read where on the first day God said, 'let there be light' I thought I understood it until the Bible said that God created the sun days later. How do you have days with daylight before there is a sun? None of that makes any sense to me. I don't mean to be disrespectful, or anything. I'm just not a spiritual person. I don't believe things that don't make sense to me."

"I get it," said the pastor, just before they got to the room.

"Is it safe for two men to come in?" John asked Emily from the doorway.

"Come on in," she replied. "I'm nursing, but I'm covered up."

"I won't ask to see Lily, because I certainly don't want to interrupt her nursing," said pastor Matt. "I didn't come to make her cry."

"Emily, maybe I should leave," offered John. "I just wanted to see how you were doing, and you seem to be doing fine. I'll leave you to talk with your pastor."

"Don't be silly," said Emily. "You just got here. Please sit down and visit for a while."

"Ok, but just for a few minutes," John replied.

"What were you two talking about while you were out?" she asked her minister "I heard you tell John that you get it. What do you get?"

"John was telling me that he had attempted to read the Bible, but that it didn't make sense to him," answered the pastor.

"I don't want to stir up things about God," said John. "I came to see you and the baby."

"No, I'm interested in your conversation," said Emily. "What didn't make sense?"

"I didn't read much of the Bible, but what I read just didn't make sense to me," replied John. "I don't want to offend either of you."

"Do you remember what it was that didn't make sense?" asked Emily.

"As I told your pastor, I started reading at the very beginning of the Bible," explained John. "First. it's hard for me to believe that God created everything that exists in six days. Science says that it took billions of years for the universe to form. That's a little easier to believe. I also told your pastor that it seemed weird that God made the sun several days after He said, 'let there be light'. It makes no sense to have days and there not be a sun. It's just too confusing. That's when I stopped reading. I figured that if the beginning of the Bible was so confusing, that the rest of it wouldn't get any better."

"I'll let Pastor Matt explain the Bible," said Emily. "I believe the Bible is true, but he is much better at explaining it."

"Let's take one aspect at a time," stated the minister.

"OK, explain it," said John.

"First of all, I believe that a God who is capable of creating the entire universe from nothing is able to do it in six twenty-four hours days – but I don't believe that's what happened."

"You don't believe the Bible?" asked John.

"I believe the Bible," said the pastor. "I personally don't believe those six days of creation were made up of twenty-four-hour days."

"How long do you think those days were?" asked John.

"I have no idea. The Bible doesn't say. Our concept of

a twenty-four-hour day is based on the earth's relationship with the sun," explained pastor Matt. "An earth day is the length of time that it takes the earth to make one rotation before the sun – from sunup until the next sunup – roughly twenty-four hours. Like you said, there were creation days before God made the sun. So, it's obvious that those creation days couldn't be the type of day that we're familiar with. This had to be a different type of day, which was unrelated to the sun. The Hebrew word *yom*, which is often translated into the English word *day*, also means time. Days are periods of time. Months and years are measurements of time. We sometimes even use the English term 'day' to mean time. When we say, 'back in my day', we aren't talking about a twenty-four-hour day. We are saying, 'back in my time.' I believe the writer of Genesis is saying that God created the universe in six periods of time, and it doesn't say how long those periods of time were."

"That makes some sense," said John. "Without the sun, there wasn't a twenty-four-hour day."

"Exactly," said the pastor. "God wasn't just making the earth; He was creating the entire universe. I'm no scientist, but I read an article which stated that the planet Venus turns very slowly. It said that a day on Venus lasts more than five thousand hours. We live on earth. We are familiar with a twenty-four-hour earth day, so we assume twenty-four-hours when we see the word day. When God said, 'Let there be light' before the creation of the sun, obviously he wasn't talking about a day that was related to the sun."

"So, what was the deal about God saying, 'let there be light', before the sun existed?" asked John. "If those creation days weren't based on light from the sun, what was that light?"

"I'm not sure," answered pastor Matt. "The Bible doesn't explain that."

"That isn't much help," said John.

"First of all, I don't believe the author of Genesis was

crazy," said the pastor. "Clearly, he understood the relationship of the sun and an earth day. Every day, he watched the sun come up and go down. He clearly understood what he was writing; that there was no sun until three creation days after God said, 'let there be light'. He obviously meant that the source of light for those creation days was something other than the sun."

"What was the source of light for a creation day?" asked John.

"I don't know," answered pastor Matt. "The Bible doesn't say. Science says there are many sources of light in the universe, but I don't think God was limited to those sources of light. When talking about himself, Jesus said, 'I am the light of the world. Whoever follows me will never walk in darkness, but will have the light of life'. Genesis says that God spoke, and light shone. In the gospel of John, John calls Jesus the Word, and he says that the Word was present when God created the universe. Christ, the Word, has always been the means of communication between God the Father and mankind. So, it's possible that Christ was the light during creation. The source of that light during creation isn't clearly spelled out in the Bible. However, the writer of Genesis intentionally makes it clear that the source of light during the creation days wasn't the sun."

"Ok, your explanation makes more sense," said John. "It would have been more understandable if the Bible just said that God created the universe in within six periods of time, but it doesn't. It said that there were days made up of light and darkness, leaving people to think of the days that involve the sun."

"The Bible never says that the days involve the sun, but people tend to read that into it," said pastor Matt.

"I guess you're right about that," said John. "So, what where the periods of light and darkness?"

"I can't really explain the periods of light and darkness for those creation days," said pastor Matt. "The Bible doesn't go into detail about it. It simply indicates that creation was done in periods of time. I'm not a scientist, but I like to read scientific articles. Before I went to seminary, my undergraduate degree was biology. I find it fascinating that both science and the Bible state that space, matter, and time began suddenly. Science calls it the Big Bang. Christianity calls it Creation. I've read scientific articles stating that there was a Dark Age of the universe that occurred after the Big Bang. So, both science and the Bible talk about the universe coming about in terms of times of darkness and light. The Bible doesn't go into detail about the source of that light, and science is learning daily about aspects of the universe. I just think it's interesting."

"So, you believe both the Bible and science?" asked John.

"Sure," said pastor Matt. "Both science and Christianity are based on the search for truth. Science focuses on the physical realm, and Christianity is the search for spiritual truth. Most of the Bible is about spiritual truth."

"What about when the Bible and science don't agree?" asked John.

"I'm not worried about it," replied paster Matt. "A physics book isn't about spirituality, and I wouldn't read the Bible to understand physics. These are two different fields of study: both seeking truth, but different aspects of truth. There are differences, but I think it is fascinating when they seem to agree."

"So, do all preachers believe what you believe?" asked John.

"I'm not sure what most ministers believe on this subject," answered the pastor. "Most of us think similarly when it comes to aspects like Jesus being the Son of God. However, we all go to different schools to prepare for ministry. Because of that, we think somewhat differently when it comes to understanding details of the Bible. I can only speak to what I think."

"Did Pastor Matt help you understand the Bible?" asked Emily.

"He certainly helped," replied John.

"So, do you believe the Bible now?" asked Emily.

"I wouldn't go that far," said John. "I'm just saying that your pastor's explanation makes more sense of it."

Chapter 11

Professionally

JOHN STEPPED OUT onto his front porch Saturday morning with a cup of coffee and breathed in the cool fall air. He closed his eyes and took in the aroma of the brew as the cup touched his lips. The slight breeze reminded him of sipping coffee with his departed wife on one of their camping trips.

I'll have to say that retirement isn't all that bad. I wish Sharon could have stayed with me long enough to enjoy it.

The peaceful setting provided relief from the stressful call he had received from his daughter.

That jerk David is making Heather miserable.

He opened his eyes and turned to find Emily rocking her new daughter on her front porch. Wearing a light jacket and Lily wrapped in a baby blanket, she gave him a smile and motioned for him to come over.

"So, is Ron back to work now?" John asked as he stepped onto Emily's front porch.

"My mother and father went home yesterday, and today Ron is back to work," she answered. "I enjoyed having my parents around for the first couple of days, but I'm now enjoying time alone with Lily."

"How are you feeling?" asked John.

"I've recovered from the delivery, but tired."

"Tired goes with the territory of being a parent. However, you won't have to feed Lily every two hours forever."

"I was told about the feeding, but I really had no idea until now," complained Emily. "It's like having catnaps all night long. Ron tried to help, but he isn't equipped to do the breastfeeding."

John chuckled. "I know doctors tell people not to do it today, but my daughter Heather slept on my chest at night. Every two hours, I would pass her over to her mother to feed. My son would have none of that. He wanted to sleep alone in his bed from the very start. It's amazing how different their personalities were from the beginning."

The cell phone in John's pocket rang. John viewed the source of the call and said, "I'd better take this one."

Placing it to his ear, John questioned the caller, "What's up?"

"I plan to drop by tonight," began Shawn. "There are new developments, but I don't want to discuss them over the phone."

"I'll be here," replied John. He sighed as he returned the phone to his pocket.

"Do you need to go?" asked Emily.

"No, a friend is dropping by tonight."

"We are so blessed to be living next door to you. I can't imagine where we would be without you."

"I'm sure you'd be fine."

"No," insisted Emily. "Without you chasing off that guy, I probably would have been another one of his victims. I would have been traumatized. Without you, I would have never made it to the hospital in time for her to be born under the care of a physician. Without you, I would still be stalked and harassed by Billy. I believe with all my heart that God had us move to this particular house so that you would be there for us."

"I just happened to be at the right place at the right time.

That's all."

"Do you really think that all of this has been just a string of coincidences?" asked Emily. "Seriously?"

"Well…"

"Can't you see that you've been God's instrument on my behalf?" asked Emily.

"Instrument of God? Not exactly. I don't spend much time thinking about God. Honestly, I'm not a very religious man. Not at all."

"God is bigger than your view of Him," said Emily.

"I'm sure that He is. You're the Christian; you would have a better understanding of God than me. Whatever God has done, I'm sure He would have done on your behalf with or without me."

"But God has chosen you to do it," said Emily. "God's hand is on you, whether you understand that or not. God has chosen you."

"Honestly, I'm glad to have been able to help, but chosen by God? I'm no Moses. I think you see me as someone who is better than I really am. It's nice to be appreciated, but please don't put me on some kind of pedestal. I can't stay on it. I'll fall off in a heartbeat, and when you see me wallowing around on the ground you'll be hurt. I don't want to hurt you."

"You mentioned Moses," said Emily. "Did you know that Moses was a murderer?"

"I believe my wife told me that," replied John. "She was a woman of faith."

"I doubt Moses understood what God was doing when he was chosen by God. God could have selected someone who wasn't a murderer, but God called Moses. When Noah got off that ark, he first built an altar to God. His sons later found him drunk and naked. It caused a real mess in his family. To us, it would make more sense for God to pick someone who always did the right thing. But God doesn't operate by our criteria. God does His own thing, in His own way."

"Well, He's God, right? God is God. I would guess that He would be a stupid god if He operated according to what screwed up people wanted. What's the point of being a god if you let dumb people boss you around? I'm a really flawed man. If He operated by my wants, my wife would still be healthy and alive. But, I don't understand what would be wrong with that. She was a faithful Christian. By my thinking, He should have let her live…but He didn't. I don't understand God."

"You don't understand why God doesn't always do the things that you think He should do," said Emily. "I get that. Me too. I don't understand everything about God."

"I think God should have taken me, instead of taking my wife," said John. "She was the one with faith. She was the one who deserved to live."

"It sounds like your wife was prepared to go to heaven. Would you have been ready to meet God?"

"No."

"If God had taken you, what would have happened to me and Lily?" asked Emily.

"God probably would have moved you next door to someone else who could have helped you."

"But God chose you."

Immediately following her words, it became apparent to them both that Lily had filled her diaper.

"Gosh, I'd better change Lily," said Emily.

"How can something that sweet dump such a nasty load in a diaper?" remarked John.

"Want to help?"

"Oh, no. I'll chicken out on that one. I've done my tour of duty with nasty diapers - twice. I'll leave all the fun to you."

"You have a pretty twisted concept of fun," said Emily.

"Yep, twisted. Told you not to put me on a pedestal. This coward is now retreating back to the fresh air of my back porch. Even my dog Zack doesn't drop poop that nasty."

Emily laughed as she made her way back into her house.

"WHAT'S CHANGED?" John asked, inviting Shawn into his home.

"Another murder, and additional wording," his ex-partner soberly answered.

"I was afraid of that. Have a seat at the kitchen table. What can I get you?"

"I'll take a beer, if you have a cold one," answered Shawn.

"Coming right up," said John.

"I'm not sure that we're any closer to catching that guy."

"Prostitute again?" asked John, handing Shawn a beer.

"No, he's gone back to stalking housewives."

"You said there was additional wording?"

"This time he carved the word 'PROFESSIONALLY' under the OPE."

"Looks like he's continuing his progression. Only Professionally. Any idea as to what the E stands for?"

"I'm not sure," answered Shawn. "Some are guessing it means 'Only Professionally Equal,' to note some kind of protest over income inequality. But what does the words 'professionally equal' have to do with pregnant women?"

"I'm not sure," said John. "It's possible that he solely uses pregnant women to profoundly grab the attention of the public. It's also possible the letters could be associated with pregnancies. Any other details?"

"This guy has a strong attention for detail, and we think he's very intelligent. He hasn't attacked pregnant women who have security systems at the house, and he hasn't attacked prostitutes in an area of the city that has cameras. What we need is video of this guy."

"You have three characteristics: strong attention to detail, he's intelligent, and an athlete," observed John. "The guy I saw was really fast. Chances are he ran track in high school."

"That's good. I forgot about your encounter. Maybe we should look at high school yearbooks, for honor students on track teams. But Atlanta has a lot of high school track programs, and there is always the chance that he's not from here."

"What do these women have in common besides being pregnant?" asked John.

"We have everything from women in retail to prostitutes. He picks on both middle-income families and poor prostitutes."

"So far, he hasn't picked on the wealthy," observed John. "But most of the wealthy would have superb security systems."

"True."

"Do the victims share common professions in any way?" asked John. "You said that some women work in retail. Could the prostitutes have worked in a different profession in the past? This second word PROFESSIONALLY may be a significant key."

"That's an idea. I'll run a background check on them."

"If he has a strong attention to detail, the words must be carefully selected by him," suggested John.

"I just don't see how a smart guy would be mutilating women's breasts," said Shawn. "He does that consistently."

"He may have an issue with breastfeeding newborns, or it could be an attention getting ploy. The second idea is my initial take."

"Any recommendations besides the background of the prostitutes?" asked Shawn.

"He is trying to say something, and all these women suffer one thing in common - pregnancy. He consistently cuts the women's breasts, so that's another common factor.

Focus on what he has given you. What is the connection between that brutal action, the pregnancies of these women and the words 'ONLY PROFESSIONALLY?'"

"Beats the heck out me," answered Shawn. "I'm not seeing it. What is professional about breastfeeding? Every kid in an underdeveloped country is breastfed."

"We don't know that he has done any of this in a third world country, but he IS doing it to Americans," said John.

"I'm in the dark," said Shawn.

"The words he is leaving, combined with the action of mutilating women's breasts, points to the messaging being important to him. I think this guy may have some kind of radical belief that involves both.

"What do you think the letter E stand for?" asked Shawn. "The third word may hold the clue, but I hate the fact that another woman will suffer for us to obtain it. I really hate this guy!"

"For now, focus on what you now have," advised John.

"What if he is simply a sadistic bastard?" asked Shawn. "Maybe he hates women. He could simply enjoy doing this to women and is using the words and lettering as a tease to sidetrack us."

"There is that,' sighed John. "But, I don't think that's the case."

"Oh, I remember you asking a while back if this pervert was raping women," said Shawn.

"I remember," said John. "He's now raping them?"

"We have reports of some guy wearing a ski mask who is raping women, but we don't really think it's the same guy," said Shawn. "The guy who rapes doesn't cut women, and he never rapes pregnant women. He threatens his victims, but he never cuts them. Also, he doesn't match the same height and build of the guy who is molesting women by cutting them."

"So, this guy raping women is trying to lead the police into believing that it's the same guy who cuts women?"

asked John.

"That seems to be the case," answered Shawn. "We believe this is an opportunist rapist who is using the molester for cover."

"We live in a sick world," said John.

"It seems to be getting sicker by the day," agreed Shawn.

Chapter 12

Educated

"I MET EMILY, the new mother next door," said Heather. "You were right about her. She's really sweet. Charlotte couldn't keep her hands off her baby Lily. She was fascinated."

"I'm glad you two get along," said John. "But stop trying to change the subject. I think David should have given you more than the $50,000 for your part of the house in the divorce settlement. That house would sell for a million dollars, easy in California."

"It's fine. We have about $150,000 equity in it. I've not been working full-time over the past few years. He's made the house payments and is responsible for building the majority of the equity."

"I would still like to kick his butt," offered John.

"Daddy, he's been fair. Besides the share of the equity, he's paying child support and alimony."

"It wasn't fair for him to cheat on you," John firmly stated.

"No, but that's water gone under the bridge, as you like to say."

"I would have liked to have seen the look on his face when you caught him dining with that little skirt, after he had told you that he had to work late with his student teachers."

"I guess he was working her, all right," said Heather. "Don't get me started. I want to put this behind me," her voice beginning to quiver.

"I'm sorry. That had to be painful for you. I sometimes don't know when to …," John was interrupted by a knock on the front door. "Hold on; I'll get that."

John opened the front door to find Shawn standing on the front porch. His eyes were full of anger.

"He killed again," Shawn whispered.

"Come in," invited John. "Let's take the conversation to the back yard. I don't want to upset Heather and the kids."

"So, Heather's come to stay?" asked Shawn.

"For a while. For as long as she wants."

The two stepped into the kitchen and informed Heather that they were going to the back yard to "talk shop." Heather's eyes brightened when she saw Shawn.

"I agree," Heather said. "If you're going to talk about what I think you are, the kids certainly don't need to hear. It's time I started supper."

John gave her a hug.

"Staying for supper, Shawn?" she asked.

"I don't know…" he stammered.

"Sure, he is," John answered, in his stead. "Look how scrawny he's become," taking hold of one of Shawn's muscular arms with both hands. "He needs a healthy meal."

Shawn nervously chuckled, as the two exited the back door.

"At least, we have the third word… EDUCATED!" Shawn blurted.

"ONLY PROFESSIONALLY EDUCATED?" John asked. "This is his message?"

"The bastard is a lunatic!" Shawn blurted.

"Worse, this time?" John whispered, attempting to quieten his ex-partner.

"He murdered a prostitute, again. But this time, he cut the baby out of the womb and placed the dead child on the lifeless and mutilated breast of the mother! I want this guy! I want him in a bad way!"

Shawn's fists were clenched, his eyes ablaze as he began to pace.

"I'm with you on that. Try to calm down," coached John.

"You didn't see what I saw."

"I get it. I still sometimes have nightmares about some of the things I saw while on the job."

"This guy took his time," said Shawn. "He cut the woman's throat and breasts, cut open the womb, took the baby girl out and cut its throat, and then placed the child on the mother's bleeding breast. On one side of the gash in her belly he carved OPE, and on the other side he carved the word EDUCATED."

"He's really sick," agreed John.

"I've never seen anything like it. Wait until the vigilante group of husbands hear about this. They'll be in a rage, fearing this guy may revisit their wives. Nobody will be able to contain those men. We're worried that they might lash out at an innocent person."

"That's a real possibility," agreed John. "So, it looks like this nut believes that only professionally educated women should have babies."

"Maybe. There are still different ideas floating around the station. It's some kind of message about the professionally educated. He's all about education, but he mutilates pregnant women. What kind of maniac does something like that?"

"During World War II, some of Hitler's men were very educated," said John. "Yet, they did horrible things to Jews. I read somewhere that Hitler had a tobacco pouch made from the breast of a Jewish woman. He had the woman's breast tanned into leather. Just because someone is educated, it doesn't mean that the person has morals. Education certainly doesn't prevent someone from being crazy. I wouldn't be surprised if this guy is highly educated."

"So, you think we should be looking for a highly educated guy who ran track in high school?" asked Shawn.

"In my mind, that would fit this guy. He may have even written a book on the subject."

"OK, I'll do an internet search for someone like that," said Shawn. "If he wrote a book, it might be easy to find."

"Shawn, there is nothing more dangerous than a highly intelligent person who is a psychopath… a brilliant person with no morals or ethical borders," warned John.

After several minutes, their conversation was interrupted by Heather calling them to supper. Her smile quickly diminished, seeing the intensity of Shawn's demeanor.

"Try to calm down," John said, placing a hand on Shawn's broad shoulder. "For the next hour, try to shift your mind to only the people at the table."

It had been years since John had such an assortment of people gathered at his kitchen table. He even had to bring an extra chair from the living room. It didn't match the other four and looked somewhat ridiculous at the table.

"I'll take this chair," volunteered John.

"It's fitting," remarked Heather. "Compared to the rest, it looks like a throne. It's your house, so you should be the king."

"Pass the butter, King John," requested Shawn, lowering his large frame onto one of the smaller chairs.

Heather laughed. A retired cop, an active and handsome detective, a mother and her two children enjoyed the company of one another. Just before dessert, Heather noticed Shawn's mood had again become sober. Everyone else continued to laugh and talk, but he was silent. When a joke was told, he would glance up and give a polite smile. Afterwards, the kids scattered back to their room to play a video game. John carried the chair back to its proper place in the next room. Alone in the kitchen with Shawn, Heather leaned close to him when she took his empty dessert plate from the table. She placed her nimble fingers on the back of his neck and whispered.

"You're off duty now. Try to relax."

He turned. Their eyes met, and he knew that she understood. She had seen her father carry the weight of the world on his shoulders when he was working a terrible case.

"It's the case," she again whispered. "There are times when you'll have to let it go. If you don't, it will drive you mad. You have to force yourself to take some down time, or it will wear you into the ground," she said placing his plate in the sink.

"This one is different," Shawn replied. "I have to figure this out and put a stop to it."

She stepped behind him and began rubbing his broad shoulders as he sat at the table.

"Oh, where did you learn to do this?" Shawn asked.

"My mother and I took turns rubbing my father's shoulders, when he had a rough day."

"What kind of hanky-panky is this?" asked John, entering the kitchen.

Shawn shot up from his chair like a missile. "No...nothing..." he nervously babbled.

John broke out into heartfelt laughter. Shawn looked over at Heather.

"Daddy, it was just a back rub," she said, smiling.

"You should have seen your face!" howled John, pointing a finger at Shawn.

Shawn's face reddened.

"You should be ashamed of yourself," Heather said to her father, giving his shoulder a punch. "He's a good man, and you're picking on him."

"Poor wuddle bitty Shawn can't take a joke," jested John, still laughing.

"Man..." Shawn mumbled.

"He only picks on people he really likes," said Heather.

"He knows," smiled John. "He's like a son to me."

"Well, you can be a pain in the butt sometimes, old man," replied Shawn, with a grin.

John slapped the large detective on the back.

"Daddy, you're undoing all the hard work I did for his back and shoulders," said Heather.

"Yeah, you were working on him all right," said John.

"Behave yourself, Daddy," chided Heather.

"Supper and dessert were fantastic," Shawn said, turning to Heather. "Thanks so much. I should be going."

"I'll walk you to the door," said John.

Heather collected the rest of the dishes, as the two men exited the kitchen. Once on the front porch, John gripped the large hand of his former partner.

"Be careful, Shawn," said John. "Heather's a bit volatile after her divorce from that butt hole in California. She's lonely."

"She's the one who gave me the back rub," Shawn defensively replied.

"I know. Just handle with care. That's all."

"I would never hurt Heather," said Shawn. "You should know that."

"You never stop being a father, even when you become a grandfather," explained John.

"I get it."

"Keep me informed about the case. Nail this guy."

"Don't get me wound up on him," said Shawn. "I would love to snatch him up by his neck and choke the life out of him."

Shawn stepped off the front porch. John turned and opened the front door of the house. Heather was standing just behind it.

"Has he gone?" she asked.

"He's heading for his car."

Heather rushed past her father and caught up with Shawn just as he made it to the car. As he reached for the handle of the car door, she placed her hand on his.

"Wait!" she said. "I brought you another piece of pie for later tonight."

"You didn't have to do that," said Shawn.

"I understand the pressure you're under. I know that you might have trouble getting to sleep. It's on a paper plate with a plastic fork, so just toss the plate when you're finished."

"Thank you," he smiled, taking the dessert in his hand. "The pie was great. You'll probably find John in there getting a second piece right now."

"Probably," Heather agreed. "Good night."

Chapter 13

Danny

JOHN TURNED THE channel on his TV from the local news to a documentary.

"Was that the case Shawn is trying to solve?" asked Heather.

"I didn't mean for you to see that," her father replied.

"Daddy, this is all over the news! It's even hit the national news. I'm guessing this is the case Shawn has been discussing with you when he comes over. You are both stressed."

"People here need to know about the danger, but I'm afraid the reporting may result in unintended actions taken by a local vigilante group made up of husbands of the victims."

"The news talked about prostitutes being attacked," said Heather. "What do you mean by husbands?"

"This jerk began with pregnant wives, and only recently moved on to prostitutes," explained John. "Now that the news has reported about this guy committing murders, some of those husbands may fear that he will return to prey on married women. But I can't say that I blame them. A while back, I caught him peeking in Emily's window and I chased him off. I wish I had been able to catch him."

"You're kidding me! She didn't tell me. I can't believe

Emily didn't even mention it. I would guess that she and her husband have been on edge."

"Fear does things to people," said John. "I'm concerned that this vigilante group will become so enraged that they'll hurt an innocent person by mistake. It's probably wise for Emily to downplay the situation, to some degree. I doubt she wants her husband involved with vigilante activity."

"I wouldn't be surprised if this criminal suffered as a child by the hand of a bad mother," said Heather.

"I don't give a damn what this guy suffered as a child!" barked John. "It can't compare with what he's doing to people."

"It's my understanding that it helps if the police understand the motive of a serial criminal," stated Heather. "I doubt Shawn has a clue as to what motivates this guy."

"I'm sorry. You have a PhD in psychology, and you're into understanding what makes people tick. But your focus was on counseling families. This guy is a total nutcase, and he is terrorizing families. I know that you're just trying to help. I agree; it's true that understanding the motive of a criminal helps an investigation."

"I'm sure it's frustrating, especially for Shawn," said Heather.

"Is that what your training in psychology tells you about this guy?" asked John. "You honestly think that he was messed up by his mother, or something?"

"It seems that his behavior would stem from something deeply personal, and his attacks are against only women," explained Heather. "The guy isn't doing anything to men or children, except for the one unborn child. He isn't lashing out from momentary anger. This seems to be methodical; it's carefully planned. He is also using these women's bodies as a medium to tell a story."

"Do you think maybe he's the child of a prostitute?" asked John.

"I don't know. Possibly. But you said that he began his

attacks on married women. So, I don't think it's specific to prostitutes. The news said that he carves messages on the abdomen of the women. The last victim had the word EDUCATED carved into her, and he cut the baby from her womb. He is saying something about only professionally educated people and it has to do with pregnancies."

"Stinking press!" barked John. "They had no business even knowing about that."

"You can't hide something like that from them. They're going to know. What's the secret? Shouldn't the public be warned about this?"

"True, but I don't like the fact that the news media are giving this pervert what he wants. It's like they are facilitating him in his effort to get his word out. The press sometimes gets in the way of police work. That gripes me. Plus, now that the husbands of victims know about what he did to this last woman, they may go nuts."

"So, have the victims been those of lower education?" asked Heather.

"So far," answered John. "How did you guess that?"

"His focus seems to be on education and pregnancy," replied Heather. "Many of the victims are prostitutes, and as a rule, most prostitutes are poorly educated. His message points to him either going after professional educated pregnant women, or he is in favor of professionally educated mothers to be. Victimizing prostitutes ruled out the former."

"Sometimes I forget how smart you are. You don't just have book sense, but you have always had a lot of common sense – street sense."

"I was raised by a cop," Heather said, giving her father a hug. "My dad is pretty smart, especially when it comes to street sense."

"Your smart dad needs to get his lazy rear end up tomorrow morning and fix the torn screen on the back door," replied John. "I meant to do that before you came, but I got sidetracked. I have no excuse, now that you and the kids are settled."

ON HIS WAY to his favorite hardware store the following morning, John decided to take a shortcut through a rough section of Atlanta. Before he arrived, his bladder began to scream for relief from the two cups of morning coffee he had earlier consumed. He spotted a convenience store and pulled into the parking lot.

This place is nasty, but I have to go - and now!

He hurried through the front door, his eyes scanning for a restroom. The only option was one which served both genders, and he found great comfort in it being available. Upon entering, the stench almost made his eyes water. He flipped on the light and reached for the lock on the door.

Busted lock! But no choice. I have to go!

Turning from the broken door latch, he found that the restroom offered a single filthy toilet.It had been days since the floor was swept and mopped. There was no partition to offer privacy, and the walls were covered by various forms of sexual artwork and vulgar graffiti. He quickly made his way for the toilet. Desperate to relieve himself, his fingers fumbled at the zipper on his pants.

Come on! I'm close to peeing myself! There was a time when I was in charge of my body. It did what I wanted. Not only am I beginning to lose coordination needed to handle bad guys, but I can't even seem to handle a stupid zipper. I'm falling apart. Getting old is a real trip. I'm ruled by a demanding bladder, and my coordination is going spastic! What's next, my brain? If that was to go...somebody should just shoot me and put me down.

He felt great relief when he accomplished the task at hand. Almost immediately after his stream of urine blasted the water in the bowl, he heard a female voice outside the restroom door, and he saw the door begin to open.

"Busy! Busy!" yelled John, quickly moving his body to

the right side of the toilet so that his back was to the door, affording himself a little privacy as he finished his business. Unable to stop the stream, urine splashed across the dirty wall to his left. The door opened to more than a foot wide, but no one came in.

"Oh God!" mumbled John, looking back over his shoulder and seeing the door had been left slightly ajar.

This is all I need. Someone may think that I'm a weirdo who purposely exposes himself. Why do I find myself in these weird situations? This reminds me of Shawn's stupid dream about a female talking to him through a bathroom door while he was taking a crap in a nasty restroom. What is this? It's like he's some kind of prophet of doom, or something. Why did he feel it necessary to tell about that stupid dream? He needs to stop sharing his weird dreams with me and focus on his case. I guess it's not his fault. He's a good man, with a fine career in his future. I'm a washed-up piece of crap ex-partner. I'm not sure why he even bothers with me.

His eyes moved up from the recently urinated area on the lower half of the wall in front of him, to find large lettering boldly scrawled across other graffiti. It read, "OPE is the answer – Danny B".

What the....? You're kidding me!

John quickly finished, flushed, and washed his hands. He moved to stand in front of the restroom door to prevent anyone from entering and took out his cell phone.

"Shawn, you need to get a forensic team here right away!"

WITHIN THIRTY MINUTES, Shawn and the team arrived. Customers of the store complained about not having a restroom available, but evidence was being gathered. There was a discussion about the need for handwriting analysis and hopes of gaining DNA from areas near the writing.

"How do you do this?" asked Shawn. "Do you have

some kind of radar?"

"What?" asked John.

"You found this out of the blue, and besides the victims you have been the only person to actually see this guy poking around someone's house," explained Shawn. "You were there for your next-door neighbor when she was harassed by an ex-boyfriend. Do you have radar, or something?"

"Man, this was just a freak accident," explained John. "I had to take a pee. Trust me, no radar."

"So, John, how did you know about this OPE information," interrupted the forensic lead.

"It's all over the news," answered John, trying to avoid mentioning that he and Shawn had been discussing this case for some time.

"The press," replied the forensic lead, rolling his eyes before walking away.

For the first time in a long time, John felt some appreciation for press coverage. As he and Shawn stepped out the front door of the store, he turned to his ex-partner.

"Coming over for supper tonight?" John asked.

"Is Heather doing the cooking?"

"You bet."

"What time?"

"How about 6:00 PM?"

"I'll be there," answered Shawn. "Thanks."

John slapped the muscular back of his ex-partner and headed for his car. After starting the engine, he pulled out his cell phone.

"Heather," John began. "Shawn's coming for supper at 6:00 tonight. Are you up for cooking?"

"You could have given me more of a heads up, Daddy! Why don't we just order pizza."

"No way. I told him that you were cooking."

"Why do you just assume that I am cooking for you?" asked Heather. "I'm not your housekeeper!"

"Would you rather that I tell him to make it another

time?" asked John.

"No."

There was silence for a few seconds.

"I can make spaghetti pretty fast," Heather said.

"Great! I'll pick up garlic bread on the way home."

"Please stop springing stuff on me," begged Heather.

"I didn't even plan on running into him today. It was just one of those things. Sorry. I love you, Baby."

"I love you too," replied Heather.

"Are you mad that I invited Shawn over?

"No."

"When I invited him, he asked if you were doing the cooking," explained John.

"He did? He actually likes my cooking?"

"He seems to. But it's also possible that he was checking to see if you would be around."

"Stop it, Daddy," Heather replied.

John never saw the smile on his daughter's face, but he could read it in her tone of voice.

Chapter 14

Adjustments

THE FOLLOWING DAY, there was pounding from a heavy hand on John's front door. Heather peered through the door peep and was delighted to see Shawn standing on the porch.

"Come on in, Skinny," she jokingly invited. "Looking for another plate of spaghetti?"

"Is John around?" Shawn asked with single-minded seriousness.

"He's out back."

"Thanks, I know my way." After a couple of steps, he turned back to her. "Sorry, Heather. I have a lot on my mind right now. It's really good to see you."

"No problem. Go on back. I'm sure you two have a lot to discuss."

Stepping onto the back porch, Shawn found John sipping a cup of coffee with Zack at his side.

"Some are thinking that there must be a connection with the pervert and the location of the nasty restroom in that crappy section of Atlanta," Shawn began.

"Duh," John replied. "That's a bit obvious, don't you think? The guy had to have written on that wall."

"No, that's not what I mean," said Shawn. "It's possible that the guy grew up in that area, or even lives in that area of town. I researched students at high schools in the area for a

Danniel B going back fifteen years. Two years ago, the city closed one of the schools down and demolished it, but I obtained a list of students prior to its closing. I found twenty-two names which could possibly point to this Danny B, but only nine who were Caucasian. Using databases available to the Atlanta police, I investigated those nine and found only two still living in the Atlanta area. I'm on my way to pick up my partner and check them out."

"Good work. I was hoping the guy was arrogant enough to leave this kind of trail."

On his way back to the front door, Shawn momentarily spotted Heather at the dining room table filling out paperwork.

"What's up?" Shawn asked, interrupting her.

"I'm applying for a position at a local university," she answered. "What did you think I was doing, Nosey?"

"I wasn't sure. So, you intend to stick around here?"

"The divorce has been hard on the kids, and they have really found comfort in my father," answered Heather. "I can't believe I'm saying that, but it seems retirement has softened him up a bit."

"He hasn't been the same since your mother died," said Shawn. "He was taking it really hard for some time, but he's doing a lot better now. I'm sure he's been good for his grandkids, but you and the kids have done him a world of good. This is the most settled I've seen him in a long time."

"I should have visited him more often," said Heather.

"I don't know. He was a bit messed up, and I doubt he would have established this solid relationship with the kids earlier. I think your timing was right."

"Maybe so, but I feel guilty for not being here for him."

"You had enough on your plate in California, and I'm not sure how helpful he would have been at the time," said Shawn. "I've known him to have a temper. If he had caught wind of your marital issues earlier, he might have visited David and done something that everyone would have regretted."

"You're right about that temper," said Heather. "My mother knew just how to cool him off when I was growing up. Without her around, it's very possible that he would have blown his stack and done something years ago. I see the relationship you two have, and I'm sure that's helped. Thanks for being here for him."

"I need to be going," Shawn said, placing his large hand on her petite shoulder. "Good luck with the job search."

"Thanks."

Heather's face was toward the paperwork, but her eyes followed Shawn's movements until he was out the front door. Shawn's touch was meant to comfort and encourage. He had no idea that it caused a rush of passion to flow throughout Heather's lonely body.

"It's been months since I felt a touch of a man," she whispered, placing both hands on her breasts. "And that man – is such a man."

JOHN WAITED FOR a thirty-minute visitation with Billy Crews at the Atlanta Correctional Facility. Soon the inmate was seated across from him.

"You're probably the last person I expected to see," began Billy, with a smirk and rolling his eyes.

"Have you had time to think about things?" asked John.

"What do you want?" questioned Billy.

"Did you know that a serial molester is running loose in the city?"

"Yeah, it's all over the news. We have TV privileges. The weirdo is terrorizing women by cutting their breasts. They are saying that he's killed a couple of women. What's that got to do with me?"

"Did you know that I spotted the guy peeking in Emily's window?" asked John.

"No, is she OK?" Billy answered. The smirk was

quickly replaced with that of grave sincerity.

"She's OK, but I wasn't able to catch him. He runs like a track star."

"I'm glad she's all right. So, why are you here?"

"Have you heard anything from your fellow inmates about this guy?" asked John.

"You think I'm a sicko who molests women?"

"No, but I am willing to bet that there are a few in this facility."

"I don't hang out with those guys for two reasons," replied Billy. "One, I'm not a pervert. Two, I'm afraid I would end up beating the crap out of somebody like that, and I would be locked up even longer."

"It was a long shot. The thirty minutes aren't up, but that's all I wanted to know."

"Hey, I heard that you aren't a cop anymore," said Billy.

"Who told you that?" asked John.

"Word gets around. If you aren't a cop, why are you here asking me questions?"

"I'm concerned about Emily" answered John. "I want this guy caught."

"Me too. I guess Emily had the baby."

"A little girl. You need to leave that family alone."

"I'll be locked up for some time, so you don't have to worry about that," said Billy. "I'm thinking that I'll probably be sent to prison this time. Listen, if you see Emily – would you tell her that I'm sorry for giving her a hard time?"

"I guess you've had some time to think. Sure, I'll tell her."

"Thanks. It means a lot. If I ever get out of here, I'll stay away. Emily is special. I've never felt like that about a woman. We have a history, but it's more than that."

"She told me about the miscarriage," said John. "I imagine that was pretty tough."

"She told you?"

"Her husband was on a job site, so she called on me to

take her to the hospital," explained John. "I asked if this was her first child. It's important. A second child can come sooner."

"I guess that makes sense," said Billy. "I'm glad that you were there for her. I hope that you'll continue to look out for her. She makes me crazy. I can't explain it. I know that I've been a real butthole with her, but I'm crazy about her."

"I felt the same about my wife. If somebody had messed with her, I would have probably gotten in real trouble."

"You're pretty tough for an old fart," said Billy.

"My temper hasn't always been good for me, and I have a tendency to stick my nose into places from time to time."

"I've never met a cop who didn't stick his nose into people's business," replied Billy.

"Well, I've probably taken it to another level."

"What was with you flipping me the finger that day?" asked Billy. "You saw that I was already riled up. You had to know that might push me over the edge."

"I did it to bring you off Emily's porch," answered John.

"You managed to do that, all right."

"Actually, I wanted to stop your harassment of Emily for good," explained John. "She has a family, and she's trying to be a good mother and wife. You're right about her being a special young lady. Emily reminds me a lot of my deceased wife, with her faith in God. If some guy had harassed my wife like that while she was pregnant with one of my kids, I'm afraid I would have done worse. I'm a bit of a butthole, as well."

"So, you wound me up on purpose," Billy stated, becoming slightly agitated. "Man…"

"You had the choice – you could have flipped me off and left or come at me. I figured you would come at me and planned to use it to put a stop to your crap."

"I was so crazy that I could have killed you," said Billy.

"That would have been pretty bad for both of us. But it

would have meant that you would never bother Emily again. You know what it means to kill a cop, right? Other cops would be looking for a reason to take you out. If you were lucky enough to be arrested, you would never come out of prison."

"Well, you've got balls, old man," said Billy. "I have to give you that."

"You can't act like that with women, Billy," said John. "In another time and place, it might have been different – but not today. You might be a young guy, but in your heart you're old school. You fight for what you want. Back in the day when men hacked each other to death with swords, that kind of behavior would have been acceptable – but not today."

"I'm thinking that you're old school too," replied Billy, calming down. "The difference between you and me is that you have a badge and gun that allows you to be who you are."

"I HAD a badge and gun, and my behavior probably has something to do with why I'm now retired. People don't put up with that today."

"You're right," said Billy. "I don't fit in with things. It's like I don't belong."

"Like I said, in another time and place you would have," explained John. "People like you have to adjust to society. You can't be who you are. Gay guys can be gay, but a man like you can't be who you are – not in today's society."

"You've got that right," agreed Billy.

"Here's the thing – you have to learn to channel who you are in order to fit into what is acceptable today," said John. "You can't do what comes natural without thinking. You have to calm yourself down and force that energy in the right direction. You're not an old fart, like me. You can learn to do it. It's not too late. Work on that while you're in jail. You'll have plenty of situations that will test you here."

"I don't think I know how to …channel, or do any of

that," said Billy.

"The first thing that you have to learn is to calm yourself down. You can't let your emotions run wild. Practice that when you find yourself tested. Just focus on that part for now."

"Is that what you did?" asked Billy.

"I've had to do that, or I would be sitting right where you are," explained John. "When you feel stuff rising up inside, think before you do. Think about calming down, about the fact that raw emotions put us in spots that get us in trouble. I think you're man enough to do that."

"I may give it a shot," said Billy.

"Give it serious effort and stay with it," advised John. "If you screw up, don't let it make you give up. You're going to screw up. Just keep practicing. It may take time to form new habits. Once you learn to calm down, you'll find out that it will help you figure out the right thing to do in situations."

"It makes sense, old man," said Billy. "You know, what you said about society not accepting somebody like me; if I had been born a long time ago, maybe things would be different."

"You can't do anything about when and where you are born, but you can adjust to what you need to do," said John. "You want to force things to happen the way you want them, but a man has to learn to control himself before he can change things in the right way."

"You're not who I thought you were," said Billy. "I thought you were just an old fart, butting in on what wasn't your business. I see that you had reasons for what you were doing. I jumped on you, but you kept your cool. You're right. I went nuts, and I'm paying for it. You were handling me. You were playing me for a fool, and I didn't know it. I didn't see it at the time."

"The important thing is that you're seeing it now," said John. "Some people don't ever see it. Some people are so thick headed that they can't see past their nose."

I don't know if I can do it, but I will give it a try. Where were you when I was growing up? You're pretty good at explaining things and you're pretty smart."

"I had to learn a few things the hard way, that's all," said John. "You're not stupid. You can learn to adjust. You just have to get your mind right."

The guard signaled that visitation time was over. As he took his prisoner by the arm to lead him away, Billy glanced back at John.

"Hey, I'm sorry that I went nuts on you," said Billy.

"We're good," replied John.

"It's good that Emily has you next door," said Billy, as the guard led him away. "Her husband Ron is pretty much a wimp. She needs a man around who knows how to handle things."

"Handle things? "John thought, as he turned to leave the room. *"That's a first. Ask anyone at the station about how well I handle things. I killed a man because I failed to handle him. It seems I can't handle hard liquor anymore. Most would say that I totally mishandled the situation with Billy and Emily. I'm glad I was around when Emily needed someone to drive her to the hospital, but that seems to be the one good thing I've handled for some time."*

Chapter Fifteen

Pastor Matt

"YOUR NEXT-DOOR NEIGHBOR, Emily, was certainly lucky to have you around," Heather told her father.

"I just happened to be at the right place at the right time,"
explained John.

"Looking back, that seems to be a pattern in your life," said Heather. "I'm so glad that you're here for me. I can't begin to tell you how much strength I've gained from your love and support."

"Loving you is easy," said John, giving his daughter a hug.

"Since she's your friend and neighbor, maybe I ought to get to know Emily better," suggested Heather.

"She is so sweet," said John. "Her faith in God reminds me a lot of your mother."

"If I pay her a visit, I should probably leave the kids here. They have little experience around newborns, and I would hate for them to wake the baby."

"I was thinking about taking Josh and Charlotte to the zoo today," said John. "I mentioned it to Josh, and he seemed to be excited about the idea. You would be free to visit."

"Go for it," replied Heather. "Charlotte loves animals. I think that's why she tries to be a vegetarian. She says that it seems mean to eat animals. Maybe she'll end up being a veterinarian."

"Josh is in the bathroom, and I have to go too," Charlotte said, interrupting the conversation as she stepped into the room.

"There's another bathroom off my bedroom," offered John.

"Is your bedroom fit for a little girl to pass through?" Heather whispered to her father.

"Of course, it is," John answered.

"Just go through my bedroom and you'll see a door to the right near the window," John told Charlotte.

The girl rushed into her grandfather's bedroom and found the bathroom. On her way out afterwards, she spotted a rolltop desk in the bedroom. She moved over to it and began running her small hands over the varnished oak. She was fascinated.

"I saw a big wooden thing in your room," Charlotte told her grandfather.

"Show me," said John.

After the two entered the room, Charlotte ran over to the roll top. She placed both hands on it. John walked over to her.

"That's a roll top desk," John said. "I bought it a few years ago from an antique shop. Would you like to see how it works?"

"Yes," said Charlotte.

John turned the key in the front of the desk and then rolled the top back, revealing the desktop and several compartments. John opened a compartment and took out a small pad.

"Would you like to have this pad?" he asked.

"I can have it?" asked Charlotte, excitedly.

"Sure, it's yours," John answered, handing her the pad.

"What's in the rest of those?" Charlotte asked, pointing to the other compartments.

"Various things," answered John. "Some are things that

I need to leave in those spots. Do you like this desk?"

"I love it!" blurted Charlotte. "I've never seen a desk like this. Maybe I can have one of these when I grow up."

"Maybe so," said John. "Are you ready to go to the zoo?"

"Yes!" squealed Charlotte.

Within minutes, John was escorting his grandkids out to his car for the zoo experience. Moments after they departed, Heather paid Emily a visit.

"Yes?" said Emily, opening her front door. "Oh, Heather! I'm glad you dropped by."

"My two children and I have decided to move back to Atlanta, and we are currently staying with my father," explained Heather.

"Please come in," invited Emily. "I'm glad you've decided to stay with your father. It'll be good to have another mother around. We'll need to be quiet. I just got my daughter Lily asleep.

"Maybe I should come back," said Heather. "I certainly wouldn't want to wake her."

"You have kids, so I'm sure you're more familiar with babies than I am," said Emily. "Please, come on in. I could use adult conversation."

"I remember my children when they were babies," said Heather. "I cherished time while they were napping."

"I'm so glad that you came over," said Emily. "Your father is such a great guy, and I don't know what I would have done if he hadn't been here to take me to the hospital."

"He's certainly unique," said Heather.

The two heard a car pull up in front of Emily's house. Emily looked out her front window.

"Oh, it's my pastor," Emily said.

"I'll leave you two," said Heather. "I'm sure that you have church matters to discuss."

"Please stay," asked Emily. "I would like you to meet him. At least stay for a while if you would. You just got here.

You're not going to interrupt anything with me and Pastor Matt. We all will just need to speak quietly, so that we don't wake Lily."

"Are you sure you want me to stay?" asked Heather.

"Yes, please."

"Alright," agreed Heather.

"Heather, this is Pastor Matt," introduced Emily. "Heather is John Rawling's daughter," she told the minister.

"Your father is an interesting man," replied pastor Matt. "He and I had a long conversation at the hospital about the first chapter of the book of Genesis in the Bible."

"Is that so?" questioned Heather. "It's not like him to have conversations about the Bible. He hasn't said a word about that to me."

"Does he usually speak to you about the Bible?" asked pastor Matt.

"No, that would have been my mother's conversation," answered Heather. "She was a woman of faith."

"What about you?" asked pastor Matt.

"My mother took my brother and I to church, but I stopped attending during my college years," replied Heather.

"I promise not to beat you over the head with my Bible," said the pastor. "But I am interested in your current faith."

"Today, I would say that I am more of an agnostic," explained Heather.

"Sadly, that's not unusual," said the minister. "Young college students often pull away from the church during those years. They are away from the norms of home. They step out into the world, and they encounter new experiences. Some have their faith challenged by college professors."

"While in college, I began to study psychology and fields of science," explained Heather. "My thoughts moved from metaphysical things to areas supported by evidence."

"Hebrews 11, in the Bible, begins with, 'Now faith is the substance of things hoped for, the evidence of things not seen'," said the pastor. "It's basically saying that belief in something unseen is a form of evidence of something in existence."

"I'm not sure that just believing something makes it true," replied Heather. "There was a time when most people believed that the sun circled the earth, but science proved that to be wrong."

"That's true," said the pastor. "However, that was a misinterpretation of evidence which was seen. I'm talking about evidence of things not seen. What about unseen truths? You can't see love. Do you believe that your mother loved you?"

"I do," said Heather.

"Where is the evidence?" asked pastor Matt. "You can't see love."

"I saw the actions of my mother," replied Heather. "Through her actions, I saw her love."

"You saw the results of her love," said the pastor. "That's like seeing a leaf being blown by the wind. We can't actually see air, but it's evidence that there air exists."

"I guess so," said Heather.

"God is a lot like that," said the minister. "You can't see God, but you can see the results of God. The Bible says that God is love. So, you believe your mother loved you because of her actions. The Bible says, 'For God so loved the world that he gave his one and only Son, that whoever believes in him shall not perish but have eternal life.' Our personal sins separate us from God. Jesus gave Himself to be punished for our sins. God placed our sins upon Jesus. When Jesus died on that cross, our sins died with Him. This action of God, of allowing His only Son to be punished and die in place of us, was an action that demonstrated His love for us. It also demonstrated His existence."

"Like I said, I'm more of an agnostic," said Heather. "I respected my mother, and I respect her beliefs. She believed in God; I'm just not sure. God could exist, but then He may not exist. I just don't know."

"That sounds like an intellectually safe place to be," said pastor Matt. "But sometimes indecision isn't safe. You see squirrels squished in the street, because a squirrel often can't decide which way to go when a car comes along. People sometimes freeze when confronted with danger. This world is a dangerous place. It always kills people; we all die. It's too late to make decisions after death. If you are looking for a safe place, regarding existence after death, then decisions need to be made in this life. Decisions like the one your mother made."

"I didn't realize that you were a hell, fire, and damnation preacher," said Heather.

"I'm not, really," said pastor Matt. "I'm more of a carrot preacher than a preacher that hits with a stick. It's just that agnostics feel safe, and I believe they are deceiving themselves. They want to be in a place where they are not attacked by atheists or believers, but that doesn't mean they are really safe. They may not offend believers or atheists, but God isn't fooled or satisfied by that stand. They still haven't taken God up on the forgiveness He offers through His Son Jesus. So, in that indecision, you are still actually making a decision to reject the offer from God."

"You are judging me," said Heather. "The Bible says, 'judge not.'"

"It does, and I'm no judge," said pastor Matt. "God's the judge, not me. I don't determine what happens to a person after death. That's God's turf. I just believe I should tell people about God's offer. You accept His offer or not. By stating that you are an agnostic, you are telling me that you haven't decided to take God up on His offer. If someone wants to give you a ticket to a concert that you might be interested in, you don't go to that concert unless you possess the ticket. You are telling me that you haven't decided whether to take that ticket. If you wait until the concert is over, it's too late. In not taking the ticket, you are making the decision not to take it. That's all I'm saying. God has gone to great lengths to provide you with something special."

"I see your point," said Heather.

"Do you have a child?" asked the pastor.

"I have a son and daughter,' Heather replied.

"If you were shopping with your son in a store, and an armed terrorist came into the store and stated that he has made a decision to kill one person in that store, would you offer up your son as a sacrifice in order to save the rest of the people there?"

"Hell, no!" exclaimed Heather. "Oh! Excuse me, pastor. I didn't mean to offend you, but there is no way I could offer my son to die. That's not happening."

"Well, that's precisely what God did," said pastor Matt. "If you were to offer your son, I bet it would have to be for someone who you greatly valued."

"There is no one who I value that greatly,' stated Heather.

"Well, God values you that much," said pastor Matt. "John 3:16 in the Bible says, 'For God so loved the world that he gave his one and only Son, that whoever believes in him shall not perish but have eternal life'. It's hard for us to get our arms around that kind of love."

"I think it is wrong for God to require death of anyone, especially Jesus," said Heather. "Jesus didn't do anything wrong. Why would a loving God require His own Son to die a horrible death on the cross?"

"I said that I'm no judge," said the minister. "I'm not judging you, but it also means that I don't judge God either. We humans tend to establish our own criteria for which we believe God should meet. God doesn't operate according to our criteria. God is God. God wouldn't be God if He had to try to live up to the criteria of billions of separate people around the world with their own ideas about right and wrong. In our arrogance, we seem to think God must meet our criteria in order for God to be just. I believe that God is the

Creator of the universe, that He has no beginning and no end, that God is in all places at once, and is all powerful. Very few of us live to see a hundred years. Our knowledge and understanding are so limited. Who do we think we are to make demands upon God to meet our short-sighted criteria? Why should God have to meet our expectations? We are created beings, who are born and die. Our live experiences and learning are extremely short, when compared to God. Who are we to judge God? What do we know that gives us the right to set criteria for God to follow?"

"I just don't understand God," said Heather.

"There are a lot of things I don't understand about God," confessed the minister. "I would have to be equal with God to understand everything about Him, and I am not even close. I try to understand God, and I think in this life I catch a few glimpses of Him. However, I believe that God has given us all the information that He believes we need to have in the Bible."

"Why death?" sked Heather.

"I don't know, but God has required the shedding of blood for the remission of sin throughout the Bible" explained pastor Matt. "Early on, Adam's son Able killed an animal and presented it to God because he had sinned. God accepted it. Able's brother Cain offered God plants, and God did not accept it. In the Old Testament, Jews shed the blood of animals and offered them to God in hopes of appeasing Him. They did this repeatedly. In order for our sins to be perfectly forgiven, a perfect sacrifice had to be made. There wasn't anything perfect on this earth, so God sent His perfect Son to be that perfect sacrifice. In this, God offered to bridge the gap between mankind and Himself. We were incapable of bridging it on our own. I understand some things about God, but my understanding is far from complete."

"You're probably right about people's attempts to judge God," said Heather. "I guess I believe I have ethical thoughts on what is right and wrong, and God doesn't seem to fit those thoughts."

"God says in Isaiah 55, 'For my thoughts are not your thoughts, neither are your ways my ways,' declares the Lord," said the pastor. "God goes on to say, 'As the heavens are higher than the earth, so are my ways higher than your ways and my thoughts than your thoughts.'"

"I remember my mother saying that," said Heather.

"God said this many years ago," said pastor Matt. "Technology has changed, and we have learned a great deal in our understanding of the physical world around us, but deep inside people really haven't changed. God's not dumb. God is well aware that it's common for people to attempt to form criteria for judging Him."

"OK, I understand your point," admitted Heather. "It makes sense that it would be ridiculous for God to try to live up to the conceived criteria that we each think to be right and wrong. God would have to live up to billions of different standards. I have a PhD in psychology with a focus on family counseling. Some people are very confused."

"Well said," said the pastor. "As a minister, like you, I've counseled many people, as you may have. We have that understanding in common. No pressure - would you consider what I said about God's offer to bridge the gap between mankind and Himself?"

"I will think about it," answered Heather. "You're probably right about agnosticism being a cop out. In trying not to offend anyone's faith or lack of faith, it's also an attempt to protect oneself from being judged by people. It's somewhat of a defensive mechanism for many. You're correct in your assessment about it still equating to a lack of decision to believe in God."

"In the long run, it doesn't matter what other people think," said paster Matt. "People think a lot of different things. What matters is the truth. Like you said, people believed the sun revolved around the earth until we discovered the truth. There is physical truth, and there is spiritual truth. Truth is truth. I'm asking you to make a decision regarding spiritual truth."

"The evidence of what is unseen, huh?" asked Heather.

"There is evidence, if you look for it," said pastor Matt. "Both science and the Bible agree that space, time, and matter suddenly came into being. Science calls this the Big Bang and the Bible calls it Creation. The difference being that when asked what initiated the Big Bang, scientists have no answer. Christians answer with stating that God did this. All of this came from somewhere, or Someone. I'm simply asking you to think about it and pray about it. Stop only searching the physical realm and begin searching your soul. If you really want to know the truth about God, you'll find Him."

"Like I said earlier, I usually try to focus on hard evidence in science and historical truths," said Heather. "My mother was an avid believer, but I'm just not so sure about the Bible and Jesus. No offense."

"I'm not offended at all," said the minister. "A lot of people have trouble with the Bible. Regarding Christ, it's a historical fact that Jesus lived in Palestine a little over two thousand years ago. It's supported by both archeological finds and hundreds of historical documents. The ancient historian Josephus documented it. Many of the books of the New Testament are records of Jesus and His followers. At least one hundred twelve ancient copies of the New Testament book of 1 John written in Greek have been found. The life of Jesus has greatly impacted the world. Much of the world measures time based on the existence of Jesus in our use of BC (Before Christ) and AD (' Anno Domini ', a Latin term which means 'Year of Our Lord' in English). BCE and CE stand for 'Before Common Era' and 'Common Era' and are alternatives to BC and AD respectively, but the measurement of time is still roughly the same. I don't believe any rational and educated person would deny that Jesus lived, any more than he/she would deny that a particular pharaoh lived in Egypt, or a particular Roman emperor lived. Oh, I'm sorry! I didn't mean to dump a sermon on you."

"Oh, I'm not opposed to the conversation," replied Heather. "I believe historically that Jesus lived, and he seemed to be a really good person. I'm just not sure about Jesus being the Son of God; you know, the entire thing about a person being deity."

"The problem many people have is in believing that Jesus Christ is the Son of God," said pastor Matt. "We live in an age where the focus is the observation and measurement of time, space and matter using the scientific method. Spirituality can't be observed and measured by scientific methods, but it is a real aspect of mankind."

"I would think that most people don't believe the existence of God to be a fact," said Heather.

"According to an article in a psychology publication, only 7% of the world is made up of atheists - those who do not believe in the existence of a god or any gods," said pastor Matt. "The vast majority of the world believes in some form of deity or believes in the possibility of a deity. Spirituality is very much a part of mankind. Deep within humans is an awareness of God."

"I also read a lot of psychology publications," said Heather. "Although, I'm not currently practicing, I have a PhD in psychology."

"Great!" stated pastor Matt, trying to keep his voice down. "We both are interesting in helping people with personal problems."

"Like I said, I'm not currently practicing," said Heather. "I hope to possibly find a teaching position at a local university. I'm just one of those people who has difficulty believing in God."

"I understand," said the minister. "Many people have issues with the idea that Jesus became alive again after He died from crucifixion. Records in the Bible state that more than five hundred people witnessed Jesus alive after His death from crucifixion. They weren't hallucinating or having visions based on wishful thinking. After His resurrection from death, people witnessed Him eating fish. Jesus showed Thomas the crucifixion scars on His body. One can intellectually read the accounts regarding Jesus, but faith involves more than just educating oneself about facts. It involves soul searching, and that has little to do with the scientific method. I can't intellectually prove it, but deep within my soul I've come to know that Jesus is the Son of God. I am thankful that His sacrifice – His death and resurrection - bridged the spiritual gap between man and God."

"I need to be getting back," said Heather. "My children have probably returned home from the zoo. They've been with my father."

"I apologize, again," said pastor Matt. "I seem to have been to be preaching a sermon! We preachers have a gift for gab, I'm afraid."

"I'll think about our discussion," said Heather. "I'll give it a day."

"*Wow! Pastor Matt is nice enough, but that man can talk*," Heather thought as she left Emily's house.

Chapter 16

OPET

"I HATE THIS!" blurted Shawn, as John led him and his new partner onto his back porch.

"I know you're upset, but try to keep your voice down," said John. "My grandkids are upstairs, and I don't want them to become upset."

"I'm sorry," replied Shawn. "That bastard attacked another pregnant housewife. Like the rest, he cut her breasts and carved letters into her stomach – but this time he added a letter – the letter T"

"OPET?" asked John.

"I want this guy!" bellowed Shawn.

"We need to think," suggested Shawn's new partner Caitlin Reeves, attempting to calm the big man. "Like John said, hold it down."

"My grandkids are upstairs playing video games," said John. "Let's make sure that we keep them out of this."

"Sorry, it's so frustrating," said Shawn, while lowering his voice.

"So, no luck while interviewing the two Danny Bs you found?" asked John.

"No!" replied Shawn. "It's like looking for a needle in a haystack. There could be a million Danny Bs."

"What's all the yelling about, Shawn?" asked Heather,

as she stepped onto the porch. "You sounded like Zack bit you or something. What's going on?"

"Zack's fine," said Shawn. "It's this pervert that's driving me up the wall. He attacked another pregnant woman."

"This time he added a letter, making it OPET," explained Caitlin.

"I've been thinking about this guy," said Heather. "He's trying to send a message, and it seems it has to do with uneducated women having children."

"Yeah, we've come to the same conclusion," said Caitlin.

"But what has set this man off?" asked Heather. "His reasoning might give an indication as to who he is. Did he have an abusive uneducated mother? Has he read books warning about the dangers of ignorant mothers? Did he hear a lecture in a university from a professor warning about problems with ignorant parents? What triggered this?"

"It's possible that he's just a sadistic bastard," suggested Shawn. "It's possible that he was just born evil and twisted. He may just enjoy giving women pain."

"Wait, Shawn," said Caitlin. "Heather has a point. It's more than just an enjoyment of inflicting pain on women. He is leaving a message with those letters. If he was inspired by some weird book or someone giving a lecture, that might narrow the search."

"I have access to a lot of books on family matters online," offered Heather. "I'll start looking through books which stress the importance of education in raising children. Maybe he read one of them."

"I suggest we consider bringing Heather in on this," suggested John. "Just on an unofficial basis, like mine."

"We're consulting with you because you've seen this guy and you're an ex-cop," said Caitlin. "You have a trained attention to detail that others may not have. Heather has a PhD in psychology. We could use expertise from a person professionally trained in that area."

"Professionally trained is what this guy is all about in his twisted carvings on women," said Shawn. "He is obsessed with it. Heather, I hope your professional education protects you from this guy. I'm a little concerned about you getting involved. You have no law enforcement training and experience."

"I'll let you guys know what I find," said Heather. My involvement will strictly be in research."

"Sounds good," said John.

As Shawn and his partner left John's house, Caitlin turned to Shawn. "When I first met Heather, I jokingly asked if she was your girlfriend."

"She's not," affirmed Shawn.

"Are you sure?" asked Caitlin. "I just heard you say that you hope her education will protect her – and I caught the tone in your voice. You really care for her, don't you?"

"Of course, she's my ex-partner's kid," answered Shawn.

"Doing the math, that 'kid' is about three years younger than you," stated Caitlin. "Plus, she's pretty. Most women who are her age with two kids don't look like that."

"She's John's daughter."

"You and I haven't been partners long," said Caitlin. "I may not be able to read you very well, yet – but a woman can read another woman."

"So."

"Heather is attracted to you," said Caitlin. "That's what is so."

"You're full of it," said Shawn.

"Not so. She is into you, you big lunkhead."

"Lunkhead? Lunkheads don't make detective at age twenty-four."

"Just promise me that you won't hurt her if she comes on to you," said Caitlin.

"I would never hurt, Heather," promised Shawn. "She's

my ex-partner's kid, remember?"

As they pulled away in Shawn's car, Caitlin spotted a smile on his face.

AS PASTOR MATT pulled his car in front of Emily's house, he noticed John sipping a cup of coffee on his front porch.

"Hi, John," the minister called out, as he exited his car.

"Pastor Matt, how are you doing?" asked John in return.

"Fine, are you busy?"

"Not so much since I retired," answered John.

"Mind if I drop over for a moment?"

"Do you want to come inside? John asked. "I have coffee on."

"I don't want to stay long this time. I was just going to visit for a minute before checking on Emily."

"Come on over," invited John. "There's another chair on the porch."

As the pastor settled into the chair, John asked "What's on your mind?"

"Emily told me that you had to kill a man in the line of duty before you retired," said the pastor.

"That's true."

"That kind of thing can be tough on people," said pastor Matt.

"How would you know?" asked John. "Have you ever killed a man?"

"No, but I've counseled veterans who have," answered the minister. "They also killed in the line of duty. Even though it was justified by war, they were still haunted by dreams."

"I guess I'm lucky, in that I haven't dreamed about it," said John.

"I'm glad it doesn't bother you now."

"Well, I think about it every now and then," said John.

"Glad to know that you're normal," said the pastor.

"So, pastor Matt, did you come here to counsel me?" asked John.

"Please, like I said earlier, you can just call me Matt," reminded the minister. "I'm not your pastor."

"OK, Matt, were you wanting to counsel me?"

"Not unless you want it," said Matt. "I was just interested in how you were managing with it."

"I seem to be doing OK. Besides, as a retired cop, I still have access to therapy by the shrink who counsels cops."

"Glad to hear it," said Matt. "Have you given more thought to your relationship with God?"

"You don't give up, do you?" asked John.

"You had your job, and I have mine. Besides, I like you, John."

"I was a cop, so most of the time I was examining hard physical evidence," said John. "Not invisible things, like God."

"So, you searched mysteries relating to crime and people," observed pastor Matt.

"I found that people can do horrible things to each other," said John. "You deal with the good people in your congregation, and I dealt with the bad people out in the world."

"We have a lot in common," said pastor Matt. "Our focus in life has been about people. I've run across some pretty evil people, as well. You said that you dealt mainly with hard physical evidence. However, you recognize that there is evil in the world, and in so doing, you are recognizing a spiritual aspect of these people."

"There are people who are unbelievably evil," said John. "There are people who do horrible things to other people and have absolutely no remorse. I'm not sure whether it has to do with spiritual matters or if they simply have twisted minds."

"People with twisted minds are capable of really odd

behavior," said Matt. "The acts of people with twisted minds can be good or evil. Even good people can have evil thoughts. Thoughts and emotions come and go. If we entertain evil thoughts until those thoughts mature into evil action, then we set evil in motion. People who are spiritually evil have no desire to disallow evil thoughts to die."

"And some of those people have no problem causing other people to die," interrupted John.

"You hit the nail on the head when you mentioned people having no remorse," said Matt. "Good people tend to stop evil thoughts from maturing into evil actions. If they commit evil, they're remorseful about it. I'm sure you can see that spirituality plays a part in evil deeds."

"Maybe you are right," said John. "There are people who think about doing terrible things, but stop themselves from carrying them out. Then, there are people who take pleasure in hurting other people. Some people are remorseful, and some don't seem to have that capacity."

"Most people only think of human beings in the sense of physical and mental, but there is something else that resides in the core of every person," said pastor Matt. "There is a spiritual aspect of a person, which is much deeper than the physical or mental aspects."

"If you say so," said John. "I'm sure you've studied spiritual matters much more than I have."

"Because of advancements in physical science, today, we tend to define a human in terms of material – atoms, molecules, cells, blood, bone, muscle…etc. However, for thousands of years the people of God viewed a human much differently. They clearly understood that our bodies have bone, muscle, organs, a brain, and blood. But they viewed a human to be much more than just a body, much more than simply material."

"It's the physical material, the human bodies, that I arrested after those human bodies committed crimes against other people," said John.

"I'm interested in why people do what they do," explained Matt. "It's my hope that the understanding may help me prevent some of those people from committing crimes against people."

"Good luck," said John. "I hope you succeed."

Jesus said in Matthew 22:37 'Thou shalt love the Lord thy God with all thy heart, and with all thy soul, and with all thy mind,'" said Matt. "That's how Jesus defined a human. Our body is a vehicle for the heart, soul, and mind. Jesus was talking about the real person who resides within the body."

"I'm sure Jesus had a lot of insight into people," said John. "I guess I spent a lot of time dealing with people with black hearts, evil souls, and twisted minds; and they used their bodies to do terrible things. If you think you can clean up their hearts, purify their souls, and untwist their minds – go for it. I wish you the very best in that."

"I can't, but God can," said Matt. "It's my job to try to introduce them to God. It's my job to let them know that Jesus can bridge the gap between mankind and God. Sin separates people from God. It's my job to let them know that when Jesus died on the cross, that God allowed the sins of all mankind to die with Him. That's our hope. That's our help in living past sin."

"Like I said, I hope you're successful in your job," said John. "I mean it."

Chapter 17

Emily's God

OVER THE NEXT two weeks, the friendship between Emily and Heather became closer. Heather's children found Emily's newborn baby to be fascinating and would do silly things to make her laugh. While visiting with Heather at John's home, Emily asked her about her marriage.

"David and I are recently divorced," replied Heather.

"I'm sorry it didn't work out," said Emily. "How are your kids taking this? I'm sure they miss him."

"His calls to the kids are rare," Heather answered, tears in her eyes. "To be honest, my father has become their primary male role model lately. I'm really surprised at how well they get along with him. David and my father are so different."

"I've had long talks with your father since we became neighbors, especially after he retired," said Emily. "I love my parents, but he has become almost a second father figure for me."

"Really? My father always seemed to be more of a man of action, not conversation. My talks were usually with my mother, but she's gone. She suffered greatly with ALS before passing away."

"Your father confided in me one day about how much he misses your mother," said Emily. "He told me that my faith in God reminded him of her. John loves his dog, Zack. The barking of John's dog was what alerted him to the guy who was peeking into my window. John told me that he has grown really attached to Zack since she passed."

"Zack is something else," said Heather. "My kids love that dog. David and I never had one. I'm really surprised at the interactions between that animal and my kids. I never thought about getting the kids a dog because David was adamant about not having one."

"Why was he opposed to the idea?" asked Emily.

"He didn't want the shedding of fur in the house, and he said that he couldn't stand the barking of an outside dog. He worked long hours and insisted on getting sleep."

"Well, your kids can now play with Zack," said Emily.

"You said that your faith in God reminded my father of my mother. Does your husband attend church as well?"

"He does," Emily replied. "I'm really thankful for his faith."

"My mother was active in church, but not my father," said Heather. "She made sure that my little brother Chris and I attended Sunday school and church, but neither of us attend church as adults."

"I stopped attending church for a while, but now I don't know what I would do without my relationship with God."

"I guess belief helps you, but I don't really understand faith in something or someone who is unseen," said Heather. "I'm not sure that God exists. I've told people that I'm sort of an agnostic, but your pastor helped me understand that I was mainly saying that in an effort not offend people. I think it was a method of dismissing the push by both sides of the issue. I didn't want to deal with it. Your pastor was right in telling me that the position of being an agnostic is still a rejection of belief in God. I have nothing against others having faith, so long as they don't try to beat me with it."

"Just because God is unseen, it doesn't mean that He doesn't exist," said Emily. "Most people believe that love exists, and you can't really see love. You can see the effects of love, by the actions of people who love one another. However, you can't really see love. God is like that. You can't see Him, but you may see the effects He has on people. In fact, the Bible says that God is love."

"You're pretty much telling me what your pastor said. I have trouble believing that God is love. Why would a loving God allow women in Atlanta to be molested and murdered?"

"There is evil in this world," answered Emily. "I guess some people would blame God for evil, and I can see their reasoning to some degree. The reason for evil in this world boils down to one word – choice. God allows choice. He gave His angels the freedom of choice and some of them elected to turn away from God and do evil. Some believe they became demons. God gives mankind the freedom of choice, and many of us elect to do evil. God could have made us all like robots, forcing us to do only good and disallowing the freedom of choice. However, most of us wouldn't really like that idea either."

"As a trained psychologist, I understand that people chose to do evil," said Heather. "I don't understand why my mother had to suffer and die from ALS. No human did that to her. Diseases like that aren't the result of evil done by humans. She was a devout Christian. Why did God allow that in her life?"

"God tried putting humanity in a perfect world, a world with no sickness, pain, or hunger," said Emily. "The Bible says that God placed two people in the perfect Garden of Eden. How did they repay God for this kindness? They rebelled and disobeyed God. Their wonderful environment didn't matter. Mankind exercised the freedom of choice to go against what God had warned about. In the process, we lost our innocence. We were no longer fit to live in that perfect world. Because of this, God sent mankind out of the Garden and into a world of death and suffering. Now, here we are. I certainly don't have total insight into the mind of

God, but this place just isn't heaven. If it was, we would probably mess it up."

"If God knows all, He must have known that mankind would screw up," observed Heather.

"I'm sure God knew. Would you rather be a robot, with no choice?"

"No, I just think God shouldn't punish people – if He loves them so much."

"Do you punish your children, if they do something that endangers themselves?" asked Emily.

"Sure, but I don't kill them," said Heather. "I don't slap them down with ALS. Who does that?"

"So, you think God should have taken a privilege away from mankind instead?"

"Yes, something like that," replied Heather.

"What privilege would that be?" asked Emily. "The privilege of choice? God told them not to do one thing, and they did it. God is the source of life. In disobedience, mankind turned away from life. God was speaking the truth to them. To turn away from life is to turn toward death. Mankind made the choice to turn toward death. The only alternative to stop mankind would have been to disallow freedom of choice. That seems to have been God's only alternative."

"Well, no. I certainly want the right to choose," said Heather. "I just think God could have been more creative - if He is the great Creator and all of that. I just don't see God as being love."

"Instead of gaining an understanding of what love is from learning about God, we have a tendency to have our own definition of love, and we try to fit God into it," explained Emily. "If God doesn't seem to fit our criteria for love, we throw up our hands and say that God doesn't seem to really be love. He isn't to be judged by our selfish and arrogant personal criteria, when it comes to what is right. This is something that I had to learn. God can't be expected to live up the different personal criteria of billions of people."

"I guess that makes sense," said Heather. "Again, that's pretty much what your pastor said."

"I think the problem is that we want God to be like us – do only what we think is best," said Emily. "We want to call the shots in the universe. How do you think that would work out? Look at what people have done to each other over thousands of years. Do you really think we are capable of running the universe? Look at the results of our actions. How smart do you think we really are?"

"I just think death is a little extreme," replied Heather.

"Jesus said that He is the way, the truth, and the life," said Emily. "Jesus offers life, and mankind rejects that life. We move away from life through the choices we make. In the Bible, John says that God created life through the Word – and that Jesus is that Word. God spoke the universe into existence. Jesus is the source of all life."

"I guess I do understand the logic of mankind moving away from life in our choices. If God is truly the source of life, I can see that the opposite direction would logically be death. I guess you are saying that we chose death and now we are stuck with it."

"We are pretty much stuck with physically dying," said Emily. However, we don't have to spiritually die. That's what Jesus is all about. God sent His Son Jesus to physically die so that we can live spiritually forever."

"I can't get my mind around spiritually living and dying," said Heather.

"I believe that each person has a soul inside their body, and that when the soul leaves the body, the body dies," said Emily. "The body can get sick and die. I believe a person's soul can become sick by sinning against God, and that sin causes spiritual death."

"I also believe people can be sick on the inside, and my profession is about helping those people become well on the inside," said Heather.

"There is only so much we can do about healing our souls," said Emily. "I think what you do is help heal the minds of people. Our souls also need help, and Jesus died so that our souls can be cleansed of that sin. God sent us His perfect sinless Son, Jesus, in the form of a human. Jesus was strong enough to handle that load. When Jesus was dying on the cross, God piled all the sins of the world - past, present, and future sins of everyone who has lived or will live – on Jesus. When Jesus died, our sins died with Him. God requires that we have faith in that act for our sins to be forgiven and cleansed."

"If Jesus took the sins of everyone, then He took the sins," said Heather. "What does belief have to do with it?"

"If I offered you a million dollars, you wouldn't have it until you accepted it from me. Right?"

"Right," agreed Heather.

"If you left me hanging with the million dollars still in my hand, that money would do you no good," Emily explained. "If you believed that the million dollars was real and that I was really offering it to you, you would want to take it – wouldn't you?"

"If it was really a gift, I guess I probably would," answered Heather. "I also might think there are strings attached to a gift like that."

"The strings attached are that God wants us to be grateful, and to love Him in return for His gift," said Emily. So, yeah – there are strings. Part of loving God is trying to live as He wants us to live."

"That's too easy," said Heather.

"No, it's not. Jesus said to His followers, 'If you love me, you will obey my commandments.' Remember, mankind got into this mess by disobeying God."

"I knew it was too good to be true," said Heather. "I tried reading all those commandments of God in my mother's Bible. I can't do that! That's an impossible life.

There isn't any point in pretending that I could keep up with all of that and do all those things. Even if I could, I would be totally miserable living like that."

"Jesus said that the two greatest commandments are to love God with our whole heart and to love our neighbor as we love ourselves," said Emily. "He said all those laws in the Old Testament boil down to these two commandments. That simplifies things somewhat."

"You sound like my mother," said Heather. "My father was right. You do remind me of her. He wasn't interested in church, but she took my brother and I to church regularly when we were growing up. To be honest, once I became a teen church bored me to tears. Once I left home for college, I was pretty much done with it. When I came home for visits, my mother still attended church. She did this on her own. The rest of the family wasn't interested. That was her thing."

"I can relate," said Emily. "My parents raised me to attend church, but I stopped going when I was a teen. Did your father tell you about my old boyfriend, Billy Crews?"

"No."

"I'm surprised. Billy and your dad got into a fight outside my house, and your dad beat him up."

"I'm so sorry!" exclaimed Heather. "I had no idea. He didn't tell me he did that. Daddy has a temper, and he probably thought that telling me might cause me not to visit with the kids."

"It's not really like that," explained Emily. "It wasn't because of your father losing his temper. Billy was harassing me while Ron was at work, and John stepped in. However, I think the incident may have resulted in him deciding to retire. The police led John off to his house and kept him there for a while. He decided to retire shortly after the incident."

"He told me that the retirement had to do with him shooting a man dead," said Heather. "My father can be a violent man, but he told me that the shooting was ruled as justified - that he shot the man in self-defense. He said that the shooting made him aware that he was getting too old to handle criminals without resorting to a gun."

"That's probably true, but the fight between him and Billy happened while he was home on leave during the investigation of the shooting," explained Emily.

"My father's tendency toward violence is the main reason my husband David and I didn't want our kids around him. David had no respect for my father and warned me about his continual involvement with violence. He had a point. Maybe it's time I found an apartment. I would hate to see my kids witness his temper. They've grown close to him."

"I'm telling you that I've never witnessed your father lose his temper," said Emily. Your father is my hero. He found that pervert who is molesting pregnant women outside my window while I was still pregnant, and he chased him off. Your father took me to the hospital to give birth when my husband was too far away to come home on time. He kept me calm. Your father was amazing. Your children should be proud of their grandfather. I don't know what I would have done without him."

"I guess, he is pretty cool under pressure."

"Initially, the incident between him and my old boyfriend Billy scared me a little," said Emily. "But, afterwards, I was glad that he stepped in. Billy Crews is crazy. Becoming involved with him was the worst mistake of my life. I hooked up with him when I was going through a wild period in my life. Believe me, there was never a dull moment with him."

"Ok, but my dad didn't have to beat him up," said Heather.

"You don't really understand what happened. When your father confronted him, he pulled a gun on your father. I'm not sure what else he could have done. Billy can be extremely violent. The court put him in jail for attacking your father with a gun, and I don't have to worry about him harassing me now."

"You're right," said Heather. "The gun puts the incident in a different light."

"Your father is my hero. He's an amazing man. I am so blessed to have him as my next-door neighbor."

"David hates him," said Heather. "He insisted that our children not be left alone with him."

"Who has really stood by you and your children, David or your father?" asked Emily.

"They're just very different people. My father is now retired, and David is extremely busy. David is much more educated. He has a PhD, like me. My dad has a degree in law enforcement from a community college."

"You didn't answer my question," said Emily. "I didn't ask you which was the more educated. I asked you which has stood by you and your children. You told me that David rarely called his kids after moving out."

"You're right," replied Heather. "My father really has come through for them. He has stood by us, and David hasn't."

"God can stand by you as well," offered Emily.

"I'll consider it," said Heather. "You've given me something to think about. I like the concept that God is love, and you've given a reasonable explanation regarding why evil is in the world. I'm an educated woman. I need to have logical explanations for things. I can't afford to let myself get carried away with feelings. I think a lot of people mess themselves over by simply following their emotions."

"I certainly messed myself over by allowing my emotions to get the best of me with Billy Crews," Emily said, rolling her eyes.

"I may have made a mistake with David, but I am so thankful for my two children. The marriage resulted in those two. They're such great kids. I would be so lonely without them."

"There is no way life could really prepare me for the

love I have for my daughter Lily," said Emily. "No one could have ever explained to me what it is like to be a mother."

"You said that God is love," said Heather. "It's natural for a mother to love her child. Maybe love is part of the unseen aspects of nature, and God is in that."

"So, belief in God makes sense to you?" asked Emily.

"I said that you've given me things to consider. I'll have to reflect on it for a while. Don't push me. Something like that requires thought and observation. I'll have to at least give it a day."

"Are we guaranteed to live to see the next day?" asked Emily.

"You and your pastor ..." Heather was interrupted by Shawn's heavy fist on the front door of John's home. Heather opened the door to find Shawn and Caitlin on the front porch.

"We need to talk with John!" blurted Shawn.

"He's on the back porch with Zack," answered Heather.

As the two detectives rushed past her, Caitlin turned to Heather and said, "Another victim and another explanation for a letter."

Chapter 18

TO

"THIS IS KILLING me!" shouted Shawn.

"Keep your voice down," coached Caitlin. "I'm sure those two young kids are around."

"She's right," said Heather, as she stepped out onto the back porch. "Shawn, the kids will be upset if they hear what are talking about. They're upstairs playing a video game."

"I'm sorry, Heather," whispered Shawn. "We need to get this guy."

"Details," said John. "Give me the details."

"He has carved up another housewife," said Shawn. "The same cutting to her breasts. He also carved 'OPET' on this victim, like he did the previous ones."

"He also carved the word 'TO' into her," added Caitlin.

"ONLY PROFESSIONALLY EDUCATED TO'? blurted Shawn. "TO what? What is he getting at?"

"Beats me," said Caitlin.

"Maybe he approves of only highly educated women nursing a baby," said John. "He seems to be fixated with breasts."

"Maybe he wants only professionally educated people to suffer," suggested Shawn. "The husband of this woman is an electrical engineer. He's highly educated."

"No!" exclaimed Heather. "None of these victims have

been highly educated. I'm guessing that he wants only professionally educated people to become pregnant."

"My thoughts, exactly," said John. "He only attacks pregnant women, and only those less educated."

"Do you think this guy is some academic pinhead?" asked Shawn.

"Possibly," said John. "However, he's not just a bookworm. He exercises. The guy I saw was not overweight and was really fast. The guy I saw was in shape."

"But it's true that he could be someone in academics," said Heather. "I've run across more than a few kookie professors in academia."

"So, is 'kookie' a professional term that you use in the shrink world?" asked Shawn.

"Good grief," said Heather. "My vocabulary has really taken a hit since moving in with my father. I should have used the word 'eccentric' or 'unique.' Kookie? I had better not use that term when interviewing for a position at a local university."

"So, you're thinking about staying here for good?" asked Shawn.

"Why not?" asked Heather.

"Your husband is good with moving here?" asked Shawn.

"David and I are done," replied Heather. "Let's change the subject. We need to concentrate on this case."

"Right," agreed Caitlin. "We have a skinny, athletic guy, who could possibly be an academic scholar?"

"That's my thinking," said John. "He could be a professor."

"I bet some of them are creepy," said Shawn.

"Cut it out!" exclaimed Caitlin. "Let's get serious. He doesn't have to be a college professor. He could be anybody that fits that description."

"That's right," said John. "The guy could even be a track coach at a high school."

"That's a thought," agreed Shawn. "I'll pursue that avenue. I can easily get a list of track coaches from the city, and I think they probably have some background information on them. I can narrow the list down to anyone with the name Danny B."

"Good idea," said John. "Shawn, you said that you'll check out the area track coaches."

"I'll get on it," said Shawn.

As Shawn and Caitlin stepped off John's front porch, she turned to her partner. "I saw the cogs turning in that head of yours when Heather said that she and her husband were done."

"Cut it out," protested Shawn.

"Just calling it as a see it," said Caitlin. "Just warning you that she might be out of your league. She's really smart, and she's kept herself in really good shape to be the mother of two kids. She's one hot mama."

"Would you let up?" asked Shawn.

"No, way!" exclaimed Caitlin. "This is too good."

"Just get in the car," said Shawn.

THE FOLLOWING WEEK, Josh walked out onto his grandfather's back porch and found him sipping a cup of coffee. Zack was curled up at his feet.

"I have a question," Josh said, reaching down to pet Zack.

"What is it?" asked John.

"If you were in the police force for many years, you must have guns. How many guns do you have?" Josh asked.

"Several," answered John. "I was issued one that belonged to the police department, but I have returned it. I have two pistols here at the house and I also own a shotgun."

"I've never seen a gun," said Josh. "My father says that guns are bad, and he told me to stay away from them."

"Things are just things," said John. "A thing is bad if it

is used to do something bad. Things can be used to do good or bad."

"When is a gun a good thing?" asked Josh. "Isn't the purpose of a gun to hurt or to kill?"

"Well, if a very bad man wanted to hurt your mother and I used a gun to scare him away," answered John. "Wouldn't that gun be a good thing, in that case?"

"Maybe," answered Josh.

"When a baseball bat is used to play baseball, it would be a good thing, right?" asked John.

"Sure," answered Josh.

"What if someone used the baseball bat to hit and hurt someone else on purpose?" asked John. "Would that baseball bat still be good?"

"That dumb bat isn't good or bad, but a person using it might be good or bad," answered Josh.

"That's exactly the right answer," replied John. "Nothing is good or evil of itself, it just depends on what people do with a thing. You're pretty smart."

"I make all 'A's in school," said Josh.

"Good grades are good," said John. "Keep it up. But not everyone who makes good grades understands things about life. You do."

"Can I see one of your guns?" asked Josh.

"That would be up to your mother," answered John. "You can ask her if you like. If she agrees, I'll will show you one.'

Josh ran back inside the house. Minutes later, he came back out pulling his mother behind him by the hand.

"Mom, says that I can see a gun," Josh announced.

"You're sure?" John asked his daughter.

"He won't leave me alone until he sees it," replied Heather. "Besides, there is no one I trust more than you to tell him about gun safety."

"You mother is right," John told Josh. "Guns can be very dangerous. You do understand that you are never to play with a gun or even touch one of my guns without me being present, don't you?"

"Yes," answered Josh. "I promise to never bother your guns, ever."

"Good," said John. "Wait here, and I will bring one out."

Moments later, John came out onto the back porch with the .38 in his hand.

"Does it have bullets in it?" asked Josh.

"No," said John. "Come over here," John told his grandson, while taking a seat.

"Can I touch it?" asked Josh. "Can I touch it while you are holding it?"

"I'll do better than that," answered John. "Sit here, and I will let you hold it in your lap."

"It feels cold and heavy," observed Josh, taking the gun in his hands.

"It's also old," said John. "It's been in my family for a long time. It's a police positive .38, and it was manufactured in 1910."

"Does it still work?" asked Josh, holding it above his head.

"Yes, it works," said John. "And put that gun back unto your lap. You asked me if the gun was loaded, and I want you to understand something. Always treat a gun as if it was loaded. Always treat a gun as if it could hurt or kill someone. Never, never point a gun at someone unless you intend to shoot that person."

"I would never shoot someone," said Josh.

"Always keep the barrel of the gun pointed downward and away from people or animals that you don't intend to shoot," said John.

"What part is the barrel?" asked Josh.

John showed his grandson the parts of the pistol. He opened the cylinder and showed him the chambers where the rounds were to be placed to load it. He showed him how the hammer and trigger worked.

"If you ever fire a gun, it should be cleaned as soon as you are able,' John told his grandson. "On another day, I can show you how it is cleaned. But this is enough for today."

"Can I pull back the hammer and pull the trigger?" asked Josh. "Will it hurt the gun to do that while it is unloaded?"

"It won't hurt this gun to do that while unloaded," answered John. "But remember - always treat a gun as if it is loaded – always. Keep the barrel pointed down and away from us and Zack while you do it."

John handed Josh the gun with the hand grip pointed toward his grandson and the barrel pointed down and away from everyone. Josh took it in both hands, keeping it pointed down and away.

The boy held the gun in his right hand and pulled back the hammer with his left hand. Carefully, he pulled the trigger until the hammer fell with a loud click.

"Wow," Josh said. "I didn't have to pull the trigger very hard. The hammer slammed down as soon as my finger pulled. Thank you, for letting me do that."

"Do you remember how to hand a gun to someone?" John asked.

"Yes, you keep the barrel pointed down and away and you give it to the person with the hand grip pointed to the person," answered Josh.

"That's right," said John. "Now, hand the gun back to me."

"I don't think I ever want to touch a gun when it is loaded," said Josh. "I'm scared that I would hurt someone. I will let you be in charge of scaring bad people away," said Josh.

"I will do just that," said John.

"Thanks for showing me the parts of the gun and how to carry it safely," said Josh.

"You're very welcome," replied John. "I'm going to put

this back, and you are never to look for it."

"I won't look for it," promised Josh.

"I trust you to keep your word," said John. "I trust you to leave it alone."

Chapter 19

David

"KIDS, HOLD IT DOWN up there!" shouted Heather from downstairs. "I don't want you to turn your grandfather's house into a gym."

"It's fine," said John. "It is really good to have some life in this house for a change. I'm loving it, and Zack really enjoys having them around."

"Josh loves that dog."

"As he should," said John. "David was a stick in the mud about not wanting an animal around."

"He thought it was too much," said Heather. "That's all."

"David was being a selfish jerk about it. Just like he is about everything."

"That's not fair," said Heather.

"Are you still defending that jerk?" asked John.

"He is still Charotte's and Josh's father," said Heather. "Don't call him a jerk, especially around the kids."

"OK, but I can think it," said John.

"You can think whatever you want," Heather said.

"Free thought, but no free speech in my own house?" poked John.

"You have a point," said Heather. "Maybe, it's time I got my own place."

"What? No way. You don't even have a job yet. I was joking about the 'no free speech' stuff. Please don't move out. Not yet, anyway."

"Ok," said Heather. "I just don't want my kids to mess up your house."

"I'm OK with my grandkids having some fun," said John.

The conversation was interrupted by a call on Heather's cell phone.

"I have no idea who this is," said Heather, observing the displayed number.

"Probably a telemarketer, trying to sell you more car insurance," said John.

"Hold on, I'll take the call," she told her father.

"Yes, this is Heather Littleton," Heather said to the caller.

There was a long pause.

"What?" asked Heather. "Is he alright?"

Another pause.

"No!" she blurted. "No! What happened?"

"What's going on?" whispered John.

"Heather held her left hand toward John while she continued to listen to the caller.

"Was he by himself, or was someone else in the car?" Heather asked, as she took a seat on a chair.

Another pause.

"Oh, dear God!" Heather said.

A pause.

"Burton Funeral Services," said Heather, her hand holding the phone trembled. "Prior arrangements have been made, and they should still be good."

A pause.

"Yes, I'll contact his attorney," said Heather before ending the call.

"David?" asked John.

"David is dead," whispered Heather, her voice shaking

and her eyes darting. "I don't know how to tell the kids, but they will have to know – and soon. I need to contact the funeral home and David's attorney before I tell them. I don't want to leave them questioning anything. I need answers."

"Speaking of answers," said John, moving close to his daughter. "What happened?"

"He was killed in an auto accident. That was the coroner. It appears he was killed outright."

"Was anyone else involved in the accident?" asked John.

"No other car was involved," said Heather. "It was a single car accident. Apparently, David lost control."

"That's good," said John.

"Not entirely," replied Heather. "Another person was involved. David wasn't alone. A female graduate student was also killed."

"I'm so sorry," said John. "You're divorced, but you were together for a number of years. You two had grown apart, but this will still impact your life."

"I'm sort of numb," said Heather. "It's like I'm in a dream or something. I need to get my head on straight before I talk to the kids."

"I'm here for you if you need to talk," said John, placing his hands on each of her shoulders.

"We will need to fly back to California for the funeral. The kids will need closure."

"You will need closure as well," said John.

Heather wrapped her arms around her father's waist and dropped her head against his chest. She was silent for several seconds. John held her tight.

"I'm sorry," he said again.

"I know."

"I'm sorry that I've said so much crap about him since you came," said John. "I sometimes say things before thinking. All I could think about was the fact that he hurt you. I didn't put some things in the right perspective. You had two wonderful children together."

"We did," mumbled Heather, still in her father's arms.

"Please let me know if there is something I can do," said John.

"I'm so glad to have you. I'm so glad the kids have you. I can't imagine the impact of this on them without you being here for them."

Heather pulled away. Her face took on the countenance of someone much older.

"That poor girl, killed with him," said Heather, wiping a tear away with her hand. "There was alcohol. I'm sure her family will be suing his estate, and I don't blame them."

"I'm sure he had insurance," said John.

"For sure," Heather replied. "That's one thing that he was a stickler about – having plenty of insurance."

"Maybe you need to sit down and rest a while," suggested John.

"No, I have to contact his attorney and then the funeral home," said Heather, pulling out her cell phone. "I have to take care of a few things before I rest."

"Like Robert Frost," said John.

"What?"

"His poem said 'miles to go before I rest'; I'm sure you remember," said john. "It was one of your favorites in high school."

"You remembered," said Heather. "I guess I better understand it now. There are things which must be handled before resting – and I have a few."

"Take a deep breath before making your calls."

"I will," said Heather. "I'll make the calls on the back porch if you don't mind."

"Not at all. Let me know if I am needed."

Heather first placed the call to the funeral home and scheduled the funeral for the coming Saturday.

"I will need a write up for the obituary," said the funeral director. "We have a website for that, but I will need the wording.”

“I’ll email you the information,” said Heather.

“Have his parents and siblings been notified?” asked the funeral director.

“Oh, God, no,” replied Heather. “I’ll take care if it.”

Afterwards she called David’s attorney to notify him of his death.”

“The will wasn’t changed after the divorce,” said the attorney. “You still inherit everything – the house and all his investments. David told me that you are in Atlanta now. The house hasn’t yet sold. Will you be moving back and taking the house?”

“No, I’m done with California,” Heather answered.

“I need a forwarding address in order to send you paperwork,” he said. “I can move on things faster if you can scan the signed documents and email them to me. But please also mail the signed originals to me.”

Heather gave him her father’s address, but then added, “I’ll be in town with the kids for the funeral. Maybe I could meet with you then.”

“It will take time for some of the paperwork,” the attorney said. “I’ll contact you as soon as they are processed.”

“Thank you.”

“I’m sorry for the loss,” said the attorney. “And I am sorry for the impact on your children. I’m sure it will be tough.”

“It will be,” said Heather. “I’m so glad that have my father here.”

“I’ll be in touch,” he replied.

With the calls made, Heather took a deep breath. Sitting on the back porch, she looked over the yard where she played as a child. Soon, her view was blurred by tears.

“I can’t believe that he’s gone,” she thought, remembering happier times with David. *“It was over with the divorce, but with death – it’s really over. There are no*

more words – no more reconciling – no more talks about the kids – nothing. I loved him, I really loved David. How did it come to this? Why?"

THE FOLLOWING SATURDAY, Heather and the kids stood at David's gravesite after everyone else had left the funeral ceremony. Josh burst into tears.

"Honey, I'm so sorry," Heather said holding him tight. She reached out for Charlotte, but she defiantly pulled away.

"If you two hadn't divorced, this would not have happened," Charlotte angrily stated.

"The divorce didn't cause this," Heather attempted to explain. "This was an accident. It was a terrible accident."

"Daddy was alone back here," Charlotte said, trying to make sense of the tragedy. "We left him here by himself."

"He wasn't alone," said Heather. "A woman was in the car with him, and she was also killed."

"I don't believe you!" shouted Charlotte. "You're making that up. You never said anything about that."

"I didn't want to tell you that," said Heather, still holding Josh.

"If you hadn't left Daddy, that woman wouldn't have been with him," Charotte accused. "It's your fault."

"No, Sweetheart, that's not true," said Heather. "Your father loved you and Josh, but he didn't really love me anymore. That's why I left him. I'm so sorry, but that's the truth."

"What did you do to make him stop loving you?" Charlotte asked. "Did you stop loving him?"

"No, I didn't," answered Heather. "I tried, but the marriage just fell apart. I am so sorry that it did, but I tried – I really did."

"You must not have tried enough!" she blurted.

"Your father was with other women," Heather coldly stated. "He didn't want me anymore. Oh, God! I didn't want to tell you that about him. I'm sorry…I shouldn't have told you that. I'm sorry."

"Why?" asked Charlotte, her eyes now filled with tears. "Why did he want other women?"

"I don't know," Heather said. "I really don't know."

"Does Grandpa know?" Charlotte asked.

"Yes, he knows," answered Heather, as she too broke into tears.

"I'm sorry, Mama," said Charlotte.

"Me too," added Josh. "I just want Daddy back."

"I know," blubbered Heather. The weight of the divorce and David's death finally crushed her. She dropped, seated on the ground – she wept bitterly. Her children now holding her, wept also. As Heather raised her eyes, about thirty feet away she saw two workmen standing with shovels standing near a front end loader and waiting to fill in David's grave. She forced herself to stand, still clinging to her children.

"We need to go," Heather whispered. "They need to finish with the grave."

"I just wish I could see Daddy again," said Charlotte.

"Me too," added Josh. "I didn't get to tell him goodbye."

"I love him," said Charlotte.

"He knows," said Heather. "He knows."

"Can he see us?" asked Josh.

"I believe he can," said Heather, trying to comfort her children. "We just can't see him."

"I love you, Daddy," Josh called out.

"Does he know what we are thinking" asked Charotte.

"Maybe," answered Heather.

"Is he happy?" asked Josh.

"Oh, I think he is happy in heaven," said Heather.

"I can't wait until I go to heaven to see him," said Josh.

"We have to wait our turn," cautioned Heather, somewhat frightened by his statement. "We aren't allowed to go to heaven until God decides it's time for us to go."

"Do you believe in God?" asked Charlotte.

"I believe in God," answered Heather, still trying to comfort her children.

"Can you tell us about God?" asked Josh.

"Preachers at churches tell people about God," Heather said.

"Can we talk to a preacher about heaven," asked Charlotte.

"We need to go now," said Heather, attempting to change the subject while leading then back to the rental car.

"Can we talk to a preacher?" continued Charlotte.

"We can, if you really want to," answered Heather.

"Do you know a preacher?" asked Josh.

"Yes, they call him Pastor Matt," answered Heather. "I met him while visiting with Emily next door. He preaches at her church."

"Good," said Josh. "I want to hear more about heaven."

"What have I gotten myself into?" thought Heather.

"WHAT DO YOU MEAN, it wasn't entirely an accident?" Heather asked David's attorney.

"The police found brake line purposely damaged when they inspected David's car," answered the attorney. "They've arrested the ex-boyfriend of the woman killed in the accident. It appears he was angry with your ex-husband over the girl, and he damaged brake lies of David's car. I don't anticipate the family filling a lawsuit against the estate, but instead I believe the family of the girl will file a civil case against the young man."

"Someone tried to kill David?" Heather asked.

"Tried and succeeded," said the attorney. "There was alcohol in David's blood, but this puts the situation in an entirely different light."

"Oh, my God!" Heather exclaimed.

"I've processed the paperwork for you," said the

attorney. "The house is now entirely in your name," stated the attorney. "I was able to move on this fast because the house had been in both your names. If you don't want to have to pay a load of California property taxes, you may want to prompt a realtor to make sure it sells soon."

"I will contact a realtor friend of mine in California," replied Heather.

"Good," said the attorney. "Put your friend in touch with me, and I can verify the ownership. You shouldn't have to come back to California to handle to selling of the house."

Chapter 20

Changes

"I'M HERE FOR William Crews," John told the clerk at the correctional facility.

"Go through the second door, and have a seat," replied the clerk.

As John waited for Billy Crews to be brought to room, he questioned himself as to whether this visit would do any good. As Billy was brought into the room and seated before him, John was surprised to find him clean cut and with a change of demeanor. He seemed to be more attentive and respectful toward the guard.

"Well, you've cleaned up somewhat," John said.

"I've had some time to think," answered Billy. "I decided that I needed to make a few changes."

"I guessing that a court appointed lawyer told you to make yourself more presentable before going before a judge on appeal," said John. "I've seen it before."

"I don't think I'm looking at an appeal," said Billy. "I attacked a cop, if you'll remember."

"I remember it quite well," replied John.

"What can I do for you, detective?" asked Billy.

"Not a detective now," replied John. "I retired."

"Then, why are you here?"

"I witnessed a guy attempting to peek in Emily's

window, and it turns out that the guy has been molesting women," said John.

"I hope they've caught him," said Billy, now taking on a more serious tone.

"They have not, and that's why I'm here," said John.

"How can I help? Anything for Emily."

"Have you heard any talk in here of a guy molesting pregnant women?" asked John.

"I don't think a guy like that would last long in here," replied Billy. "Most of these guys are crap, but there are two things they can't tolerate – somebody sexually messing up kids and anybody attacking a pregnant woman. They will take care of a guy like that if he isn't protected by being put in solitary."

"I want you to have your ear to the ground regarding anyone talking about somebody on the outside molesting women; that's all," said John. "Can you do that?"

"I can do that," said Billy. "I can make a call to my lawyer, if I hear something. He can get a hold of you. His name is Childers, Fred Childers."

"I know who he is," replied John. "He hangs out at jails looking for clients. I'm not sure how great an attorney he is. Most good attorneys don't do that."

"I'll contact him and give him my number," said John. "I'll let him know that I'm expecting to hear from you. I can't guarantee that information from you will help your situation in here, but it might."

"I don't expect any change," said Billy. "I'll do this for Emily and those women. Nobody in here would fault me for giving information on a guy like that."

"So, you decided to clean up your act a bit?"

"It's not an act," said Billy. "I've had some time to think. Emily went for a good guy, and she deserves a good guy. If I had changed sooner, maybe she would still be with me. I was crazy about her, you know."

"I know," said John. "Cleaning yourself up can't hurt."

"I'm trying to learn self-control and listen more," explained Billy. "You were right. I can't keep flying off the handle whenever I get riled up. I'm trying to calm down and listen to people, instead of reacting. I read a book about that."

"That's good," said John. "I should listen to my own advice and do a better job myself."

"The book said that when you practice listening to other people and calming yourself down, it can also calm other people down," said Billy. "The book calls it de-escalation."

"I've read books about de-escalation, but I've had trouble practicing it," said John. "As a cop, we had classes on it."

"You should try it," said Billy.

"I should try harder," agreed John.

"I made another change," said Billy. "I'm trying to get people to call me by my middle name – Ian."

"Ian?" asked John. "What made you decide to do that?"

"Everybody knows Billy as somebody that isn't who I want to be anymore," explained Billy. "I want to make a clean break from all that. Would you mind calling me Ian?"

"Sure, if that's what you want," answered John. "From now on, it's Ian Crews."

"Thanks," said Ian. "I've gotten the guards call me Ian, but only a few of the guys in here do. Some of them refuse. I don't think it's such a hard thing to ask."

"Wow," said John. "What else have you been doing?"

"I started reading the Bible," answered Ian. "I had never read it, but a preacher visited me and gave me a copy. He also gave me a list of scriptures to read."

"I've met a number of guys in jail who started reading the Bible and began working that angle to impress a judge," said John. "They tell folks that they are a changed man, but it's an act. They hope it will sway a judge to give them lighter sentences or grant them parole. Sometimes, it works in their favor."

"It's no act," said Ian. "I'm serious; you'll see."

"I'll have to admit that some of them actually change," said John. "Ian Crews – Bible man! Regardless of what you are trying to do, you could be doing worse. Keep up the good work of calming yourself. Listening to other people isn't as easy as people say, but it's a good practice."

"This isn't a game," said Ian. "You'll see. I'm not expecting anyone to change my situation."

"While practicing your listening to people, don't forget to keep your ear to the ground about a guy who molests women," reminded John.

"Absolutely," said Ian.

"GOOD GRIEF," thought John, as he exited the facility. *"That was weird. Maybe he will seriously make a change – who knows? I had better tell Emily about his name change, in case someone named Ian tries to contact her. I wouldn't put it past him."*

Chapter 21

OPETRC

"I'M SO GLAD to have you and the kids here with me," John told his daughter.

"Now that David has passed away, there is absolutely nothing for me in California," replied Heather.

"Has it gotten any better?" John asked.

"David disrespected me by going after other women and he became less involved with our children, but it wasn't always like that," she answered. "Memories of better times sometime flood my mind. I believe we really loved each other during those early years. But I am quickly reminded that those times were short lived, and I often wonder how real they were. David may have been pretending. It's so sad."

"It seems that when someone passes away, it's normal to tune out the bad experiences and remember mainly the good ones," said John. "At least, that's been my experience."

"Experts in psychology have detected changes in a variety of brain regions during times of grief via neuroimaging," said Heather. "I know the facts, and I've both studied and counseled the stages of grief. However, experiencing it is a different matter. It was different when Mom passed, because she deteriorated over a longer period of time. I was somewhat prepared. David's death was so sudden."

"I'm sorry," said John. "I didn't like the guy, but I am so sorry that you and the kids are having to go through this."

"One minute I am sad over the fact that there is no longer a chance to reconcile and reestablish solid relationships for our children's sake, and the next minute I am angry over David's terrible choices," Heather explained. "His actions not only resulted in the end of our marriage and the destruction of our family, but the death a graduate student. If he had never been involved with her, the ex-boyfriend would have never tampered with that car. Now, his life is also ruined. David's selfishness has caused immeasurable pain and suffering, and I'm angry."

"You have a right to be angry," said John.

"It's just so senseless," complained Heather.

"I agree. Listen, I think the kids need a break. There is a new children's movie now showing in theaters. I'd like to take them to see it this afternoon."

"I'm sure they would enjoy that," replied Heather. "They've been through too much. The divorce, David's sudden death, and the crazy talk on the news about women being molested. Thank you, they need a distraction."

"You're welcome to come too," offered John.

"They need quality time with you," she said. "Plus, I could use a couple of hours of down time."

"OK, I'll…" John's sentence was interrupted by the familiar heavy-handed knock on his front door by Shawn. Opening the door, John found Shawn and Caitlin on the porch.

"It seems we may have the complete message now!" blurted Shawn, as he entered the home. "More letters and more explanation."

"Let's take this to the back porch," advised John. "There are two children upstairs, and they don't need this."

The four adults moved to the back porch in silence.

Once there, Caitlin provided more details.

"Another victim, but this time he added two letters instead of just one. He added the letters 'RC', so that the entire abbreviation is OPETRC. He carved OPETRC above her jelly button, and he added the words RAISE CHILDREN directly below the belly button. So now, the pervert's entire message appears to be 'ONLY PROFESSIONALLY EDUCATED TO RAISE CHILDREN."

"This guy is completely crazy," stated John. "In the US, we have some of the most educated parents on the planet. This isn't like children being raised in third world countries."

"You can say that again," agreed Shawn.

"I think we're missing what this man is attempting to communicate," added Heather. "I don't think his message would be to third world countries, because he probably doesn't believe that higher education is within the power of those people – they aren't offered the education. His problem is with parents here in the United States, where ample education is available. It's possible, that he believes this country is squandering the ability to devise a very different form of raising children."

"What do you mean?" asked Caitlin.

"I think we are still missing something," answered Heather. "I think this man blames the crime rate, the chaotic rise in mass murder, and troubles of our current society on parents who are currently raising children in the US. I think he wants to change our educational system."

"There may be something to that, but you don't fix it by mutilating women," said Shawn.

"I believe the mutilations are about gaining attention," said Heather. "He has attacked women of lesser education, and he has done it in a way that shocks the public."

"I think he would have more credibility if he wrote a book about his concerns," said Caitlin. "What he is doing is causing people to fear and hate him."

"I don't think this is the end of his message," said

Heather. "Now that he has our attention and has made a general statement, it's possible that he has more to say."

"So, you don't believe this victim to be his last," said John.

"Unfortunately, I do not," answered Heather. "I frankly don't think that he will stop until he is stopped. These women are his medium of communication, and I don't believe he will stop until he sees the changes that he desires."

"What changes?" asked Shawn. "He wants parents to be better educated? What the hell does that mean?"

"Shawn's right," said Caitlin. "Education can always be better. At what point would this guy be satisfied?"

"I think the guy enjoys inflicting pain on women," said Shawn. "He's disgusting. I want to strangle the life out of this sick bastard."

"Shawn has a point," said John. "He could have tied these women up and taped a manifesto to them. He didn't have to inflict such pain and fear in these poor women. Whatever his message may be, he didn't have to do this. This jerk thinks it's acceptable to hurt women as a means to send a message, and I think he likes it."

"All of that may be true," agreed Heather. "However, I think it will continue until he sees massive change or until he is stopped. It's very possible that he has grown to enjoy this. If so, it will continue until he is caught."

"I think this guy loves torturing women, and this message thing is simply an excuse." said Caitlin.

"The message is important to him," said Heather. "Rather than post the same message on each victim, he has methodically spelled more and more of it out over time. I don't think he is finished with providing more details of that message."

"Oh God!" blurted Shawn. "This could go on forever, if he isn't stopped. I had hoped that this was last victim."

"OK, continue to keep me in the loop," John told Shawn and Caitlin. "I need to cool off a minute before taking my grandkids to a movie.”

“That’s so sweet,” said Caitlin. “You’ve really grown into this granddad thing.”

“I am so grateful for the opportunity to spend time with them,” said John.

“OK, we’ll let you know if something else materializes,” said Shawn before leaving the back porch.

TWO DAYS LATER, John answered a phone call from Shawn.

“Heather was right,” said Shawn. “It was like this guy was listening to our conversation.”

“How so?” asked John.

“That manifesto you talked about was taped to this guy’s last victim,” explained Shawn.

“What did it say?” asked John.

“There’s too much,” said Shawn. “Caitlin and I will need to pay you another visit. You’ve got to see this.”

Within two hours, Caitlin and Shawn were again talking to John and Heather on John’s back porch. Caitlin took a seat on the outdoor couch and opened her laptop.

“Here we go,” said Caitlin. “Take a look at this.”

The four viewed a photo of the manifesto which had been taped to the stomach of a pregnant redhead. Bloodstains could clearly be seen on the note.

“I’m guessing he cut her up like the others,” said John. “Bloodstains are visible.”

“He did,” answered Shawn. “He doesn’t have to keep doing this. He has our attention. He enjoys doing this!”

“Did he murder this victim?” asked John.

“No, she’s alive but terribly shaken,” said Caitlin. “He cut her and left the note.”

“It looks like a typewritten note,” said Heather, attempting to focus attention on the manifesto.

It read:

"Children must be removed from the households of parents and be placed in institutions where only those professionally trained in raising children are allowed to guide them into adulthood. The destructive practice of allowing unlearned parents to teach and instill social ethics must be stopped. It is clearly obvious that the methods employed for the past thousands of years are not working. We now have the technical means to bring this change about and it must be implemented immediately."

"He's out of his freaking mind," said John. "This guy wants strangers to be in charge of raising kids. He wants people who don't love them as parents do to raise them. I think I've heard it all."

"This isn't the first time I've heard this," said Heather.

"What?" asked Shawn.

"Years ago, there was some talk about giving institutions more influence in guiding children," said Heather. "There was only a little talk about placing them full-time in institutions, but there has been a lot of talk about having public schools taking a stronger role in both educating and instilling ethical behavior in children. It's happening more already."

"Schools teaching ethics?" asked Shawn.

"The federal Department of Education has a division dedicated to ethics," said Heather. "The focus is on ethics for employees of the Department of Education. However, there is an effort by the department to teach ethical behavior supporting LGBTQ and transgender youth. Some parents like it, and some do not. Many of the parents of children in those categories like this idea. Other parents believe that public schools should focus only on areas of education, and object to time being taken from that to instill ethics. Some parents want to be solely responsible for teaching their children ethics because they disagree with the ethics being taught in the schools."

"The question is, whose children are they?" asked John. "Historically, it's been the responsibility of parents to teach things outside of academics to children. What's wrong with that? Why not have the schools teach reading, writing, history and math – and let the parent teach ethics?"

"What if parents are not teaching ethics to their children?" asked Caitlin.

"That question is the basis for the federal effort," said Heather.

"I don't have kids," said Shawn. "However, if I did, I don't think I would like to have a school undermining or overriding what I am teaching my kids about ethics."

"That's one of the reasons why private schools have grown so rapidly in this country," said Heather. "The other main reason is that many parents do not believe the public schools are adequately teaching academic subjects. National achievement test scores have dropped in some areas."

"Before school starts for Josh and Charlotte, maybe you should consider private school," suggested John. "I'd help pay for it. I understand that parents have more involvement with what is happening in the classrooms."

"I need to spend more time researching the public and private systems of education in the Atlanta area," said Heather.

"Let's not get sidetracked from this note," reminded Caitlin. "Let's focus on the task at hand. Heather, you were right about this guy having more to say. What happens now?"

"That's a good question," said Heather. "I'm not sure what his next move will be."

"Heather, do you know of books which advocate what this guy wants done?" asked John.

"I'm going to take a look at that," Heather answered.

"You're right, John," said Shawn. "We need to find out where this guy got his ideas. We need to get inside his head, and we need to find out whether there is a movement in support of his whacky ideas."

Chapter 22

Hollands

"I'VE FOUND SOMETHING," said Heather

"What did you find?" asked John.

"I found a book written in 1969 by George Hollands, who obtained PhDs in both Psychology and Philosophy, stating that the uneducated have no business raising children," said Heather.

"1969 was a long time ago," said John.

"In the description of the book, it says the author promoted the idea that the uneducated have no business raising children," said Heather. "It also advocates for the dissolution of the institution of marriage and promotes the idea of raising all children in institutions staffed with those professionally trained to raise children. Does this sound familiar?"

"Too familiar," answered John.

"In the bio of the author, it says that he was a university professor for more than fifty years," added Heather.

"Have you ever run across a nutjob professor spouting this kind of crap?" asked John.

"I'm familiar with wide varieties of points of views espoused by university professors," replied Heather. "You would be surprised."

"If this is what is being pumped into college kids, God

help us," said John. "You said that he carries PhDs in both Psychology and Philosophy?"

"Yes," answered Heather.

"What might be more concerning is the idea that some of these same people are counseling individuals who have mental and emotional issues," said John. "Do you think maybe the guy molesting women was counseled by someone like this?"

"Maybe, but it's also possible that he simply took a college class or read a book promoting these views," replied Heather.

"Maybe Shawn should interview this twisted professor," suggested John.

"That would be difficult because he passed away in 2021," explained Heather.

"Do you think the library has a copy of the book?" asked John. "Shawn wants to get into the head of this guy."

"I don't know, but I could buy a copy online," replied Heather. "I'm looking at a source offering it right now."

"That might be better," said John. "We wouldn't have to worry about returning the book. We could use it however we want and as long as we want."

After a few clicks on the keyboard of Heather's laptop, she announced. "Done. I've ordered a copy."

"I'm going to give Shawn a call," said John. "But first, I need to take care of business. Those two cups of coffee are screaming to get out of my body. I'm off to the bathroom."

Afterwards, he entered the room where Heather was still reading about the professor. He waved his cell phone to capture the attention of his daughter.

"Going out back to give Shawn a call," John told Heather as he reached for the back door.

Heather gave her father a thumbs up.

"What's up?" asked Shawn, answering John's call.

"Heather has found a book written in 1969 by a college professor advocating that only educated professionals be allowed to raise kids," said John.

"You're kidding," said Shawn.

"I'm not kidding," replied John. "Reading that book may help you get inside this guy's head."

"Exactly!" exclaimed Shawn.

"The author of the book had two PhDs," stated John.

"A college professor with two PhDs?" asked Shawn. "It's hard to believe that someone with that kind of education could be so stupid. You used the word 'had'. I take it that the professor is dead."

"Died in 2021, so there's no chance for an interview," said John. "It's a long shot, but it's possible our molester read this book or one like it. It's also possible that he took a class under this professor."

"Wow!" exclaimed Shawn.

"Heather ordered a copy of the book," said John.

"Good, how's Heather doing? asked Shawn, changing the subject.

"She's fine," answered John. "Would you like to come over for dinner Saturday night?"

"Maybe," answered Shawn. "I don't want to put more work on her. She's pretty busy with the kids and also looking for a job."

"Does lasagna sound good?" asked John.

"You know it!" exclaimed Shawn. "Heather makes great lasagna. Are you sure?"

"Yeah, come on over at 6:00," encouraged John.

"I'll be there," replied Shawn. "Back to the case, tell me more about this guy and his book."

John proceeded to give Shawn the title and details around the book and suggested that he contact bookstores to see if anyone had ordered or purchased the book within the last two years. Shawn said he would ask Caitlin to check with online sellers.

Heather stepped out onto the back porch and asked her father if he was still speaking with Shawn.

"I am," confirmed John.

"I'd like to speak with him," requested Heather.

"Sure," John replied, handing her his cell phone.

"It's possible that this criminal took a class taught by this professor, but it's also possible that he attended a lecture given by him," Heather explained to Shawn. "It might be tough to link this molester to the professor, but I'll send you the contact information for the university associated with him. You may want to check the class enrollments covering the last decade the class was taught."

"Thanks," Shawn told her. "I'll be looking for that contact info. I'm also looking forward to your lasagna Saturday night."

"What?" asked Heather, giving her father a glare.

"John invited me over for lasagna, Saturday night," said Shawn. "He knows that I really like your lasagna."

"That will be fun," said Heather, giving her father a middle finger before ending the call.

"When were you planning to tell me that you invited Shawn over for Saturday evening, and that he expects me to cook lasagna?" Heather asked her father.

"Even you just said that it sounds fun," replied John, wearing a grin. "I just thought you could use a little fun."

Daddy!" Heather blurted, while punching her father's shoulder with her slight right fist.

"Do you want me to call it off?' asked John, still grinning.

"No."

"I thought you liked having Shawn over," said John, still smiling.

"Daddy."

"I think I see a smile coming," teased John.

Heather punched her father's shoulder again. As she turned to walk back inside, she stopped. Turning back to her father she said, "I don't know what I'm going to do with you."

"You'll have fun," said John.
"I know," replied Heather, now smiling.

Chapter 23

Shawn

HIS GRANDKIDS Josh and Charlotte wiggling on his lap, John opened a children's fantasy book. It had taken a couple of minutes for them to stop fighting for positions that satisfied them both and was comfortable for John. Heather had decided to slightly limit the time her children spent playing video games. John eagerly volunteered to occupy more of their time on Saturdays by reading to them.

"Does the book have a wizard?" asked Josh.

"We'll have to see," teased John.

"What about a princess?" asked Charlotte.

"Same answer," replied John. "We'll have to see."

"Wizards are scary," said Charlotte. "They put people under spells and turn children into frogs."

"No, they're not!" argued Josh. "A princess is dumb. All she does is sit around looking pretty and waiting to be kissed by a prince. Yuk! Princesses are boring."

"You're boring," Charlotte said to her brother.

"Do you two want me to read or not?" asked John.

"Read," answered Charlotte.

"OK, read," said Josh.

Josh mumbled a couple of sentences under his breath about princesses. Charlotte nudged her brother and gave him a condescending look. Once John began reading, he felt the bodies of both children relax. Charlotte placed her head on his shoulder. After thirty minutes, John closed the book.

"You just got to the good part," protested Josh.

"Both my legs are going numb," explained John.

"Can we read more later, after your legs are better?" asked Charlotte.

"We'll see," answered John. "I don't want to hear any more arguing."

"We won't argue," said Charlotte.

"And you, Josh?" asked John.

"No arguing," promised Josh.

"Ok, up you go," instructed John. "I need blood flow in my legs."

"Can I see your desk again?" asked Charlotte.

"Maybe later," answered John.

"What desk?" asked Josh.

"Grandpa has a roll top desk in his bedroom," said Charlotte. "It's beautiful."

"Good grief!" blurted Josh. "Who cares about an old desk. You're weird."

"Enough, you two," said John. "Time for you to go upstairs."

After the children ran up the stairs, John placed the book on the coffee table. Standing, he rubbed his legs.

"I have a cup of coffee for you," offered Heather.

"Thanks so much," John replied, taking the cup. "You know me pretty well."

"The kids love having you read to them," Heather said. "Their reading has improved since you began reading stories to them which are understandable but above their reading levels."

"Finding a book that interests them both is the kicker," said John. "I think I found one this time."

"Thank you," said Heather.

"I invited Shawn over for dinner tonight."

"Again!" blurted Heather. "I haven't even planned anything."

"I told him that you would make lasagna," said John.

"Daddy!" blurted Heather. "Don't do that to me, again. I haven't even purchased the ingredients for lasagna."

"You know that's his favorite," said John, with a wink.

"Stop doing this to me," complained Heather.

"So, you don't want him to come over?" asked John.

"I didn't say that."

"I can call him and tell him that we've called it off," suggested John.

"No, I just need more heads up – that's all."

"I didn't invite Caitlin, just Shawn," said John. "Do you want me to invite her also?"

"No, having only Shawn over is fine."

"Are you sure that you don't want Caitlin, too?" asked John.

"I said that's fine just having Shawn."

"You read me and my desire for coffee pretty well, but I can read you too," said John.

"What do you mean?" asked Heather.

"You can't stop looking at Shawn when we get together to discuss the case," said John. "I know that look."

"Stop it."

"You don't look at Caitlin the same way," said John.

"Good grief! Give me a break."

"Are you trying to tell me that you don't like looking at Shawn?" asked John, giving his daughter another wink.

"Cut it out!"

"You know, Shawn asks about you just about every time we have a phone call," said John.

"What does he ask?" questioned Heather.

"He wants to know how you are doing," answered John. "He cares about you."

"You and Shawn were partners for years," said Heather. "Partners always care about family members."

"No, he cares about you," repeated John.

"I care about him too," said Heather. "I've cared about the safety of all your partners over the years."

"Now, it's my turn to tell you to cut it out," said John.

"What?"

"You've never looked at other cops the way you look at Shawn," said John.

"Well, he is easy on the eyes," admitted Heather, sporting a smile.

"If you say so," said John. "Personally, I think all those muscles are kind of ugly – don't you think?"

"What muscles?" asked Heather. "Now, that he made detective, he's in plain clothes and wears a coat. I wouldn't know if he had muscles or not."

"I doubt he will be wearing a coat when he comes over for dinner tonight," said John.

"Dinner!" exclaimed Heather. "I've got to go shopping for dinner."

"Here are the keys," offered John, tossing Heather his car keys. "Maybe buy a bottle of wine, while you're at it."

SHAWN PROMPTLY ARRIVED at 6:00PM carrying a bottle of wine. John had been correct in his assessment of Shawn's clothing. He was wearing a tight golf shirt and jeans.

"Heather's is finishing up," said John, ushering Shawn into the dining area of his home.

"Shawn, go ahead and take a seat," offered Heather, taking the bottle from Shawn's huge hand. "I like Rose. Thank you so much."

Heathers slight fingers purposely brushed against Shawn hand as she took the bottle from him. Holding the bottle, her eyes quickly scanned his powerful hands and body.

"I couldn't come empty handed," said Shawn.

"Oh, my God!" thought Heather, noticing Shawn's well-defined muscles bulging under the tight golf shirt. *"He has the body of a Greek god, and I can think of several things I would like for him to do with those hands!"*

"Thanks so much for inviting me over," said Shawn.

"I enjoy having you…over," replied Heather, stumbling to get the words out.

"Are you hungry?" asked John.

"Absolutely," answered Shawn, watching the movement of Heather's body under her slacks as she turned to go back into the kitchen.

Turning his attention back to the table, he nervously fumbled with his fork and knife. Placing them back onto the table, he attempted to refocus his attention on John.

"So, John, when do you think the book Heather ordered will arrive?"

"Not sure," answered John. "You would need to take that up with Heather."

"I heard my name," said Heather, returning to the dining area with a platter of hot buttered rolls.

"When do you think the book by that professor will arrive?" asked Shawn.

"Tracking says that it should arrive Wednesday," answered Heather.

Shawn intently watched her, as Heather walked to the bottom of the stairs to call her children to the table. He quickly turned back toward the food on the table as she turned to make her way back.

"Man, this looks good!" exclaimed Shawn.

"I hope you enjoy," Heather said, as her children scurried down the stairs and ran to their places at the table.

"So, Josh, how is school?" asked Shawn.

"It's a new school, and I don't know anybody," Josh answered. "I've never gone to a private school before."

"Most of the kids are nice," added Charlotte.

"You don't say," Shawn said. "That's good."

"I don't like Tiara," said Josh. "She kicks me at recess."

"I remember having a girl kick me in school," said Shawn. "She didn't wear tennis shoes. Hers had hard soles, and she left bruises on my shins."

"She probably liked you," said Heather.

"I don't kick boys that I like," said Charotte.

"Do you like a boy at school?" asked Shawn.

Charlotte nervously smiled, but didn't answer his question. Throughout the meal, Heather's children engaged in conversation with Shawn. He laughed at their jokes, and they laughed at his. By the end of dinner, Heather felt more drawn to Shawn than ever before. As he left John's house that evening, she stepped out onto the front porch with him.

"Josh and Charlotte seem to really like you,' said Heather.

"I get along with kids pretty well," said Shawn. "You have great kids. You're really a great mom."

"Not all the time," said Heather. "I don't think I've ever seen them take to an adult like they did tonight."

"I think I'm probably on the same mental level as your kids," said Shawn.

"No, you're not."

"I grew up with six brothers and two sisters," explained Shawn. "I was the oldest, so I was around kids a lot."

"Your mother had nine kids?" asked Heather.

"Yep, and we were a handful," said Shawn. "My father left us right after the youngest was born, so everything was on my mother. She had to be tough, but not a one of us doubted her love for us."

"I didn't know that," said Heather. "I'm sorry. My brother and I had it good with my dad and mom, I guess. They really loved each other."

"You were lucky," said Shawn. "I helped raise my brothers and sisters."

"You're something else, Shawn Stone," said Heather.

"You're something else, Heather Littleton," Shawn

replied.

"You just like my lasagna," said Heather.

"I do, but I actually like everything about you," said Shawn.

"You don't know everything about me."

"I like everything that I see."

"So, what do you see? I loser who couldn't keep her husband? A mom of two kids, who lives with her father? I would say that you're looking at a loser."

"I see a beautiful woman who is far more brilliant than I could ever hope to be," said Shawn.

"I don't even have a job," said Heather.

"I don't care," said Shawn. "I don't think the timing is right. You've been through a lot. Take it easy on yourself."

"Why are you so nice to me?" asked Heather.

"Maybe I like you," Shawn answered.

"I like you too," said Heather.

"Does that mean that you plan to kick me during recess?" asked Shawn.

"No," answered Heather. "I would kiss you, except for the fact that without heels I am too short to reach your lips."

"I can take care of that," said Shawn, bending down to kiss Heather.

She wrapped her arms around his neck. He reached his powerful arms under her hips and lifted her off the porch. Their embrace became heavier, and Shawn returned her feet to the porch.

"What's the matter?" asked Heather.

"I'm afraid of myself," explained Shawn.

"What's to be afraid of?"

"I can't begin to tell you what you do to me," said Shawn.

"Tell me."

"I want to start taking your clothes off, and that can't happen on John's front porch," said Shawn.

"What would the neighbors say?"

"I'm more concerned with what your father would say," said Shawn.

"It was my father who invited you over," said Heather.

"So, you didn't want me to come over?"

"I didn't say that."

"So, would you like to come over to my place sometime?" asked Shawn.

"Maybe."

"Maybe?" asked Shawn. "So, what's the problem?"

"I don't have a car," explained Heather. "I sold mine before moving to Atlanta."

"That's why you don't have a job!" blurted Shawn. "Why would they hire someone who can't get to work?"

"I can take MARTA," answered Heather.

"You don't want to have to rely on the subway and buses," said Shawn. "Besides, bad things sometimes happen on those buses."

"So, what do you advise?"

"I would advise you to buy a car, but you don't have a job," answered Shawn. "I'm not sure they would give you a loan."

"I should have money soon from selling the home in California," answered Heather. "I won't need a loan."

"How about if I take you car shopping when you get the money?" offered Shawn.

"That's awfully nice," she replied. "Are you sure?"

"Absolutely," answered Shawn. "Afterwards, maybe I could take you to diner."

"Are you asking me out on a date?" asked Heather.

"I am."

"OK, under one condition," said Heather.

"What's the condition?" asked Shawn. "I should have known there would be strings attached."

"On the condition that you take me to see your apartment after dinner," said Heather.

"I can make that happen," said Shawn.

"Good," said Heather. "Are you going to kiss me again or talk all night?"

Chapter 24

Auto

"NO LUCK finding a car?" John asked his daughter.

"I just can't decide," said Heather. "I've conducted some research regarding safety and reliability, and I've narrowed it down to four. I just haven't found what I want in my price range."

"You received a letter in the mail from David's attorney," John said, handing her the letter.

"There's no telling," Heather said, opening it. "He has the power of attorney to close on my house, he is handling David's investments, and I had him draw up a new will for me."

"That's my girl," said John. "Safety and reliability are important aspects if you are driving my grandkids around. You have a PhD, but you also have a lot of practical common sense."

"Well, this may help expand my price range for a car a bit," she said, smiling. "The house in California sold for $1,240,000, and the profit after closing costs comes to $420,500. It has been deposited digitally into my savings account. So has another $156,400 from David's investments. It comes to a total of $576,900."

"Good Lord!" exclaimed John. "I didn't even know that you heard from the realtor."

"She called to tell me that she had a buyer, and she told me what it sold for last week," said Heather. "When I was growing up you told me not to count my chickens until they hatched. Looks like they've hatched."

"Wow!" John exclaimed. "My little girl is loaded!"

"Daddy, at some point I plan to buy a house here," said Heather. "That money needs to be reinvested in a home, as to avoid being heavily taxed on the profit."

"Have you checked your account to see if it's there?" asked John.

"That's just what I'm about to do," said Heather, opening her laptop.

"You're right about buying a house for you and the kids, but I will really miss having you here with me," said John. "You and the kids need to have a life for yourselves."

"Daddy, it's not like I would be moving to California," said Heather. "I don't intend to live very far from you."

"You probably shouldn't buy in this neighborhood," said John. "With that kind of money, you could live in a really nice neighborhood."

"I'm not in a hurry," said Heather. "Is it OK for us to stay here for a while longer while I look for a home?"

"Are you kidding?" replied John. "I wish you would live here forever, but you need to move on with your life at some point."

"Looks like it's all there," said Heather, closing the laptop.

THE FOLLOWING SATURDAY, Shawn picked up Heather again to shop for a car. She couldn't contain her smile, as she dropped into the passenger seat of his car.

"What's going on with you?" asked Shawn. "What's with that sly smile?"

"I told you that my house in California sold," replied Heather.

"Congratulations, again," said Shawn. "I bet that's a load off your mind."

"It is," she replied. "It also means that I have a little more when it comes to buying a car."

"Well, OK! What kind of price range are we looking at?"

"The lawyer in California moved the profit from the house sale and other funds into my savings account," answered Heather. "I moved $50,000 into my checking account."

"What?" burst Shawn. "You have $50K cash for a car?"

"No, I want to keep the price down to around $40,000," she answered. "I don't want to spend it all on the car."

"That's smart," said Shawn. "Your father told me that you have a good head on your shoulders – and a pretty one, at that."

"I don't want to do something stupid," Heather said. "There has been so much going on - the divorce, and David dying."

"So, where to?" asked Shawn.

"I want to go back to the Kia place," answered Heather. You've made up your mind?" Shawn asked.

"I have."

"You've settled on a South Korean car?"

"I was looking at a smaller SUV – a Toyota, but I think I want to go ahead and buy a Telluride," she said.

"It's probably a nice ride," said Shawn. "I would think a larger SUV would be safer for the kids."

"My thoughts exactly," said Heather.

"I usually try to buy American, but it's your money and your decision," said Shawn.

"The research that I've done shows it to be very reliable and safe," said Heather. "Plus, these are manufactured in Georgia. I'm supporting Georgia jobs."

"You're something else," said Shawn.

"I hope you mean something good," said Heather.

"You're the best," said Shawn. "You are one in a million. I don't know what you see in me. You have a PhD, and a great career ahead of you. I'm a cop."

"What's wrong with someone on the force?" asked Heather. "My father was a cop, remember. I'm over the moon about my father."

"If you find a smart guy that treats you really well when you find that job teaching at a university, I wouldn't blame you," said Shawn.

"You're trying to get rid of me?"

"No way! I'm just saying…"

"Pull the car over!" interrupted Heather.

"What?

"Pull the car over!" she shouted. "Are you deaf?"

"No, I hear you," said Shawn, pulling into a parking lot.

Heather unbuckled her seat belt.

"You're getting out?" asked Shawn.

Heather quickly launched herself onto Shawn's lap, straddling him. He raised his hands his hands from the steering wheel, as an act of surrender.

"You can be an idiot," Heather said, moving again to engage in a long passionate kiss.

Shawn lowered his hands and took hold of her hips, pulling her close. She left his lips and began caressing his neck. Shawn began breathing heavily. Heather stopped and locked her eyes on his.

"Does this look like I am jumping out of the car?" she asked.

"Well, no," answered Shawn.

"You listen to me, you lunk," Heather began. "I married an academic, and it didn't work out at all. I may have a PhD, but I come from a cop family – are you listening?"

"I'm listening," Shawn whispered.

"Do you want me or not?" she asked.

"There's no question about that," answered Shawn. "You have no idea what you do to me. Want you is an understatement."

"Then act like it and stop with that dribble about me hooking up with a professor," she said. "Done that, and I'm not going back to it. Do you hear me?"

"Loud and clear," said Shawn.

"If you want me, act like it," she ordered.

"Yes, Ma'am," replied Shawn.

Heather planted another long and passionate kiss on Shawn. After a couple of minutes, she quickly left his lap and buckled her seat belt.

"I'm ready to shop for a car," she announced. "Are you ready?"

"Girl, you have my head spinning," said Shawn. "You're a fireball, you know that?"

"Is that good or bad?" Heather asked.

"Oh, good," answered Shawn.

"Are we going or not?" she asked.

"We're going," said Shawn, dropping his car into gear.

"Hey, I want your opinion on the Telluride," said Heather. "I can do research, but I don't know much when it comes to looking under the hood."

"You've got it," said Shawn. "I'll do my best."

"Thank you."

"What did you earlier call me?" asked Shawn. "A lunk?"

"That's right."

"What's a lunk?"

"It's short for lunkhead," answered Heather, smiling.

"It's probably fitting," Shawn said.

"I was kidding when I called you a lunk, but you didn't seem to get it," said Heather.

"Get what?"

"Get that I like you a lot," answered Heather.

"I like you a whole lot," said Shawn.

"Good," said Heather. "I'm glad we have that settled."

"Like I said, you're something special," said Shawn.

LATER THAT AFTERNOON, Heather pulled into her father's driveway in her Kia Telluride. Shawn left his car on the street. She and Shawn moved up the steps and stood at the front door for a moment before going inside.

"I want to tell him about the SUV," said Heather.

"Absolutely," said Shawn. "This is your show."

Opening the front door, she called out, "I've got a new car! Who wants to go for a ride?

"I do!" shouted Josh.

"What kind is it?" asked Charlotte.

"Come and see," answered Heather.

The kids raced out the front door and began squealing loudly. John turned off the TV.

"Are you coming, Daddy?" asked Heather.

"Coming," he replied. "Are you sure that you have enough room for all of us?"

"It seats eight," answered Heather, proudly.

"You don't have eight butts to seat in that vehicle," replied John.

"True, but it has plenty of room for the butts in my family and more," she said.

They all gathered around the vehicle, exchanging comments. Shawn leaned against his car.

"Are you getting in?" Heather asked Shawn.

"Sure," he answered, opening a back door and squeezing himself into a third-row seat.

"You don't have to sit way back there," said Heather.

"The old man gets shotgun," replied Shawn, turning his long legs to the side as he dropped into the seat. "I've got plenty of room."

On the second row, the kids found a car seat for Josh and a booster seat for Charlotte. They scrambled into their seats and buckled up. John was at the front of the SUV, still looking it over.

"Are you coming, Daddy?" asked Heather.
"I wouldn't miss it," he answered.

Chapter 25

Call

ZACK SAT CURLED at John's feet, as his master sipped on a cup of coffee on his back porch. Fall's cool morning air graced John's face. The sun was just beginning to lighten the sky with a red hue which cast a warm glow on the neatly manicured back yard. The trimmed azaleas were no longer blooming, but the grass was neatly cut and the bed below the bird bath was weed free.

"I never imagined my life could be so good after losing Sharon," John thought. *"Though it would be heaven to have her still with me sharing Heather and the grandkids."*

Within an hour, the peaceful setting was interrupted by kids scurrying around preparing for the school day. Heather was calling them to the kitchen table for breakfast. John came back inside for a fresh cup.

"Good morning," chirped Heather.

"You're in a pleasant mood," observed John.

"That's unusual?" asked Heather.

"Does it have anything with that date you had with Shawn last night?" asked John. "I noticed it was about 3:00AM when you came home."

"I'm sorry to have woken you up," said Heather.

"You never came in that late when you were in high school," said John.

"I'm a big girl now," replied Heather. "I hope you don't plan to ground me."

"I'm afraid it's a little late for that," replied John.

"Things are nice," said Heather while giving her father a tight hug. "I need to take the kids to school."

Heather coached her children through the morning ritual of brushing their teeth and hair before rushing them out to the Telluride. When she returned to her father's house after taking them to school, she found him seated at the kitchen table with another cup of coffee.

"How many cups does that make?" teased Heather.

"It's coffee, not bourbon," replied John. "It's one of my joys of retirement."

"I have to get dressed in an hour," stated Heather.

"You are dressed," said John.

"I have an interview with Georgia State University at 10:00AM," she explained. "I don't plan to go in sweats."

"Great!"

"I think I have a really good shot at teaching two psychology classes," Heather said. "This is actually the second interview. I didn't tell you about the first because I didn't want you to get your hopes up."

"Of course you have a shot at it," said John.

The conversation was interrupted by a call from the correctional facility. Glancing at the number, John announced, "I need to take this."

"Ian, good to hear from you," John said as he stepped out onto the back porch.

"First of all, my lawyer is here with me," began Ian, as he spoke to John on the phone. "I don't have much, but this older guy was talking about someone he knew who talked about how kids should be raised in institutions."

"Keep talking," encouraged John.

"This old man was a pimp when he was younger, and he told us about a kid years ago who belongs to one of his prostitutes," explained Ian. "Before this kid's prostitute mom died from an overdose, this teenager went crazy and threatened the other prostitutes who refused to have an abortion. He advocated abortion for all uneducated pregnant women and said that all children should be placed in institutions until they reached the age of eighteen. Does this sound like this molester?"

"Sounds like similar talk," answered John. "Go on."

"He said the kid raved about what this pimp called "a stupid book he was reading," said Ian. "He estimated this kid would probably be about twenty-five now – that is, if he is still alive."

"That's interesting," said John.

"He said that the kid's name was Danny Barker," added Ian.

"Danny Barker?" asked John. "Are you sure about that name?"

"That's what he said."

"Ian, I really appreciate the call," said John. "If anything comes out of this, I will see if there is anything that I can do for you."

"Thanks," replied Ian. "And thanks for calling me Ian instead of Billy."

"Billy Crews isn't around anymore, is he?" asked John.

"No, only Ian Crews," answered Ian.

"OK, Ian, stay on that good path," advised John. "Talk to you later."

After hanging up, John called his ex-partner Shawn.

"Shawn, it's possible that we may have a name."

"Really?" asked Shawn.

"See if there is anything on a Danny Barker, about age twenty-five," said John. "If you find anything, you may need to get a court order to open juvenile records on this guy to get more information."

"Where did you get this name?" asked Shawn.

"Not every guy that I put away is looking for payback," said John. "There are a few who are looking for a reduced sentence."

"So, what's the connection to this guy Barker?" asked Shawn.

"Several years ago, word is that he was advocating for uneducated pregnant women to have abortions and that all children be raised in institutions by professionals," answered John.

"Wow!" said Shawn. "How do you do this?"

"Do what?" asked John.

"Run into these clues," answered Shawn. "You're retired and you're finding messages on sleazy restroom walls and obtaining names from guys you busted. How do you do this?"

"I told you back in the day, I was born to be a cop," answered John. "I guess it's just who I am. I hope this pans out, but it may be nothing. Let me know what you find."

"Daniel Baker is a common name, but I will run this down," said Shawn.

"It may prove to be nothing," said John.

THE FOLLOWING EVENING, John and Heather heard the pounding of Shawn's heavy hand on his front door. Opening the front door, there was excitement in Shawn's eyes as he and Caitlin entered.

"Caitlin and I found six guys in the Atlanta area named Daniel Barker in their mid-twenties," Shawn said.

"Come into the kitchen," said John.

"We ran down all six yesterday, and one of them was this skinny guy who worked in a bookstore," explained Shawn, as he placed a notebook on the kitchen table.

"That guy is a possibility," said John.

"We went back to the bookstore today for a follow-up interview, and the owner told us that the guy didn't show up for work," said Shawn.

"Bingo!" exclaimed John. "You may have spooked

him."

"It gets better," explained Caitlin. "The owner has photos of all his employees, and he allowed us to have a copy of this guy's photo.

"Does this look like the guy you saw at Emily's window?" asked Shawn, as he opened the notebook to reveal the photo of the missing bookstore employee.

"It could be him, but I didn't get a good look at his face," answered John.

"The owner gave us his address and we paid him a visit today," Shawn said. "The guy wasn't at home. We have two cops watching the place tonight, and tomorrow we should have a warrant to go inside."

"Great work!" said John.

"I have to say the same for you," added Caitlin.

"My father's the best," said Heather.

Chapter 26

Note-2

"I DON"T LIKE oatmeal," complained Josh, sitting at the kitchen table.

"So, what do you want for breakfast, cold cereal?" asked Heather.

"Grandpa made us pancakes Saturday," said Josh.

"We don't have time for pancakes this morning," explained Heather. "We have ten minutes before we need to leave for school."

"Where is my necklace?" Charlotte called out from upstairs.

"When did you last wear it?" Heather shouted up the stairs.

"I don't remember," whined Charlotte.

"*What a morning!*" thought Heather as she finally rushed her kids out the door of John's house. "*All I need is crazy traffic to top this off. We're going to be late.*"

She stopped in her tracks, as she approached her Telluride. There under the driver side wiper was a note.

"Oh God!" she whispered in fear.

"Go back inside!" she ordered her children.

"You said that we are late for school," complained Charlotte.

"Just go back inside for a few minutes," Heather

ordered again.

"Make up your mind," complained Josh.

"Just do it!" barked Heather.

As the children stomped back to John's front porch in frustration, Heather reached for the note. She glanced up and down the street, fearful of spotting the person who had placed it under the wiper. Seeing no one, she carefully opened the note. It was more verbose than the previous note.

YOU THINK YOU'LL BE SAFE IN YOUR NEW
SUV?
BUT SEPARATED FROM JOHN YOU'LL ONLY
BE.
NICE UNIFORMS IN PRIVATE SCHOOL THEY
WEAR,
BUT I'M WATCHING YOUR CHIDREN OF
WHOM YOU CARE.
THINK YOU'RE PROTECTED BY YOUR
BOYFRIEND COP?
THERE WILL BE A TIME WHEN HIS BIG BODY
WILL DROP.
YOUR FATHER AND SHAWN WILL BE GONE
ONE DAY,'
AND ATTENTION TO ME YOU'LL HAVE TO
PAY.
I'M WATCHING.

Heather ran to the porch where her children were standing. "Get inside!" she shouted.

"What's going on, Mom?" asked Charlotte, as her mother pushed them inside John house. Heather locked the front door behind them.

"Up to your rooms for a few minutes," she said. "Please, just for a few minutes."

As the kids moved the stairs, Heather hurried to her father who was sipping coffee on the back porch. She burst out the back door and showed him the note.

"Another note!" she cried out.

John quickly set the cup on the outdoor coffee table and scanned the note.

"I'm driving you and the kids to school this morning," he said.

"Take the Telluride," said Heather, her voice shaking. "It has the car seats."

"Wait here for a moment," said John.

John quickly went inside his house and returned with a plastic bag.

"Put the note in this bag," instructed John.

Heather did so.

"Now, grab the kids and I'll meet you at your SUV," said John, taking the keys from her hand.

Standing beside the SUV, he placed a call to Shawn. John read him the words on the note.

"We've stirred this guy up," said Shawn.

"That's my thinking," said John. "But why my daughter? She's not pregnant, and I wasn't the one checking him out at his workplace."

"I don't know," replied Shawn. "I doubt he knows where Caitlin or I live, but he does know where you live. You spotted him from your backyard, and you called him down."

"This guy is a real weirdo," said John.

"You said it," agreed Shawn. "If he ever approaches Heather....I don't know...I'll kill him! We have to get this pervert!"

"I think you're flushing him out," said John. "He's going to make a mistake. Try to calm down. I'll be here for Heather and the kids. You focus on your end."

"We're about to search Danny Barker's apartment," said Shawn. "I'll keep you informed."

"Good!" replied John. "I've got Heather and the kids; you just focus on that apartment."

THAT EVENING, SHAWN and Caitlin visited with John and Heather to report on the search of Danny Barker's apartment. As Shawn spoke, Heather's eyes watered and her hands shook.

"This guy is certainly a neat-freak," said Shawn. "It's almost like he didn't live there. Everything was spotless, even the bathroom."

"What about his clothes?" asked John.

"This guy has cleared out," said Shawn. "The clothes are gone. We think he even took the dirty clothes hamper."

"Wow!" said Heather, still shaking.

"There is almost no furniture," said Shawn. "No pots and pans in the kitchen. Nobody could move everything out that fast. We figure he only keeps the basic necessities in an apartment, and eats carry out all the time. He lives in a manner that allows him to quickly cut and run."

"So, he expects to be caught by the police," said John. "He's nuts, but not stupid."

"What about the note?" asked Heather.

"It's certain that you and your kids are being watched," said Caitlin. "Do you own a firearm?"

"No," answered Heather. "As a daughter of a cop, I've been around them all my life. My father took me to a range frequently when growing up and taught me to shoot. Each time, he taught me to clean the weapon when we returned home. That said, I'm afraid to own a weapon now. I have kids, and I could never forgive myself if they were ever to take hold of a gun and hurt themselves or someone else."

"I see," said Caitlin. "I don't have kids. Maybe I would feel the same way, if I did."

"At least carry pepper spray," suggested Shawn. "It would be difficult to protect Josh and Charlotte without some help."

"Maybe you're right," agreed Heather. "The worst the

kids might do is to burn their eyes a little with that stuff. It's not deadly."

Chapter 27

Gun

"I DISAGREE," insisted John "I think a handgun would offer more protection than pepper spray. You were saying that you're afraid of firearms, and you should be. Too many people fail to have a healthy respect for the capability of a deadly weapon. I know you. I taught you. You're as careful as it comes."

"I think the pepper spray can be as effective as needed," argued Heather.

"Have you ever even used pepper spray or mace?" asked John. "That stuff is just as likely to blow back on you in the wind and mess you over."

"I'm just not ready for a gun," Heather defiantly said.

The next day, Heather went to a shop that advertised pepper spray. She watched women coming out of the shop carrying their purses with short straps coming off their shoulder.

"I would bet that each one has pepper spray in those purses," she thought.

"I'm looking for pepper spray," she told the clerk

"Our best seller is the size of a magic marker," he explained.

"A magic marker?" asked Heather. "What about kids mistaking it for a magic marker and accidentally spraying themselves?"

"Well, like any sort of weapon, you have to keep it away from children," said the clerk. "The difference is that this isn't lethal. It sprays a stream up to sixteen feet and it contains a dye.

Once hit in the face, the assailant's face will be dyed orange – making it easy for law enforcement to identify him."

"That's interesting," commented Heather.

"It has ten shots," said the clerk. "In case you miss the first time, you have plenty more chances of hitting him."

"OK, I'll take two," Heather said.

"You won't be sorry," replied the clerk.

Upon returning to her father's house, Heather immediately went to the back porch.

"Daddy asked if I had ever used pepper spray," Heather thought, while standing at the top of the steps and pointing one of the pepper spray devices directly downward toward the yard. *"Let's see what this thing does."*

Heather fired the spray and immediately began coughing. Within seconds, her eyes began to burn, and she retreated back into her father's house.

"Good grief!" she called out between coughs. "I made sure that thing … *cough, cough* … was pointed down and away. How … *cough, cough* … did that blow back onto me?"

She ran to the bathroom and began washing her eyes. Still coughing, she dried her face with paper towels from the kitchen.

"What's all the commotion about?" asked John, entering the kitchen.

"You were right," Heather mumbled between coughs. "It blew back on me…I bought pepper spray…aimed it downward toward the backyard…this is awful."

"You washed your face, didn't you?" asked John.

"Yes."

"Well, it should pass within about half an hour," said John, soaking a clean wash rag under water. "Here, wipe your eyes."

"How did you know?" she asked.

"Years ago, I bought some of that stuff for your mother," explained John. "She was against having a gun. She did the same thing. When she tried it, it immediately blew back on her. You aren't alone."

"Good grief!"

"Now, what do you think about having a firearm?" asked John.

"Is that what my mother did?" asked Heather.

"No, your mother could be as stubborn as they come," answered John. "The difference being that no one was leaving threatening notes on windshields."

"I guess you made your point," agreed Heather. "Maybe I should shop for a gun – maybe one of those small ones. I just don't know."

"Come with me," instructed her father.

John escorted his daughter into his bedroom. Standing before his nightstand, he pointed to the small electronic gun safe.

"Watch," John said, reaching out for the safe. "It's programmed for my fingerprint only."

The safe opened to reveal a small nine-millimeter handgun. John took it out.

"Is this small enough?" he asked.

"Daddy, that's yours," Heather said, objecting.

"Now, it's yours," said John. "I have another one."

"I'm not surprised. How many do you have?"

"They are all secure," said John, pointing to his closet.

Heather proceeded to walk over to the closet and open it. In the back of the closet was a large upright gun safe."

"That one has a combination lock, and only I know it," John said. "Your kids could never open that if they wanted to. I doubt they even know that it exists."

"I should have known," said Heather.

"I have a handgun in the locked gun case on my nightstand," offered John, opening the gun case and taking it out. "Take this nine-millimeter and feel the weight. It's small and light. You should have no trouble using it."

"It IS light," she said, taking the gun.

"Good, it's yours," said John. "So is this small electronic safe."

"You should put the gun back in your gun safe until I can buy one for myself," said Heather. "You should keep them both."

"No need," explained John. "I'll simply reprogram this one for your fingerprint. Hear, I am unplugging it, and we'll take this to your bedroom to reprogram it. This shouldn't take long. I have another gun in a safe in the top of my closet."

"Thank you, Daddy," said Heather.

"As long as I am alive, I will do everything in my power to protect you and the kids," John promised. "You should take the gun to a range and brush up."

"I will," said Heather. "I know a guy who might want to take me."

Later that afternoon, Heather gave Shawn a call.

"I need a favor," she began.

"Anything," Shawn replied.

"You don't even know what I'm going to ask," she said. "You'd better be careful."

"OK, what do you need?" asked Shawn.

"I have a nine-millimeter, and I need to practice," said Heather. "I bet you have access to a range."

"You would be right," said Shawn. "I can't bring you to the police range, but I have access to a private range."

"Perfect, when can we go?"

"How about Saturday morning?" Shawn asked.

"Are you asking me out on another date?" asked Heather.

"No," Shawn stated emphatically.

"No?"

"No, you were the one asking me out on this date – if I remember correctly," he said.

"I guess you're right," said Heather. "I seem to be taking advantage of you."

"Baby, you can take advantage of me anytime you want," said Shawn.

THE FOLLOWING SATURDAY morning, Shawn picked Heather up at 9:00. As they drove away, Heather nervously mentioned that she felt she should tell him something.

"What's on your mind?" Shawn asked.

"I told you that my house in California sold," she began.

"Yeah, you bought the Telluride with that money," said Shawn.

"Well, I made a little bit more than that on it," she said.

"Great!" exclaimed Shawn. "You deserve it."

"To be honest, I made a lot more than that on it," she said.

"Good, your money is not really my business," Shawn said. "You're worth way more than what you made off that house."

"I also have David's investments," Heather explained.

"Good."

"At some point, I want to buy a house in the Atlanta area," said Heather.

"You should," agreed Shawn. "Houses here aren't as expensive as those in California, and you might be able to make a good downpayment. That could possibly save you from paying PMI. That would be really good."

"No, you don't understand," said Heather. "I have enough between the profit from the house sale and David's investments to BUY a house."

"Buy a house?" asked Shawn. "You mean, like buy a

house – just buy the thing?”

“Yes,” she replied. “I used $40,000 for the Telluride, but I still have a little over $580,000.”

“What?” Shawn blurted. “You have more than half a million in cash?”

“I do,” she replied. “And I need to invest it back into a house for me and kids within a year in order to avoid paying huge taxes on it.”

“Wow! You could have bought something much more expensive than that Telluride.”

“I don’t need something more expensive,” she said. “The Telluride is safe, comfortable, and it has plenty of room. It seats eight.”

“So, are you planning on having another five kids?” Shawn asked.

“No, but I expect Josh to begin playing sports at some point, and I will need lots of room for gear by putting down the third row of seats,” Heather explained.

“You have all this figured out, don’t you?” asked Shawn. “You’re something else. You’re smart academically and you have loads of common sense, and on top of that – now you are telling me that you’re rich!”

“That money has to go into a house,” said Heather. “I won’t have it after I buy a house. Besides, I don’t even have a job yet.”

“You told me that you interviewed for a job with Georgia State,” said Shawn.

“I did, but I haven’t received an offer yet,” said Heather.

“Of course, they are going to hire you,” said Shawn. “If they don’t, they would be a bunch of idiots.”

“I don’t have the job yet, and I can’t really think about looking at houses until I have a job,” Heather explained.

“You could buy a nice house in Gwinnett County with $580K,” Shawn told her.

“I’m not sure about Gwinnett County,” said Heather. “The traffic is terrible.”

"A lot of people are moving out there," said Shawn.

"I don't really want to be really far away from my father," she explained. "I want to be far enough away to have privacy, but not so far away so that it takes a long time to visit."

"Your father's neighborhood isn't as safe as it was when you grew up there," said Shawn.

"My father's house is safe because my father is there," said Heather.

"I can't argue with that."

"And Emily is safe in her house because my father lives next door."

"True, but I just hope you'll buy somewhere safe," said Shawn.

"What about where you live?"

"My neighborhood isn't as safe as it once was," Shawn replied.

"That's a shame," Heather said. "I was thinking that we could get together easier if I lived nearby."

"You want to get together more?" asked Shawn, wearing a grin.

"Yeah, we could cook out on the grill and such," said Heather.

"That would be nice, but I'm not sure about that neighborhood."

"You don't plan to keep me safe?"

"Sure, but I'm not home all the time," said Shawn. "I work, sometimes long hours."

"You don't work much at night, do you?" asked Heather.

"Not usually," replied Shawn.

"Then you could maybe hang around at night?" Heather asked. "We could maybe have sleep overs. You know, like pajama parties and such."

"If I was to hang out long with you at night, I would have no intention of either of us wearing pajamas," said

Shawn.
"What if I became cold?"
"I wouldn't let that happen."

Chapter 28

Games

"IT'S NOT FAIR!" shouted Charlotte.

"You and your brother are spending too much time playing video games," explained Heather.

"I only played for two hours yesterday," complained Charlotte.

"From now on, you need to limit it to only one hour each day," said Heather. "I want you to spend more time reading."

"I hate reading!" blurted Josh.

"Reading or playing board games," said Heather.

"What about card games?" asked Josh.

"Card games are fine, as long as you increase your reading time."

"Why are you doing this?" asked Charlotte.

"I've been reading articles on the effects of video games on developing minds," explained Charlotte. "One article stated that scientists have collected and summarized studies looking at how video games can shape our brains and behavior. Current research suggests that playing video games can change the regions in the brain responsible for attention and visuospatial skills, making them more efficient. However, other articles say that those games can be addictive and lead to relationship issues. They can also cause poor academic performance."

"What does visuospastic.. whatever that word is – what

does that mean?" asked Josh.

"Visuospatial," said Heather. "It refers to cognitive processes necessary to identify, integrate, and analyze space and visual form, and spatial relations in more than one dimension."

"You're not helping," said Josh. "I don't know what the crap all that means."

"What the crap?" questioned Heather. "Where did you hear that phase?"

"I don't know," answered Josh.

"From your grandfather?" asked Heather.

"I said that I don't know," replied Josh. "Maybe at school."

"I don't think so," said Heather. "Visuospatial skills are those like being able to tell how far things are away from you."

"Why didn't you just say that?" asked Charlotte.

"You're right," said Heather. "I should have just said that. I read the article and those were the words used in the article. But it really doesn't hurt you to learn new words."

"Nobody at my school says visuospastic," said Josh giggling.

"Visuospatial," corrected Heather.

"Kids would think we were nuts for using that word," said Charlotte.

"Possibly," answered Heather, smiling.

"Mom, I have a question," said Josh.

"Can you buy me a visuospastic card game?" he said as he burst out laughing.

"She said 'visuospatial'" said Charlotte, smiling.

"Very good, Charlotte," said Heather. "And to answer your question, Josh, I doubt I'll have any luck finding that game."

"I bet Shawn could find it," said Josh. "He's so big that he has to be visuospastic," he said laughing.

"You're impossible," Heather said, giving Josh a tight

hug.

"You're going to squeeze all my guts out and leave me all visuospastic!" Josh shouted.

"Good grief," Heather said, leaving the bedroom of her children.

THE FOLLOWING SATURDAY, John, Heather and her children were busily playing a board game on the kitchen table when Heather heard a heavy knocking on John's front door.

"That has to be Shawn," said Heather. "He and I plan to go to the gun range today. I'll get it."

"Are you ready to go?" asked Shawn stepping into the house.

"She's playing Monopoly!" shouted Josh from the kitchen. "Want to play?"

"Maybe later sometime," answered Shawn.

"Maybe you're too busy being visuospastic," said Josh.

"What?" asked Shawn.

"Cut that out, Josh," said Heather.

"What did he say to me?" asked Shawn.

"I'm trying to have them spend less time playing video games and more time reading and playing board games," answered Heather.

"But what was Josh talking about?" asked Shawn.

"I've been reading studies on the effects of video games on children during their formative years," explained Heather. "One study said that too much exposure to video games during those years effect visuospatial skills."

"What the crap is that?" asked Shawn.

Heather could hear Josh laughing in the kitchen.

"So, he learned that phrase from you?" asked Heather.

"Don't change the subject," said Shawn. "Explain what you're saying in English."

"It affects the ability to do things like judge distances,"

said Heather.

"You could have just said that," said Shawn.

"By this time, both Charlotte and Josh were laughing loudly.

"I give up," said Heather.

She returned to the kitchen to kiss her children before leaving out with Shawn for the gun range.

"Shawn, make sure that you don't get yourself shot," said John.

"I'll take every precaution," promised Shawn.

Heather went to her bedroom and came back out with the unplugged small gun safe. She gave her father a wave with the other hand, before leaving with Shawn.

"That looks like John's gun safe," observed Shawn.

"It's mine," said Heather. "He gave it to me."

"Good man," replied Shawn.

"Let's go," said Heather.

"Will that safe open if it's unplugged?" asked Shawn.

"It has a backup battery that lasts for up to four hours," explained Heather.

Within firing ten rounds at the gun range, Heather's childhood training with firearms came back to her.

"You're pretty good," said Shawn, as the two left the range.

"You had better be careful, if you know what's good for you," Heather replied.

"So, tell me more about the studies on video games," said Shawn.

"The researchers also looked at studies exploring brain regions associated with the reward system, and how these are related to video game addiction," explained Heather.

"I can believe that," said Shawn. "Even adults can get pretty sucked into those games."

"Adults are responsible for themselves," said Heather. "I'm responsible for Josh and Charlotte."

"True," said Shawn. "They've had a tough time with the

death of their father, but they have no idea how lucky they are to have you."

"I'm just trying to do the best I know how for them," said Heather.

"You ARE the best," said Shawn.

"Now that I'm packing, you're just trying to get on my good side," said Heather. "Scared?"

"Maybe, just a little," answered Shawn, smiling.

"Keep it that way, big boy," said Heather.

"So, do you want to go back to John's and play board games with the kids?" asked Shawn.

"Is that what you want to do?" asked Heather.

"I'm fine with it," answered Shawn, starting the engine of his car. "I enjoy spending time with your kids."

"I guess that's one option," said Heather.

"What's the other option?" asked Shawn.

"We could go back to your place and play other games," suggested Heather.

"What, like Bingo?" asked Shawn, trying to maintain a straight face.

"I had other ideas," said Heather.

"Like what?" asked Shawn.

"Like this," answered Heather, as she quickly jumped in his lap and straddled him.

"How do you play this one?" asked Shawn.

"Like this," she said before planting a passionately long kiss.

"I don't think that's a board game," said Shawn, as he came up for air.

"You had better not be bored!" threatened Heather, as she dug one of her fingers into his ribs.

"This is a violent game!" cried Shawn.

"Yes, and you had better do everything I demand of you," said Heather.

"Yes, Ma'am," said Shawn, reaching for her hips.

Chapter 29

Note-3

WHEN I COME, YOU'LL HAVE NO TIME TO USE
A GUN.
YOUR FATHER CANNOT HELP; YOUR KIDS
WILL YELP.
NO GUN WILL KEEP YOU SAFE.
EVEN IF YOU WEAR IT WHERE IT MAKES YOU
CHAFE.
YOUR COP BOYFRIEND WILL PROVIDE NO
HELP.
WHEN I AM DONE, HE WILL ONLY YELP.
YOU CAN NOT PROTECT THE GIRL AND BOY,
AND EVENTUALLY YOU WILL BE MY TOY.
I WATCH EVERY MOVE YOU TRY TO MAKE,
BUT YOUR LOVELY BODY I WILL TAKE.
YOUR INTELLECT AND STRENGTH ARE UP
FOR DEBATE.
YOU WILL NOT UNDERSTAND UNTIL IT'S TOO
LATE.

The 3rd note threatening Heather and the kids was found on the windshield of Heather's car by Emily as she and Lily came to John's house to visit with Heather.

"I thought someone had left an ad for a service on your windshield," said Emily, handing the note to Heather. "This is creepy."

"It's worse than creepy," said Heather, terrified.

"I'm glad you decided to take me up on having the nine-millimeter," said John. "I hope you'll put it in your purse each time you leave the house."

"Oh God!" thought Heather, *"I honestly can't imagine using a gun on a person. I hope it never comes to that!"*

"In the note he says that he is watching every move you are making, Heather," noted Emily.

"It's possible this guy has bugged my house while we were out," said John. "That does it! "I'll call Shawn, and he and I will turn my house upside down looking for bugs or camera feeds."

THAT EVENING, JOSH and Charlotte were late going to bed. Their bedroom was searched by John and Shawn first, before diligently searching the rest of John's house for bugs and camera feeds. By 10:00 PM, the two decided to call it a night and Heather put the kids to bed.

"John, I'll be here first thing in the morning to help you finish searching the outside of the house and the property," promised Shawn.

"I think we're all tired," said John. "Tomorrow, we can also give the inside another once over."

"I'll be here," promised Shawn.

"Thanks, brother," said John.

Heather escorted Shawn out onto the front porch. There, apart from her children, she finally burst into tears.

"Shawn, I don't know what to do," she said, sobbing. "The kids don't understand, but they know something is up. It may take half the night for them to fall asleep. They don't deserve this – especially after all they've been through."

"Your dad and I know what we are doing," said Shawn.

"I'll let Caitlin know about this note, and I'm sure she'll be glad to help. We'll make sure this place is clean, including your vehicle."

"I felt safe with my father after coming to Atlanta, but now I have to carry a gun around with me everywhere I go," said Heather. "I don't know if I can live like this. I don't know if I can put the kids through this."

"Are you wanting to go back to California?" asked Shawn.

"I don't know if that would help," said Heather. "If this guy is really after us, and he is watching, it's possible that he might follow wherever we go."

"You're exactly right," said Shawn. "If you are asking me, you might be better protected with your father and me."

"I don't want to leave," Heather said. "I don't want to leave my father…and I don't want to leave you. But my kids…"

"This is going to be tough for a while," said Shawn. "You can relax while you are at the house with John. However, you need to pay careful attention to detail when you are outside the home. You need to make the school your kids attend aware of this situation. They must also be vigilant regarding the safety of Josh and Charlotte. I hate to say this, but you need to talk to your kids and let them know that they must be under adult supervision at all times – and only by adults trusted by you."

"I hate this!" blurted Heather.

"This is temporary," reminded Shawn. "We will get this guy. This mess will come to an end. You have to stay the course. I will be here for you."

"When I take the kids to school tomorrow, I'll make the principal aware of the situation," promised Heather. "You're right. I'll explain to the kids that they must stay under adult supervision for a while. I don't have to go into the things contained in the notes, but they need to take care. They're already aware that there is a really bad man threatening the safety of people."

"Good,' said Shawn, taking Heather into his powerful arms.

"Thank you," she said. "I just needed a plan of action. My head was spinning, and I just needed help focusing."

THE FOLLOWING MORNING, Heather met with the school administrative personnel and informed them of the specifics regarding the threat to her family. Every staff member was put on notice. When she returned back to her father's home, she found John, Shawn, and Caitlin scouring the property for surveillance items.

"So far, we've found nothing," said Shawn. "We plan to spend another couple of hours searching the place. Now that you're home, I'm going to conduct a thorough search of your Telluride. We've already checked out John's car."

"Thanks so much," said Heather.

"I plan to put up some surveillance equipment of my own," said John, joining Heather and Shawn. "A neighbor, Tom Griffin, shared with me the type of security system he has. I plan to buy the same system and install it myself. Tom has offered to help me put it in."

"Now, that's a great idea!" exclaimed Shawn.

"Thank you, Daddy," said Heather, giving her father a hug. "Thank you, so much."

"I should have done it a long time ago," said John. "I've recently been concerned that some guy might be taking advantage of my daughter on my own front porch."

"Who would do such a thing?" asked Shawn, grinning.

Chapter 30

Secure

"I HAVEN'T HEARD anything on the news about the molester in weeks," said Heather.

"He's probably lying low," replied John. "But I'll admit that I'm somewhat surprised."

"How so?' questioned Heather.

"It seemed to me that this guy expected to be caught," answered John. "I expected him to accelerate his behavior until he was caught."

"Do you think possibly one of the vigilante groups found him and got rid of him?" asked Heather.

"I have little doubt whether they would leave him alive, but those husbands and other family members of the victims would want the women of this city to know he was dead," explained John. "They would want women to understand that they no longer need to fear him. Plus, they would probably want copycat criminals to understand their own fate should they attempt to do the same thing. They would want to send a message, and I expect that message would be brutal."

"It's somewhat a breath of fresh air to not hear about more attacks on women," said Heather.

"It's important that you don't put your guard down," said John. "Please tell me that you're still carrying the gun when you go out."

"I am, but I'm sick of living like this," replied Heather.

"I'm sure you are," said John.

"I just want things to go back to normal."

"I hate to be the one to say it, but this may be a new normal for a while," said John. "But rest assured, we'll get this guy. If not today, soon. Give it a day."

"There have always been serial criminals," said Heather. "Once they are caught, things should go back to normal."

There seems to be a sickness spreading across the planet," said John. "We've always had a serial violent criminal from time to time. London had Jack the Ripper. Today, irrational violence has become common. I can remember when there weren't mass killings. Back in the day, people didn't march into a school playground and murder masses of innocent children. People didn't go into movie theaters and start slaughtering people they didn't even know."

"Maybe it's time we rethought the abundance of guns," suggested Heather.

"In Japan, someone used poisonous gas on a train," said John. "In England, someone used a samurai sword to attack people. Guns just seem to be a popular weapon of choice in mass killings. If all guns went away, I'm sure they would simply use some other weapon. You're the psychologist. You tell me why it has become common for people today to slaughter strangers."

"I'm not really sure," answered Heather. "I've read theories suggested in psychology publications, and most seem to agree that perpetrators are more likely to be angry people who seek retribution for some perceived harm done by some person, group, or institution. These incidents are generally premeditated and often planned well in advance. But, you're right. There have always been angry people, but they haven't always lashed out in mass at innocent strangers.

People seem to have lost the ability to cope."

"We have mass insanity," said John.

"All of this begs the question, why have people lost the ability to cope?" asked Heather. "I can't help but think it's a failure of our current society and culture. Some think it's the increased use of video games. Others point to people avoiding personal contact. Some people feel more comfortable communicating with another person over an electronic device than in person, face to face. I think it's important that we understand why."

"Your mother and Emily would probably say it's because people no longer believe in God," said John. "Here's the thing about that, there have always been people who didn't believe in God – and they weren't out murdering masses of people that they didn't really know. What is going on with people?"

"I wish I had an answer," replied Heather. "I don't. It seems that many people today have lost empathy for other human beings, but I can't say why."

"Are we still on for having everyone over for board games this Saturday?" asked John.

"I've invited Shawn and Emily's entire family over," said Heather.

"So, it's going to be me, you, Shawn, Josh, Charlotte, Emily and Ron?" asked John, counting all seven out on his fingers.

"Yes, and Emily will be bringing Lily of course," answered Heather. "Your dinning room table seats eight, so we should have plenty of room."

"That's great!"

"Emily is really excited, and she has suggested that we make this a regular Saturday thing," said Heather.

THE FOLLOWING SATURDAY, there were eight seated around John's dining room table, including Lily who was being held by her mother. Bowls of potato chips and popcorn were stationed at various locations between people. Zack, hoping for morsels to be dropped on the floor, curled himself under the table. Within an hour of play, baby Lily began to fuss.

"I may have to take Lily home," said Emily. "She needs a nap. I'm sorry, but the rest of you should continue playing."

"Hold on, there," said John. "Heather, please bring down a sheet and three pillows from the hall closet upstairs."

Once Heather returned with the items, John placed the folded sheet on the carpet along the wall of his living room. He placed the pillows on the remaining three sides.

"I raised two kids," John began. "Just place Lily on the sheet between the pillows. I bet she'll be fine."

Emily did so. Kneeling beside her daughter, she placed her hand on the child. Within a couple of minutes, Lily was fast asleep.

"Where did you learn that?" whispered Emily.

"Necessity is the mother of invention," replied John. "Parents learn to come up with ideas for the sake of sanity and rest."

They returned to the board game on the table. Periodically, Emily would excuse herself to check on Lily.

"This is so nice," said Emily. "It's peaceful, really peaceful."

"I bet your arms were getting tired while you held Lily at the table," stated Heather. "I can remember hanging on to Josh with one arm and holding Charlotte's hand with the other. After a while, it became exhausting."

"I can imagine," said Emily. "I can become exhausted with only the one."

"John, I hear that you put in a security system," said Ron.

"I did," replied John. "Tom Griffin helped me put it in and it's provided a measure of peace."

"To be honest, I'm not sure that I can afford one," said Ron.

"This company has initial systems which can be expanded over time," said John. "You purchase the system and install it yourself. The cost is very reasonable. Before you leave, I'll show it to you."

"OK," said Ron.

"It also doesn't hurt that I have two men trained law enforcement around," added Heather.

The group enjoyed two more hours of board game activity before they broke up. Ron promised John that he would consider purchasing the basic home security service. Everyone agreed to make the playing of board games a regular event for each Saturday, and they established start and end times to avoid encroachment on other Saturday activities. Hearing the commitment, Josh jumped around the living room in excitement. Charlotte was busily touching Lily's soft skin, as she was being held by Emily.

THE FOLLOWING AFTERNOON, Heather found her father dragging a large box through the front door of his house.

"What is this?" she asked.

"If the board game activity will be regular and ongoing, we need to do this right," he answered. "Isn't it obvious?" he asked, pointing to the large lettering on the box.

"You bought a playpen?"

"Yep, and it's going right against that wall," John answered. "It didn't cost much. Emily doesn't have to resort to pillows and a sheet."

Heather felt a wave of calmness and security sweep over her. "*It's not just the home security system or the presence of Shawn and my father,*" she thought. "*There's something about a sense of community in having a close relationship with good neighbors.*"

Chapter 31

Spotted

HEAVY KNOCKING on John's door alerted him to the presence of his ex-partner. John opened the door to find Shawn and Caitlin standing on the porch.

"I didn't expect to see you on a Saturday morning," greeted John.

"Another victim," said Shawn. "This time, he attacked a woman who lives less than two miles from your house."

"Come through to the back porch," said John, escorting the two through his home. As soon as the three were seated on the back porch, Zack curled up at his master's feet.

"Is this the first time that he's struck in this part of town?" asked John.

"We believe so," answered Caitlin.

John pulled out his cell phone and called his daughter who was upstairs reading to her children.

"Shawn and Caitlin are here on the back porch," began John. "I think you should join us. I recommend that the kids stay in their room during our conversation."

Within a minute, Heather was seated with the other three. Caitlin informed her of the new attack and of its location.

"Do you have suggestions?" asked Heather.

"Keep the windows and doors locked," said Caitlin.

"And don't leave the house without that gun," added Shawn.

"That's been standard procedure over the past month," said John.

"How is the woman who was attacked?" asked Heather.

"Terrified, as expected" answered Caitlin. "She is being kept at Grady's hospital for observation, and they are administering antibiotics to her intravenously. I believe she will be kept there for at least a day."

"He cut her just like the last victim," said Shawn. "Cuttings on both breasts, and the same abbreviation letters of 'OPETRC' across her abdomen. He left the same manifesto taped to her."

"So, he didn't show any signs of progression?" asked Heather.

"No," answered Caitlin.

"Was this woman less educated, like the others?" asked Heather.

"High school educated, and works part time as a waitress," said Shawn. "Her husband is a truck driver, and he is currently away on runs to New Jersey and Pennsylvania."

"We believe that he watched this family for a while, noting work patterns of the husband," said Caitlin. "He drives for two weeks, and then he is home for a week. Looks like he waited for him to be away."

"Interesting," said Heather. "He's completed his message, and now he is reemphasizing it with another victim"

"Do you have any ideas about his next move?" asked Shawn.

"My guess is that he will strike periodically and randomly, just to make sure the public stays aware of the message," said Heather.

"Why randomly?" asked John.

"He's not ready to be caught, and there is shock value in the public never knowing when he will strike," answered Heather. "That's my opinion."

"I don't like the fact that he attacked someone so close to us," said John. "Are there any patterns to the areas of town he hits?"

"It's hard to tell," answered Shawn. "We don't know if he doesn't strike repeatedly in previous areas to avoid alerted neighbors in the vicinity or if he is moving purposefully toward an area."

"Remember the notes left on our vehicles," said John. "Has anyone else had these notes?"

"We've not heard of any," answered Caitlin. "That's puzzling. I'm not sure what to make of that."

"Why us?" asked Heather, looking at her father.

"I'm guessing it's possible that I'm the only one to have actually seen him without the ski mask," said John. "Maybe he took that personally and is trying to make me back off."

"Maybe, but it's weird," said Shawn. "Anyway, you need to be aware of something else. As we speak, another vigilante group has spun up today in the neighborhood of this last victim. It's led by a friend of the husband of this woman. He too, is a truck driver."

"Yes," said Caitlin. "Since the attack was so close to you, it's possible that their patrolling may cross over into your neighborhood. Just be on the lookout. These guys are armed to the teeth with handguns, hunting rifles and AR type weapons."

"I'm glad I have a brick house," said John. "If these psyched up guys start shooting at something, we have a better chance of the brick stopping a few rounds."

"You're not making me feel better," said Heather. "You sound like we are in a war zone."

"In the minds of some of those men, their neighborhood has become one," said Shawn.

"I feel for the people living in that neighborhood," said

Heather.

FOUR DAYS LATER, John received a call from Shawn.

"We believe that molester has been spotted in your neighborhood," said Shawn. "A couple of streets over from you, a man spotted a slightly built man peeking in a window of a home."

"Crap!" exclaimed John.

"However, there is good news this time," added Shawn. "The man pulled out his cell phone and yelled at him. When the jerk turned, he took a photo of his face. We ran it and we've confirmed that it is Danny Barker. His face is about to be spread all over the news and on billboards around town."

"That IS good news!" shouted John. "I'll pass this on to Heather."

As soon as he was off the phone with Shawn, John knocked on Heather's bedroom door.

"What is it?" stammered Heather, still half asleep. "Couldn't this wait an hour? It's five in the morning."

"Good news, and bad news," answered her father. "I think you want to hear this."

"What's the good news?" Heather asked.

"The police have a clear photo of the molester's face, and it's going to be plastered all over the news," answered John.

"That's great," whispered Heather, making sure that she didn't wake her children. "What's the bad news?"

"The photo of this pervert was taken in this neighborhood," said John.

"Oh, God!" blurted Heather, no longer mindful of her sleeping children.

Within hours of the first broadcast on the news showing the face of Danny Barker, a neighborhood watch group was formed in John' neighborhood. Hearing that John was a retired cop, he was approached by the watch group leader, Tom Griffin.

"We could really use a man like you," said Tom. "I'm in charge of organizing our neighborhood watch group."

"I'll sign up for a patrol," said John.

"I thought you would," said Tom. "Your next-door neighbor, Ron, told me about you when he signed up."

"Ron signed up for a patrol?" asked John.

"He was eager," said Tom. "He told me that you caught this pervert peeking through a window at his wife when she was pregnant."

"Ron's a good man," said John.

"Emily told me about how you drove her to the hospital to have the baby when Ron couldn't make it," said Tom. "She raved about you. They both told me how fortunate they felt to have you next door."

"I just happened to be at the right place at the right time, that's all," said John.

"I just hope you'll be at the right place if this jerk shows his head around here again," said Tom. "Thanks for signing up."

"Glad to do it," replied John. "And thanks again for helping me install the security system."

"What's going on?" asked Heather, as she walked into the room.

"John has just signed up to be on patrol with our group," said Tom.

"What group?" asked Heather.

"Since that molester has been spotted in this neighborhood, we've formed a group to patrol our area of town," explained Tom.

"You've formed a vigilante group?" blurted Heather.

"No, it's just a neighborhood watch group," answered John. "Ron, next door, has joined as well."

"Ron?" she questioned.

"I'm telling you, that it's a neighborhood watch group,"

said John. "It's not a vigilante group. We're signing up to take turns patrolling the neighborhood. I've signed up to patrol twice a week, Tuesdays and Thursdays, 1:00 – 3:00 PM each of those nights. Ron is still working, so his watch is 8:00 – 10:00 PM on the same nights, as to not interfere with his sleep."

"Did Ron tell this group that he doesn't even own a gun?" asked Heather.

"Gun ownership isn't a requirement," said Tom. "We're a watch group. If this guy is spotted, a group member is to call law enforcement. This is a watch group, not a vigilante group."

"I'll be carrying," said John. "I have a license to carry."

"That's fine," said Tom. "You're trained in law enforcement, and we are happy to have you carrying a weapon."

"Have women signed up?" asked Heather.

"Not yet," answered Tom. "Would you like to be the first?"

"Your kids might be more comfortable if you stayed with them at home," protested John.

"I have a license to carry, as well," Heather told Tom.

"It's your call," said Tom. "If you are licensed, I have no problem with you taking a patrol or two."

"Think about it," John advised his daughter.

"I'll think about it for the time being," Heather told Tom. "My father has a point. My children might become upset if they knew I was away patrolling the neighborhood."

"We have patrol hours during the day," offered Tom.

"I'll think about it," replied Heather. "Thanks so much for all that you're doing, Tom."

"It's the least I could do," said Tom. "You are more than welcome to join."

"I have a question for you, Tom," said John.

"What is it?" Tom replied.

"When are you going to let a woman make an honest

man out of you?" asked John. "Isn't the bachelor life getting old?"

"Not yet," answered Tom. "I haven't found the right woman, but I'm certainly on the lookout for her."

"I'm sure you have a number of women interested in you, Tom," said Heather. "You're a catch. "You're an engineer with a solid income, and you're not bad looking."

"Well, I have a type of woman in mind," said Tom. "So far, my type hasn't shown any interest."

"I hope you find the right one," said John. "There's nothing like having the right woman."

"Thanks again, for stepping up to keep everyone safe," said Heather, placing a hand on Tom's shoulder.

"You bet," said Tom, reaching for the front door to leave.

As Tom left John's home, Heather turned to her father.

"Tom seems to be a nice guy, but I think his main problem in finding a wife is that he also seems to be shy."

"That, or maybe he's wise enough to be careful," said John.

Chapter 32

Ron

"WHY IS THIS perverted guy hanging around in this neighborhood?" Heather asked her father.

"I can't answer that," replied John.

"You saw him peeking in Emily's window, he has left notes on our cars, and now he has been spotted again in this area," said Heather. "All of this can't be a coincidence. What disturbs me the most are the notes. Why is he going after me and my children? I'm not pregnant and I'm very well educated. This makes no sense."

"Nobody said that this nutjob was rational," said John. "Uneducated mothers have been raising children since before recorded history. Why would an educated fool of a university professor think strangers who have no family-based love for a child would do a better job than mothers who have committed themselves to carrying a child for nine months and then enduring painful childbirth? Can you explain that to me? Shouldn't he know better? If you can explain that nonsense, then maybe we can better explain the thinking of this pervert."

"All of what you said are valid points," said Heather. "However, why is his attention on me? Shawn said that none of the victims mentioned having received notes from him. Why is he writing me notes? Why threaten me and my children? Why is he going to such great lengths concerning me and my children? Why am I even on his radar?"

"I honestly don't know," answered John. "I'm at a loss, except for the fact that I spotted him that day and you are my daughter. I'm going to call Shawn."

John contacted Shawn using his cell phone and asked him if the molester had issued threatening notes to the person who photographed him.

"So far, we've heard nothing regarding notes sent to anyone but Heather," answered Shawn. "Since the photo taken by this guy has been posted all over the news and the internet, I would think that this pervert would be after him the strongest. However, so far, there has been no reported backlash on the guy who took the photo."

"Then, why is he specifically threatening Heather and the kids?" asked John.

"You spotted him at Emily's window, and you spotted the writing on that nasty restroom wall," said Shawn. "Until this photo, you were the primary cause of him being identified. That was my thinking regarding the notes about Heather and the kids. But you're right about him not showing the same vindictiveness toward the guy who photographed him. It's not consistent with his previous behavior."

"Heather is spooked."

"As she should be," replied Shawn. "Maybe she and the kids should go back to California for a while."

"She is adamantly against that," said John.

"The molester doesn't attack men, in any way," said Shawn. "He only goes after women. Maybe that has something to do with why he hasn't gone after the guy who took the photo. Maybe he blames only women for the problems in the world."

"I've heard of religious nutjobs who blame all of the world's problems on Eve; you know, Eve in the Garden of Eden," said John. "There are guys out there who blame everything on women."

"This guy has never mentioned God," said Shawn. "He has never referenced anything out of the Bible. So far, we have no indication that he is religious in any way."

"But you make a really strong point about him never throwing blame on men," said John. "Maybe that's why he didn't threaten me. Instead, he has gone after my daughter."

"Then again, it's possible that he didn't go after you because the pervert is a wuss," said Shawn. "He picks on women."

"There are men who rape women because it's a power thing," said John. "Some of them aren't sexually motivated, as much as it being a turn on from simply overpowering a woman."

"I have no tolerance for crimes like that," said Shawn. "I have a deep hatred for guys who sexually attack women or children. It wouldn't bother me in the least if someone tied the guy's pecker to the bumper of a truck and floored the truck. I would never do it because of my respect for law and order, but that kind of thing sets me off. I have to focus on controlling myself when it comes to those guys."

"I understand," agreed John. "Most criminals in prison have little tolerance for guys who sexually prey on women and children. They may beat the crap out of a woman or child, but never do that."

"Any man who violently beats a woman or a child, isn't a man – in my book," said Shawn.

"Absolutely," agreed John.

"Hey, we had better change the subject before we find ourselves getting mad and flying off the handle," said Shawn.

"I wouldn't mind somebody flying off the handle with this pervert," said John.

"I hear you."

"Let me know if you hear any reports of this guy being in my neighborhood again," said John.

"You got it," replied Shawn. "I'll contact you immediately if I hear anything."

"The guys in the neighborhood have formed a watch group," said John. "This isn't a vigilante group, only neighbors patrolling the place. They are to contact law enforcement if they spot anything."

"That's not a bad thing," said Shawn. "But caution them not to try to take this guy down themselves. He could hurt somebody."

THE FOLLOWING SATURDAY, Shawn was visiting with Heather and the kids at John's house. Before long, the five of them were enjoying a game of monopoly on the dining room table. Late that afternoon, Heather asked Shawn if he would stay for supper.

"I may be wearing out my welcome," said Shawn.

"Lasagna is on the menu," said Heather, giving him a wink.

"You play hardball," said Shawn. "You know that I can't resist your lasagna."

"So, you're going to stay?" she asked.

"I think you're twisting my arm hard," Shawn replied, holding out his powerful right arm.

Both Josh and Charlotte attacked his arm, attempting to pull it behind his back. Within seconds, Shawn allowed his arm to be pushed behind his back.

"I give!" Shawn blurted. "Don't hurt me anymore. I give up; I'll stay for supper."

Charlotte squealed in delight. Josh threw his arms up in victory and danced around the room like Rocky in the movie.

"I think I'll take Zack for a walk before supper," said John. "Do you folks think you can behave while I'm gone?"

"I'm completely subdued," said Shawn, dropping to the floor and laying spread eagle. Seeing the opportunity, both kids jumped on him. Shawn acted as if he was pinned to the floor, unable to escape.

While John walked Zack, Danny Barker was spotted by two neighborhood watchers a few blocks away in the opposite direction. The watchers called the police and began following him in a vehicle, but Danny escaped them on foot by cutting through yards. While running down John's street, Danny saw Emily rocking Lily on the front porch of her home. He remembered being stopped at her window earlier by John, and rage began to grow within him. Forgetting the neighborhood watchers, he decided to finish what he had planned for her while she was still pregnant. He pulled a box cutter out of his pocket and walked towards her. Seeing Danny, Emily screamed.

While watering shrubs on the other side of the house, Ron heard the screaming. He dropped the hose and ran to her aid. Seeing Danny approaching Emily near the foot of the steps, he tackled him. As they began wrestling on the ground, Emily continued screaming for John to help.

"Emily's screaming!" shouted Heather, clearly hearing the commotion next door.

Shawn leapt up, leaving both kids rolling across the floor. He sped from John's house in the direction of the scuffling men. Danny rose from the ground with Ron still clinging to his leg. Seeing Shawn quickly approaching, he sliced Ron with the box cutter. Blood squirted from Ron arm. Ignoring the pain, Ron refused to let go.

"Drop it!" yelled Shawn, as he barreled toward the much smaller man.

As Danny pointed the box cutter in Shawn's direction, Ron rolled his body twisting the leg of the molester causing him to be off balance momentarily. As Danny turned his attention to Ron and raised the cutter for another slice, Shawn sent him flying backwards with a powerful blow to the side of his face. Blood still gushing from his arm, Ron's grip was unyielding. Shawn placed his heavy knee on Danny's chest and quickly disarmed him.

"You can let go now," Shawn called out to Ron.

Ron finally released the leg and clamped his right hand over the gash on his left arm. His face began to grow pale.

"You're a good man, Ron," said Shawn. "You did good, brother. I have him now."

Still controlling the man, Shawn contacted his station on his cell phone to alert them of about the molester. He called out to Heather, who was viewing the confrontation from her front porch.

"Ron's cut and needs help," he yelled. "I have the guys at my station on my cell phone. Call for an ambulance."

Heather immediately contacted the emergency number for an ambulance. Several of the neighborhood watchers parked their vehicles in front of Emily's house.

"Need help?" yelled one watcher.

"Thanks, but I have him," said Shawn. "I'm an off-duty detective."

Shawn glanced down to find Emily holding Lily in one arm and attempting to stop Ron's bleeding with her other hand. Tears were rolling down both her checks.

"You have a good man, Emily," said Shawn. "A man never knows what he is made of until he is faced with a situation. Ron proved himself today."

Heather raced to help Emily, relieving her of Lily.

"That's it, Emily," coached Shawn. "Keep pressure on the wound. An ambulance is on the way."

Returning from the walk with Zack, John immediately saw Ron's condition. "I'll be right back," John said, racing off to his house. Within a minute, he returned with a roll of duct tape. John tightly taped Ron's wound with the tape, and the bleeding was contained.

"I used to give you a hard time about you using duct tape on things instead of actually fixing them, but it looks like that stuff can be a life saver," commented Shawn.

Within minutes of the scuffle, Danny Barker was in custody and enroute to the police station. Ron, Emily and

Lily were on their way to the hospital. Other officers questioned Shawn about what had happened.

"I'm going to tell you the truth," began Shawn. "Ron Johnson was a real hero today. He saved his wife, and after being sliced open with that box cutter, he held on to that pervert like a bulldog biting down on a steak. I'm proud to know that man."

Ron was treated and released from the hospital, and that evening the incident was on every news broadcast. The following morning, the street in front of his and Emily's home was lined with news trucks. Reporters stood on her front porch, asking for an interview. Emily stepped outside to quieten them.

"Please, my baby is sleeping, and Ron needs rest," she told the mob of reporters.

"So, your husband tackled the molester?" asked one reporter.

"He saved me and our child," Emily answered.

Ron stepped out onto the porch holding Lily in his good arm. Cameras turned on him like sharks going after bleeding prey.

"They woke her up," Ron told Emily, handing Lily to Emily.

Reporters insisted that they have photos and videos of the family standing on the front porch. Ron allowed it on the condition that they limit the questions and filming to twenty minutes.

After the news coverage of the interview, the following day cars were lined up and slowing passing the Johnson house bumper to bumper. It wasn't limited to the local people of Atlanta. There where cars with tags from various parts of Georgia and some even from out of state. People hoped for a glimpse of the man who captured the serial molester. Ron's life would never be the same. During the next month, advertising representatives from various companies tried to obtain contracts from him to endorse their products. After hiring an attorney to handle the offers, Ron eventually selected three.

Chapter 33

Peace

"I'M NOT SURE what we are going to do," Emily told Heather. "Ron is pulling in big money from these contracts, and he has become somewhat famous."

"Is that bad?" asked Heather.

"No, the money is a real blessing," said Emily. "However, we continuously have strangers coming to the door asking to speak with him or have a photo taken with him."

"So, it's become a privacy issue," observed Heather.

"It's to the point that I can no longer rock Lily on the front porch," explained Emily. "Our attorney warned us about the possibility of some weirdo attempting to abduct Lily, thinking that he could hold her for ransom. Life was so much more peaceful when we were scraping by each month."

"I'm sorry to hear that," said Heather.

"Ron wanted me to let John know that we will be having a privacy fence built around the back yard," said Emily. "I hate cutting you and John off as neighbors. I've really enjoyed our talks over the chain link fence."

"Maybe you'll find some peace with the fence," said Heather. "I'll tell you that the rest of the neighborhood is enjoying peace without being in fear of the molester."

"I'm glad they are," said Emily. "The news said that the city is considering a celebration of Danny Barker's capture. If so, I wouldn't be surprised if they asked Ron to speak at it. I'm glad the guy has been put away, and I'm glad women in Atlanta no longer fear him. All of that is great, I just want to have privacy again."

"I hope the fence helps," said Heather. "I've heard that most of the vigilante groups around town have disbanded."

"I heard that also," said Emily. "Ron thinks that the neighborhood watch group will remain in place, and he plans to continue taking his watch patrols on Tuesdays and Thursdays. Tom Griffin has volunteered to continue his leadership of the group."

"My father said he would also continue with the group," said Heather.

"Ron says there is now less anxiety within the members," said Emily.

"I'm sorry that things are complicated for you, but I have been able to relax again with my kids," said Heather. "Don't make this public knowledge, but I've stopped carrying the gun in my purse."

"I haven't seen Shawn at the house as often," said Emily. "Are you two still seeing each other?"

"I'm going over to his place more often," explained Heather. "I feel more comfortable leaving the kids with Dad. Josh and Charlotte have begun to settle down now that the molester is no longer on the news."

"I'm so glad," said Emily.

"Shawn plans to take me and the kids to the zoo Saturday."

"That sounds really nice," said Emily.

WHILE STROLLING THROUGH the zoo, Heather informed Shawn that she had become serious about finding a house for herself and the kids.

"Have you settled on a location?" asked Shawn.

"There are nice places in Cobb County," replied Heather.

"So, you've totally ruled out Gwinnett?" he asked.

"I absolutely can't stand the traffic, and I can get to work at Georgia State quicker from Cobb," answered Heather. "Besides, it would make it easier to see my father."

"I'm glad that you feel that you no longer need his constant protection," said Shawn.

"The kids and I will always need my father, and I'm so glad that we are now able to spend time with him," said Heather. "David's gone, and I'm done with California. It's time that I began having a life of my own."

"You'll make yourself at home in that fancy house and forget all about me," fretted Shawn. "Within a year, I see you settled into that house with a university professor."

"Been there, done that," said Heather. "That's not happening."

"Seriously, you deserve a new life," said Shawn.

"I have a new life," replied Heather. "And I plan to share it with you."

Heather stopped walking and turned to face him. She reached up and began playing with the back of his neck.

"You had better watch out with that," warned Shawn.

"I have plans for you," she said.

"What kind of plans?"

"You'll see," answered Heather.

"Tell me about them," said Shawn.

"They aren't the kind of plans that I can tell you about in public," she replied with a smile. "They're the kind that I have to show you in private."

"Show me?"

"These are not zoo plans," said Heather. "Tonight, when I come over to your place...I can show you then."

"Mom and Shawn!" yelled Josh. "I see monkeys ahead! Hurry!"

Charlotte grabbed Shawn by the hand and started pulling him in the direction of the monkey exhibit. "Come on, you big gorilla," teased Charlotte.

"Gorilla?" asked Shawn. "Who are you calling a gorilla?"

Looking back at Heather, Shawn shouted back to her, "I hear that I'm now a gorilla - so, you're good with showing what you have planned to a gorilla?"

"Especially, gorillas," answered Heather.

"Good to know," he called back, glancing back at her.

"Look where you're going, ape man," she shouted. "You're going to trip over one of my kids."

"Yes, Ma'am," he replied. "Do I need to prepare anything for tonight?"

"Just make sure your big ape self is available," she called to him.

Chapter 34

Randy

RANDY JENKINS WAITED, crouched behind Heather's Telluride parked in John's driveway. John had taken Zack for a walk.

"Come on, we're running late," coaxed Heather, herding her two children toward the vehicle.

"I forgot to brush my teeth," complained Charlotte.

Just as Heather opened the rear door of the SUV, Jenkins lunged at her, driving her hard to the ground.

"Mommy," Charlotte choked out in fear.

Momentarily confused, Heather struggled to her feet.

"Run back to the house!" she commanded her children.

It was too late. Jenkins grabbed Charlotte from around her small waist and reached for Josh with his free hand. Josh wiggled free and fled for his grandfather's front porch.

"Take your filthy hands off my daughter," Heather ordered the man.

"*God, I wish I still had that gun,*' she thought.

"Call your boy back here," ordered Jenkins.

"Why are you doing this?" she franticly asked.

"Why are you doing this?" mocked Jenkins.

"Stay where you are, Josh!" Heather called out.

"Get that boy back here and then shut up before I cut your daughter," Jenkins threatened, pulling a knife from his back pocket.

"Please," mumbled Heather.

"If you get that boy back here, I promise that I won't hurt your kids," stated Jenkins. "You had better not try me."

"Please put her down and take me, instead," she pled.

"I don't want that boy rousing up John," the man stated. "You better get him back here," he threatened, flipping the knife open with his thumb.

"Don't," pled Heather. "Why? I don't even know you. Do you know my father?"

"I know John Rawlings, all right," growled Jenkins. "We go way back."

"Did you put the notes on my windshield?" asked Heather.

"I don't want to use it," said Randy, moving the knife closer to the girl. "Don't make me."

"I don't think you really want to hurt us either," said Heather, attempting to calm the situation. "Why can't we just talk?"

"I have to keep him talking until my father notices that I didn't start the engine," thought Heather. *"Try to calm him down."*

"Are you going to get that boy back here or am I going to have to start cutting?" threatened Jenkins. "I don't want to, but I will if I have to."

"Tell me what you want," Heather calmly said.

"Get these kids in the backseat of this SUV, hand me the keys, and you get in the passenger side," stated Randy Jenkins.

"What do you want with my kids?" she asked, still trying to remain calm.

"I just want to drive you to the place where your father ruined my life," explained Randy. "You don't know the things your father has done, and I need you to understand."

"My children don't need to go," said Heather. "Let them stay here, and only take me."

"What's the boy's name?" Jenkins asked.

"Josh, and he's no concern of yours," she said.

"Josh, do you want me to hurt your sister?" Jenkin's called out.

"No sir," Josh answered.

"You're a good boy," Jenkins said. "You know your manners. I know you will do what is needed to make sure your sister is safe. Come here."

As Josh began to slowly make his way toward the man, Jenkins tossed Charlotte into the backseat. "Stay there, and you won't get hurt," he told the girl.

"Get in the backseat with your sister, Josh," Jenkins demanded.

Josh cautiously made his way toward the stranger, while Jenkins continued to point the knife in the direction of Charlotte who was terrified in the backseat.

"Just do what I say, so your sister stays safe," ordered Jenkins. "My name is Randy, and I want to take you kids and your mother for a ride. That's all."

"Randy, please leave them here," begged Heather. "There's no need for them to be involved."

"Come on, Josh," coaxed Randy. "Here, I'll step away from the SUV and you just get in."

Randy stepped back from the Telluride and motioned for Josh to get in the backseat. Josh cautiously made his way to the SUV and climbed in. Jenkins closed the rear door. As he turned back in Heather's direction, she rushed him knocking him off balance. Without hesitation, Heather began punching him in the face with her slight fists. Jenkins swung and connected squarely on Heather's jaw, sending her flying backwards onto the ground. He began to move toward Heather, holding the blade toward her. Heather suddenly heard a shot and the man's head seemed to explode. He dropped like a sack of potatoes.

"Are you alright?" she heard her father call out.

"I don't know," she said, dazed.

John rushed to her, still carrying the police positive .38. He glanced in the direction of his grandchildren, still in the backseat.

"Stay in the backseat!" John called out to them. "Everything is OK, just stay seated and don't look out the window. Promise me that, and we'll go for ice cream a little later."

He whipped out his cell phone and called Shawn, while placing the revolver in a pocket of his jacket. Bending down to help Heather to her feet, he quickly explained the situation to his ex-partner.

"Get the police to the house," John told Shawn, before quickly ending the call.

"He said that his name was Randy," said Heather.

"I remember Randy Jenkins," said John.

"He said that you ruined his life."

"Are you alright?" asked John. "I saw him hit you – he hit you really hard."

"The kids…" stammered Heather.

"In the SUV," said John. "I told them to remain seated and to not look out the windows. I'll take them out the other side of the vehicle and tell them not to look back in this direction. Are you OK?"

"My head is beginning to clear, but my face is beginning to hurt like hell," Heather answered.

"Shawn's on his way," said John.

"I don't want him to see me… I feel like my face is one giant bruise," said Heather. "I feel like crap, so I must look like crap."

"Can you walk?" asked John.

"I'll try," she said attempting to stand. Her legs buckled.

"I have you," said John. "I'll help you to the front porch, and then I'll go back for the kids. Put your arm around my shoulder and lean on me."

John helped Heather to stand, and together they made it to his front porch. He went inside the home and momentarily came out carrying a bag of ice in one hand and a bed sheet under the other arm. He gave Heather the bag of ice for her face. Once back at the Telluride, he covered the body of Randy Jenkins with the sheet before moving to the passenger side of the vehicle.

"Ok, time to come out," John instructed his grandchildren, opening the rear door. "Your mom isn't feeling well, and she is resting on the front porch. When she is feeling better, I plan to take everyone for ice cream. You two, go run and see about your mom."

Josh and Charlotte quickly exited the SUV and ran to the front porch of John's home. He had successfully redirected the attention of the two from the body.

"Are you OK, Mommy?" asked Charlotte.

"I'll be fine," she answered, hugging both children. "I was a bit dizzy, but there's no need to worry."

Within minutes, Shawn, three police cars, and an ambulance were at the scene. Shawn lifted the sheet and quickly observed the body before making his way inside John's house.

"Are you OK?" Shawn asked Heather, kneeling beside the chair where she was sitting.

"I'll be fine, but I feel like crap," she said, her left eye swelling.

"Where doesn't it hurt?" he asked.

"My feet feel fine," she answered, attempting to smile.

Shawn kissed the top of her head, and then reached out to Josh and Charlotte who were both standing on the other side of their mother. Charlotte launched herself into his arms. Josh gave him a polite wave with his right hand, but never left his mother's side.

"I'll have the paramedics check you out," Shawn said, releasing Charlotte before standing.

Within a few minutes, Shawn returned. He was accompanied by a paramedic and two police officers. As the paramedic began examining Heather, John suggested that the officers interview him first.

"Let's take this inside the house," John told the officers.

"We hear that you shot the victim," stated one of the officers.

"Let's keep our voices down, so that we don't further upset the kids," John told them. "I had to kill Randy Jenkins. He threatened my daughter and grandkids with a knife. He convinced the two kids to get into the rear seat of my daughter's SUV. Heather saw an opportunity to attack him, but in the process, he managed to hit her extremely hard. I saw her go to the ground and I saw the blade in his hand. I killed the bastard."

"Why did Mr. Jenkins have those kids in the rear seat of your daughter's vehicle?" asked the other officer.

"You could ask that son of a bitch, but I don't think he'll be talking," replied, John, still furious at the thoughts of anyone endangering Heather or his grandchildren.

"We're asking you," the officer stated.

"I thought he was trying to abduct them," said John, attempting to calm himself. "My daughter later told me that Jenkins said that he wanted to drive them all to a place. She said something about showing them the place where I 'ruined his life,' or some sort of crap like that. He wasn't going to take my daughter and grandkids anywhere, and he certainly wasn't going to take a knife to them!"

"Randy Jenkins was released from prison seven months ago, and we understand you were the arresting detective who put him there," said an officer.

"I arrested him; a court of law put him in prison," stated John. "You're both cops. I'm sure you understand that there are times when someone you've arrested wants payback after they are released from prison."

"It happens," said an officer. "Do you think this was an act of reprisal by Mr. Jenkins?"

"Possibly," answered John. "Listen, it's one thing if some dirtbag wants to come after me, but nobody is going to come after my daughter and my grandkids. That's what I witnessed. That's why I took this bastard out. He had beaten my daughter, and he threatened her and my grandkids with a knife. That's not happening."

"I glanced under that sheet," said one of the officers. "What did you shoot him with?"

"The .38 was loaded with hollow points," answered John, handing the revolver over to the officer.

"All of this will be in our report, sir," said an officer. "We need to obtain a statement from your daughter now."

John and Shawn sat on the steps of John's back porch, each holding a child, while the officers questioned Heather inside the house. On the back porch, the eyes of the children were successfully shielded from seeing the police and paramedics examine the body of Randy Jenkins.

"So, what flavor of ice cream do you plan to get?" John asked Charlotte.

"Chocolate, for sure," she answered.

"How about you, Josh?" asked John.

"Chocolate and raspberry," the boy replied.

"Both?" asked Shawn.

"I like to mix them all together," Josh explained.

"Maybe, I'll try that," said Shawn.

"You'll like it," said Josh. "Mom thought it was gross before she tried it, but now she likes it."

"She's just trying to be nice," said Charlotte. "It IS gross. It looks like poop."

"It looks like your poop," teased Josh.

"Maybe I'll try some poop ice cream," said John.

"You're sick, too!" blurted Charlotte. "I thought you would like caramel, like Mom."

"Your mom liked caramel ever since she tried it as a little girl," said John. "I'm the one who introduced it to her."

"Mom likes both caramel and poop ice cream," Josh nervously giggled.

"Are the police going to arrest Mommy?" asked

Charlotte, large tears forming in her eyes.

"No, honey," answered Shawn. "Never! They are just asking her questions about that man who hurt her."

"That man needs to go to jail," said Josh.

"You don't have to worry about that man," said John. "He will never hurt your mother again, and he will never make you scared again."

"How can you be sure?" asked Charlotte.

"If your grandfather says that he will never hurt your mother or scare you, you can be sure that he won't," said Shawn. "I've known your grandfather for a long time. If he said it, you can be sure about it."

"Good," said Charlotte.

Chapter 35

Ghosts

AS JOHN SAT in his bedroom after the police returned his revolver two weeks after he surrendered it to them, cleaning the police positive .38. He thought about how he had repurposed the gun. Once reserved for suicide, it had now been used to take out the criminal Randy Jekins. It had protected his family.

Jenkins had the choice of enjoying his freedom or allowing revenge to take control of things. He chose poorly, just like the guy in that movie I saw. If I had used this gun to commit suicide, I would have chosen poorly – and it would have horribly impacted Heather and the kids. How could I have been so stupid? Why did I allow myself to get so wrapped up in my own crap? What was wrong with me?

Once the gun was cleaned and oiled, John placed it back inside the small gun case. He hesitated before closing the lid.

If this gun hadn't been on me, Heather might have been knifed or beaten to death. This thing is old, manufactured in 1910, but it's as lethal as the day it was made. I wonder how many modern nine-millimeter guns will be around in one hundred years. They made things to last back in the day.

John closed the lid, locked the case with the key and placed it back on the shelf in his closet. The electronic gun safe containing the nine-millimeter, which had been returned by Heather, was now back on his nightstand. With the immediate threat of the molester now gone, Heather no longer wanted the gun in her possession. She had also mentioned to her father her desire to purchase a house for herself and her children.

Heather feels comfortable moving into a place of her own now. I hate to see her go. She and the kids have brought life into this place again. But she's right. She needs to make a life for herself, but I'm really going to miss them.

John found Heather seated on his back porch enjoying a cup of coffee. The aroma of the brew and her presence brought a sense of peace to him.

"I see you decided to take up my habit," John said to his daughter. "You can't beat a cup of coffee on a cool fall morning."

"I made a pot," said Heather. "Get a cup and join me."

"Sounds like a terrific idea," replied John.

While inside pouring himself a cup of coffee, he glanced up at the cabinet that once held his bourbon. It seemed like a lifetime ago.

"So much has happened since that time," John thought, as he moved to the door leading to his back porch. *"So much as changed."*

"I appreciate the invitation," John said to Heather, while taking a seat beside her.

"I decided to enjoy it while I'm still here," said Heather.

"Have you found the house that you want?" asked John.

"Maybe," answered Heather. "The kids haven't seen it yet. Whatever I find, they will not want to leave here."

"Not everything they've experienced here has been good," said John. "They experienced the death of their father while living here. They heard the continual talk about the molester; and to top it all off, they were threatened by that dirtbag Randy Jenkins. What a piece of crap that guy was!"

"What was going on with him?" asked Heather. "Why did he blame everything on you?"

"Because I arrested him, I guess," answered John. "I'd never seen the violent side of him until he hurt you. He was a thief, a habitual thief. He had a long rap sheet of stealing everything from TVs to cars. I arrested him on a charge of theft. His ex-girlfriend called the police and complained about him stealing her car. When I arrested him, he told me that he needed it to get to his job. He asked if I would allow him to simply park it and walk away from it."

"Was that an option?" asked Heather.

"I called it in, and I was told that the ex-girlfriend was pressing charges against him," explained John. "At that point, I had no choice. I had to arrest him. With his long history of stealing, the judge threw the book at him. Jenkins was given fifteen years. He must have behaved himself while in prison, because he was out in ten."

"So, he blamed you for not letting him walk away," said Heather.

"Randy Jenkins made his own bed," said John. "This wasn't a first offence. He had been stealing since he was a kid, but I kind of felt for the guy. He was caught up in a fight with his girlfriend and they broke up. Jenkins thought she wouldn't call the police if he took the car to go to work. He wasn't the sharpest tack in the box. The guy was as dumb as a rock. If he hadn't made such a long criminal record for himself, it wouldn't have turned out like that. I can't blame the judge."

"I'm teaching a class on human behavior," said Heather. "This tragic situation would be a good example of how poor behavior can result in terrible consequences. Speaking of consequences because of behavior, I'm sitting here drinking coffee and I'm about to cause my kids to be late to school. Plus, I may be late to my first class at Georgia State."

Within ten minutes, Heather had her children loaded in the Telluride and she was enroute. After they left, John poured himself a second cup of coffee. Upon returning to the back porch, John spotted Zack soaking in the sunshine which spilled across the backyard. Hearing the back door close, the dog sprang up and made his way to his master.

"Well, Zack, it's just me and you for a few hours today," John told the dog.

His relaxation with Zack didn't last long. Within a half hour, John heard a knock on his front door. John left the peaceful setting of the back porch to answer it.

"Mind if I come in" asked Pastor Matt.

"Sure," answered John, inviting him in. "What's on your mind?"

"Emily told me that you had to shoot a man," said Matt.

"I killed a man, if that's what you want to know," said John.

"Would you mind if we talked about it?" asked Matt.

"Suit yourself," answered John. "Would you like a cup of coffee?"

"Thank you," answered Matt.

"Mind if we take the conversation to the back porch?" asked John as he handed the minister the filled cup and then opened the back door.

"I'm good with that," answered Matt, exiting the door.

"Take seat," said John. "I like it back here. It's away from the small amount of traffic we now have on this street. With the privacy fence put up by my neighbor, it's become really peaceful."

"Speaking of your neighbors, Emily and Ron told me that the man you killed threatened your daughter and grandkids," said Matt.

"He did, but he won't threaten them again," said John.

"True. Is this the first time that you've had to take a person's life?"

"No. I killed a man threatening me with a knife shortly before I retired."

"Both killings due to threats by knives," remarked Matt. "How common is it that people are threatened by knives?"

"More than you think," answered John. "Gun crime is

more sensational, so the press covers those cases more thoroughly."

"I didn't know that."

"There were more than one thousand six hundred murders last year by knives," said John. "But it's true that there are many more homicides by use of guns than knives. With a knife, the attacker has to be in very close proximity. It's not so with guns. Someone can be murdered using a gun from a very long distance."

"I guess that would be the primary reason for so many murders committed by guns," observed Matt.

"A person can murder with a gun from a safe distance," said John. "It's much more cowardly. Knives are used in hand-to-hand situations, and there is much more risk for the attacker."

"Why would anyone use a knife?" asked Matt.

"There are two main reasons," answered John. "Usually, it's because of opportunity. Almost everyone owns kitchen knives, but much fewer people own guns. Secondly, it's used because it's more silent than using a gun. Gunfire attracts attention. In the case of Randy Jekins, he was a felon. It's against the law for a felon to own a gun."

"Do you think that the man who threatened Heather and the kids intended to kill them?" asked Matt.

"I don't know, but I couldn't allow the situation to escalate to the point that it was obvious he fully intended to kill them," explained John. "It would have been too late."

"I'm fortunate that I've never had to kill a person," said Matt.

"I'm sure that the people in your family were law abiding and peaceful citizens," said John.

"I didn't say that," replied Matt. "My older brother is in prison. He hasn't murdered anyone, but he is a violent man. He was a promising football player in high school until he almost beat a kid to death for trying to take his girlfriend. He was kicked off the team. Without success on the field, he became extremely frustrated, and he stayed in fights."

"To what do you attribute the difference in the two of you?" asked John.

"I was a fair athlete, but he was extremely good," said Matt. "Without football, my brother seemed to sink. His grades were poor, and mine were good enough to obtain a scholarship to a community college. After graduating, I worked in finance at a small company and took graduate courses from a seminary."

"When did you become interested in being a preacher?" asked John.

"I became a Christian while attending the community college," explained Matt. "A fellow student led me to Christ. By that time, my older brother was in jail for car theft. I visited him there and tried to talk to him about faith, but he would have nothing to do with it. After talking with a high school friend of mine about my conversion, that friend decided to become a Christian. That's when I decided I would spend more of my time trying to convince people who were more receptive to the gospel than my brother."

"Why is he currently in prison?" asked John.

"He hasn't changed; he almost beat a man to death," answered Matt. "While in a bar, the man pushed him. I'm guessing heavy drinking was involved. It didn't take much to set my brother off. He beat him unconscious and then stomped him with his boot. The man was in ICU for several days. The judge took one look at my brother's criminal record and gave him ten years."

"I'm familiar with the type," said John.

"To me, he's more than a type," said Matt. "He's my brother."

"I'm sorry," said John. "I've seen so much of it over the years. It must be tough."

"I visit my brother once each week," said Matt.

"That's a real commitment," replied John. "You must be close."

"We are," said Matt. "Regardless of the direction in life we each have taken; he is still my brother. I know him better than anyone does. I believe he knows me better than anyone does. He's not all bad. He knows things about me that no one else knows. He is exceptionally loyal to me. He always has been."

"Loyalty is hard to find today," said John.

"I'd like to change the subject," said Matt.

"Alright," replied John.

"What did you do with the gun after shooting the man?" asked Matt.

"After the police returned it, I cleaned it and put it away," answered John.

"There are no feelings attached to the weapon?" asked Matt.

"What do you mean?"

"For me, I would have always associated the gun with killing a man," said Matt. "I would have probably relived the shooting each time I viewed the gun. Maybe you've used it so many times that here is no association with violence regarding the weapon."

"It's the first time I've ever killed someone with it," explained John. "The gun has been in my family for years. It was manufactured in 1910, and it belonged to my grandfather."

"It must be well kept," observed Matt. "That's an old gun. It must have had a special purpose. I would have expected you to carry something more modern."

"With the molester around, I let my daughter borrow my nine-millimeter," John told the minister. "So, I carried the .38, and it was a good thing that I did. She might not be alive if I hadn't."

"You said that this was the second person that you've killed," said Matt. "I understand that the police department has counselors on staff. Did you receive counseling after the first situation?"

"I did."

"Was the counseling helpful?"

"No," replied John. "I had issues which ran deeper than a killing in self-defense."

"Can you talk about those issues?"

"I've heard that a priest has to hold all confessions in confidence," said John. "Does that apply to you?"

"There's no policy like that in my church," answered Matt. "However, holding things in confidence is personal with me. People can tell me things in confidence. If I swear confidence, then I never speak of it."

"I see," said John.

"What's bothering you?"

"I think I'm over it," replied John.

"You think, or you know?" asked Matt.

"I think," said John.

"OK," replied Matt. "Do you want to talk about it?"

"No," John emphatically answered.

"Ok," said Matt. "If you ever want to talk about things, I'm a good listener."

"I will tell you about one thing," said John.

"What's that?"

"I didn't like the feeling I got this morning when I walked down the driveway while taking Zack for a walk," answered John.

"What was the feeling?"

"Do you believe in ghosts?" asked John.

"I think our souls go before God when we die," answered Matt. "But there are a lot of aspects about death that I don't understand. Why the question about ghosts?"
"I felt a chill when I walked past the place in the driveway where I killed Randy Jenkins," explained John. "I got the feeling that his ghost was maybe hanging around that place where he died on my property, and it gives me the creeps."

"Like I said, I don't understand everything about death," said Matt.

"Does the Bible talk about ghosts?" asked John.

"It seems that the disciples of Jesus believed in ghosts," answered Matt. "When they saw Jesus walking on water, the Bible says that at first they thought they were seeing a ghost."

"Damn!" exclaimed John. "Oh, sorry for the cussing, preacher. So, maybe there was a ghost out there on my driveway."

"I'm not saying that I believe you sensed a ghost," said Matt. "Personally, I'm not concerned with ghosts. You asked a question, and I gave you a truthful answer. I don't really understand some aspects of the Bible, and that includes the subject of ghosts."

"You may be the first preacher that I've ever heard say that he doesn't understand parts of the Bible," said John.

"I think there's a lot of people who don't understand things about the Bible and about God," said Matt. "We are beings created by an all-knowing and all-powerful God, the Creator of the universe who has no beginning and no end. Honestly, I can't get my mind around the concept of eternity. I believe God is eternal and I believe people will be eternally in heaven, but I have difficulties comprehending the concept of eternity."

"I can't get my head around that either," said John. "What else does the Bible say about ghosts?"

"Well, I'm not sure whether it is talking about a ghost or not, but it tells of something done by the witch of Endor," answered Matt.

"You're telling me that there are witches in the Bible?"

"Yes, but don't think that I'm an authority on witches," answered Matt.

"What did it say?" asked John.

"It talks about it in 1 Samuel 28," said Matt. "Saul was having difficulties in battles he was waging, and he wanted advice from the prophet Samuel. The problem was that Samuel was dead. God forbade people from consorting with witches, but Saul decided to consort with the witch of Endor in an attempt to make contact with Samuel."

"Saul was wanting to make contact with somebody who was dead?" asked John. "Like a séance?"

"That's exactly what he was trying to do," answered Matt. "I really don't understand it, but it seemed to have worked. The witch described to Saul the person she saw who appeared to her as a ghostly figure from the dead, and Saul understood it to be Samuel. Samuel informed Saul that God had become his enemy, and that he would be defeated in battle. The Philistines killed Saul's sons, and Saul killed himself by falling on his sword."

"It sounds like God isn't happy with people who consort with witches and attempt to contact the dead through a séance," said John.

"That appears to be true," said Matt. "If I were you, I would avoid any thoughts of contacting the ghost of Mr. Jenkins," advised Matt.

"Sounds like good advice," agreed John. "The next time that ghost feeling comes, I plan to ignore it."

"So, you believe in God?" asked Matt.

"I've always believed there was a God," said John. "I'm not an idiot. All this stuff – the world and life in the universe – came from somewhere. I figure it would be stupid to think that all of this just randomly came about by accident. That would be a ridiculous long shot. In my mind, there has to be something or someone behind it all. So, I believe in God. It's just the Bible and all the things about Jesus being God's Son that I have trouble believing. My wife was a faithful believer in all of that, but I'm just not there."

Matt brought up Romans 1:20 on his cell phone. He showed it to John.

"You are talking about exactly what is said in Romans 1," said Matt, handing his cell phone to John. "Would you mind reading this aloud?"

"For since the creation of the world God's invisible

qualities—his eternal power and divine nature—have been clearly seen, being understood from what has been made, so that people are without excuse," read John.

"The Bible says that people understand that God exists because they see what God has made," said Matt. "I believe this is what you were saying."

"That is what I was saying," replied John. "I generally believe in God because I see what has been created by God. I just don't know that I can believe the Bible."

"You believe the verse that you just read to be right, don't you?" asked Matt.

"That one makes sense, but there are a number of things in the Bible that make no sense, at all," said John. "Like I said, my wife was a woman of faith. She tried to explain the Bible to me, but I just didn't see it the same way. It didn't make sense to me."

"I really enjoy visiting you, John," Matt said. "I enjoy hearing your detective stories. You're not a member of my congregation, but you always put me at ease when I'm around."

"I would imagine someone living a pastor's life would have to be on guard 24/7," observed John.

"You really have no idea," said Matt. "Even pastors screw up. We happen to be human beings like everyone else. I try hard not to let people down, but the expectations are enormous."

"You don't have to be a fake around me," said John.

"I didn't say that I was a fake around the members of my congregation," said Matt. "I just don't want to do anything to discourage new Christians. I recently shared from the pulpit a bit of wisdom given me when I was a young Christian. I had been discussing with a man how much I admired particular ministers in the faith. He told me not to put anyone on a pedestal. He said that if I knew someone who had not failed me, it was only because I hadn't known the person long enough. People mess up. We are all flawed beings."

"That's good advice," agreed John. "Did your congregation listen?"

"Hopefully, some may have listened," answered Matt. "However, one new Christian came to me after the service and told me that he didn't believe that I would be one of those ministers who fail people. I assured him that I was far from perfect, but I don't think he really accepted it."

"You can always be yourself when around me," assured John. "I've absolutely failed people."

"I enjoy our talks," said Matt.

"Well, to be honest, there are a few things about myself that I don't care to share with anyone," said John.

"Same here," said Matt.

"I don't' think your failures could possibly be in the same league with mine," said John.

"I wouldn't be so sure," said Matt. "Maybe one day, I'll be able to talk to you about some of mine."

"I'm here," said John. "You're welcome to come by anytime."

"You told me that there were aspects of the Bible that didn't seem to make sense to you," said Matt.

"I think there are quite a few things in the Bible that don't seem to make sense," said John.

"Would you like to discuss the things in the Bible that don't make sense to you?" asked Matt.

"No, not right now," answered John. "I'm enjoying the coffee and just sharing stories with a friend this morning. As for the Bible, let's give it a day."

THE FOLLOWING WEEK, Heather finally settled on a home in Cobb County, Georgia. Before the move, the kids complained about moving out of John's home, but quickly adjusted to the new place. Within the first day, Carlotte became excited about having her own bedroom. Josh still complained during the first week of living away from this grandfather. Shawn gravitated to spending more time at Heather's place and less time visiting John.

TWO MONTHS LATER, Heather and Shawn were married by Pastor Matt at his church. John's eyes were filled with tears as he led his daughter down the aisle.

"He's a good man," John whispered to Heather, as he released her hand.

John kept his grandchildren at his house while Heather and Shawn enjoyed a short honeymoon on Dauphin Island, just south of Mobile, Alabama. Since the two kids had become used to having separate bedrooms in the new house, he allowed the practice to continue in his own home. When Heather and Shawn returned to collect her children, Josh told Shawn," Now, you don't have to sneak in and out anymore – you can officially move into our house."

Chapter 36

Wealth

THE MONOPOLY GAME played on John's dining room table was interrupted by the ringing of his doorbell. The eyes of Heather and John became fixed on the door.

"Who in the world could that be?" asked Shawn. "It's been a long time since I've heard your doorbell. I didn't even know that it still worked."

"That's because you always resort to slamming the front door with those big meaty hands," said John.

"My hands aren't meaty," said Shawn, defensively.

"Enough," said Heather moving to answer the door.

"We have a surprise that we wish to share!" blurted Emily, upon Heather opening the door.

"Well, OK," said Heather. "Come on in and tell us about it."

"Is that Emily and Ron?" asked John, from the dining room.

"You guessed it," said Ron, entering the dining room with a thick manilla envelope under his arm.

"What do you have there?" asked Shawn.

"Guess!" exploded Emily, in excitement.

"I wouldn't have a clue," said John.

"Guess!" repeated Emily, this time giggling.

"You bought a new car, that that's the paperwork,"

guessed Heather.

"It's a contract for a book!" blurted Emily.

"A what?" asked Shawn.

"A writer wants to write a book about Ron capturing the molester!" shouted Emily.

"Really?" questioned Shawn.

"Did a lawyer read over this contract?" asked John.

"Oh, yeah," answered Ron. "When I was first approached by this writer, I had doubts. My father knows a small-time publisher back in Birmingham, and he asked him about it."

"I forgot that you were originally from Alabama," said Heather.

"That small-time publisher knows people at a much larger publishing house, and they gave him the name of a local lawyer in Atlanta who is supposed the be the best when it comes to these kinds of contracts."

"I bet that guy wasn't cheap," said Shawn.

"He wasn't," said Ron. "But I believe it was worth it. The lawyer reviewed the contract and said that it was very fair. But he had them sweeten it up even a little more. I get fifteen percent from sales profits of hard copies and twenty-five percent of digital sales. I also retain movie rights."

"Movie rights?" asked John. "Did they talk about that?"

"No, that's pretty much the standard," answered Ron. "There wasn't any serious talk about a movie, only the publishing of the book."

"Congratulations!" shouted Heather. "This is great!"

"I can't think of a better guy for this to happen to," said Shawn.

SIX MONTHS LATER, Ron began to have large checks deposited into an account of his. Again, strangers began to appear on his front porch – this time, wanting him to sign copies of the book.

"I'm not sure what to do about this," Emily told Heather. "This isn't like the last time. These aren't just locals, and it's happening more often. Our lives are disrupted constantly by people from several states away. Lily's naps are interrupted, and she becomes cranky. Now, people are even waiting outside Ron's workplace. His manager told him that the owners of the company have said that it's causing problems for other employees who are having to wade through these people to get to their cars after work. Customers and business partners are blocked from entering through the front door of the company. It' a mess."

"I don't know what to say," said Heather. "I've never encountered that kind of problem."

"We can't entirely put a stop to it," said Emily. "Ron says that he is making far more money off of book sales than he makes at work."

"I doubt this will last forever," advised Heather. "It has to die down, at some point."

IT DID DIE down, temporarily. Four years later, the book was made into a movie. Ron and Emily were thrown into the national spotlight like never before. They felt that they had to move to have privacy. They had tried moving to a condo, but now they decided it was time to make another move.

"We've purchased a house in a gated community," Emily told Heather over the phone. "Our condo in Buckhead is on the market. Things have become crazy even there. Privacy was impossible when we were living next door to your father. I'm hearing that people are driving by to see the old house again."

"My father has been telling me about how the entire neighborhood has been swamped with people and reporters," said Heather. "Even he has considered moving. It just isn't the same. He told me that one person was in the yard of your old home digging up grass in the spot where the molester was held by Ron and Shawn."

"How is Shawn?" asked Emily.

"Fine," answered Heather.

"I hope your father will be at your home Saturday," said Emily.

"He plans to be here," replied Heather. "Shawn insisted on Daddy being there.

"I miss those days of playing board games on your father's dining room table," said Emily. "Your father has played such a huge roll in my life. I can't imagine how things would have turned out without him."

"He really enjoys having you drop by to see him from time to time," said Heather. "Are you sure that you'll be able to come to our house Saturday?"

"I wouldn't miss it for anything," answered Emily. "Maybe your father can bring one of his board games."

"I'll mention it to him," said Heather.

Chapter 37

Confession

JOHN HAD JUST started the coffee pot when he heard the doorbell ring. Hearing Zack paw at the back door, he let the dog outside before answering the front door.

"Do you have time for a visit?" asked Pastor Matt.

"Sure," answered John, inviting him inside.

"Is that coffee I smell?" asked Matt.

"Sure is - I just put a pot on," answered John.

Within a couple of minutes, the two men were seated on John's back porch sipping fresh coffee.

"Have you seen Emily lately?" John asked.

"I see her and Ron on Sunday mornings," answered Matt.

"I would think that you'd visit them more often," said John. "I remember frequent visits when they lived next door."

"It's a bit of an ordeal visiting at the gated community, and it's pretty far from town," explained Matt. "Plus, it's a bit of a pain getting past the gate."

"I saw them last Saturday at Heather's," stated John. "It had been a while since I had seen little Lily. She's running all over the place now. So, what's on your mind?"

"I have aspects of my life that I don't talk about," said

Matt.

"I would say that most people do," said John.

"You and I have gotten to know each other better over time, and something has been on my mind continually over the past few days," said Matt. "I would like to share with you something that I've never told anyone. I've never even told my wife. I've certainly never told anyone in my congregation."

"Why would you tell me something like that?" asked John.

"I don't know," answered Matt. "I just have a feeling that should tell someone about it, and I always feel comfortable when talking with you. Maybe God is prompting me to tell you about it."

"Why me?" asked John.

"I don't know," replied Matt. "I have a peace in my heart about telling you. Can I trust you to keep this between us, and not share this with another living soul?"

"I have the ability to keep secrets," answered John. "Whatever it is, your secret is safe with me."

"I can't believe that I'm about to tell you about this, but here goes," said Matt. "When I was fifteen and my brother was seventeen, we were shooting off fireworks on the 4th of July. A lot of people were. We had bottle rockets and roman candles. In a park down the street, we decided it would be fun to have a battle with the bottle rockets, so we were shooting them at each other. We ran out of the bottle rockets, but we weren't sure whether we should battle with the roman candles. I don't know where my brain went to, but I decided to test the roman candles against an old house. Standing about five feet from the house, I fired a roman candle at it. One of the fireballs exiting it lodged between two boards of the siding, and the house caught fire. Scared out of our minds, we ran like crazy. To make a long story short, the house burned down, and an old man living there died."

"Oh, my God," said John.

"His neighbors saw the two of us running away, and reported us to the police," continued Matt. "When we were questioned, my older brother took the blame. That incident began his criminal record. He was charged with manslaughter and spent time in juvenile detention. I went on to gain a scholarship, and his life took a very different direction."

"Why did he take the blame?" asked John.

"He is my older brother," said Matt. "He always looked out for me, and he always took responsibility for things when we were got in trouble together as kids. People see me as a successful man – a good man who lives for God and tries to help people. The public sees my brother in a different light. But if the truth be told, he is an inspiration for me. His sacrifice that night made all the difference in the world of my life. My grades were excellent, and his were poor. His hope for his life was in sports. I think he felt that his life was going down the drain after being kicked off the football team, and he didn't want mine to do the same."

"That's some story," said John. "Is it true? I've heard preachers on TV tell all kinds of stories, and I think a number of them are made up."

"For me, an oath before God is a very serious thing," said Matt. "I swear before God almighty that it's the truth."

Matt sipped his coffee in silence. He felt the cool fall breeze brush his face. After a few moments, John spoke.

"The .38 revolver wasn't just a family item," he said. "It was also kept for a special purpose."

"I'm guessing that purpose was personal," said Matt.

Silence.

"I don't know what got into me," said John. "After my wife passed away, things were never the same. I began drinking heavily."

Silence.

"I figured that if it ever came to ending things, that gun would be my choice," John said, glancing downward at the sleeping dog by his feet.

"Is that still the purpose?" questioned Matt.

"No, it was repurposed to protect my daughter and grandkids," said John. "But I think it should have a different purpose now."

"What would that be?"

"When my grandkids are a bit older, I want to use it to teach them gun safety," answered John. "If they're interested, I can use it to teach them how to shoot, clean, and oil a weapon. It needs to have a more positive use than killing. It's served that use, and it's time for it to be retired from that type of active duty."

"Retired, like you," said Matt.

"Something like that," said John.

"If you want, what you told me about it's original purpose will remain between only you and me," said Matt.

"I would like that," replied John. "Thank you."

"Thank you for sharing," said Matt. "I feel honored that you would share that with me."

"Well, you're it," said John. "I've never before told a soul, not even my partner. Then again, I've shared things with Shawn that I would never tell anyone else."

"I feel even more honored," said Matt.

Chapter 38

Sponsor

IAN CREWS SAW a familiar face when he walked out of prison. *"There's no mistaking John Rawlings,"* thought Ian.

"Do you have a place to go?" asked John.

"I do," answered Ian. "I was about to flag down a cab."

"No need," said John. "I'd be glad to take you wherever you need to go."

"What if I said that I was going to California?" asked Ian."Not happening," said John. "I was a cop, remember. You have a probation officer here in Georgia."

"I should have known that I couldn't fool you," replied Ian, wearing a sheepish grin.

"My car is right over there," said John.

As soon as the two were seated in John's car, Ian told him the address of the apartment.

"I know the area of town," said John. "What kind of job do they have lined up for you?"

"I'll be working as an accountant for a nonprofit," answered Ian.

"An accountant!" blurted John. "How in the world did you manage that?"

"I had some time on my hands while in prison," explained Ian. "So, I spent a great deal of my time earning a four-year degree in accounting. I took online courses. The prison has a deal worked out with a college."

"I had no idea something like this was funded by the government," said John.

"It wasn't entirely funded by the government," said Ian. "There was a program that was heavily funded in the 1970s, but most of that program went by the wayside in 1994. However, in 2016 the government put together Pell Grants again for those in particular prisons, but people in this facility didn't qualify until 2020. I began taking classes earlier than that."

"So, how did you begin taking classes before 2020?" asked John.

"You could take classes if you had a sponsor willing to pay the tuition and books," answered Ian.

"Who was your sponsor?" asked John.

Ian's eyes began to water.

"Promise me that you won't tell anyone," said Ian.

"Ok, I promise," said John.

"No, I'm serious," said Ian. "I really mean it, don't tell anyone – ever. He wants to keep it a secret."

"I promise," John seriously said. "I can keep a secret."

"Ron Johnson, Emily's husband," whispered Ian.

"Ron?" asked John. "He has money now, but he didn't have it back then."

"Ron paid as much of it as he could afford, but he convinced a group of people at his church to help pitch in to pay for the rest of it," said Ian.

"Ron has never mentioned a word to me about this!" blurted John.

"That's Ron Johnson," said Ian. "The man's a saint. Emily is lucky to have him."

"Wow!"

"Ron is involved in a prison ministry," said Ian. "It began with me. At first, I was suspicious of what he was trying to do. But I quickly found out that he was for real. You may have wondered why I changed. Now you know why."

"Is Emily involved?" asked John.

"No, this is Ron's thing," answered Ian. "Emily didn't even know he was coming by to visit with me. She didn't find out until Ron began drumming up financial support for me at his church."

"Is his pastor Matt Wright involved?" asked John.

"That guy has been visiting me regularly for years," answered Ian.

"Why didn't I know this until now?' asked John. "I can't believe they were doing this and not publicizing it."

"Ron isn't someone who brags about the good he does," said Ian. "The guy is amazing. He is the one who is sponsoring me to work at the nonprofit. He assured them that I would be a good employee. I owe that guy, but he doesn't see it that way."

"Ron Johnson sponsored you to work at a nonprofit?" asked John.

"He did," answered Ian. "I didn't ask him to do it. He just did it. You think Ron is a hero for his part in capturing that molester, but he is a much bigger hero than you think."

"Emily has never said a word about this," said John.

"Ron asked her not to tell anyone," said Ian. "He asked his pastor Matt not to tell people. Ron's is well known for the time he was badly cut while capturing the molester, but he takes other risks as well. He couldn't avoid the publicity about the molester, but he does most of the good he does in secret. I asked him why he keeps everything a secret, and he shared a verse out of the Bible with me."

"What verse?"

"Matthew 6:6," answered Ian. "In that verse, Jesus told his disciples this – 'But when you pray, go into your room, close the door and pray to your Father, who is unseen. Then your Father, who sees what is done in secret, will reward you'."

"You have that verse memorized?" asked John.

"I don't have many memorized, but I have that one,"

said Ian. "Ron told me that verse inspired him to do good in secret."

"So, the verse you just quoted says that God rewards what is done in secret," said John. "Ron has certainly been rewarded. The guy is loaded."

"Ron never did any of this in secret expecting money," said Ian. "The guy isn't like that. I bet if you looked at his bank account, you would see that he gives a lot of what he has to charity. I don't think I'm the only person who has benefited from Ron Johnson."

"People should know about this," said John.

"No, they shouldn't!" shouted Ian. "That's the point. Ron doesn't want people to know. He would be upset with me if it turned out that I was the cause of people knowing. Please don't tell people. Please."

"Alright,' said John. "I know how to keep a secret."

"Good," said Ian. "Please keep that one. Pease don't discuss it with him, or Emily, or his pastor Matt - nobody."

"It's obvious that Emily knows how to keep a secret," observed John.

"She loves him, and Ron deserves her," said Ian.

"It's obvious that Pastor Matt knows how to keep a secret, as well," thought John.

Chapter 39

Faith

"I CAN'T BELIEVE that I've lived to be in my sixties," thought John, as he sat on his back porch. *"How could I have ever been so stupid as to consider suicide? I'm glad I listened to my own advice. I always tell people to give it a day. I would have missed out on reestablishing things with Heather and my wonderful grandkids. I doubt Heather would have ever had Shawn for a husband. I believe God sent Zack into that bedroom just in time to rescue me, even when I had little to do with God. Thank you, God, for helping me."*

Reaching down to his dog lying at his feet, John scratched the dog behind his ears.

"Thank you, Zack," John told his dog. "We both are turning a bit gray, I'm afraid – your face and my head."

John's hand ran over the .38, now strapped in the shoulder holster he was wearing. He pulled it from the holster and felt the weight of it in his hand. Opening the chamber, he viewed all six rounds. Snapping it shut, he slid it back into the holster. John rose and entered the house. In the top drawer of his dresser in the bedroom, he found a Bible. He closed his eyes, opened it to 2 Corinthians 6:2 and read the verse aloud.

For he says, "In the time of my favor I heard you, and in the day of salvation I helped you." I tell you, now is the time of God's favor, now is the day of salvation.

John placed the Bible on top of the dresser and dropped to his knees beside his bed. He called out to God.

"Oh, God! I am so sorry for ignoring you," he began. "I should have squared things away with you while Sharon was still living. I should have listened to her. What a stupid idiot I've been! I always tell people to give it a day. I should have never put you off for even a day. Thank you so much for my life. Thank you so much for saving my life. Please, God, I ask you to save my soul."

John wept for close to ten minutes and afterwards a sensation of peace came over him. He sensed the Almighty like never before. There on his knees, his soul bathed in the presence of God.

He rose from his position at the bed and removed the .38 from the shoulder holster. He retrieved a box of rounds from the bottom drawer in his nightstand. Unloading the gun, he slipped each round back in the box. John placed the .38 back in the gun case and locked it with the key. After placing the gun case and box on a shelf in his closet, he removed the shoulder holster and hung it on a nail in the closet. He raised his eyes to view the gun case on the shelf.

"Old friend, like me, you are now in retirement," he spoke to the gun resting in the case. "Maybe I'll pass you down to my grandson Josh as a family heirloom. You have earned your rest. Like me, you're an antique, even much older. You've served me well, and it was by the grace of God that I didn't cause you to be the end of me. Sleep now in peace."

I thought I would feel a bit naked after being unarmed, but I don't. Maybe it's because I know that I have the nine-millimeter in the other safe, but I don't think that's it. I no longer feel that I'm on duty. Shawn is now there to protect

Heather and the kids. If something was to ever happen to me, I'm ready to meet my God and my wife Sharon. It's like a load has been lifted. I've never felt so free.

John returned to the back porch. He knelt beside his sleeping dog, and stroked Zack's head. After several minutes, he stood. He felt his right knee pop and both knees ached.

"Zack, maybe I shouldn't have done that," he mumbled. "Getting back up wasn't any fun, at all. My knees aren't happy with me after kneeling so long by the bedside. Well, it was worth it. It was worth every minute of aching joints and popping in the knees. I bet you're feeling it now too."

The leaves in the backyard had fallen from the trees, allowing more sunlight to spill across the grass. He walked out into the sunlight. The cool winter air felt wonderful on his face. John took off his jacket and dropped on the yard, then unbuttoned his shirt and removed it from his body. A mix of warm sunlight and cool air made him feel alive. John slowly turned in circles, coating all sides of uncovered skin with sunlight. He stopped, eyes closed, facing the sun. He felt Zack's head rub against his leg. Reaching with one hand to pick up his shirt from the grass, he reached out with the other to touch his dog.

"It's good to be alive," he told Zack. "It really is good to be alive."

He shook the dead grass from the shirt and put it back on. Looking back at his house, he took a deep breath.

"This is where the best things have happened," he told Zack. "This is where I lived with the love of my life, and we raised our kids. This was it. It wasn't the exiting times in the field chasing thieves and killers. It wasn't nights out with the guys. It was here – right there, in that home."

John retrieved his discarded jacket. He reached down and patted the dog's back. Straightening up, he began talking to Zack again.

"This place is also where God moved you to come into

my bedroom at the right time to save me from doing something stupid. You're the hero. You were at the right place at the right time, and you did what was needed. There are dogs on the force who are heroes. You're not trained like them, and you're not on the force. But you are my hero. You're the one who helped me live long enough to turn to God. I thought Shawn was my best friend, and he has done a lot for me. Shawn has been there as my partner, and he is there for Heather and the kids. But you have been there too. It looks like you were smart enough to listen to God when I was too dumb to listen to Him. Thank you, buddy."

The retired detective and his dog returned inside the house. John opened the refrigerator and found nothing that he wanted. After opening almost every cabinet, he turned to Zack and said," "I'm getting hungry, old boy. How about you? I don't see anything here that I want, and I'm sure you're tired of dogfood. What do you say about me ordering a pizza to be delivered? Does that sound good?"

Zack wagged his tail.

"OK, then it's a deal," John told his dog. "I'll order double meat and double cheese! We'll split it."

John never again placed that Bible back in the top drawer of his dresser. From that day on, for the rest of his life, it was left on top of the dresser and John read from it each morning and each evening before sleeping.

Chapter 40

Illness

"MY NECK HURTS, Mommy," Lily told her mother.

"Where?" asked Emily.

Lily pointed to the spot. Two weeks later, the child began to spill things more often at the dinner table. Seeing no improvement during the third week, Emily decided to take Lily to their family doctor.

"I'm going to refer you to a neurologist," said the doctor, handing Emily the name and address of the specialist. "I'm going to set up an appointment for Lily with Dr. Vandenhausen. I would place my child under his care if he was having these symptoms."

After examining Lily during the first visit, the neurologist ordered an MRI for Lily. The scan showed a tumor on Lily's spinal cord.

"Lily needs surgery," said Dr. Vandenhausen. "If the tumor expands and creates compression within the spinal cord, your child may experience decreased motor skills. I believe this is already happening, so surgery should be done as soon as possible. I am scheduling the surgery for Thursday of next week."

ON THE MORNING of Lily's surgery, Emily was worried

sick. Turning to Ron, she said, "We have more money today than I could have ever imaged four years ago, but all the wealth in the world can't cure Lily's sickness."

She pulled out her cell phone and informed pastor Matt of Lily's condition.

"I'll begin praying now, and I am on my way to your home," Matt said.

"Thank you, so much," replied Emily, almost in tears.

Next, she called Heather, who told her that she would also be in prayer, but that she was unable to leave class at Georgia State to spend more time in conversation.

"I promise I will get back to you as soon as I can," said Heather.

Though comforted by the presence of her husband Ron and the prayers of Matt and Heather, Emily still felt powerless. Tears flowed down her face and her hands trembled.

ON THE MORNING of Lily's surgery, Emily dialed another number on her cell phone.

"John," Emily spoke.

"Emily, it's so good to hear from you," said John. "How are things."

"Lily is about to have surgery this morning," Emily stammered. "She has a tumor on her spinal cord."

"Oh, no!" blurted John. "When did all of this happen?"

Emily explained about Lily's neck pain and loss of coordination. She told him about the findings of Dr. Vandenhausen.

"She's in the hands of the neurosurgeon and in the hands of God, right now," said Emily.

"I'll begin praying as soon as we get off this call," said John.

"Thank you, John," said Emily.

"Let me share a scripture with you," John replied. "It's

meant a lot to me, and maybe it can of help for you too. Hold on, let me look it up. It's 2 Corinthians 6:2."

"Thank you," said Emily.

"For he says, 'In the time of my favor I heard you, and in the day of salvation I helped you.' I tell you, now is the time of God's favor, now is the day of salvation,'" read John. "I believe God steps in at our hour of need, on the day that we need Him."

Suddenly, an unexplained peace came over Emily. For the first time in days, her hands and voice became steady.

"Thank you, John," she said. "I think I needed that verse."

"I hope you called Pastor Matt," John said.

"He is to meet us at the hospital," replied Emily. "John, I am so grateful for you. You have always been there when I needed you. Thank you."

"I just have happened to be at the right place at the right time," said John. "Nothing more."

"It's more than that," said Emily. "You're more than a friend to me. You're like family. I mean it. It feels like you are my grandfather, or something like that."

"Ok, I'm old – but not that old!" said John. "I'm not ninety."

"I know," said Emily. "It just feels that way. Both of my grandfathers have passed away, and you're a little older than my parents. It's true that you're not old enough to be my grandfather, but I feel that way about you when I'm around you and when I talk with you. I love you like family."

"I love you too, Emily," said John. "I can call Heather, if you want. I'm sure she would want to know about Lily."

"I've already called her," said Emily. "I called her just before calling you."

"Good. Please let me know how the surgery goes."

"I will," said Emily.

"God is able to take care of Lily," said John. "She's special."

"Thanks for being there," Emily said, ending the call.

"You seem to be feeling better," Ron told his wife after her call to John ended.

"I am," said Emily. "There is something settling about talking with John."

"Maybe I should call him," said Ron. "I'm anything but settled."

Emily laughed. The tension within her had passed.

"I told John that he was like a grandfather to me," said Emily. "But nobody on this earth is like you in my life. I am so thankful for you."

"I'm thankful that I found you," said Ron. "I love you."

"If there is such a thing as a soulmate, you're the one," said Emily. "You are my man. You are my best friend. I love you like I love no one else in this world."

Lily was taken for surgery. Emily and Ron were shown the waiting room, and they seated themselves there. Emily rested her head on Ron's shoulder. Within minutes, Pastor Matt was with them in the waiting room.

"Any word yet?" asked Matt.

"No, she was just taken into surgery," said Ron.

"How are you holding up?" Matt asked Emily.

"Surprisingly well," she answered.

"She just got off phone with John," said Ron. "That guy has a calming effect on her, for some reason."

"John is certainly an interesting guy," stated Matt.

"Thanks for being here," said Ron.

"I'm no John, but want to always be there for you two," said Matt.

"Thank you, for being here," said Emily.

"Would you let me lead us in prayer?" asked Matt.

"Please," answered Emily.

"WE WERE ABLE to get all of the tumor," Dr. Vandenhausen told Ron and Emily, as he met them in the waiting room.

"Thank God!" shouted Emily. "And thank you so much, Doctor Vandenhausen. Thank you so much!"

Emily gave the doctor a hug, and then turned to bury her face in Ron's chest. Pastor Matt stood silently behind the couple.

"Thank you so much," said Ron, extending his hand to Dr. Vandenhausen.

"Lily's recovery isn't going to be easy," said the doctor, taking Ron's hand. "The tumor is gone, but it will take time for her to gain coordination and strength in her hands and arms. She'll have to have physical therapy for about two months."

"They give physical therapy to children?" asked Ron.

"Yes, they do," answered the doctor. "It's doing to be difficult for Lily, but she must persevere."

"We'll see to it," said Ron.

"I'll make the arrangements with physical therapy and get back with you," promised Dr. Vandenhausen.

"LILY IS SO sore after therapy," said Emily, during her family's visit with Heather and Shawn.

Shawn moved his huge frame to kneel next to the chair where Lily was sitting. Looking directly into Lily's eyes and holding her sweet face between his powerful hands.

"You can do this," Shawn told Lily. "I know it hurts, but I know you can do this. Where does it hurt?"

"Here," answered Lily, pointing to her arms and hands.

"You are so good, and the hurt is your body trying to push the bad out," said Shawn. "Keep working at the therapy until you've pushed all the bad out. Then you will feel a lot better. Can you do that?"

"Is that how you became to big and strong?" asked Lily. "Did you work until all the bad got out?"

"I was born to be bigger than some, but yes – I do work

to be strong," answered Shawn.

"I'll work to be strong," promised Lily.

"Even if it hurts?" asked Shawn.

"Especially when it hurts," answered Lily. "I want all the bad to go out."

Shawn kissed the little girl on the forehead. "I know you will," Shawn said.

Over the next two months, Shawn visited Lily twice per week. She enjoyed periodic visits by John and pastor Matt, but her eyes would light up when she saw Shawn come through the door of her home twice each week. The two developed a bond.

"Do you have time to come to the house for coffee?" John asked Matt, after the two ended a visit to see Lily.

"Absolutely," said Matt. "You make a great cup of joe."

"Great," I'll get the pot started as soon as I get home," said John.

"Since both of us seem to visit Lily on the same days, how about if I pick you up to visit her on Mondays, Wednesdays, and Fridays?" Matt asked John. "I love your coffee. When bring you home, I'll hang around a bit for a cup or two. The church will see that as visitation, but it will give me an excuse to come by three days each week for coffee."

"It's a deal," said John. "You supply the gas for the visit, and I'll supply the coffee."

DURING THE TWO months of Lily's therapy, she became stronger and pain free. Lily would squeal and run to be lifted into Shawn's powerful arms when he visited, and John and Matt became the best of friends. In the process, John agreed to join Matt's church as a member.

Lily's struggle brought everyone together again. John, Matt, Heather, Shawn, Charlotte and Josh begin to meet at Ron and Emily's home for supper and board games on every other Saturday night and supper and prayer time on the other Saturday nights.

"I love seeing Lily and everyone else for board games, but I'm not sure that I belong in a prayer session on those other Saturday nights," Shawn told Heather. "That's great for the rest of them, but our family doesn't go to that church."

"I know," agreed Heather. "I feel a bit awkward, as well."

"I want to do what I can to encourage Lily, and I like the people," said Shawn. "John is like a second father to me, but I feel awkward while sitting there when the rest of them are praying. It doesn't feel right."

"They've never pressured us to join in prayer," said Heather. "It's another chance for Charlotte and Josh to be with their grandfather. They became close when we lived with him. I don't want them to drift away. They need him."

"OK, you're right," said Shawn. "It's a great time for the kids to be with John. They don't seem to mind the prayer times. I guess it's just me. And you're right about them not pressuring me to be all holy and all. You're right, we should continue meeting with them."

"What did you just say about me?" asked Heather.

"What?" blurted Shawn. "What are you talking about?"

"You said something about me," said Heather. "I think the word you used began with an R. Did you say that I was right?"

"Ok, don't let it go to your head," said Shawn.

"No, you said it three times," said Heather. "I counted them. You said that I was right three times in one conversation. That means you're emphasizing that fact. Thank you. I'm glad that you've finally seen the light!"

"I'll tell you what I want to see," Shawn said, lifting his wife off the floor and into his arms.

"I want to see your nude body on that bed upstairs," he whispered in her ear.

"You do?" she asked, while kissing his neck. Shawn quickly carried Heather upstairs.

Chapter 41

Larry

"I'M GOING TO check the mail," Heather called out to Shawn.

I'm going out front as well," replied Shawn. "I need to check on the maple tree I planted last week."

As Heather reached to open the mailbox, she heard a speeding car suddenly come to a stop beside her. As she turned toward it, a man jumped out from the front seat and grabbed her. Heather began screaming.

"Shut up!" the man yelled at her, struggling to pull her toward his car.

Heather struggled and continued to scream, and the man sent a heavy blow to her face with his fist. She dropped to the ground unconscious. The man opened a rear door to his car. Just as he turned to retrieve his helpless victim, he was sent reeling by Shawn's huge fist. Shawn continued to pound the man until he lay unconscious beside his car. Shawn lifted the man against the car and continued to beat him. The man's bloody face was almost unrecognizable. Hearing his wife moan, Shawn dropped the attacker to the ground.

"Are you alright?" Shawn asked Heather, dropping to one knee beside her.

"I don't know," answered Heather.

"It was a good thing I was outside," said Shawn. "You

were attacked as you checked the mailbox."

"In our neighborhood?" stammered Heather, dazed.

"Looks like it," replied Shawn, still knelling beside his wife. "Don't try to stand yet. I'm calling an ambulance."

Shawn quickly called for an ambulance and then called the police at his station.

"My face hurts," said Heather, raising a hand to her cheek. The skin over her left cheekbone was split open from the blow, and her face was beginning to swell.

"That guy hit you pretty hard," said Shawn.

"What if he comes back?" asked Heather.

"He's not going anywhere soon," replied Shawn, turning to point to the unconscious bloodied man lying beside the running car.

"Oh," moaned Heather, as she tried to lift her head to see the man.

"I don't think he saw me standing by the maple tree," said Shawn. "I think he was focused only on you."

"Who is he?" questioned Heather.

"I don't know, but if I'm sure we'll find out," answered Shawn.

Within minutes, paramedics were examining Heather, and three patrol cars were on the scene. Those treating Heather determined that it would be best to take her to the emergency room at a nearby hospital for scans to see if there was internal damage.

"Good God!" said another paramedic who was examining the man beside the car. "This guy is messed up pretty bad."

A second ambulance was called for the attacker. A uniformed officer reached into the man's back pocket and retrieved a wallet.

"Larry Kaufman," the patrolman said. "Anybody here familiar with a Larry Kaufman?" he asked, looking directly at Shawn.

"No," said Shawn, as he walked beside the paramedics

who were moving his wife toward the ambulance. "I've never heard of him."

"Looks like he's still alive," said the patrolman. "Were you the one who beat the living crap out this guy?"

"You bet," answered Shawn.

"We'll need to question you and your wife," the patrolman said.

Shawn turned and flashed his badge at the patrolman and a look that could kill. "Not now!" bellowed Shawn, in his deep booming voice. "I'm following my wife to the hospital. We'll talk later. You're welcome to follow me there, but my concern is my wife. This guy attacked her as she was opening our mailbox. You bet I beat the hell out him!"

"Alright detective, I'll follow you there," said the officer. "That's enough of a statement to begin with. I'll be right behind you, and I'll get a complete statement there."

"Thank you," replied Shawn.

While Shawn and the patrolman sat in the ER waiting room, Shawn gave a complete statement.

"I'll still need to talk with your wife, when she is available," said the patrolman.

"Absolutely," replied Shawn.

After about an hour, a doctor met Shawn in the waiting room. Shawn stood and moved quickly to join him.

"The scans showed no broken bones in Heather's face, and we found no brain trauma," said the doctor. She needs rest. Your wife gave me the location of the pharmacy that you use, and I've called in prescriptions for pain and an antibiotic. She's going to be sore, but she should heal well with the ten stitches I tightly placed. I believe her scarring will be minimal."

"Thank you so much," said Shawn, placing his huge hand on the doctor's shoulder.

As the doctor walked away, Shawn examined the stitches in his wife's face. Her eye was turning black, and her cheek beneath the stitches was badly swollen.

"I look like Frankenstein," Heather said.

"You'll heal," said Shawn. "It will just take some time."

"What an afternoon," said Heather.

"Come on," said Shawn. "We need to drop by the pharmacy on the way home. I want you to be as pain free as possible."

"I was given something for pain already," said Heather. "They numbed up my check before sewing me up."

"Let's get that prescription filled and get you home," said Shawn.

"I want to stop for a chocolate shake before the pharmacy," requested Heather.

"Shake first, and pharmacy next," promised Shawn.

The shake was finished by the time Heather and Shawn arrived back home. She objected to Shawn's suggestion to go to bed and positioned herself instead on the couch under a blanket. In less than an hour of returning to the house, a patrolman knocked on the front door.

"I need your wife's statement," explained the officer, as Shawn ushered him inside. "How is she?"

"She's on the couch," replied Shawn.

The officer apologized for disturbing her rest, and Heather told him that she understood. After giving him the details she remembered, the officer provided the two of them with information on the assailant.

"Heather, Larry Kaufman was arrested by your father twenty-five years ago," the officer began. "He was recently paroled from prison because of good behavior. The guy is now fifty-four years old, but he is exceptionally strong from daily workouts in prison. Records show that he has never killed anyone, but your father arrested and charged him for beating a woman badly, to the point of disfiguring her. It seems he has a thing for beating women."

"What a piece of crap!" blurted Shawn. "Any guy that beats women is a wuss! I hope they don't let him out this time."

"He'll be in the hospital for a while," said the patrolman. "He's conscious, but he's not yet talking. I'm guessing he attacked you Heather because he wants revenge on your father for putting him away."

"Sometimes guys want revenge," agreed Shawn. "But it really takes a low life to go after a cop's family."

A few days later, Shawn learned more. While planning revenge and scoping out John's home, Larry Hickman spotted Heather while she was visiting her father. Hickman decided she would be an easier target. As she left her father's house later that day, he followed her from a distance to her home in Cobb County. For days he drove by the house, looking for opportunities. That day, he saw her at the mailbox and decided to grab Heather and take her. Larry never saw Shawn, who was standing at the maple tree.

Two months later, both Shawn and Heather testified at his trial. Because of his record, Larry was given twenty more years in prison with no chance of parole.

Walking from the courtroom, Heather turned to her husband. "I wonder how many more people who were arrested by my father want revenge."

"Unfortunately, there is no way of knowing," replied Shawn. "It's part of the job. There are serious stresses on people in law enforcement, and the stresses aren't limited to cops. Some of these guys decide to go after lawyers when they get out."

"Growing up, I never saw that part of my father's career," said Heather.

"I'm sure he hid a lot of things from you," said Shawn. "I kid doesn't need those stresses. It's possible that he confided in your mother about some of those things, but most cops don't want to lay much of that on a wife. Things like that can contribute to stress in a marriage. A number of cops end up divorced."

"You're not going to get rid of me that easy," said

Heather. "I grew up in a cop family. Even though my father didn't often discuss cases with the family, I learned to know when he was under a lot of stress. We hung tight. Our family was a team. You and I are a team, the kids too. I'm not going anywhere."

"You're the best," Shawn said, taking Heather into his arms.

There's another aspect of growing up in a cop family," said Heather.

"What's that?" asked Shawn.

"My father taught me to shoot from an early age," answered Heather. "If you ever try to run out on me, I'm a crack shot."

"I saw that when I took you to the range," said Shawn. "I know better than to cross you."

"You had better be afraid," she said.

"What can I do to keep you happy?" Shawn asked, taking her into his powerful arms.

"I'll let you know later tonight," answered Heather.

"Yes, Ma'am," replied Shawn.

Chapter 42

Crisis

TIRED AFTER A trying day of detective work, Shawn finished his last report on a case. He had already sent his partner Caitlin home an hour before, promising her that he would handle finalizing the report. Shawn had earlier called Heather to warn her that he would be coming home late. Now, he placed a second call.

"Ok, I'm finally done and on my way home," he told his wife.

"It's dark, and the kids have already eaten supper," Heather said.

"Do you want me to pick something up for us on the way home?" asked Shawn.

"No, I'll heat up the supper I prepared for them," she replied. "There's plenty, and it's late enough already."

"Sorry about the late work," apologized Shawn for the second time.

"It happens sometimes. Just come on home."

Shawn rubbed his eyes. He grabbed his jacket before turning off the light on his desk.

"Are you leaving so soon?" poked a second shift officer, James Golden, seeing Shawn walking toward the back door of the station.

"I've had enough," Shawn replied. "Good night."

Good night," he heard Golden reply as he stepped out the back door.

The partially lit station parking lot reserved for law enforcement was quiet. Shawn stood momentarily on the steps before remembering that his car was parked near the back of the lot. He didn't see the car at first, but then spotted it in an exceptionally poorly lighted area. Shawn wearily walked over to it and opened the front driver side door. Suddenly there was a sharp pain from the side of his head, and everything went black.

Because there was so little activity in that parking lot at night, Shawn lay bleeding profusely from his head for two hours. His chance of being seen was also hampered by his car being parked in the poorly lit back area of the lot. Patrolman Golden had stepped onto the back steps to smoke a cigarette and while lighting up he heard the sound of a cell phone ringing in the lot. That's when spotted Shawn lying beside his car.

"Are you OK," the patrolman asked, nearing Shawn.

Silence.

"Oh shit!" blurted officer Golden, tossing the cigarette onto the asphalt.

He quickly notified the desk inside the station.

"Officer down!" Golden yelled. "Officer down in the back parking lot! Call an ambulance and get your asses out here! Detective Shawn Stone is hurt pretty bad."

Careful not to move Shawn, the patrolman reached into the large detective's jacket to search for the cell phone he had heard. Finding the most recent calls, he dialed the number. The screen on the phone displayed the name Heather.

"Oh God, it's his wife," thought the patrolman.

"Shawn?" answered Heather.

"This is patrolman James Golden," said the officer. "I believe you're the wife of Shawn Stone?"

"Yes, is Shawn alright?" she asked.

"Ms. Stone, he's been hurt, and an ambulance is on the way," explained Golden. "As soon as I'm informed as to which hospital he will be taken to, I will let you know.

"What happened?" asked Heather, now trembling.

"It looks like somebody attacked him from as he was getting into his car," answered Golden. "I've checked and he's breathing, but unconscious. The ambulance will be here soon."

"Where is he now?" asked Heather.

"Shawn was attacked in the back parking lot of the station," answered Golden. "I'm here with him. Don't come to the station. I believe the ambulance will have taken him before you get here. Just be ready when I call back with the location of the hospital."

"I will," said Heather. "Thank you."

In a state of shock, Heather fumbled at a coat in her hall closet. She gathered her purse and placed the keys to the Telluride in her coat pocket. She quickly called her father.

"Daddy, Shawn has been hurt badly," she told him.

"Where are you?" asked John.

"At home, waiting for them to let me know which hospital he'll be taken to," she answered. "He was attacked in the back parking lot of the station. A patrolman found him."

"Damn!" blurted John. "I told those idiots that the lighting in that parking lot was crap two years ago, and the security cameras don't adequately cover that area. As soon as you hear, let me know where they are taking him, and I'll join you at the hospital."

"Would you please instead come to the house and stay with the kids?" asked Heather.

"Of course," answered John. "I'm on my way now."

Heather immediately called Emily and told her about the situation. "Please pray," Heather asked her friend.

"I will, and I will call pastor Matt," replied Emily.

"Thank you," said Heather.

She awoke Charlotte and Josh. She told them that their father had been hurt and was being taken to a hospital and that their grandfather was on his way to stay with them. Within five minutes of telling her children, she heard from patrolman Golden that Shawn was in route to Grady Memorial Hospital. She quickly informed her father, as she got into the SUV.

WHEN HEATHER ARRIVED at the hospital emergency room, she was told that Shawn was alive but severely injured. One side of his head was slightly caved in.

"Your husband has been badly beaten in the head repeatedly with a heavy object," said the doctor. "Scans show a number of bone fragments dangerously near his brain."

"Can I see him?" asked Heather.

"He's currently in the hands of a trauma team," answered the doctor. "I'll keep you informed. You can see him, once it's been determined that he's in a stabilized condition. I know that this is difficult, but I'll have to ask you to wait in this waiting room for now."

"Is Shawn going to be alright?" asked Heather, wide eyed.

"It's honestly too early to tell," answered the doctor. "He needs neural surgery to remove the bone fragments, and soon."

"I want Dr. Vandenhausen to perform the surgery," said Heather. "Please contact Dr. Vandenhausen. He successfully helped the child of a friend."

"I'll do what I can to contact him," promised the doctor. "But your husband needs to have the surgery done soon. We have great neural surgeons on call, and we will have one of them come in."

Heather nervously took a seat in the waiting room. She fumbled around with a couple of magazines, but she found it impossible to think of anything other than Shawn. Within thirty minutes, Emily and pastor Matt joined her.

"How is he?" asked Emily.

"Not good," answered Heather, her eyes filling with tears.

"Would you like us to pray?" asked pastor Matt.

"Please," stammered Heather through trembling lips.

The three of them joined hands in prayer. *"Pease God, please save Shawn's life,"* Heather silently pled. *"Please don't take my husband."* Two hours later, the neurosurgeon came out to the waiting room.

"We believe your husband will live, but he is going to have a long recovery," said the doctor. "There has been damage to the Primary Motor Cortex of his brain, but only time will tell of the extent."

"What does that mean?" asked Heather.

"His motor functions may be affected," answered the doctor. "He may have trouble walking, but it's hard to determine at this point."

"But Shawn's going to live?" Heather asked.

"We believe so," answered the doctor.

"When will he be going to a room?" Heather asked.

"He'll be in ICU for some time," answered the doctor. "We believe the bone fragments have been removed, but your husband may need additional surgeries. There's a good chance we will need to put a plate in his head, but getting him stable is our primary concern at this time. I suggest that you go to the ICU waiting room."

"Thank you, doctor," said Heather.

All three of them went to the ICU waiting room. Heather called John, who informed her that he planned to stay the night with the kids.

AFTER TWO MORE surgeries to remove bone fragments and to place a plate in Shawn's skull, he and Heather were told that he would require months of physical therapy. Shawn's arms were mostly functional, but he lost a significant degree of motor control of his legs. The physical therapy began while he was still in the hospital. Shawn quickly regained his coordination and strength in his arms and hands. He was fitted with leg braces, given forearm crutches and taught how to walk using that equipment. Shawn was released after three weeks in the hospital, but he was informed that he should expect months of physical therapy. He and Heather were told that the chances were slim that he would ever regain the full use of his legs.

Chapter 43

Severance

"PHYSICAL THERAPY IS brutal," Shawn told his wife. "I understand the value of it. I know that my mobility depends on it, but physical therapists have no mercy."

"I never knew I married a whiner," replied Heather.

"You wouldn't last two sessions," said Shawn, wearing a grin.

"I know it has to be frustrating," said Heather, wrapping her arms around Shawn's neck as he sat at the kitchen table.

"I'm sorry that I'm not the man you married," said Shawn.

"Oh, you are the man I married," said Heather. "You've just become whinier."

"You know what I mean," said Shawn. "My legs are pitiful. I'm a cripple. You deserve more than a cripple."

"I'm so thankful to have you still alive," said Heather.

"Well, if you decide to trade me in on a working model of a husband, I wouldn't blame you."

"Oh, I still have a working model," Heather said, as she moved her hand up the brace covering his leg and stopping her hand inside the thigh of her husband.

"You know and I know that it's not the same," said Shawn.

"I like being on top," she whispered in his ear. "I have

you right where I want you."

"You'd better watch that hand of yours. We don't have time for that. You need to get me to the station for the last time."

"Soon you'll be able to drive yourself," said Heather, removing her hand. "Your car will be fitted with hand controls next week. Then you can visit your buddies at the station anytime you want."

"It won't be the same," said Shawn. "After today, I'll no longer be a detective. My career in law enforcement ends today."

"I'm so proud of you," said Heather.

"I'll be useless," said Shawn. "I never planned on early retirement. Who wants a crippled ex-cop? I have no idea as to how I'll bring income for this family."

"Don't worry about that for a while," said Heather. "Just enjoy your retirement ceremony today at the station, and then enjoy the party we have planned for you tonight with our friends and family."

SHAWN STRUGGLED IN pain as he slowly made his way up to receive his retirement plaque at the station. He had become able to walk with the aid of his leg braces and forearm crutches, but the pace was excruciating and slow. He had regained coordination and strength in his arms and hands, but continued to have difficulties walking. Shawn focused intently on each step, making sure that he didn't fall. Heather patiently walked behind him. Standing before Captain Don Evans, he awkwardly extended his hand. The station erupted in applause as Shawn and Heather were seated in the front of the room. Captain Evans made mention of several heroic deeds performed by Shawn over the years. At the end of the speech, Caitlin brought Shawn a plaque and a box of well-wishing cards signed by officers. Again, applause thundered.

"Caitlin, I have something else that I want you to present to your partner," said Evans, as he handed her an envelope. "Please present this to Shawn."

"I have no idea as to what's in the envelope," she said, handing it to Shawn.

"Thanks," Shawn replied.

"Are you going to open it?" Caitlin asked.

"I'm not sure whether I'm supposed to open it right now," Shawn replied.

"Go ahead, open it," advised Evans, smiling.

"Well, OK," replied Shawn, as he opened it.

"Oh, my God!" Shawn blurted.

"You deserve it," said Evans. "It's both the most and the least we could do."

"Well, what is it?" asked Caitlin. "You big lug."

"It's a severance check for two hundred thousand dollars," Shawn answered.

The entire station erupted again. Everyone but Shawn was on their feet. The applause lasted for a full minute, until Shawn motioned for them to stop.

"Thank you, so much," Shawn said. "This is going to make a huge difference."

THAT EVENING, HEATHER welcomed her father, pastor Matt and Emily's family into her home for Shawn's retirement party. He wanted it to be small. Heather's children and Lily were seated first, then the adults.

"I told you that I needed a table that seated ten," Heather told her husband, as he awkwardly took his seat at the head of the table.

John sat at the other end of the table, and a large cake was positioned in front of Shawn. Once everyone was seated, John asked if pastor Matt would lead the group in prayer.

"Dear God, we want to thank you for the life of Shawn

Stone," pastor Matt began. "We pray for his continued health and healing, and we pray that you bless the fellowship that we enjoy here tonight. We also ask that you bless us as we partake of this fine cake. Amen."

"Amen, dig in," added Josh. "I want a piece with a lot of icing."

"Just you cool it, young man," advised his mother. "There's plenty of cake for everyone."

After everyone was given a piece of cake, each person gave a short statement regarding Shawn. When it came down to Lily's turn, she hopped off her chair and stood beside Shawn while holding her arms up.

"Can you still pick me up?" she asked.

"Sure," answered Shawn, picking her up and placing her in his lap.

"Mama said that you're having a hard time in physical therapy," she began.

"Oh, I'm fine," Shawn replied. "I just complain too much."

"No, you don't," Lily said, placing a small hand on each side of his face. "It's OK if you spill your drink once in a while. When I had therapy, I did that a lot. You can do anything that you put your mind to. I love you, but you have to work to become strong. You have to work at it until all the bad goes out of your body."

"I think I've heard those words before," said Shawn.

"YOU said those words, silly," teased Lily. "You have to work hard."

"Even if it hurts?" asked Shawn.

"For sure," said Lily. "The hurt means that the bad stuff is leaving your body. I want you to be heathy and strong."

Shawn pulled her close, wrapping his huge arms around the tiny girl. "Thank you, for reminding me about that," he told her. "It's a deal."

"Ok, then let's eat cake!" she shouted.

After cake was consumed, the children went upstairs to

play as adults enjoyed coffee around the table.

"Do you think you were attacked by someone you once arrested?" asked pastor Matt.

"It's possible," answered Shawn. "That happens more often than people think. Heather has been attacked twice by guys arrested by her father."

"Don't remind me," said John. "I can't tell how that makes me feel."

"I'm fine now, Daddy," said Heather. "Those two will never bother anyone again."

"I heard that you were given a substantial severance package," said Ron.

"Where did you hear that?" asked Shawn, glancing over at Heather.

"I told Emily," confessed Heather. "I had to tell someone!"

"Good grief," mumbled Shawn. "Who else has heard about this?"

Every adult at the table raised a hand.

"You told everybody?" asked Shawn.

"Well, not everybody," answered Heather.

"Who didn't you tell?" asked Shawn.

"I didn't tell my students at the university," replied Heather.

"Well, I'm certainly finished with detective work," said Shawn.

"Seems like I remember someone advising me to do something after I retired," said John. "You may want to take your own advice."

"If you haven't noticed, I'm a cripple now," Shawn told his father-in-law.

"You're not dead," said John. "If you want to, you could set up a private investigation business with that kind of money."

"And do what?" asked Shawn.

"You know as well as I do that all investigation isn't

done with your feet pounding the pavement," answered John. "There is a lot you can do online and by making phone calls. You could hire a couple of investigation grunts to do the legwork."

"Like you?" asked Shawn. "You want to work for me?"

"I can think of worse people to work for," answered John. "I wouldn't mind doing something part time – like some consulting work for you. I know other retired cops who are in far better physical shape than me. Hire a couple of them."

"That doesn't sound bad," added Ron. "That's not my field, but it doesn't sound like a bad deal for you."

"Your years of experience would be valuable," said pastor Matt. "Don't sell yourself short."

"You could set your own hours, and be your own boss," said John.

"Hey, Shawn already has a boss," joked Heather.

"Well, Mother, may I?" poked Shawn.

"Yes, you may," replied Heather.

"I think it's a great idea," said Emily. "You're a natural. Plus, I would bet that a number of female detectives might be interested in working a day job or even part time, so they can be home more with their kids. Instead of two full-time employees, you might consider four part-time investigators."

"I doubt many people would want to leave the force to work in the private sector," said Shawn. "They wouldn't want to give up a pension for this."

"You don't know that," said John. "Some on the force may be married to someone with great retirement benefits, and don't need the pension. Some cops might want to moonlight on the weekends to earn extra money."

"You could start off small," said Heather. "You might start off working out of our house in the beginning."

"You want me to turn our home into an investigation business?" asked Shawn.

"Not permanently," answered Heather.

"She has a point," said John. "You could work mainly out of the house until your health improves. Later, you could rent a small office space for a couple of part-time investigators. You could see if the business expands into something bigger. You wouldn't have to invest all of the severance money at once. Think about it."

"Heather and I would have to think about this for a time," said Shawn.

"OK, let me think about it," said Heather, placing a finger against her chin. "OK, now I've thought about it and I'm good with it. It's your call. I think it's a great idea."

SHAWN'S CAR WAS fitted with hand controls, and he began to drive his car. He told Heather that he was just practicing his skills with the new controls, but Shawn was also looking for a small building in which to begin a private investigation agency.

Chapter 44

Promotion

AS HEATHER EAGERLY opened the letter from Georgia State University, she heard Shawn enter the back door of their Cobb County Georgia home. Shawn kept weights used to strengthen his upper body there. Like John, Shawn enjoyed relaxing on his family's back porch. Away from the city of Atlanta, the peaceful setting west of the Chattahoochee River provided a haven for her family.

"I'm thinking about building a privacy fence in the back yard for the kids," said Shawn. "I certainly have the money now."

"What about the idea of starting a private investigation agency?" asked Heather.

"I'm still considering it," answered Shawn. "The fence will only slightly dip into that money. It's relatively safe here, but I can't forget you being attacked out front. The kids could freely play in the back yard without us having to watch them so closely. Our neighbors are great, but there are really crazy and violent people in the city of Atlanta. There is nothing to prevent them from driving out here."

"You have a point, but are you sure you want to spend your money on that?" asked Heather. "I mean, Charotte is a teenager and Josh is eleven. I don't see them playing often in the backyard now."

"Well, what about when they leave for college?" asked Shawn.

"What?"

"When the kids leave for college, you could be nude in the backyard if we had a privacy fence."

"Is this what you're thinking about?" Heather asked, punching Shawn on his broad shoulder.

"You're really violent," he replied. "I didn't think you where the type to beat a cripple."

"You certainly don't act like a cripple."

"What's in that letter you're holding?" asked Shawn.

"I was just about to read it. It's from the university, and I hope it's what I think it is."

Heather paused the conversation as she read over the letter. Suddenly, her eyes brightened.

"Good news?" asked Shawn.

"I've been granted tenure at the university," said Heather. "I've been awarded the position of full professor!"

"Great! Congratulations!

"It comes with a significant increase in my salary," said Heather.

"It shouldn't have taken them six years to figure out that you deserve it," said Shawn. "Back to the earlier subject we discussed, would you consider being nude in the back yard if I put up a privacy fence?"

"You should know that people have drones now," replied Heather. "There isn't much privacy anymore."

"You're right about that, but a guy can dream – right?"

"You need to make yourself busier," said Heather. "You need something to occupy that mind of yours."

"OK," said Shawn, as he hobbled away using the forearm crutches.

"So much has happened in my life over the past six years," thought Heather. *"Divorced from David, moving back to Georgia, David now dead, remarried to Shawn, and look at all that Shawn is dealing with now – I could have*

never guessed all of this. And Charotte – she certainly isn't the same child. Where did that sweet little girl go? I guess the hormones have kicked in. It had to happen at some point. I hate the fact that she and I aren't close anymore. It's good that she has Shawn. He seems to be the only one she will listen to now. She adores that man – and so do I. Physically, he isn't the same – but that man is a rock. She needs him. We both do."

"WAKE UP!" HEATHER shouted at Shawn. "You're having one of those dreams again. Everything is OK. It's alright."

During his nightmare, Shawn had thrown off the covers of their bed. Heather looked at his once powerful legs which had begun to atrophy from limited exercise. He didn't wear leg braces while sleeping or showering. Without the braces, Heather had to help her husband into the shower, where they had placed a handicap stool for him to be seated while showering.

"His arms are stronger than ever, but it's probable that he will never regain the full use of his legs," thought Heather. *"What will happen when we grow old? How will I manage getting him into the shower, then? Will we need to hire someone to look after him? I don't think he could ever handle that emotionally or mentally. It's humbling enough that he has to rely on me. I'm not sure what we will do. Thank God that I bought this home with a downstairs master bedroom. It would take him half an hour to go upstairs, and there would always be the chance that he would fall while attempting to go down the stairs. We'll cross that bridge later. These horrible nightmares of his – I hope they pass."*

"It's OK," Heather comforted her husband while pulling the bed covers back over him. "Everything is alright. It was just a dream."

Shawn's weary eyes gazed at his wife, as he lifted one

of his large arms. Heather moved close and rested her head on his powerful chest.

"I'm sorry," Shawn whispered. "In the morning, you'll begin your first day as a tenured professor. You certainly don't need to start off with little sleep."

"I'll be fine," replied Heather. "Go back to sleep. Everything is alright."

"I don't know what I would do without you," said Shawn. "You didn't bargain for this. I have the severance, but I can no longer help support this family without being in the field."

"I'm glad you're no longer in the field," said Heather. "You have no idea how much I worried about you. I never knew whether you would come home in the evenings or if I would get a call telling me that you had been shot to death by a violent criminal. You have no idea."

"You did get a call," reminded Shawn.

"But you're still alive," said Heather. "That's what matters. I love you so much. I can't lose you."

"You would be better off with a man who could walk without crutches and braces," said Shawn. "I'm a burden to you and to the entire family."

"You are the man I love, and the kids need you," said Heather.

"The kids are growing up fast," observed Shawn. "They will be grown and on their own before we know it."

"You're twice the father David was," said Heather. "Josh thinks you're a god, and Charlotte loves you. She and I no longer talk like we did in the past. You're the only one she'll listen to. She needs you more than you can imagine."

"Charlotte's a great kid," said Shawn. "She's just in those teen years, and it won't last forever. You'll be close again. She's at a very volatile age. I've tried to warn her about teenage boys. They are really nuts at that age. I remember when I was a teen. It was like my brains had leaked out of my head and I was running on hormones. I was crazy, and fortunate that I lived to adulthood."

"I'm so glad that she listens to you," said Heather.

"She listens to what she wants to hear," said Shawn. "Like most teens, she focuses on what she wants to hear and will only slightly consider the rest. That's why in my conversations with her, I always let her know that I see her as being both smart and pretty."

"I remember being thirteen," said Heather. "Boobs and legs are growing, and a girl hopes she'll turn out like Barbie with a brilliant mind who can twist boys around like a pretzel."

"Your boobs and legs certainly twist my head around like a pretzel," said Shawn, moving a hand to one of his wife's breasts.

"That's all you think about," said Heather, placing her slight hand on his.

"You had better believe that's all those teenage boys think about," said Shawn. "I warned Charlotte about them. They think with the head that's between their legs."

"It wouldn't take much for her to make a serious mistake," worried Heather.

"That's true," agreed Shawn. "But she's smart, like her mother. I'm not so worried about her, as much I am concerned with the boys in that school. But I sent them a message."

"What do you mean?" asked Heather.

"Why do you think I volunteered to take the kids to school after I became proficient with the hand controls on the car?" asked Shawn. "I wanted those boys to see me. I wanted them to see who they would be messing with, if they didn't control themselves. I wanted to scare the hell out them."

"What?"

"The first time I dropped Charlotte off, I spotted a guy checking her out," explained Shawn. "I mean, he was looking her up and down, really hard. I whistled in his direction, and when I had his attention, I motioned for him to come around to my side of the car. I let down my window, hung my arm out of it, and told the kid that I was a retired detective and that I look out after Charlote."

"You did what?" blurted Heather. "You tried to intimidate a kid?"

"I didn't try, I did intimidate him," said Shawn. "It only takes one. That kid will pass the word among every teen boy in that school. I wanted to scare the shit out him."

"You'll scare every boy away from her," said Heather. "She'll never be asked out on a date during her high school years."

"She'll only be asked out on a date by guys who respect her," said Shawn. "I told you that the boy was checking her out really hard. There will be a host of guys wanting to ask her out, but I don't want slimeballs asking her out. She'll have guys that are smart enough not to take advantage of her asking her out."

"Did Charlotte see you intimidate that kid?" ask Heather.

"I'm not sure if she noticed, and I made sure that my conversation with that kid never made a scene," explained Shawn. "I would never embarrass Charlotte, but she knows that she can count on me if needed. I just quietly put the fear of God into that boy. At his age, that's what speaks to him. Remember, I know boys. I was one."

"You're ridiculous!" laughed Heather.

"I put the fear into that one guy, and I'm sure that word got around to the rest of them," said Shawn. "Believe me, Charlotte will never be lacking in boys who want to ask her out. We need to make sure the right kind of boy feels comfortable asking her out."

"So, now that you you've put the fear of God into every young man in Charlotte's school, can you focus on the idea of a private investigation agency?" asked Heather.

"John has already agreed to come on as a consultant,"

answered Shawn. "I just needed to establish my priorities. Charlotte comes first."

Chapter 45

Church

JOSH WAS BRILLIANT. His raw intelligence surpassed even the minds of his mother and biological father. However, his physical abilities were nothing like what Shawn once had. Charlotte's grades were excellent. She was attractive and she easily became popular in school. Unlike his sister, Josh was picked on by the boys in middle school. As he grew older, he felt a disconnect with his stepfather and gravitated toward his grandfather John.

"Would it be alright if we started attending Grandpa's church?" Josh asked his mother.

"What brought this on?" asked Heather.

"Since moving out of Grandpa's house, we don't see him as often," answered Josh.

"Well, it would be an opportunity to stay in touch with your grandfather," agreed Heather. "Also, I would be better able to stay in touch with Emily. Since we both moved from your grandfather's neighborhood, Emily and I rarely talk."

"Would Shawn go with us?" asked Josh.

"I'll bring it up with him," answered his mother. "As partners on the police force, Shawn and your grandfather were very close. He may think it's a good idea, as well."

"Great!" exclaimed Josh. He avoided the main reason for his wish to attend the church. Josh hoped to find friends his age who were kind. Later that evening, Heather brought the subject up to her husband.

"Josh and I were talking, and it might be a good idea to attend my father's church," said Heather. "It would be an opportunity to better stay in touch with him."

"I miss John," said Shawn. "Are you sure that church would want us there? We're not exactly holy roller people, you know."

"No!" exclaimed Charlotte, listening to her parent's conversation. "I've met a few kids that go to that church at school and there is nothing cool about them. If I start seeing them at a church, then they'll start coming up to me at school. I don't want them to hang around me. God no!"

"That's not the kind of attitude I've taught you to have," said Heather. "I never expected you to be mean to other people."

"I don't want to be mean to them," said Charlotte. "That's why I don't want them hanging around me. I know that I'll lose my patience with them and end up being mean to them. It's better if I go my way, and those kids hang out with kids like them. It's better for them and it's better for me."

"We'll talk more later," said Heather.

After supper, Shawn found Charlotte sitting on the back porch playing a video game on a handheld device. He struggled to sit next to her.

"I don't want to go to church," said Charlotte. "I know that you're coming out here to talk me into it."

"You know me," said Shawn. "Have you ever known me to be the church type?"

"No, but you love my mother, and you love Josh," said Charlotte. "You're just trying to make them happy."

"And I don't care about you one bit, do I?" asked Shawn.

"I know you care," Charlotte said, leaning her shoulder against Shawn's massive frame.

"You seem to be concerned with the uncoolness of those church kids rubbing off on you," said Shawn. "That's not going to happen. You should know that. I mean, look at you. You're turning into a drop dead gorgeous young lady, and you're not dumb. Listen, you have it. Nobody can take who you are away from you. You should have more confidence. I know that at your age, confidence is something that may be hard to find. I understand. You're changing, and you're not so sure about what you will be changing into at the end of all this."

"What do you know about it?" asked Charlotte. "You were never a girl."

"No, I have never been a girl," agreed Shawn. "However, I've dated a lot of girls. I do know guys, and I've seen how those guys look at you when I drop you off at school. That's why I spend so much time warning you about them. Those guys think that you're hot, and there is only one thing on the minds of those guys. There is nothing in the world you could do to turn those guys off from you. They're idiots at that age. You should have confidence in yourself. That's the secret to being cool. It's not who you hang with, it's knowing who you are and having confidence in yourself. It's like a magic shield. As long as you have it, they can't rock you."

"That's easy for you to say," said Charlotte. "I remember the first time I saw you; I thought you looked like a Greek god or something."

"I'm a cripple now," said Shawn. "I'm not so much like a Greek god or anything like that now. Do you think that I'm still cool?"

"You'll always be cool," said Charlotte. "You're a hero. You've saved people. You're not afraid of anything. Grandpa told me that you've handled some the worst people on the planet."

"So, I'm still cool?" asked Shawn.

"Of course," answered Charlotte.

"But the church kids aren't cool at all?" asked Shawn.

"I just don't have anything in common with them," said Charlotte.

Have you ever thought about the possibility of your cool rubbing off on those church kids?" asked Shawn. "Nobody can take your cool from you, but you might help some of those kids."

"I don't know," said Charlotte. "I just don't like them."

"How many of them have you talked with?" asked Shawn.

"I've seen them acting weird with each other, and I don't want to talk with them," explained Charlotte.

"Would you be willing to do me a favor?" asked Shawn. "For the sake of peace, would you give attending the church a try? No one is demanding that you sit next to these kids. We would be sitting with John. Would you please give it a try?"

"Alright," promised Charlotte. "It would be nice to see grandpa more often. Just don't expect much more from me."

"Thank you," said Shawn, as he gave Charlotte a hug with his powerful left arm. "I owe you one."

"I'm going to hold you to that," replied Charlotte. "I'll be thinking of ways that you can pay me back."

"God help me," mumbled Shawn.

Charlotte laughed.

THE FOLLOWING SUNDAY, Heather and her family sat on the same church pew as John. Pastor Matt's sermon was based on Ephesians 4:26-27. "26 In your anger do not sin: Do not let the sun go down while you are still angry, 27 and do not give the devil a foothold."

After the service, John joined his family for lunch at Heather's home. She had tried a new recipe of chicken spaghetti cooked in a crockpot, and it had been cooking while they were in church.

"This is really good," Shawn told his wife.

"I second that," said John. "I'll have a little more, if you don't mind."

"Of course," replied Heather, while placing more on John's plate. "I'm glad it turned out alright."

"What did you think about the church service?" asked John.

"It's a nice church," said Shawn. "The acoustics are really good."

"What about the sermon?" asked John.

"I think that it's difficult to not be mad at some people," said Josh.

"I agree," said Charlotte. "Some people deserve to have people mad at them. Some people are awful. Why let bad people off? Especially people who don't apologize and those who continue to do bad things to people. What's wrong with being mad at them?"

"Did you hear what pastor Matt said about allowing other people to have power over you?" asked John. "If you are mad at someone, who is really being hurt? Most of the time, the person you are mad at doesn't care that you're mad. You're simply upsetting yourself and making yourself unhappy. In a sense, you've let that person control your happiness."

"I can see that," said Josh. "I'm just not sure how to stop being mad at a person. Like Charlotte said, what if the person keeps doing bad things to you?"

"That verse from the Bible doesn't say that we can't be mad," explained John. "It's important that we learn to not allow negative situations get the best of us. We need to learn how to channel our emotions to do something that has positive results, instead of allowing anger to eat at us for days."

"Maybe it's easy for a grownup to do," said Josh.

"Have you forgotten what Randy Jenkins did with us?" asked Heather. "He allowed anger at your grandfather to fester for years and look what happened."

"I doubt I'll ever forget that," added Charlotte, who had been sitting quietly. "I've never been so scared in my life. He beat you and tried to kidnap me and Josh. I hate that guy."

"That guy is dead," said Shawn. "Hating him only messes you over. He got what was coming to him. It's over. Try not to let it continue to hurt you."

"I'm not hurt!" blurted Charlotte. "I'm still mad at that guy. What a jerk! What had Mom ever done to him? I'll never forgive how he hurt her, and I'm surprised that you can."

"I'm not saying that I forgive the guy, but I'm just trying to move on," said Shawn. "Jenkins is dead. What more could be done to him? It's over. There is no use in making myself miserable still. He got what was coming to him."

"How do you think that made me feel?" said John. "It was all because of me arresting him. Jenkins hurt my daughter and my grandkids to get back at me. But Shawn is right about moving on. I can't do anything about all of that now. All I can do is try to learn from things and move on. The man is dead. All bad feelings can do now is only make us unhappy."

"I'll never forget it," said Charlotte.

"I'm sure you won't," said John. "But it's best that you don't let it continue to upset you. Hating Randy Jenkins does no one any good. It's best if we take bad situations like that one and learn from them. That's the only good that can come from it."

"Heather, I bet you are more aware of checking to see if there is someone hiding behind your car now," said Shawn. "I should have been more aware of that. If I had, it's possible that I wouldn't be a cripple now."

"You were tired that night," said Heather. "You are usually aware of things like that. It was just one of those terrible things."

"Why does all this crap happen to us?" asked Charlotte.

"I bet no other kids at school have had a criminal try to kidnap them. I bet none of them have seen a jerk beat their mother to the ground. I bet none of them have a family member who was beaten from behind and left for dead in a parking lot. What the crap?"

"Part of it comes with a career in law enforcement," answered Shawn. "We understand the risk we are taking. I doubt many of us really understand the risk we place on family members until something happens. It's like most things. People think it will happen to someone else, not them or their family."

"Shawn's right," said John. "I'm so sorry Jenkins took things out on you two and your mother. There are really bad people out there, and someone has to protect the public from them. I can't tell you how it makes me feel to think that protecting the public resulted in harm to my family. I'm sorry."

"It's not your fault, Grandpa," said Josh. "It was the fault of Randy Jenkins. He didn't have to do that. He could have decided to move on and make his life better. He didn't."

"So, you see how hanging on to anger can be devastating to you and others?" asked John. "It's OK to get mad, but only give it a day. Don't let your anger simmer and build into bitterness or hate. Settle it that day and decide what you can do to change things."

"I think it was nice when the pastor stopped the service and told the people to greet each other," said Josh. "A couple of kids came up to me and introduced themselves. They seemed to be nice."

"I'm glad that happened," said Heather. "Maybe you'll find a friend there.'

"I'm not sure that I like that part," thought Charlotte. *"I don't want to get to know those people."*

WITHIN THREE WEEKS of attending John's church, Josh

made several friends. Two of them called him regularly and invited him to a church youth ice cream function. Charlotte was surprised to meet one girl who seemed to be popular at her school. One evening several weeks later, while John and Shawn talked and sipped coffee on her back porch, Heather went into the bathroom attached to the master bedroom. While seated there, she considered the impact the church had made on Josh's life.

"Thank You, God, for bringing friends into Josh's life," she began. "Thank You for saving the life of my husband. I thank You for my father; for his influence on my children and what he brings to my life. He was there when I needed him, even after years of ignoring him. I am so blessed."

Suddenly, an inexplicable warmth came over Heather. For the first time in her life, she sensed that God was actually listening to her. She began to weep. After leaving the bathroom, she knelt beside her bed.

"Thank you, God, for all you have given me," she prayed. "I can't explain it, but I know You are there and I know that You are listening to me. I don't really understand it. I sense You all around me. I'm sorry for ignoring You all these years. Mom was right. I wish I had listened more to her. I wish I had shared a belief in You when I still had her. Pastor Matt said that all the sins of everyone who had ever lived were placed on Jesus, and when He died on the cross our sins died with Him. Thank You, Jesus, for doing that. I believe that You took my sins away, and I ask You to have my soul. I give my soul to You. You deserve it. You have done so much for me. I believe in You. Please help my kids. Protect them from all that may come their way. Protect them from harm and help me to guide them into adulthood. Please help Shawn. He is in such pain and misery physically, and he is tormented in his dreams at night. Please give him peace. Thank You, God."

Chapter 46

Charlotte

SHAWN KNEW SOMETHING was wrong when he picked up Charlotte and Josh from the middle school they attended. Charlotte usually greeted him with a smile, but today she was silent as she sat beside him. Shawn wisely waited. As they pulled onto the street from the school, Josh opened up.

"Christie Taylor was killed in a car accident last night while riding with her family," Josh said.

"Everyone else in the car were only bruised a little, but she was killed," added Charlotte. "Someone who was speeding ran a traffic light and hit their car at the spot where Christie was sitting. She died while being taken to the hospital."

"I'm sorry to hear that," said Shawn. "Were you two close friends?"

"Yes," answered Charlotte.

"That's horrible," said Shawn. "I can't imagine what her parents are going through."

"Her brother and sister weren't at school today," said Josh.

"Christie was in my math class, and we heard about the accident in that class," said Charlotte. "By the time school let out, that was all everyone could talk about."

During the remainder of the drive home, both kids were

silent. Shawn tried twice to change the subject, but it was no use. When Heather returned home, Shawn told her about the situation.

"The kids are pretty upset," Shawn began. "A friend of Charlotte was killed in a car accident last night."

"Oh, no!" exclaimed Heather. "Is Charlotte in her room?"

"I think so," said Shawn. "They're both upstairs. It's difficult for me to make it up those stairs, or I would have gone up."

"I'll talk with them," said Heather.

When Heather arrived at the top of the stairs, she found Charlotte's door closed and Josh's open. She approached Josh, who was playing a video game.

"I heard about what happened," Heather began. "How are you doing?"

"I'm doing Ok, but I didn't know Christie as well as Charlotte did," answered Josh.

"Shawn said that she was the only one killed in the accident," said Heather. "Is that right?"

"It's really weird," said Josh. "The rest of the family members were banged up a little, but it killed her. She just happened to be sitting at the spot where the other car made impact. She took the full force of the accident. I can't imagine sitting beside someone who was killed. Her sister was seated right beside her and was only bruised. Pretty freaky, isn't it?"

"I'll say," said Heather. "How are the other family members?"

"Her brother and sister didn't attend school today," answered Josh. "Christie's brother and sister are twins. They're my age. I honestly didn't know them all that well. Those kids are popular, and I'm not usually welcome in that crowd."

"How is Charlotte?" asked Heather.

"She's torn up," answered Josh. "She and Charlotte

were close."

"Are you sure that you're alright?" asked Heather.

"I'm fine," replied Josh. "It's just weird."

Heather gave her son a kiss on the top of his head and left his room to check on her daughter. Standing at Charlotte's door, she said a quick prayer before knocking.

"*God, please help Charlotte*," she silently prayed. "*And please help me to help her*."

"It's unlocked," Heather heard Charlotte mumble from inside the room.

"I heard," said Heather, shutting the door behind her.

"It's terrible," said Charlotte. "Why Christie? She was such a cool girl, and really nice to people. Why didn't it happen to someone else. Why her?"

"I can't answer that," said Heather.

"It was so stupid," said Charlotte. "I could better understand it if it had happened on I-20 or I-75, but it happened on a city street in Atlanta. Some idiot was trying to make a red light and hit them. He was speeding, while trying to make the light. That idiot killed her. Don't tell me not to be mad at him. Don't remind me about the preacher's sermon about not staying mad at someone. I'm mad at that guy. That idiot killed my friend."

"I'm so sorry," Heather said, while taking a seat on the bed beside her daughter.

"I don't understand," whispered Charlotte, as tears ran down her face. "Why?"

"I don't know the answer to that," said Heather.

"The preacher talks about God's love and all that," said Charlotte. "If God exists, why would He take Charlotte – of all people? She was good to me. She was a popular girl who included me. Christie pulled me into the popular crowd at school. She was cool, but she was nice. Why would God take her? Why did He do that? I think I hate God."

"Not everything that happens is God's fault," said Heather.

"He's God, isn't He?" blurted Charlotte. "Doesn't God call the shots? Why isn't it God's fault?"

"I'm no authority on God," said Heather. "But I will give you the explanation that Emily once gave me. When Jesus taught His disciples to pray by giving them the Lord's Prayer, Jesus said that we should pray for God's will to be done on earth just like God's will is done in heaven. If God's will is always done on earth, why would Jesus tell His disciples that they should pray for God's will to be done on earth? Look around. Do you see God's will being done? Do you see people loving God and loving each other? No. People are basically selfish. Most people are about themselves, not God and others."

"I guess you're right," said Charlotte. "I really don't think about making God happy, and I only sometimes think about making other people happy. I guess I should blame that stupid jerk who tried to selfishly make that red light instead of blaming God."

"That guy had more to do with what happened than God," agreed Heather. "But try not to hate him either. It won't do any good."

"I don't know what to do," said Charlotte.

"It's going to be difficult," said Heather.

"I realize that getting mad at that guy won't help anybody," said Charlotte. "It won't bring Christie back. Do you really think there is a heaven? Do you really believe that we go to heaven when we die?"

"The Bible says there is heaven," said Heather. "Like I said, I'm not an authority on God or heaven. I believe that God and heaven are real, but I can't prove that to anybody else."

"When did you start believing in God?' asked Charlotte. "You always told people that you are an agnostic, that you just don't know if it's real."

"It's hard to explain," answered Heather. "One night, I just knew. I just knew deep inside that it's all real. My mother tried to explain it to me for years, but I didn't listen. I wish I had listened, but I didn't. I can't prove it to you, but I know."

"Do you think pastor Matt can explain it to me?" asked Charlotte. "I want to know if Christie is in heaven."

"I don't know," answered Heather. "Would you like to talk with him?"

"I think that I would," said Charlotte. "Do you think he would come over tonight? Maybe he can come for supper."

"I'll ask, if you really want me to," offered Heather.

"Please, I want to know," said Charlotte.

"Ok, I'll give him a call."

Heather went downstairs and explained the conversation she had with her daughter with Shawn.

"Call the guy," said Shawn. "Whatever he can do to make her feel better. I'm all for it."

Heather stepped out onto her back porch and called the pastor using her cell phone. She explained the death of Charlotte's friend and told him that her daughter wanted to talk with him about heaven. She invited him for supper.

"We're having an early supper right now," said the pastor. "Would it be alright if I came over a little later tonight?"

"Sure," answered Heather. "Please do. I've been meaning to tell you that I prayed for Jesus to forgive my sins. I gave my soul to God a few nights ago."

"That's great!" exclaimed Matt. "I'm so glad."

"I haven't told Shawn, so please don't bring it up with him," said Heather.

"My lips are sealed," said Matt. "How about if I come over at 7:30 tonight? Would that be too late?"

"No, That's fine," said Heather. "I'll let her know."

"See you then," promised Matt.

Heather entered the house and found her husband seated in a recliner, with his braced legs raised.

"The pastor is coming at 7:30 tonight to meet with

Charlotte," Heather told Shawn,

"Great!" he replied. "I hope the conversation with her helps. Charlotte is really upset."

"I need to tell you something," said Heather, while sitting on the armrest of the recliner.

"What?" asked Shawn.

"I believe in God now," said Heather. "The other night, I prayed for God to forgive my sins, and I gave Him my soul."

"Wow, that pretty heavy," said Shawn. "I don't know much about giving your soul away. I hope you'll let me have the rest of you," he said, giving her a wink.

"You have my body and heart," said Heather.

"In that case, I'm all about it," said Shawn. "So, why don't you hand that body over to me right now. I can get out of this chair in a New York minute."

"Do you want supper, or not?" asked Heather.

"OK," said Shawn. "First supper, then your body for dessert?"

"We'll see," said Heather. "First Charlotte."

"First Charlotte," agreed Shawn, now taking on a more serious tone. "I hope the preacher can help."

At 7:30 that evening, pastor Matt was there as promised. He and Heather's family enjoyed apple pie with ice cream, before beginning the discussion about the death of Charlotte's friend. Once the pie and ice cream were consumed, Matt suggested that Charlotte and he have a private conversation on the back porch.

"I would like that," said Charlotte.

Once seated there, Charlotte explained that after she talked with her mother, she no longer blamed God for the accident killing Christie.

"I don't blame God, and blaming that guy in the other car won't bring Christie back," said Charlotte.

"You're absolutely right," said Matt. "Your mother gave you good advice."

"What I want to know is whether heaven really exists and if Christie is there," said Charlotte.

"I strongly believe in the existence of heaven," said Matt. "I believe that people are more than just a collection of chemicals and matter. I believe that each of us has a soul that rides around inside our body, and that when we die our soul leaves this realm to live forever in another realm. We call that realm heaven."

"So, you believe that Christie is in heaven?" asked Charlotte.

"Only God determines where a soul goes after we die," answered Matt. "The Bible says that some souls go to heaven and other souls go to a place that isn't as good."

"Are you talking about hell?" asked Charlotte.

"That's believed to be the other place," answered Matt.

"Charlote can't be in hell," said Charlotte. "She was probably the nicest kid in our school."

"It's certainly good to be nice," agreed the pastor. "But being nice isn't what qualifies a person for heaven."

"What qualifies a person?" asked Charlotte.

"Faith," answered Matt.

"What do you mean?"

"The Bible says that all people sin, and that sin separates people from God," explained Matt. "We can't be good enough to qualify for heaven, and God knows this. God allowed His Son Jesus to die on the cross to take away our sins. God placed all the sins of everyone on Jesus, and when Jesus died our sins died with Him. We have to have faith in what God did for us in allowing Jesus to do that."

"So, God took away Christie's sins?" asked Charlotte.

"Do you like rides at the fair?" asked Matt.

"Some of them," answered Charlotte. "I like the Ferris wheel. I like to see the view and feel the sun and wind."

"Well, you need a ticket to ride the Ferris wheel," explained Matt. "You have the ticket, but you have to use it in order to experience the ride. God has given us the ticket for heaven, but we have to use it. We use it by faith. That ticket is the means to have our sins forgiven. Think about the Ferris Wheel ride. We have faith that He has provided the ticket, and we have to have enough faith to give it the person running the ride, and we have to have enough faith in the ticket to actually get on the ride. If we just stand around with the ticket, it doesn't do us any good. In that case, we would just waste the ticket. We have to have faith that God has provided us a ticket to heaven by what He allowed Jesus to do for us, and then we have to use that ticket. We need to ask God's forgiveness and trust him with our soul, that when we die will take that ride to heaven. Does that make sense?"

"That sounds too easy," said Charlotte.

"If it was really all that easy, wouldn't more people take that ride?" asked Matt. "Have you asked God for the ticket? Have you trusted God with your soul?"

"Not yet," she replied. "Is that all there is to it?"

"Not entirely," answered Matt.

"I knew it," said Charlotte.

"Doing good things and being nice to people won't earn us a ticket," said Matt. "The ticket is free. But to use it, we need to have faith that the ticket will work. That faith is what prepares our soul for heaven. It's free, but because God has done so much for us, we should love God in return. Doesn't that make sense?"

"It does," answered Charlotte.

"Jesus said that if we love God, we should obey God," explained Matt. "In gratitude for God, we need to do what we can to please God. Jesus said that there are two simple rules. We are to love God and love other people. In loving other people, we are to forgive other people. Jesus said that if we don't forgive other people, God will not forgive us. That can sometimes be difficult. Do you think you can forgive the person who caused the accident which killed Christie?"

"I knew there was a catch," said Charlotte.

"Can you?" asked Matt.

"If it will make God happy and if it will mean that I can see Christie again in heaven after I die," said Charlotte. "I will do my very best."

"Good," said Matt. "I can't guarantee whether or not Christie is heaven. That's between her and God. Would you like to pray to God asking for forgiveness and giving God your soul?

"Yes," answered Charlotte.

"Do you accept that ticket that Jesus bought for you by suffering and dying on that cross to take away your sins?" asked Matt. "Do you want to pray that prayer?"

"Yes," Charlotte answered. "But I'm not sure that I'll say the right words.

"The Bible says that God's Holy Spirit helps us pray in words that can't be heard," said Matt. "Whatever words we lack, the Holy Spirit can fill in. What matters is that you are honest with God."

Pastor Matt led Charlotte in prayer to accept Jesus Christ as her Savior. After Matt and Charlotte entered the house, she walked over to her mother and whispered in her ear.

"I asked God to take away my sins. I want to go to heaven when I die."

Heather smiled and gave her daughter a long hug.

"Here we go with women's secrets," said Shawn.

"I want to go to heaven when I die," Christie told him. "I have faith that Jesus has bought me a ticket to heaven."

"Well, let's not rush the dying part," said Shawn.

"I'm here for you if you need me," said Matt, as he stepped toward the front door.

Heather followed him out the door and thanked him for coming. She hoped that Charlotte understood and meant her prayers.

"*Only time will tell*," Heather thought.

"Maybe it would be a good idea for you to call your

grandfather and talk to him about it," Heather suggested to her daughter.

"I think I will," said Charlotte as she ascended the stairs to her bedroom.

The entire family continued to attend Matt's church, but two members of Heather's immediate family gave no indication of a desire to profess faith in Christ.

Chapter 47

Conflict

OVER THE NEXT two months, Charlotte and her grandfather became closer. Their shared faith grew, and she called him often. Charlotte made sure to sit next to him during church services. Like silly teens, they sometimes passed notes to each other during the sermons. She maintained her relationships with the popular teens at school, but her circle of friendship grew to include those from her church.

"Would you lay off me about all that Jesus stuff?" Josh told Charlotte. "I go to church. I like the people there, but I'm not buying all the Jesus stuff. I have nothing against you, Mom and Grandpa having faith in God, but just leave me and Shawn out of it."

With Charlotte and John having shared faith, Josh turned more to Shawn. His conversations with his grandfather became fewer.

"Shawn isn't all that bright, but at least he has sense enough to not fall for all that spiritual stuff," Josh thought. *"I don't know what has come over my family. I understand Charlotte being just torn up still about Christie dying. She hopes to see her friend again in some afterlife. But Mom? Crap, she has a PhD. She should know better. What's with her?"*

"I'm glad you haven't bought into all that holy stuff," Josh told Shawn.

"It's Ok," said Shawn.

"You don't have Charlotte beating you over the head with the Bible," said Josh.

"I mean, it's OK for them to have faith if they want to," said Shawn. "I'll go to church. It's important that we stick together as a family."

"I see that, but you don't believe in God, do you?" asked Josh.

"I can't say that I believe God exists, but I can't swear that He doesn't," said Shawn. "It's possible that there is a god, but I don't really understand spirituality. I simply don't know."

"That's what Mom thought until recently," said Josh. "That makes sense. We both thought the same. Now we're sort of split up. It's like you and me against the rest of them. I don't like it."

"Your Mom is still your mom," said Shawn. "She loves you like she always has. That's what counts."

"All my life, it was me, Charlotte and Mom – together," said Josh. "Now, it seems like Charlotte and Mom are teaming up against me."

"Your mother and sister still love you," said Shawn.

"Yeah, but they are always conspiring behind my back to try to convert me," said Josh. "I hate it. I would consider not going to church, but those kids seem to be my only friends."

"I'll have to say, those kids at the church seem to do you right," said Shawn.

"So, you don't have plans to go holy on me?" asked Josh.

"I have no plans to change," said Shawn. "I have enough on my plate just trying to walk," he said with a grin.

The tension in the home continued to grow. Josh began to avoid his mother, sister and grandfather.

"I THINK I want to become a nurse," Charlotte told her mother.

"What brought that on?" Heather asked. "Nursing is a noble career, but you've got plenty of time to think about it."

"We've had different professionals speak to us at the school about their careers," said Charlotte. "Since then, I've watched surgery procedures on TV and on the internet. I'm amazed at the human body and how it works."

"I've had several biology and anatomy classes in college," said Heather. "It really is amazing."

"I want to take anatomy next year," said Charlotte.

"Well, you have time to explore a number of fields and careers," said Heather.

"When will Emily and Lily be coming over?" asked Charlotte.

"We see them each Sunday at church," said Heather.

"But I miss having them over regularly," said Charlotte.

"Maybe we can have them over Saturday for board games," suggested Heather. "You used to like that."

"I would, and I am fascinated with babies and childbirth," said Charlotte.

"Just make sure that you hold off on your own birthing of children until the right time," said Heather.

"I'm not stupid," said Charlotte. "I'm not dumb enough to get pregnant."

"A lot of girls say that, but then they slip up with a guy and become pregnant," said Heather. "That can greatly impact your life."

"I'm not dumb and I know that God doesn't want me to have sex before I'm ready," said Charlotte. "They talked about sex outside of marriage in Sunday school. The Bible says that God isn't pleased with that. I want to God to be happy with me."

"Good thinking," said Heather.

"She is serious about her faith in God," thought Heather. *"I'm so glad."*

"I wish Josh was a Christian," said Charlotte. "I don't know why he thinks having faith is dumb."

"I was the same way when I was younger," said Heather. "For years, my mother tried to convince me to turn to God. I just didn't see it at the time."

"So, maybe Josh will see it when he's a little older?" asked Charlotte.

"I hope so," answered Heather. "If a relationship with God is real, it seems to happen when people are ready. It's not really an intellectual thing, and I think that's why Josh doesn't see it. He can't figure it out. People come to God when they allow God's Holy Spirit to reach into their soul and touch them from within. It's not so much an intellectual decision as it is a spiritual one."

"Yeah, but people have to think about God in order to come to Him," said Charlotte. "Thinking has to be involved, doesn't it?"

"Pastor Matt mentioned human beings a few sermons ago," said Heather. "He talked about a person having a heart, soul, and mind. He said that we are much more than just a body made up of chemicals and matter. He's better at explaining it."

"Would it be OK if I called him and asked him about it?" asked Charlotte.

"I'm sure it would be fine," said Heather.

"Can I do it right now?" asked Charlotte.

Heather pulled her cell phone from her back pocket and dialed the pastor's number.

"Here, it's ringing," said Heather, handing the phone to her daughter.

"Hello? Pastor Matt?" questioned Charlotte.

"Yes," he answered.

"This is Charlotte Littleton, from church," Charlotte said.

"You're the daughter of Shawn and Heather Stone, right?" asked Matt.

"Yes, but I have my birth father's last name," said Charlotte.

"What can I do for you?" asked Matt.

"Pastor Matt, can you explain the part about people having a heart, soul, and mind?" asked Charlotte.

"Sure," replied the pastor. "Matthew 22:37 talks about Jesus saying that the greatest commandment is this: Thou shalt love the Lord thy God with all thy heart, and with all thy soul, and with all thy mind."

"What about the body?" asked Charlotte.

"Most of us see a person's body and we think that's the entirety of the person," explained Matt. "But like I said in a sermon a few weeks back, human beings are more than matter and a mixture of chemicals. When it comes to love, it is a much deeper matter. Chemicals can't love, can they?"

"I wouldn't think so," answered Charlotte. "Chemicals might affect the emotion of love."

"Matter can't love, can it?" asked Matt.

"I don't think so," answered Charlotte.

"But there are aspects of a person which have the ability to love," said Matt. "Jesus said that we are to love God with all our heart, with all our soul, and with all our mind. All three of those aspects of humanity can love."

"I understand loving with our heart, but I don't understand loving with the rest," said Charlotte.

"The New Testament was originally written in Greek, so what we currently read in the Bible was translated to English from an original language," explained Matt. "Sometimes the full meaning of Greek words doesn't come across when scripture is translated."

"So, what does it all mean?" asked Charlotte. "Can you explain what is meant by a person's soul?"

"Well, if you want to get into the technical matters of theology, the Greek word for soul is psuche," said Matt.

"The psuche or soul is what makes you alive, according to theology. It's the spark that causes your body to be alive. When your soul leaves the body, the body is no longer alive. It's sort of the real you which rides around inside your body."

"OK, I think that makes sense," said Charlotte. "What about our mind?"

"The Greek word for mind is nous, and it basically is a person's reasonable faculty or mind," said Matt. "The meaning is captured fairly well in the translation."

"And the heart?" asked Charlotte.

"The Greek word for the English word heart is kardia," said Matt. "It's what drives a person's behavior, a person's nature or character. This is the core of what makes you – you. Your personal nature or your personality. It's unique to every person. A person's soul, heart, and mind are internal characteristics. We can see the body with our eyes, but not those three. We can recognize the mind of a person on an intellectual level, but not so much the heart and soul of a person. Those are more spiritual."

"So inside of us are three parts, which are not physical," observed Charlotte.

"That's right," said Matt. "We have those three aspects that make up a person on the inside. If you will remember, God has three aspects or persons which we call the Holy Trinity. God is made up of the Father, the Son who is Jesus, and the Holy Spirit. Genesis says that God made mankind in His own image. God is made up of three aspects and mankind is also. We both are made up of a trinity. You are Charlotte. Your soul that gives life to your body is Charlotte. Your heart is Charlotte and your mind is Charlotte. There are three aspects which make up Charlotte, but there is just one Charlotte. God is like that. God is made up of the Holy Trinity, but there is just one God. We are made in the image of God, both made of a trinity."

"I never understood what was meant by God making

people in His own image," said Charlotte. "I thought maybe we looked a bit like God, or something."

"Well, the bodies of men and women are different, right?" asked Matt.

"Of course," answered Charlotte.

"Well, then God wasn't talking about what we look like when He said that both men and women are made in His image," explained Matt.

"That makes sense," said Charlotte.

"In Genesis 1 God said, 'Let us make mankind in our image,'" said Matt. "God was letting us know that He is a trinity by using the word 'us' in describing Himself. God is made up of three persons, and we are made in God's image. Jesus called out the three aspects of mankind when He talked about us loving God."

"All of that makes sense," said Charlotte. "I'm not sure that I understand it all, but it is beginning to make sense. Thank you."

"So, it's our soul that goes to heaven when we die," said Charlotte. "We are dead when our soul leaves our body, but that soul lives on in heaven."

"That's it," said Matt.

"So, when my friend Christie died in a car accident, her soul is still alive," said Charlotte.

"That's right," said Matt.

"Good," said Charlotte. "That makes me feel better. I wish Josh understood this, but he just isn't interested in God. Maybe I shouldn't have said that. I'm not sure that he wants people in the church to know that isn't really serious when it comes to faith."

"I won't tell anyone," assured Matt. "But I'll be praying that Josh becomes interested."

"Thank you," said Charlotte. "I'll pray for that too. He and Grandpa were close until my grandfather found faith in God. Now, they hardly talk. He seems like he is mad at me and our mother, too. I don't understand that."

"It happens," said Matt. "You and your brother are still brother and sister on the physical level, but on a spiritual level you are somewhat at odds. There is conflict. Jesus talked about that too. Your brother still loves you, but things are not the same on a spiritual level. I'm sure he finds it frustrating."

"You can say that, alright," agreed Charlotte.

"Josh will be in my prayers," said pastor Matt.

"Thank you," said Charlotte.

Chapter 48

Death

JOHN WAS AWAKENED by the sound of a loud thud on the side of his house, followed by two loud barks from Zack. He quickly slipped on the jeans which lay at the foot of his bed, and he then took the nine-millimeter from the small electronic gun safe on his nightstand. He glanced out the bedroom window before proceeding to the front door of the home.

"What in the world?" John silently questioned.

He viewed the front yard from the living room windows before quietly opening the front door. His gun was the first to move through the opened door, as he cautiously scanned the front yard. Confident that there was no danger in front, he moved down the steps and to the side of the house where he heard the loud sound.

"Nothing," John thought.

With the gun pointed ahead, he stepped onto the side yard. He took two more steps before two sharp pains griped his back and chest.

"Oh, God, I've been shot," he thought.

Breathing was all but impossible, and he began to feel faint. Turning to his right, everything suddenly went black.

AFTER THE SUN rose that morning, a neighbor called

Heather, who was busily trying to get her two children ready for school.

"Heather?" said the voice over the phone.

"Yes?" said Heather. "Who is this?"

"It's your father's next-door neighbor, Patti," said the caller.

"What's going on?" asked Heather.

"It's your father," Patti said. "It's bad. He was found shot in his side yard this morning."

"Is he…?" Heather couldn't bring herself to finish the question.

"I'm sorry," said Patti. "He was pronounced dead on the scene."

"Oh God!" exclaimed Heather. "Where is he?"

"He is being taken to the county morgue on Pryor Street," said Patti. "At least, that's what the police said. The place is still crawling with police. There must be ten officers, including K-9."

"Thank you," said Heather, somewhat dazed.

"I would have called earlier, but I just found out that it happened," apologized Patti. "I heard all the commotion and stepped out to find the police everywhere. It looks like the ambulance is just now leaving."

"Thank you," said Heather.

"I'm so sorry," said Patti, as Heather was ending the call.

"Shawn!" Heather called out, stepping into the bedroom.

"What!" called out Shawn from the master bedroom bath. "I'm about to get into the shower."

"It's Daddy," said Heather, opening the bathroom door. "He's been shot. He's dead."

Heather dropped the cell phone and began to weep uncontrollably. She placed her right hand over her mouth.

"No!" blurted Shawn. "No. What happened?"

Heather was unable to talk. She stepped back into the

bedroom. Shawn grabbed a towel, wrapped it around himself, and slowly hobbled from the bathroom while holding onto the wall. Heather dropped onto the bed, and Shawn managed to sit beside her.

"What happened?" Shawn asked.

"I don't understand," Heather said, between sobs. "His neighbor Patti called. She said… that he was found shot in the side yard of the house…. He's dead."

"Shawn pulled her to him with his powerful arms. Heather broke into loud and hysterical weeping. After a few minutes, she calmed down.

Still in tears, she told her husband, "You find that son of a bitch that killed him! Do you hear me? Find that bastard."

"I'm on it," promised Shawn, reaching for his cell.

Within minutes, officers from Shawn's old station were at the house. Shawn called the school and informed them of the death of the grandfather.

"Charlotte and Josh will not be in school today," Shawn informed someone in the school administration. "Their grandfather has been brutally murdered."

Heather took her children to the back porch and informed them of John's death, while Shawn talked with members of law enforcement.

"We'll get that bastard," promised one officer. "John was one of our own. We won't rest. We'll get him."

After the police left the house, Shawn joined Heather and the kids on the back porch. Heather was trying to remain calm, but both children were weeping uncontrollably.

"I want to know everything!" Heather barked at Shawn. "I want to know everything they told you."

"Right now?" asked Shawn.

"Yes, right now!" demanded Heather.

"OK, it looks like John was shot twice in the back and once in the side of the head," Shawn bluntly told her. "The police on scene found a large rock on the side yard. The side where the neighbor Patti has those hedges which run between her yard and John's. The police think that whoever did this was hiding behind those hedges and drew your father out by hitting the side of his house with that rock. They believe the person shot him from those hedges. John probably never saw it coming."

"Nobody heard the shots?" Heather asked. "Half the neighborhood should have heard those shots. Why wasn't he found until morning?"

"They think it's possible the killer used a silencer with the weapon," suggested Shawn.

"So, do you believe this was a professional hit on my father?" asked Heather.

"I don't know," answered Shawn. "It's a possibility. It's possible that someone he arrested in the past hired a hit man. I don't know."

"You find out whether any of the people Daddy arrested had a record of killing for hire," demanded Heather. "Do you hear me? You get on this, and you find out who could have done this."

"I'm on it," promised Shawn.

Before talking with law enforcement, Shawn had slipped on a pair of pants. However, he was still barefooted.

"I'll place a few calls, and then get fully dressed," said Shawn. "I want this guy. I want him bad."

"If you find him, shoot his ass," said Heather.

"Mom!" blurted Charlotte.

"I'm sorry, Honey," said Heather. "I didn't mean it. I'm just so upset."

"I want Shawn to shoot his ass, too," said Josh, his lip quivering. "I want that shithead shot dead."

"Language, Josh," Heather said to her son. "I was wrong to say that and use bad language. It just slipped out before I thought about what I was saying."

"I've thought about, and I want the shithead shot dead," said Josh. "I'll never get to talk with Grandpa again," Josh said, his voice breaking. "I wanted to talk with him. I needed to talk with Grandpa. I needed to tell him that I am sorry for not spending time with him lately." Josh broke into tears. "It's too late."

"We'll see him in heaven," said Charlotte.

"You may," said Josh. "You may believe that, but I don't know about whether all of that is real."

"I believe your Grandpa is in heaven," said Heather.

"OK," said Shawn, stepping back out onto the back porch.

"I've called Emily, and she and Lily are on their way over. Your father's body is with the Fulton County Medical Examiner on Pryor Street. We need to meet with the people there and let them know what to do with John."

THE FAMILY WAS still crushed, as Pastor Matt conducted the eulogy at John's funeral. The church was packed with police officers. Before Matt began, Captain Don Evans spoke about the heroism John exhibited during his career in law enforcement. Police cruisers led the way to the cemetery for the graveside service. Police officers lined each side of the way leading to the grave. Six officers carried a flag draped coffin from the hearse to the grave. At the conclusion of the ceremony, an officer played taps on a bugle. Heather noticed tears in Shawn's eyes.

Josh was shaken by the loss. During the graveside event, he sat between his mother and Shawn. After the service, Heath Vickroy, a teen member of the church youth group talked with Charlotte. Comforted by him, Charlotte continued to call him in the days which followed.

"So, tell me about that boy you've been calling," Heather said to Charlotte.

"You mean, Heath Vickroy?" asked Charlotte. "He's a strong Christian who is a member of our church."

"I've seen you two after services," said Heather. "Are

you and Heath serious about each other?"

"We aren't having sex, if that's what your concerned about," said Charlotte. "He's a good friend, and he's helped me a lot after Grandpa died."

"I wasn't inferring that you were having sex," said Heather.

"Yes, you were," said Charlotte, smiling. "Don't worry. I'm sure that you know that he's fifteen. He's a couple of years older than me, but you can trust me with him. I'll be attending his high school next year. Mom, he is a very serious Christian."

"OK," said Heather. "If you ever want to talk, I'm here."

"I think you need to be more concerned with Josh," said Charlotte. "He is so angry, all the time."

"I'll talk with him," said Heather.

Heather found Josh sitting alone on the back porch of the house. He wasn't playing a video game, as usual. He was just staring off into the back yard.

"How are you?" asked Heather, taking a seat beside her son.

"I'm OK," Josh answered.

"Are you still angry about Grandpa?" asked Heather.

"Yep, but I remember him telling me to channel my emotions," answered Josh. "He said that I should channel the energy from anger into doing something good."

"That's sound advice," said Heather.

"I'm considering becoming a prosecutor when I'm an adult," said Josh. "I hate people who murder other people. I think I would like to make sure they go to prison."

"Law school is a long road," said Heather. "You're plenty intelligent enough for it, but it takes a lot of discipline."

"I want to get the bad guys," said Josh. "I will never have the physical strength Shawn has, and I don't see myself chasing down criminals like Grandpa. I think I'm better suited to using my brain to handle criminals. I will have to work with the strengths I have, and I have the capacity for study and to become an attorney."

"You're not just academically smart," said Heather. "You think things through. You're exceptionally rational for someone your age."

"I know," said Josh, smiling. "And I'm modest, too, right?"

"I'VE REVIEWED THE security camera feeds of your dad's system, and I haven't seen anything," Shawn told Heather. "It seems that side yard isn't covered by cameras."

"Our neighbor Tom Griffin helped my father install that system," replied Heather. "Daddy probably should have hired a professional to install it."

"Maybe," said Shawn.

"Tom is an engineer, but I'm not sure whether he is an expert with home security systems," said Heather.

"Well, that was a do-it-yourself system," said Shawn. "Not all DIY products are all that they are advertised to be."

"Also, some men have problems following the instructions," said Heather. "Tom may have decided that with his engineering background that he didn't need to read the instructions."

"Tom probably installed it the same way he did his own," said Shawn.

"I'm glad we have Zack now," said Heather, changing the subject.

"The guys are coming to build that privacy fence for the backyard, tomorrow," said Shawn. "Zack should enjoy it back there. He has a back porch, like your father's house."

"The lawyer has given me power of attorney to sell my father's house," said Heather. "The official reading of Daddy's will is to be Thursday. Daddy's house is to be sold and the profit split between Chris and me. Chris has agreed for me to put the house on the market tomorrow. We'll settle the rest later. It seems weird selling that house. It has so many memories."

"It does, for us both," said Shawn. "You grew up there, and John and I spent a lot of time there when we were partners."

"It's just a place," said Heather. "It's not the same. Without Daddy there, it's just a place. Maybe another family can enjoy it."

"Maybe," agreed Shawn. "I can't believe that your brother Chris didn't bother to show up for his father's funeral. What's wrong with that guy?"

"I don't know," answered Heather. "He blew it. Now it's too late for them to mend their relationship. What a waste. I tried to talk him into it, but he said that one of his big technical inventions was about to hit the market."

"He has several inventions, but he only had one father," Shawn said.

"I know," agreed Heather. "He's in his own world. He hardly has time for my calls, and he shows no interest in the kids – except during Christmas. Chris still sends them stuff for Christmas."

"But Charlotte and Josh hardly know him," said Shawn. "I don't get it."

"You don't see your older brother often," said Heather. "Granted he's in prison."

"Yep," said Shawn. "Prison put a damper on things, for sure. We certainly went our different ways. We were close, but not so much now. Whenever I do visit him, he wants me to jeopardize my life by doing something illegal for him. It's not the same, anymore."

"I guess that explains why you stopped visiting him as often," said Heather.

"That's it," said Shawn.

"What have you found about my father's killer?" asked Heather.

"The people he arrested over the years have been checked out," said Shawn. "Some have been arrested again, so they are out of the picture. Some have gone straight and are still on the outside. None of them seem to have the capability to be a professional hit man and none of them have the money to hire one."

"That's not much help," said Heather.

"What we do know is that whoever this guy is, he is smart," said Shawn. "He knows security systems. He knows the blind spots and can spot the cameras a mile away."

"Sounds a bit familiar," said Heather. "The guy who attacked you knew the areas not covered by cameras in the station parking lot."

"You think it could be the same guy?" asked Shawn.

"I don't know, but I see similarities," said Heather.

"I knew you were book smart, but you could have been a great detective," said Shawn.

"It's in my blood, right?"

Chapter 49

Will

EVERYONE WAS SHOCKED to see Heather's brother Chris at the official reading of John's will after the probationary period. He made sure that he was seated next to his sister. All funds in John's accounts were to be split evenly between Heather and Chris. The house was to be sold, and the proceeds split evenly between brother and sister. There were several stocks owned by John worth a little over ten thousand dollars, and they were to be split evenly between Chris and Heather.

"Now, we come to the itemized portion of the will," stated the attorney. "Charlotte Littleton is to be given John's rolltop desk, including all items within the desk. Josh Littleton is to be given the 1910 police positive .38 caliber revolver, but it is to be kept for him by his mother until he reaches the age of eighteen. Christ Rawlings is given John's baseball signed by Hank Aaron. Heather Stone is given John's dog Zack and any furniture in the home and on the rear porch of the home. That's it."

"I expect my share of the proceeds from the house, the stocks, and my half of the accounts," said Chris. "He made you the executor and you were given power of attorney, so I trust you to handle this."

"I will," said Heather. "It's so good to see you, Chris. Would you stay for dinner?"

"No, I have a flight out at 5:00 this evening," Chris answered. "Yeah, good to see you too. I just have a lot on my plate with work and I need to get back."

"That's a shame," said Heather. "I was hoping to catch up."

"Josh, the baseball is yours," Chris said to Josh, turning to his nephew he hardly knew.

"Thanks," replied Josh.

"Charlotte, I don't have anything to give you from the will," said Chris. "However, I haven't forgotten that you have a birthday coming up. I'll send you something nice."

"Thank you, Uncle Chris," said Charlotte.

"That rolltop desk is nice," Chris told Charlotte. "You should enjoy that. It's an antique. I wouldn't have minded that, but I'm glad you have it."

"I wish you could stay," said Charlotte.

"I'm sorry, I have to be going," replied Chris.

The parties left the attorney's office separately. Chris waved as he opened the door to his rental car. Heather's family climbed into her Telluride.

Before Heather dropped onto the driver seat, her brother called out to her. "I'm too busy with work. Once things die down, I'll give visiting you some consideration. Like Dad always said, "I'll give it a day.""

"I hope you will," said Heather, blowing her brother a kiss.

"Why doesn't Uncle Chris ever visit?" asked Josh. "I'm not sure that I would have recognized him, if you hadn't called him by name."

"I don't understand that either," said Charlotte. "Why isn't he interested in family? He's not even married. Uncle Chris is alone in California."

"That's the way he wants it," replied Heather. "I can't explain it. It's just the way it is."

"I'm with you two kids," Shawn chimed in. "I don't get Chris at all. He has a fabulous sister and rock star nephew and niece, and he doesn't seem to appreciate it."

"You have a brother, don't you Shawn?" asked Charlotte. "Why don't we have him over."

"He's in prison," answered Shawn. "He doesn't get out much for dinner."

"I 'm sorry to hear that," said Josh. "It must be hard."

"There are lots of things about being an adult which aren't easy," said Shawn. "You two have endured your own hardships. You've lost both your biological father and your grandfather this year. That's tough."

"So, are you and Mom going to have more kids?" asked Josh.

"I don't believe so," stated Heather, cutting into the conversation.

"What about you?" Josh asked Shawn. "Do you want kids with Mom?"

"I'm happy having you two," said Shawn.

"Yeah, but we aren't your kids," said Josh. "You haven't even adopted us."

"Is that something that you want?" asked Shawn.

"I'd be good with it," volunteered Josh. "You don't have to adopt us both. You can just adopt me, if you want."

"I think that's something that the entire family needs to discuss," said Heather.

"I thought that was what we were doing," said Charlotte.

"Ok, then," said Heather. "What are your thoughts on the subject, Charlotte?"

"I would like to be adopted by Shawn," she answered. "But only if he never leaves you. He would have to be serious about this family."

"Oh, I'm serious alright," said Shawn. "I'm as serious as a heart attack about this family. Where would I go? I'm a cripple, right? I can't even get up the stairs."

"I'm serious," said Charlotte.

"I'm also serious," said Shawn. "Your mother would

have to kick me out, and then I would be hanging on to the front porch rails for dear life. I don't ever want to leave this family. Never."

"Ok, Shawn is cool with it," said Josh. "What about you, Mom?"

"There would have to be legal papers drawn, and details ironed out," said Heather. "I'm not sure how long it would even take in the state of Georgia."

"It can take up to a year in this state," said Shawn.

"How do you know that?" Heather asked Shawn.

"I don't have a PhD, but I can read," said Shawn.

"So, you've been reading up on it?" asked Heather.

"Sure," answered Shawn. "I just didn't know if others were interested."

"I think Josh Stone would be a cool name!" shouted Josh.

"I don't think you have to change your name if you don't want to," said Shawn.

"I want to," replied Josh.

"I do too," said Charlotte. "I like the last name Littleton, but if we are going to be a Stone family we should have the name."

TWO DAYS LATER, the rolltop desk was moved to Charlotte's bedroom and Heather placed the .38 revolver in its case in the top of her closet. She retained the key on her key ring. Inside the rolltop, Charlotte found John's journal containing all the arrests he made, and a novel begun by him.

"It's a crime novel, based on the journal," said Heather, as she reviewed it with her daughter. "Daddy started it."

"What's this?" asked Charlotte, pulling a slip of paper from between the pages of the novel.

"It's a note from Daddy," said Heather. "He wants me to complete his novel. The note says that the novel is based on actual accounts of criminals he dealt with. He gave fictional names instead of the actual names. The novel is to tell of his many experiences as a detective, the loss of his wife, the reconnection with his daughter and grandchildren."

"I want to see what's inside that gun case," said Josh.

Opening the gun case for the .38, Josh and his mother found a note written specifically to Josh telling him how this gun was owned by John's grandfather, passed to him, and was used to protect the family from Randy Jenkins. John charged Josh with caring for it and retaining it as a peaceful family heirloom.

Chapter 50

Salvation

"SO MUCH DEATH," Josh said to his mother. "Grandpa, my biological father, Christie at school – gone. There'll never be a chance to talk with Grandpa again; no opportunities to ask him questions."

"I believe my father is in heaven," said Heather. "I think I'll see him again, but you're right about it not being the same. Those opportunities to spend time with him and others in this life are over."

"Do you really believe there is a heaven?" asked Josh. "You're smart. You're very educated. Don't you have doubts about placing faith in something that can't be seen or touched in this world?"

"I did doubt it for a long time," explained his mother. "I can't explain it. It's nothing that can be proven by intelligence and rational thinking, but deep within me I know that God and heaven are real."

"Really?" asked Josh. "If there's no evidence to be proven by rational thinking, what evidence is there for it?"

"Hebrews 11 in the King James version of the Bible begins saying 'Now faith is the substance of things hoped for, the evidence of things not seen,'" answered Heather. "If there was scientific proof, then faith wouldn't be required. Instead, it would be scientific fact. Spiritual truths require faith to observe them. It's not like the study of physical evidence."

"I don't know," said Josh.

"Look around you," said Heather. "Do you really believe that the universe and life just accidentally came to being? Really? What are the chances of something like that happening? Be honest with yourself. We have no real evidence that it all came about without any intelligent design. To be honest, to believe that is a real stretch of faith. Do you really believe that the universe is an accident? Both science and the Bible hold that space, time, and matter suddenly came into being. Science calls it the Big Bang, but when asked what caused it science has no answer. Christianity says that God caused it. Science has established a number of truths about this realm in which we live, but do you really think that science has all the answers? Do you really think there is no chance that other realms don't exist, simply because we have no scientific method of measuring them? You're very intelligent. I hope you don't limit your understanding to only what you can touch or see."

"I have to admit that there is no evidence against the existence of other realms or realities," admitted Josh. "It's very possible they exist. Charlotte told me about what pastor Matt said about a person having a soul, heart and mind. Those are interesting concepts. Regarding a person's mind, I believe the mind is based on chemical reactions within the brain. I see that as more of a physical thing than something spiritual. People have self-awareness. Animals like Zack have self-awareness. Our human brains are simply larger and more complex."

"How do you explain love?" asked Heather.

"I'm really unsure," answered Josh. "I believe love exists because I see the actions of people who experience love. I'm not sure if it's just chemically based, like hormones, which are released into the body and mind or whether there is more to it."

"The question is, why do people love?" asked Heather.

"I don't know," answered Josh. "I'm guessing it has a lot to do with preservation of a species. People care for human children, and even dogs care for pups. I think both experience love of some type. Maybe it's why both people and dogs still exist on this planet."

"The Bible says that God is love," said Heather. "God created all life based on His Love for us. Without that love, I doubt there would be anything in this universe or this realm of ours."

"So, you're saying that life came about because of love?" asked Josh.

"You certainly came about because I loved your father," answered Heather. "I can't explain it, but the moment I saw you after giving birth I fell in love with you. I still love you."

"I love you too," said Josh.

"Thoughts?" asked Hather.

"God is love," said Josh. "That is another interesting concept. It sounds like the Bible contains several interesting concepts. It may be an interesting read, but I became totally bored when reading past Genesis."

"I suggest that you begin reading with the New Testament book of John," said Heather. "It begins with stating that there is a part of God called the Word. The Word is how God communicates with mankind, and it says that the Word became flesh. The Word became flesh in the person Jesus. It says that the Word was involved when God created the universe. The Word is like the voice of God. God spoke the universe into existence."

"The creation of the universe is something science is actively trying to explain," said Josh. "I've read several online articles on the subject."

"God created time and matter," said Heather. "God created a realm where mankind could exist, and it's possible that other life exists in the universe. However, God the Father resides outside this realm that He created for us. The

Bible says that God's Son, called the Word, is God's method of contact with us in this realm. God the Father sent the Word, Jesus, to help us see into that other realm - the realm of God the Father. The Word was sent to bridge the gap between God the Father and mankind."

"Wow!" said Josh. "That's heavy stuff. OK, it makes sense that if someone created the universe, he would do it from outside the universe. And it makes sense that, in order to have any kind of relationship with those in this universe or realm, he would have to establish some method or tool of doing it. This is all hypothetical. This is assuming that God exists at all."

"Where do you think all of this came from?" asked Heather.

"I don't know," said Josh. "But OK, I admit that it's rational to believe that something or someone is behind it coming about. It is a little irrational to believe that somehow order came from disorder or came from nothing. Assuming that a god did this, why would God create the universe?"

"That, I don't know," said Heather. "Do you really think that our puny little human brains could comprehend this? Do you really think we created beings can really understand the vast mind of God almighty, the Creator of the universe?"

"I guess not," admitted Josh. "Any being with that capability would be so far above our minds that it would be impossible."

"So, you see the need for God the Father to send His Son, the Word, to help communicate with mankind?" asked Heather.

"It would make sense," said Josh. "I think I understand."

"I came to the same conclusion," said Heather. "I reached out to God. I seriously reached out to Him and asked Him to help me. I can't explain it. I can't explain why I know all of it is real, but deep inside I know it to be true."

"How would I go about making that connection to

God?" asked Josh.

"Since the bridge is Jesus, I pray to God in the name of Jesus," said Heather. "The Bible says that our sins separate us from God, and that when Jesus died on the cross God placed our sins on Him. When Jesus died, our sins died with Him. We must have faith in this act by God of healing that separation. We must confess that we believe Jesus to be this Savior of mankind and ask God to forgive us of our sins in Jesus's name."

"That's it?" asked Josh.

"Yes," said Heather. "We can't reach God by our own incapable efforts. God makes that connection for us when we have faith in what Jesus did for us. Jesus, the Word, went back to the realm of heaven, but we were sent the third person of God – the Holy Spirit, to reside in this realm with us. Jesus made it possible for that bridge to be crossed, but the Holy Spirit is here to help spiritually guide us. Jesus paid the price for our ticket to heaven, but we must have faith that He has done so. Much like rides at the carnival, we must accept the ticket, and we must get on the ride. Actions are required on our part. If we just stand there with the ticket in our hand, it does us no good."

"So, just believe and ask?" asked Josh.

"That's what is required for us to use that ticket to heaven that Jesus provided, but in order to stay on the ride to heaven we are to do two things. In gratitude for all God has done for us, we need to love God and love other people. Part of doing this is forgiving people."

"What if I don't want to forgive some people?" asked Josh.

"We are required to forgive," said Heather. "Jesus said that if we want God to forgive us, we must forgive people. The forgiveness from God is to flow through us to others."

"I guess that makes sense," said Josh. "If I pray for God's forgiveness, what will happen? Will I hear God's voice or something? If so, is that scary?"

"God speaks to us internally in most cases," said Heather. "Not so much in words of English, but in a deep knowledge and understand from within. It's spiritual understanding."

"That also makes sense," said Josh. "God isn't a person in America who speaks English. He would be above all of this. See, I knew you had a reason for believing in God. I knew you weren't just stupidly believing in something just because you heard someone tell you about it. It had to make sense, and it does."

"So, are you willing to believe?" asked Heather.

"It makes sense, so I think should believe," said Josh.

"So, would you like to pray?" asked Heather.

"Right now?" asked Josh.

"Why not?" asked Heather.

Josh dropped his young head. Heather reached out and took her son's hand in hers.

"Ok, God," Josh began. "I believe You exist. I believe you created everything in this realm. Mom, says that Jesus is the bridge between You and humanity. Who am I to doubt that? In the name of Jesus, God please forgive me for doubting you and for anything that I've done that displeases you. Help me to forgive the person who killed my Grandpa. I don't want to forgive him, but I understand this is part of the deal. I give You my soul, and I ask You to take me to heaven in Your realm when I die. I want to see Grandpa again. Amen."

Heather held her son tight.

"So, was that prayer alright?" asked Josh.

"Perfect," said Heather, still holding him.

"Grandpa used to say, 'Give it a day,'" said Josh. After we talked, I thought it best not to give this another day."

"I'm so glad," said Heather.

"Now, if you'll let go of me, I'd like to tell Charlotte that

I've joined the Jesus club," said Josh.

"You do that," said Heather, laughing.

Charlotte was ecstatic when Josh told her of his newfound faith. She danced around her bedroom in excitement.

LATER THAT WEEK, Ron and Emily invited Matt, Heather, Shawn, Charlote, Heath and Josh over for a time of reflection and board games. After they talked about the impact of John's life on everyone present, Matt remembered John's thoughts of suicide.

"John's life has meant a great deal to everyone here," thought Matt. *"We're all so fortunate that he didn't commit suicide years ago."*

"John shared something very personal with me," Matt told Shawn. "John told me this in confidence, and I'm able to keep secrets. You and John were very close. He loved you like a son. He didn't want to burden you, but he was really struggling. I won't go into details, because he shared with me in confidence. He was frustrated with his life, and he greatly missed his wife. John really loved you, Shawn. He was hurting badly, but loved you so much that he didn't want to burden you."

The big man began to cry like a baby. Between sobs, he told Matt how much he missed John.

"I can't tell you how much John loved Sharon," said Shawn. "He wasn't the same man after she died. I loved that man."

"John is in heaven, now," said Matt.

"He's finally with Sharon, again," said Shawn, with tears in his eyes. "She was really a believer in God. I'm telling you, she was a serious Christian."

"John isn't suffering anymore, and he's at peace," said Matt. "He is now in the presence of God, and all of his heartache is gone. The Bible says that in heaven all our tears are wiped away."

"You really believe in God and in heaven?" asked Shawn. "John certainly seemed to believe it before he died."

"I do believe it," said Matt. "I can't say that I understand everything there is to know about heaven. It exists in a realm that is much different than the realm in which we live. I admit that I understand only a few things about heaven. I've never been there."

"It seems like I'm the only one around who isn't bound for heaven," said Shawn. "I'd like to see John again. Maybe you could help me understand what I need to do to be able to go to heaven when I die. I can see the impact of God on the lives of everyone in this family. Can you help me?"

Matt placed his hand on Shawn large shoulder and led him in prayer. Afterwards, Shawn asked God's forgiveness and gave his soul to God.

"I'm glad I did this," said Shawn. "John's death made me think a lot about what happens when we die. Seeing the impact of faith on members of this family, I realized there is something about it. I saw the change in Charlotte. I saw the peace that she now has. When we talked here tonight, I decided I just couldn't give it another day."

The two men went inside and shared Shawn's prayer of salvation with the others. Heather hugged him so hard that Shawn almost lost his balance with his forearm crutches. He had to reach out and clutch a doorframe to keep himself from toppling onto the floor. Once stable, he put his other powerful arm around Heather.

"John's in heaven now," Shawn whispered to his wife. "Your faith will allow you in heaven when you pass away. I don't ever want to be anywhere without you."

"I love you, Shawn," Heather said, still holding him tight.

Chapter 51

Again

"WHAT'S THIS?" HEATHER thought while nervously reaching for a paper tucked under the windshield wiper of her Telluride.

"No!" she screamed, when she began to read what was contained. It was a poem titled "Ode to Hot Heather."

JOHN'S BLOOD RAN RED, AND HEATHER IS
BLUE.
YOU DON'T KNOW ME, BUT I KNOW YOU.
YOU THOUGHT IT WAS BARKER AND YOU
THOUGHT IT WAS JENKINS,
YOUR FAMILY IS SMART, BUT WITHOUT THE
RIGHT THINKINGS.
I'VE SEEN YOU UNDRESSING RIGHT
THROUGH YOUR WINDOW.
MEANT FOR SHAWN, BUT YOU GAVE ME A
SHOW.
I COULD NOT HEAR THE WORDS YOU SAID,
BUT I'VE WATCHED YOUR NUDE BODY UPON
YOUR BED.
WITH CAMERA ZOOMED, I'VE SEEN EVEN
YOUR NIPPLE.
YOU NO LONGER HAVE JOHN, AND SHAWN IS
A CRIPPLE.

LAY NUDE AND I'LL DO ALL YOU WANT ME
TO DO.
SWEET DARLING HEATHER, I'M COMING FOR
YOU.
YOU WON'T KNOW WHEN AND YOU WON'T
KNOW WHERE.
BUT YOU'LL ENJOY WHAT I DO TO YOU
THERE.

"Shawn!" she called out as she quickly made it back inside her home. "Oh God!"

Shawn's crippled body shook with anger as he read the poem. "What the hell?" he blurted.

Shawn quickly called his old partner Caitlin at the station. Within minutes Caitlin and her new partner Rod Nelson were at the house. She carefully bagged the paper as evidence."

"Caitlin, I need you to study every arrest that John and I have made over the years," Shawn told his ex-partner. "My guess, this is somebody wanting revenge, and he sees Heather as a target. I can't let another sicko attack her."

"You got it, Shawn," promised Caitlin. "You know that I'll be on this like a duck on a June bug. Even if it is assigned to someone else, nobody can stop me from pursuing this after hours. I'm on it."

"It's just like before," said Heather. "The same stupid poetry, placed under the wiper of the SUV."

"Heather, I promise you that I won't rest," said Caitlin.

"Thank you, Caitlin," Heather told her, still shaken. "I thought these notes were behind us after Randy Jenkins died."

"It appears that he may not have been responsible for the earlier notes," said Caitlin.

"Then who?" asked Heather.

"That's what we have to find out," said Caitlin. Caitlin turning to her ex-partner, she said, "Shawn, I promise you that I won't let up. This guy has to be brought down."

"Thanks Caitlin," said Shawn. "I'll rack my brain trying to come up with ideas as to who could be behind these notes. I'll let you know if I come up with someone. But if I get my hands on him, I'll beat him half to death with these stupid crutches."

"He'd better hope that you don't find him first," said Caitlin. "Crutches or no crutches, nobody wants to get on the bad side of you – especially by screwing around with your family."

"I wish meeting you was under better circumstances," Rod said, reaching his hand out to Shawn.

"Me too, brother," replied Shawn, taking his hand before the two detectives left the house.

"I guess I should be glad that it's a Saturday morning," said Heather. "At least the kids didn't have to see that note. Both are still sound asleep."

"That's true," Shawn said, his eyes still ablaze with anger. "I want to get my hands on him. I hope I do get ahold of that bastard before Cailtin finds him."

"We should pray," Heather reminded Shawn.

"OK," he agreed, taking a deep breath. "You're right. We need God's help on this."

Heather placed her head against Shawn broad and powerful chest. He balanced himself on one forearm crutch and wrapped his other arm around her.

"God, you are bigger than the man who placed this note," began Heather. "No one can hide from your eyes and your arm is not so short that it can't save. I ask you stop this man. We ask you to take control of the entire situation and we pray for his soul."

"You're beautiful, you know that?" said Shawn. "I want to kill this guy and you're praying for his soul."

"God is bigger than this guy," said Heather.

"You looked pretty upset, earlier," said Shawn.

"I was, and it is unsettling," said Heather. "But I

remembered God. I remembered a verse in Isaiah that I was reading a couple of days ago. It said, 'Surely the arm of the Lord is not too short to save, nor his ear too dull to hear.' I remembered that verse and a peace began to come over me."

"Yeah, but bad things happen to good people," said Shawn. "I've seen a lot of it."

"That's true," said Heather. "But if it's my time to go, then it's my time to go. If God decides to take me, there's nothing much I can do about it. My life is in His hands, not just my soul, but my entire life. My life is His to do whatever He wants."

"Ok, I recently prayed to give God my soul, but I think God wants me to use my wits and skills in this life," said Shawn. "If a man pulls a gun on me, I don't think I should just say, 'If you want to shoot me, that's OK.' I think God wants me to defend myself. If somebody tries to do something to you or the kids, I think God would want me to stop the guy."

"I'm not saying that we are to kiss our brains goodbye, just because we are Christians," said Heather. "I'm just saying that I have put my life in God's hands, and that God is big enough to handle things."

"OK, you had me worried there," said Shawn. "It's good to trust God, but you're going to be careful, right?"

"Absolutely," answered Heather.

"Good, I feel better," said Shawn. "I pan to find this guy, and when I do, I don't plan to preach a sermon to him."

"If you find him, try to search your heart about what God would want you to do," said Heather.

"If I find him, and he is not actively threatening anyone, I'll take him in," said Shawn. "I will want to beat him into the ground, but I will just take him in. I promise."

"Good," said Heather. "I wouldn't mind having him in a place where I can give him a piece of my mind."

"What about all the talk about that guy's soul?" asked Shawn.

"I'll talk with him about the state of his soul, after I give him a piece of my mind," answered Heather.

"That's my girl," said Shawn.

Chapter 52

Elimination

A WEEK PRIOR to Heather finding the fourth note on her windshield, Shawn had installed camera surveillance on their Cobb County home. After reviewing the digital capture of a man placing the note on the windshield, Shawn threw up his hands in frustration.

"The cameras I installed are of high quality, but the recording isn't good enough to identify the face of the guy who put the note on your windshield," Shawn angrily told his wife. "The guy was obviously on foot. He either lives in the area or he parked his vehicle somewhere and walked to our house."

"Do you think the police will have better equipment which can determine who he is from the video?" asked Heather.

"No, the guy is smart," said Shawn. "It's like he understands where each camera is located and the effectiveness of those cameras. The guy is clearly wearing a hoodie, and he keeps his head down while the camera is on him. He wears gloves, as to not leave fingerprints on the note and to not allow the camera to clearly identify his skin color. He knows what he is doing, damn it."

"Is he tall or short?" asked Heather.

"He is average height and sort of average build, but it's

hard to determine his build clearly because of the loose sweatshirt type hoodie he was wearing," said Shawn. "I've looked at this recording all morning to see if the guy came by the house at other times in an effort to scope the place out. Nothing."

"Do you plan to give the recording to Caitlin?" asked Heather.

"Absolutely," said Shawn. "I'll share it with her this afternoon. I need to also run into town today to a hardware store located at a shopping center in Atlanta. You know the one. I've been going there for years. I want to pick up a different saw blade. The one I have is fine for ripping boards, but I need a blade that makes a cleaner cut for a project that I have in mind."

"There are hardware stores in Cobb County," said Heather.

"I know, but I trust this guy in this particular store," said Shawn. "I'll be back by supper."

WHEN DROPPING THE recording off with Caitlin, she had lots of questions for Shawn. When she had been at his house the day before, her interests were purely professional. She had limited her discussions with him and Heather regarding the threat being posed by the note. Now, she saw an opportunity to catch up on the things going on in her ex-partner's life. The two talked for an hour. By the time Shawn arrived at the shopping center containing the hardware store, dusk had already begun to settle in.

"Crap!" Shawn shouted from within his car. "Even this late, all the handicap parking places are taken. Selfish jerks! I don't see a handicap indicator on a single vehicle parked in those spots. Maybe they would think about it if they were on crutches for just one day. Jerks!"

Shawn had to park further back in the parking lot.

I'll be sweating like a pig by the time I get inside that

store. Oh well, it is what it is.

Shawn struggled with his forearm crutches as he moved across the parking lot. By that time, only a few cars were left in that area of the parking lot. Shawn was glad that he no longer had to carefully squeeze between parked vehicles, to avoid scratching the paint with his crutches. He was still angry when he finally made his way inside the store. Some of the lights in other areas of the huge parking lot were beginning to illuminate when he exited the store, but none were yet on where he parked. He carried the bag containing the saw blade in his right hand, while also gripping the forearm crutch. Arriving at the truck, he was exhausted. He moved the bag with the saw blade from his right hand to his left. Reaching for the door of the truck with his right hand, he suddenly found himself off balance and he fell against the side of the car. At the same time, he felt severe pains shoot through his left shoulder. No longer able to hold himself steady with the left forearm crutch, he fell onto the asphalt parking lot. Shawn quickly glanced down at his left shoulder, and he saw blood. Realizing that he had been shot, he quickly whipped out his nine-millimeter from his shoulder holster. Shawn spotted a man wearing a hoodie stepping from behind his car. As the man raised a pistol equipped with a silencer in the direction of the wounded cripple lying on the pavement, Shawn fired two shots directly into the man's chest. Pieces of sweatshirt flew, and the man took two steps back. Shawn then fired a third shot that hit the man squarely in the forehead. The man's head jerked back from the force of the bullet, and he then dropped like a sack of potatoes to the asphalt less than a dozen feet from where Shawn lay.

"Oh, God!" mumbled Shawn. "I've been shot, and it's bad."

In agony, Shawn struggled to lift his head attempting to make sure his assassin was still down. Releasing the gun, he reached into his pocket with right hand and found his cell phone. He first dialed 911, then Caitlin.

"I've be shot," Shawn told her.

He quickly gave Caitlin the address of the shopping center. By the time the call ended, he was feeling weak. He called Heather.

"I've been shot," he stammered.

"What!?" blurted Heather. "Where are you?"

"Hardware store, you know the one," said Shawn.

"Are you badly wounded?" asked Heather.

"Ambulance on it's way," mumbled Shawn. "I saw him."

"You saw who?" asked Heather.

"I saw his face," mumbled Shawn, now beginning to lose consciousness due to loss of blood.

"Shawn!" yelled Heather. "Keep talking to me until the ambulance arrives."

"I'm here," Shawn weakly moaned.

"Don't you leave me," whimpered Heather.

"I'm here," Shawn said again. "I'm still here."

Heather heard the phone drop onto the asphalt.

"No!" she cried out. "Pick up that phone…pick it up, do you hear me!"

Heather heard vehicles pull up, people talking, and then a man call out to someone else. She heard someone call out that a man had been shot dead.

"No!" she screamed into the phone.

"He's lost a lot of blood!" she heard someone else shout. "Get that Stryker over here. And we need to get a line in quick!"

Heather tried to get the attention of someone on the scene.

"Talk to me!" she yelled over her cell phone. "Somebody, talk to me!"

After several seconds, she heard a voice.

"Is there someone on this phone?" the person asked.

"I'm his wife!" blurted Heather. Is Shawn alive?

"We have him, and we are leaving with him now," the person said while getting into the ambulance.

"Who are you?" Heather asked.

"I'm the guy who is about to take your husband to the ER," he said. "Listen, I need to focus on driving, not talking."

"Just tell me where you're taking him," she said.

"Grady," said the man. "Grady. Now I'm hanging up and I'm going to get him there."

"Thank you," Heather whispered as the call ended.

She sat dazed for a moment, before remembering her children. She quickly went upstairs and told them both what had happened, and that Shawn was enroute to Grady Memorial Hospital.

"I need to call Emily to come stay with you," said Heather.

"No, you're not!" shouted Josh. "Not this time. We are going with you!"

"I'm going to be there into the late hours," said Heather.

"Mom, it's a Saturday," Charlotte said. "There's no school tomorrow. It doesn't matter how late it is. We are coming with you this time. We are not going to sit around this house wondering whether Shawn is dead without having you with us."

"OK, hurry, get in the SUV," Heather commanded them.

AS HEATHER PARKED the Telluride in the ER parking lot, she got a call on her cell phone.

"Heather, this is Caitlin," the caller announced.

"Shawn's been shot, and I'm just now getting to Grady," said Heather.

"I've been on the phone with the people at the hospital, and they have him in stable condition," said Caitlin.

"Thank God!" said Heather.

"When you get seated in the ER, give me a call back on this number," Caitlin said. "I need to fill you in."

"I will," promised Heather. "Thank you so much."

Heather spoke to the personnel at the ER desk to verify Shawn's condition, and then found a place to seat herself and the children in the ER waiting room.

"Shawn's in stable condition," she assured her children.

"He's going to live?" asked Josh.

"He is stable, and I believe he'll live," said Heather.

"Thank You, God," said Charlotte. "I've been praying since we left the house."

"Me too," said Josh.

"Listen, I need to call Caitlin back," Heather told her children.

"Shawn's partner?" asked Josh.

"That's the one," replied Heather. "Let me make this call," she said while calling Caitlin.

"Caitlin, this is Heather," she said. "You were right, Shawn is in stable condition. I can't go back there yet, but I will as soon as they let me."

"I want you to know that Shawn got the guy who shot him," said Caitin. "Apparently, Shawn was still able to pull his weapon, and he shot the man dead."

"Do you know who the man was and why he shot Shawn?" asked Heather.

"As for why, I haven't a clue at this point," said Caitlin. "However, we have identified the man. His name is Tom Griffin."

"What?" blurted Heather. "I know a Tom Griffin who was heading up the neighborhood watch group in my father's area of town during the time of the molester."

"That's the guy," said Caitlin.

"No way!" shouted Heather.

"Mom, keep it down," warned Charlotte. "The lady at the desk is looking at you."

"OK, honey," Heather replied quietly while glancing at

the women at the desk.

"Listen, I believe Shawn's training kicked in," said Caitlin. "It appears Shawn shot him twice in the chest, but the man was wearing a jacket with Kevlar plates under his sweatshirt. If Shawn hadn't realized it and taken a third shot to his head, I doubt your husband would be alive."

"Thank God," said Heather.

"We are on our way over to the guy's house," Caitlin told Heather. "We plan to search the house tonight. I'm not waiting until morning. Not when it involves Shawn."

"Tom Griffin helped my father install a security system in his house," said Heather. "I can't believe he shot Shawn."

"He did," said Caitlin. "He shot Shawn twice in the back. It's possible that Griffin has been involved in other crimes. I'll let you know what we find."

"Thank you, Caitlin," said Heather.

"Anything for you and Shawn," Caitlin said before ending the call.

"Heather Stone," the woman at the ER desk called out.

"Yes, I'm Heather," she said, moving toward the woman.

"Your husband is being moved to a room in ICU," said the woman. "He's out of surgery and awake."

Thank you so much," said Heather. "I apologize for being loud a few moments ago."

"That's fine," said the woman. "I've certainly heard worse on this job."

After obtaining Shawn's room number, she and her two children headed for his room in ICU.

"Are these Mr. Stone's children?" asked the nurse in ICU.

"These are my children, and I am Mr. Stone's wife," explained Heather.

"We'll be very quiet," promised Charlotte.

"See that you do," said the nurse. "Mr. Stone is awake, but he needs rest. Please remember that there are patients here who are in much worse shape than Mr. Stone."

"We will," promised Charlotte, smiling.

Heather and the children found Shawn slightly sedated when they entered the room. The two children stood at the foot of the bed, as Heather moved beside her husband.

"Are you awake?" Heather asked.

"Just barely," mumbled Shawn. "Apparently, I was in surgery for some time. One bullet shattered my left shoulder blade. They had to repair it. I'm really drugged up."

"Are you in pain?" asked Heather.

"A little, but like I said, a lot of drugs," answered Shawn.

Heather leaned over and kissed him on the lips.

"I'm afraid that I'm not up for any of that right now," Shawn mumbled.

"The kids are here," Heather told her husband.

"Where?" asked Shawn.

Both Charlotte and Josh moved to be near Shawn. Charlotte reached out and took his huge right hand in hers.

"We're right here, Dad," Josh said.

"So, I'm Dad now?" asked Shawn.

"That's the way I see it," answered Josh.

"Me too," added Charlotte, gently stroking his hand.

"Well, I'm absolutely good with that idea," said Shawn.

"It's time to let Mr. Stone get some rest," said a nurse when entering the room.

"Come here," Shawn said to his wife. Lean down, I need to say something. Two things."

"I'm here," Heather said while leaning down near his face.

"I love you," Shawn said.

"I love you too," replied Heather.

"I got him," whispered Shawn. "I got the guy, and it was Tom."

"Caitlin told me it was Tom," replied Heather. "She called and she is now searching his house."

"Good," mumbled Shawn, almost drifting asleep. "Caitlin's a good detective. She'll do a good job."

"Get some rest," said Heather. "We'll talk more later."

THE FOLLOWING DAY, Heather got another call from Caitlin.

"I don't think you'll have to worry about getting another note on your windshield," said Caitlin.

"Why not?" asked Heather.

"We're pretty sure Tom Giffin was the one putting them there," answered Caitlin. "Without getting into the details of the evidence that we found in that house, I'll just say that he was obsessed with you."

"What?" said Heather.

"He has lots of digital photos and recordings of you," said Caitlin. "Are you sitting down?"

"I am now," answered Heather.

"That guy had a few digital recordings of you and Shawn in bed," said Caitlin.

"How?" blurted Heater. "How in the world could he get those?"

"Tom Griffin had a collection of expensive cameras, and he's been spying on you for a long time," explained Caitlin. "Some with night vision. They are very sophisticated, and he knew how to use them well. Photos and video were taken of you and Shawn in the bedroom of your current house. We are thinking that he took them from a distance with a zoom lens, possibly from a hill across from your home. There are also photos of you and the kids when you were living with your father. I'm thinking that he used his position as head of the neighborhood watch as a cover to spy on you. Nobody would have given it a second thought if he had been caught with a camera in John's neighborhood. He could have chalked it up to part of his watch duties."

"That sick piece of garbage!" said Heather.

"That, he was," agreed Cailtin. "It was the perfect cover at the time, while pretending to protect. We found evidence that he was a perverted rapists of more than ten women in the Atlanta area. The jerk took photos of the women after he was finished with them. It's believed that he used a ski mask while raping the women. We will be able to solve several crimes with this evidence."

"I'm creeped out," said Heather. "You said earlier that you believe he took photos of Shawn and me possibly from a hill. Come to think of it, there are empty streets on a hill not far from our home where they were preparing for a new neighborhood to be built. Construction was stopped because they found some environmental concerns."

"We also found a couple of guns," said Caitlin. "The one that he shot Shawn with had a silencer. We are going to run these through ballistics to see if we find a match which might solve other crimes."

"Good grief," said Heather. "Nobody would have thought that about Tom Griffin."

A WEEK LATER, Shawn was resting somewhat comfortably in a regular hospital room when he was visited in the hospital by Caitlin. She handed a file to him.

"What's this?" asked Shawn.

"It's a file on Tom Griffin," said Cailtin. "Turn to page six."

"It says that ballistics matched Tom's gun to the one used to murder John," said Shawn, somewhat stunned.

"Heather told me that Tom helped install her father's security system," said Cailtin. "We believe he was well aware of the gaps in that surveillance system."

"He could have set it up to have gaps," observed Shawn. "So, he was the one who threw the rock against the side of John's house to lure him out."

"And he shot him in the back from the hedges next

door," said Caitlin.

"Heather told me about the kinky recordings he took of us," said Shawn. "What a sick pervert! Now, I find out that he murdered John. Why?"

"He was obsessed with Heather," Caitlin told Shawn. "He wanted her for himself. When she hooked up with you, we now know that he planned to murder John and then you. Once you both were gone, he intended to gain her affection afterwards by giving her comfort. He had a detailed plan for the elimination of anyone standing between himself and Heather."

"That sick bastard!" said Shawn.

"He was sick, alright," agreed Caitlin. "We also found evidence that he had been in contact with Larry Kaufman. It's possible that Tom Griffin hired Larry to kidnap Heather. After that failed, he probably decided to simply finish you off."

"Does Heather know?" asked Shawn.

"Not yet," said Caitin. "Do you want to be with her when I tell her?"

"You bet I do," said Shawn.

"I thought so," replied Caitlin.

"I've had enough!" blurted Shawn. "I'm checking out of this hospital right now. Do you have time for me to notify the staff here that I plan to check out and then collect my stuff?"

"Absolutely, Shawn," Caitlin said. "Anything for you."

Chapter 53

Reflection

AFTER SHAWN HEALED from the gunshots, he contracted with two retired detectives and rented a small place in a rundown shopping center on Mooreland Avenue in the east part of the city. Shawn spent the majority of his workday in the office and oversaw bringing in new business, while the other two conducted the field work. Heather and Shawn regularly made time to meet for lunch.

"Each day with you is a gift," Heather told her husband while at a small dinner.

"You are the greatest gift God could have given me," said Shawn.

"I don't take a minute we have for granted," said Heather. "Not with you, and not with the kids."

"Seven years ago, could have you have imagined all that has happened?" asked Shawn.

"No way," answered Heather. "I was in such a different mindset before moving back to Atlanta."

"You even had a different man-set," joked Shawn.

"That was a different world," said Heather.

"Same here," said Shawn. "You were the piece I was always missing. At the time, I didn't realize it."

"Josh had another bad dream last night."

"I hate that," said Shawn.

"Yours seem to have subsided," stated Heather.

"I'm sleeping like a baby," said Shawn. "I don't understand why. I was shot. Tom meant to kill me, and I had to kill him. I'm the one who shouldn't be sleeping."

"The grace of God," said Heather.

"I think you're right," agreed Shawn. "I pray God grants sleep to Josh.

"I miss my father so much," said Heather.

"You and me, both," said Shawn.

"He viewed you as a son," said Heather. "I loved it when my father joined us in playing board games with the kids. Do you miss those times we shared with Emily's family?"

"That was really nice," said Shawn.

After lunch, Heather placed a call to her old friend Emily.

"How is Shawn doing?" asked Emily.

"He's doing good," replied Heather. "He's fully recovered from being shot and he actually started up that private investigation agency."

"Good," said Emily. I'm so glad he's doing well."

"Would you and your family like to come over for board games this Saturday night?" asked Heather.

"That sounds wonderful!" answered Emily. "I'll tell Ron. I'm sure he would love to."

OVER THE NEXT two years, the families of Heather and Emily continued the old practice of meeting at Heather's home for board games on the first Saturday of each month. Initially, an empty chair was left in John's honor. After a short time, Lily was given the place at the table where John once sat. Charlotte always sat beside the little girl. Whenever a new board game was introduced, Charlotte helped Lily learn how to play.

Before supper was ready one Saturday, Charlotte and

Josh played with Lily in Heather's fenced backyard while the adults discussed dangers faced by those in law enforcement.

"John never gave up on a case," said Shawn. "He was like a bulldog. He used to have a saying – if we don't catch the bad guy today - give it a day – we'll get him."

"You're right, 'give it a day' was one of his favorite sayings," said Heather. "We never know what each day will bring, so it's important that never take our blessings for granted."

"We aren't guaranteed another day on earth," said Emily. "It's also important that we not put off things which are important."

"My father is no longer here," said Heather. "I look back on every day that I spent with him at that house as precious. It's important that we tell our loved ones that we love them every day that we are given with them. We should be thankful. Every day is a gift from God."

"I completely agree," said Ron.

"Do you expect a visit from your brother Chris anytime soon?" Emily asked Heather.

"He's still very busy with his work," answered Heather. "He recently received a prestigious award and was featured in a scientific journal."

"Wow!" said Emily. "I knew he was smart, but I didn't realize."

"Hopefully, he'll get a break from work long enough to visit," said Heather.

"We were just saying that John's favorite saying was 'give it a day,'" said Shawn. "Sometimes it's wise to give things a day, but there are things which shouldn't be put off. Chris needs to make time for family. Some things may not be available, when given an extra day."

"I would like to meet your brother," said Ron.

"After the reading of my father's will, Chris told me that he would consider visiting us," said Heather. "But I don't want to nag him about it."

"Sometimes it's wise to take time to make a decision, but some opportunities may not always be available in the future," said Shawn. "For example, my athletic days of running or playing sports are over for me. It's foolish to assume that we can always do something in the future. John is no longer with us. We no longer have opportunities to spend time with him. I loved and respected that man, but regarding some things it's not always wise to give it a day."

Don't miss these other books by Rob Williams

Cabin by the Stream
Three Days in Brandon Springs
In Search of Brandon Springs
Rest in Brandon Springs
A Gathering of Six
Sins of Variance

About the Author:

Rob Williams, currently residing in Nacogdoches Texas, has served in multiple roles supporting the Christian community. Included in this long list of mentorships was his service as youth director of an inner-city church in Atlanta and working with children in some of the toughest housing projects in that city. Rob worked at a rehabilitation center for five years, where he became better acquainted with the homeless. The center helped those who were physically and mentally handicapped and those on work release from jail. He has taught adult Sunday school classes for more than thirty-five years and led youth in Boy Scouts and Cub Scouts for twenty years. Retired from the high-tech industry in Huntsville Alabama, he writes Christian fiction and science fiction in his free time. Rob is a husband, a father of four, and a grandfather. He is the author of the three novel *Brandon Springs* Christian fiction series, the dystopian science fiction novel *Sins of Variance*, the Christian mystery *Cabin by the Stream*, and Christian crime novels *Gathering of Six* and *Give It a Day*.

www.ingramcontent.com/pod-product-compliance
Lightning Source LLC
Chambersburg PA
CBHW070405310726
48977CB00003B/564